SPARK OF PASSION

" 'Fore God, we're as ill-matched as a pair of fighting cats! For a girl on the threshold of marriage to a man she patently abhors, you're mighty calm, Mistress."

Judith's smile was slight. "One must bow to the inevitable to retain dignity."

Quentin's temper rose. He reached out and took her chin in a firm grasp. "Dignity? By God, Mistress, I don't look for dignity, but some small spark of emotion. Is that beyond you?"

Judith raised her brows and regarded him steadily. He read the cool question in her eyes, and frustration snapped his control. She should be taught that marriage to Quentin Tarrant was not to be entered into so lightly and mockingly. His hands dropped to her shoulders and he pulled her roughly toward him.

"Emotion, Mistress," he snarled, "like this."

One hand rose to the back of her neck, forcing her face forward. The gray eyes blazed into hers for a moment, then the lips came down fiercely on her mouth. . . .

Other Leisure Books by Marjorie Shoebridge:

RELUCTANT RAPTURE
DESTINY'S DESIRE

MARJORIE SHOEBRIDGE

Bride
OF THE
Saracen
Stone

LEISURE BOOKS ✿ NEW YORK CITY

A LEISURE BOOK

Published by

Dorchester Publishing Co., Inc.
6 East 39th Street
New York, NY 10016

Printed in the United States of America

Part I

1

From a distance of five miles, Tarrant Castle could be seen, its walls stark and unrelieved save for the moss and lichen that time had bestowed upon it during the last century. It stared down with hauteur over the fair countryside of Sussex, a grim reminder of the power of England's invader, Duke William of Normandy. The first knight of Tarrant had built and held it for William, and now, a century and a half later, the Lords of Tarrant were still in residence.

A mile from the castle, Judith Bradley drew her palfrey to a halt and regarded her future home somberly. Her maidservant, Lucy, observed the look and sat her pony quietly beside her mistress. She, too, regarded the castle with misgiving. It lacked the mellowed warmth of the stone and timbered manor they had left two days ago, but it was the home of her mistress's betrothed, the elder son of the house, Quentin Tarrant.

Judith glanced at Lucy and her smile was wry. "But for circumstances and the pressing invitation of Lord Tarrant we should not be viewing this sight until next month." She looked at the castle and then back at Lucy. "I trust it is not as harsh within as it appears from without."

"It would be difficult, Mistress." Lucy returned in the same wry tone.

Judith laughed. "I'm glad you're with me, Lucy," she said impulsively. "You are my last and only link with Bradley."

Lucy's round, good-natured face was as familiar as her own, and they had come to know each other well across the sickbed of Mistress Bradley, Judith's mother. Death had hovered, then claimed its victim, leaving Judith stunned and bereft. Lucy had been there just as she was here, a country girl who viewed sickness and death with the calm acceptance of every peasant family.

"Well, it is no use sitting here and filling our minds with foreboding," Judith said on a brisker note. "The sun is losing brightness and I would be indoors by nightfall, whatever the condition."

Lucy pointed to the distant gatehouse as the thin sound of a horn drifted toward them. "His Lordship has sighted us, Mistress, and sends out an escort."

A single horseman was galloping across the drawbridge, spurring his mount into headlong flight, a tall figure, slim and dark.

"Is it Master Quentin, Mistress, who rides to you in such haste?"

Judith narrowed her eyes to observe the fast-approaching figure more closely.

The sergeant-at-arms riding slightly behind the two girls spoke. " 'Tis Master Henry, Mistress. Master Quentin waits upon His Majesty in Winchester."

Judith nodded and smiled at the sergeant, then looked forward again. There was an air of relaxation about the armed men who had come to Sherborne to act as escort for this new bride of Tarrant. Green and gold flashes were on every breast, and beneath the dark surcoats each man wore ringmail. For most of the journey she had been closely surrounded by silent, helmeted men with riders in van and rear, more spread widely on the flanks. They were glad to be at the end of their journey, but for Judith it was only the beginning.

The horseman reached them and circled his mount to draw level with Judith.

"Welcome to Tarrant," he gasped, his breathing a little harsh and his cheeks flushed from the ride. "Father waits to receive you on the threshold as a good host should, but I was determined to ride out and express my deepest sympathy at your loss, and assure you of my support and affection at all times."

Judith smiled and reached to touch Henry's hand. "Thank you. It was good of you to ride out. My mother's sudden death was a great shock, but pray God she finds happiness in reunion with my late father."

For a moment Judith's face clouded as she recalled the moving ceremony in the crypt of the Bradley chapel a week ago. Her mother had looked forward to being her companion on this journey that would result in the marriage of her only child to Quentin, heir of Tarrant. They had been betrothed for ten years, since Judith was six and Quentin a sullen boy of thirteen.

From that day to this they had met but once and that was five years ago on the eve of his departure to the Holy Land with King Richard. At eighteen, Quentin had become a lithe, well-muscled man of more than average height. Dark-haired and with a tanned skin that spoke of much outdoor activity, he had, even then, acquired an air of authority, backed up by a hard, commanding stare from gray eyes.

Judith had not, at the time, known the reason for his rough attitude toward her as she, at her mother's behest, attempted to show him courtesy and friendliness. Only later had she discovered his rebellious anger at the prospect of being forced to leave the company of his fellows being taught the knightly skills in the castle of some Yorkshire baron to attend his betrothal ceremony.

Judith, riding beside Henry, compared the brothers in her mind. Henry was two years Quentin's junior but in height and looks very similar, save that Henry was slimmer and more delicate in looks.

Above in the darkening April sky, the banner of the Tarrants caught the breeze and spread wide, green and gold on an azure field. It held for a moment, as if to remind all about that Tarrant held them in its power.

Judith's palfrey lifted a hoof and placed it delicately on the planking of the drawbridge. Henry followed, then Lucy and the escort. Through the archway a wide court-yard spread before them. A few wall torches were already alight. Lord Tarrant, on the steps before the great hall, was waiting to greet Judith as Henry helped her to dismount. He descended the steps and bowed to Judith's curtsey.

"Welcome, my dear. It is a joy to see you, though a sad occasion for us both with the passing of your lady mother, God rest her soul."

"Thank you, my lord," murmured Judith. "I feel the loss of her most keenly."

Lord Tarrant led her into the great hall. Tapestries and banners crowded the walls, the banners stained or shredded, their strange devices bearing witness to the valor of earlier Tarrants in foreign fields. Shields, from the round to the long triangular of early Norman hung tarnished above the wide hearth. The musky scent of aging animal skins vied with the aroma of baked meats. Rushes lay thickly on the stone floor.

Judith was glad to approach the hearth, for it was still only April and the wind had gusted coldly on their journey. She accepted the stool that Lord Tarrant directed her to, then gazed into the strong face of her future father-in-law. He was a tall, powerfully built man of middle years, square-jawed and keen-eyed. His tunic was richly braided, but the colors were muted and he wore no jewelry save a crested signet ring of heavy gold.

Lord Tarrant handed her a glass of wine, then took the seat opposite while Henry stood leaning an arm on the back of the settle, his very slimness and dark clothes giving him an air of elegance.

"As you know, my dear, Quentin is in attendance on the king. His service bars him from returning earlier to Tarrant, though I daresay he will come with all haste as soon as the king releases him." He smiled upon her, and Judith nodded, returning the smile politely, but in her heart she acknowledged that Quentin's absence was not a thing that threw her into despair.

King Richard had decided to be crowned afresh in Winchester following his release from captivity in Germany. During his absence, his youngest brother, John, had assumed control, and it was widely believed that nothing would have pleased him better than to have Richard die in captivity. But the golden giant, idol of the people and hero of the Second Crusade, had returned.

As Judith changed from her traveling clothes into a gown more suitable for the evening meal, she wondered about Quentin. He had fought in the Holy Land with Richard Plantagenet. A man needed to be strong to survive a four-year campaign in that country. She visualized an extension of the boy, and now, at twenty-three, he held a privileged position with his king. Courtier and soldier. Could she hope that the soldier had acquired a courtly gloss when they met? One thing she knew with certainty, a fact he had made plain at their last meeting. Quentin did not want a wife, but the House of Tarrant required an heir. Had her betrothed been Henry, how much better that would have suited her. But Quentin was the heir, and a man must protect his inheritance by ensuring a continuation of his line by legitimate means, and she was the means to this end.

She set her headrail in place before the polished steel hanging on the wall. A slender, dark-haired girl looked out of a fine-skinned oval face. Arching brows lifted over a pair of blue eyes and her reflected expression was grave. Then she smiled and a little color flushed her cheeks. She had almost a month before the wedding took place. It was spring, she was sixteen years old, and Henry Tarrant was to be her friend and companion during that time.

She raised her arms as Lucy tied her silver-thread

girdle about her waist.

"What jewelry do you choose, Mistress?"

"The gold chain only, Lucy. We dine quietly and I will not be long from bed."

Henry met Judith at the head of the main stairway. He smiled and she read admiration in his eyes, but he said no word as he led her to the hall. The trestles were set up, cloths were spread under dishes of roast fowl and sliced beef, wooden platters and bone-handled knives at each place.

Lord Tarrant met them and his gaze ran approvingly over Judith. "How pretty you look, my dear. Come, sit by me, Mistress. You will be hungry after your journey, I don't doubt."

With Henry seated on her right, Judith surveyed Lord Tarrant's household, these people she must come to know when she was Quentin's wife. His chaplain and administrators were present, and a fair sprinkling of the nobler knights he housed as part of his duty to the king.

Lord Tarrant was jovial and Henry charming, but the cloud that was Quentin hovered inexorably over her head. She dismissed it resolutely. She was tired, that was all. Turning to Henry, she smiled.

"I hope you have plans to entertain me royally now that I am here. I have well-nigh forgotten the gardens and walks. I look forward to reviewing them all again." In spite of her resolution, her forced gaiety communicated a message to Henry.

"What troubles you, Judith? You have nothing to fear, for you are amongst friends. You must forget your sadness and look to the future."

"Yes." The word fell flatly and Henry looked at her closely.

"Ah, yes, I understand but the future will go well, I assure you."

She was comforted by his presence. "I am acting like a foolish child," she said, smiling. "Forgive me. My spirits will be quite recovered tomorrow."

A good night's sleep did much to restore Judith's composure. She should not have betrayed her feelings to Henry, but he was so gentle and understanding. She rose as Lucy came in with hot water. She dressed in a fine woollen tunic that fell gracefully to her ankles. It matched in color the plaited silk fillet that held her headrail in place. A fine gold chain over the high neck of the tunic supported a pendant of sapphires and diamonds. She broke her fast with the wine and honey cakes Lucy had brought, then left the bedchamber, a light cloak over her shoulders, for castles were drafty places and Tarrant no exception. Down the stone steps that curved round the castle walls, she made her way to the hall.

Lord Tarrant was there with his gentlemen. His thick hair was barely touched with gray, and his stride as he crossed the flagstones to confer with his falconer was strong and surprisingly light for a man so well-made. Thighboots, already spurred, suggested the hunt.

He turned, drawing on a leather, gauntleted glove and his gaze found her standing by the log-fire hearth. His smile was affable.

"Good morning, Mistress. A fine day for hunting, and I would judge the worth of my new falcon, Pluto. Henry will be down directly, and I leave you in his care." With that he was gone, his attendants hurrying to keep pace with that long stride.

Judith smiled and seated herself on the settle. It was a beautiful day and she anticipated a pleasant stroll with Henry. He did not keep her waiting long. As he approached, she was struck by the similarity of his soft stride, the same lithe movement as his father's. But unlike his lordship, Henry was not ruddy-complexioned. As he smiled, she noted again the pale, drawn look. She rose and took his hands, holding back any comment, aware that her concern would be unwelcome, for he was also a Tarrant and proud.

Henry reached her, smiling. "The gardens, you said.

Then let it be so." He offered his arm, and Judith laid a hand on his wrist, feeling the fine bones beneath the lace at his sleeve-edge.

"His Lordship hunts today. Do I take you from that pleasure?"

He shook his head. "My lord of Tarrant goes like the wind and expects to be followed in like manner. I have learnt to preserve my own wind for more leisurely pursuits, though I disappoint him by my lack of achievements." His mouth twisted wryly. "He must content himself with one son in his own mold."

Judith looked into his eyes, but there was no bitterness there.

"But I ride well enough to escort a lady around the environs of Tarrant as my sire bids me," he finished solemnly, and his voice held a note of amusement.

Judith kept her own expression grave. "Since you are bidden by His Lordship, you must obey, and I, for my part, will seek to express enjoyment, should His Lordship require report."

Henry laughed, and for a moment he was the sixteen-year-old Henry of five years ago, gently protective toward the child who stood abashed under the lash of his elder brother's tongue. She had loved him then for his championship, wondering that he dared denounce the impolite behavior of his hard-eyed brother. Quentin had frowned, then laughed suddenly, begging her forgiveness, but Judith had known even then that his softening had been on Henry's account, not hers. She pushed back the memory, determined to gain as much happiness as she could in Henry's company until Quentin arrived to honor the bond of betrothal.

For a week she succeeded in holding that memory at bay. The weather held fair, and the days were filled with explorations of garden and wood, leisurely canters over the Tarrant property and evenings in the solar where Henry delighted her by proving himself a most accomplished lute player.

The blow fell most unexpectedly. She had risen to another clear day and, assisted by Lucy, had dressed and descended to the great hall, anticipating another leisurely day in Henry's company. Lord Tarrant, dressed for hunting, had just given her greeting when the sound of hooves on the approach road to the castle was plainly heard by them both.

Lord Tarrant's head jerked up as he listened. The note of a horn blared, and nearer at hand came the answering call from the gatehouse tower. His Lordship's brows rose.

"God's love, who comes in such haste? 'Tis no cause for alarm, Mistress. Were it so, the watchtower would play a different tune." He dropped his gloves on the stool and made swiftly for the outer door, his booted feet sending the rushes flying.

The wooden drawbridge resounded to the thud of many hooves. A fair body of riders, Judith judged, then the courtyard was alive with sound, the creak of leather as men dismounted, the blowing of horses and the stamp of booted feet. Voices came nearer, Lord Tarrant's the most dominant. Judith rose from the bench and waited, hands clasped, her eyes watchful on the entrance arch.

The party came into view and spread wide in the great hall. Without exception they were hardy-looking men with little more than a score of years apiece. Swords and daggers were strapped or hung from tight-belted riding tunics. The badge of the Plantagenets on every sleeve proclaimed their allegiance.

Judith felt a prickle of unease as she sighted Lord Tarrant's beaming face. Holy Mother, not Quentin! And yet the badges showed plain that some officer of King Richard had led these men to Tarrant. The noisy talk quietened as men caught sight of the erect figure by the settle.

"Be seated, gentlemen," Lord Tarrant was saying, "and avail yourselves of refreshment." He gestured to his steward who had already instructed his underlings, even now moving in with loaded trays.

One man remained by Lord Tarrant's side, and Judith stared at him. Surely, please God, not Quentin? This man was not in the least as she had imagined these five years. It could not be he. This man was of a height with Lord Tarrant, but his skin was darkly tanned and his hair a glossy black. The face was hard and watchful, the lines too many for a man of his apparent years. His dark brow rose in question as Lord Tarrant placed a hand on his arm to draw him apart from the others.

Then he moved forward, and the strides of the two men were so alike that Judith's doubts fled in a surge of terror. Lord Tarrant stood before her, his hand still on the man's arm.

"Now, here's a pretty surprise for you, Quentin. Behold your betrothed, the Mistress Bradley. Judith, my dear, we have Quentin come unexpected home so luckily."

Judith curtseyed, though her legs trembled. "With your father I give you greeting, sir," she murmured in a flat voice. He was staring at her so blankly that she could not bring herself to call him by name.

His bow was of the briefest. A frown sketched a thick black line above his eyes. "Mistress Bradley? I did not suppose to find you here." Though his voice was controlled, Judith sensed the shock in him. He had not expected to come upon her under his father's roof.

She raised her chin and eyed him coolly, her own shock subsiding and pride taking its place. "Nor did I expect to be here, sir. Only my mother's sudden death and the insistence of my Lord Tarrant brought me sooner to this place than I intended."

"I was not aware of it, for my business for the king has taken me far these last months." His gray eyes were cold, like the waters of a flat wintry sea. "I would not have known you," he said and the even tone suggested neither compliment nor insult. She could read nothing in his expression, save, perhaps, complete indifference.

He turned toward Lord Tarrant so sharply that Judith was startled by the abruptness.

"Where is Henry?" he demanded. "Not ill, I hope?" There was a hint of concern in the harsh voice.

"Henry is well. I don't doubt he will join us directly."

"I'll go up to him." Quentin glanced quickly at Judith. "Your pardon. I must speak with my brother."

He was gone with the quick, lithe step of the Tarrants. His father gazed after him for a moment, then shrugged and smiled at Judith."

"He is greatly attached to Henry. Forgive his brusqueness, my dear. I fear I was at fault in not preparing him for this meeting. He is tired, I think, and has been in the company of his fellows overlong. Excuse me, Mistress, I must see to the gentlemen as neither of my sons is in attendance."

As he moved away, Judith turned her shoulder to the room and gripped the back of the wooden settle, fighting back the cold desolation that swept through her. Was she not worth a few words of welcome, a polite smile one might bestow on any visitor, however undesired? A small hot feeling began to grow, filling the emptiness within her. Tired, was he? That was no excuse for treating her so curtly. He had not expected to see her, that was obvious. Surprised was too tame a word. His expression had been shocked! Why, for the love of God, had her presence shocked him? They were betrothed and due to marry within three weeks. Her knuckles whitened on the back of the settle. Quentin showed little courtesy to his betrothed. What less could he show to a wife? And this was the man who would own her, body and soul, when the bond of marriage had been solemnized. Mother of God, what of her future?

2

Henry Tarrant was brushing his sleep-disordered hair into place when his brother came silently into his chamber. Henry glanced over his shoulder.

"On my soul, 'tis brother Quentin! What brings you up here so swiftly? I heard the arrival and thought to meet you downstairs, with father beaming all over his favorite son."

There was no malice in Henry's voice, just amusement, and Quentin grinned, cuffing the slim shoulder affectionately.

"I came to inquire after your health. Some fellows have all the luck, lazing about in idleness at Tarrant while I get sent flying up and down the country on Richard's business."

"Were you at Sandwich when he landed last month?"

"Yes. I thought to find him somewhat subdued by fourteen months' captivity, but no such thing. I gather his confinement was pretty rigorous, both by Leopold of Austria in his castle at Diernstein, then by the German emperor who held him as strait in Trifel. Leopold was not happy to give up his prisoner, but the command of his suzerain forced obedience."

"And neither gentleman exactly enamored of Coeur de Lion," Henry commented dryly.

Quentin laughed and the harshness left his face. He looked barely older than Henry as the brothers grinned at each other.

"For a man so full of charm as our golden Plantagenet,

he has a great facility for making enemies. And Philip Augustus is currently the favorite."

Henry's eyes narrowed. "And what does he intend?"

Quentin shrugged. "You know Richard. He is set on avenging the wrongs done him by Philip. He sails for Normandy next month to reaffirm his sovereignty."

"So your journeys around the country have been with that aim in mind?"

Quentin nodded, then stretched, dropping down on the edge of Henry's bed. "I've been in the saddle for weeks, rousing the barons."

"God's bones, the man has only been home a month!" Henry exclaimed.

Quentin shrugged. "A second crowning in Winchester to wipe away the stain of imprisonment and he's spoiling for a fight with the French king." He yawned and stretched out on the bed. "By the Saints, I'm weary."

Henry stared down at his brother. "And you, Quentin? He'll expect you by his side."

"I intend to be there."

"Are you crazed, man? What of your wedding? Does that wait until another war is over?" He paused and looked at Quentin keenly. "You do know she is here?"

"I know." Quentin nodded. "It came as a shock, for I hoped to have the thing settled before she left her home." His eyelids drooped. "That's what I want to talk to you about. The wedding can still take place."

"But sooner, you mean. Yes, I see your point, but will your bride take happily of the idea of your going to war so soon after the wedding?"

Quentin opened one eye. "You miss my point, Henry. I don't want the wedding sooner."

"Then what the devil is your point?"

"A change of bridegroom, Henry. That's all. You're fond of the girl. She's yours with my blessing."

Henry drew in a sharp breath. "Damn you, Quentin! You sound like some Syrian merchant bartering away the life of a slave girl. Father will never allow you to break the agreement, and I shall not help you. Just think of the distress you will cause Judith."

Quentin spoke lazily without opening his eyes. "We are practically strangers as it is. Why should she be distressed? One bridegroom is as good as another."

"You've forgotten one important factor, Quentin. You are the Tarrant heir. I hardly think the Bradleys would bestow their daughter and her fortune on a second son."

"They're in no position to object. I understand the girl is orphaned, therefore has no champion for her cause."

The callousness of his remark robbed Henry of breath for a moment, then he recovered, turning fiercely on Quentin.

"How can you speak so despicably of a girl you have been betrothed to these ten years?"

"Don't be simple-minded, Henry. The families arranged it all when we were children. Did we have any choice? The girl expected to marry whomever she was told. Had I died in the Holy Land, the Bradleys would have sought another groom and she would have married him as obediently."

"That would have been different. You didn't die and you are still betrothed to Judith. She's beautiful and intelligent, Quentin. Even if you ignore her fortune, will you throw away the chance of marrying a girl so suitable to become Lady Tarrant?"

Quentin opened his eyes and smiled faintly into Henry's indignant face.

"She can still become Lady Tarrant, Henry. You are my heir and sole beneficiary. I drew up those papers before Palestine. Marry the girl, Henry, and if I don't survive France, you will be the Tarrant heir with a wife and fortune to go with it."

Henry moved abruptly to the window. His hands clenched on the metal grill and he stared unseeingly over the countryside. Quentin's voice followed him lazily.

"You spring to the defense of the girl so hotly, my Henry, that I'd hazard a guess she's a maid after your own heart."

"This is madness, Quentin. You survived Palestine. Why should you not survive France? Only your death will make me father's heir, and 'fore God I've no wish to become so in that manner."

"But you're fond of the girl? Tell me truly, Henry. Would you be content with her if you were, in truth, the elder son? Say you would not take her under any condition and I'll cease this talk at once."

Henry rested his forehead on his hands still clasping the grill. "I will not lie to you, Quentin. I have envied your betrothal to Judith since I became a man and took note of these things. She is sweet and charming, and a man would be a fool if he could not find happiness with such as she. You will rue the day if you discard her so lightly, Quentin. She is everything a man could desire." He drew himself erect and turned. "There you have it, Quentin. I love Judith, but I am aware of my duty. What cannot be altered must be endured, and there is no way out for either of us. Father will make sure of that."

A sign of exasperation came from the bed. Quentin stretched out and linked his hands behind his head.

"I should ill serve a wife while I serve Richard. Think you our father could smile on the idea of reversing our roles?"

Henry gave a short laugh. "Now I know you're crazed! Father will never consider it. If you broach such an out-landish notion to him, you'd better be prepared for powerful argument, at best. At worst, he'll have you confined for a madman until this foolish fancy has left you."

He turned back to the window and stared out. It could never be, he knew that very well, but how sweet the thought of Judith as his wife. Had Quentin loved her, he would have denied his own feelings, claiming mere brotherly affection. But had Quentin loved her, this conversation would not have taken place, he reflected wryly. Quentin was a grown man and a hardened soldier. There was nothing wrong with his wits, either. But how, in the name of all that was holy, did he expect a proud parent to consent to this madness? He dropped his hands from the grill. He, too, must put aside this foolish fancy. Judith could never be his. Reality must be faced. Next month she would become Quentin's wife.

He walked slowly over to the bed. "Come, Quentin. Father will expect—" he paused. The face of his brother was relaxed, the hard lines smoothed away as if by a gentle brushing of an angel's wings. His breathing was slow and even, the fingers of his hands still curled round his head. He was asleep, deeply and peacefully.

Henry smiled and lifted a soft covering from the foot of the bed to lay over his brother. Let him sleep. Father would understand. Perhaps sleep was best. When he awoke with a refreshed mind he would admit the foolishness and futility of their conversation. It need never be referred to again.

Henry stepped quietly out of the room, letting down the latch without a sound. He glanced down the corridor. Matthew, his own body servant, was approaching, clean linen sheets over his arm. Henry raised a hand to halt him.

"Later, Matthew. My brother has fallen asleep on the bed and it would be as well not to disturb him. Let him sleep it out, for he says he has been in the saddle for weeks."

"Very good, sir." The man studied Henry's face with a hint of anxiety in his eyes. "And you, Master Henry? Have you recovered enough to join His Lordship at table?"

"I'm well enough, Matthew. You know these bouts don't last long." He smiled and glanced down at the sheets. "Poor Matthew. What trouble I put you to. 'Tis only a touch of fever that makes me sweat so. You should hang out the sheets to dry and save the washer-woman the task. She'll be thinking me too nice in my ways to sleep on wrinkled sheets."

"She's not paid to think, Master Henry, but to do as she's told, and I'll not have you risking your health by sleeping on damp sheets. Her Ladyship placed the care of you on me when she passed away, God rest her soul. You were fourteen years at the time, and I've done my best ever since, pray God."

Henry nodded, smiling. "Indeed you have, Matthew, but my years are now twenty-one and you still treat me like that fourteen-year-old."

"Aye, you're a man, sir, but some things don't change with age no matter how much you treat them lightly. There's no excuse to be neglectful." Matthew's voice held reproach, and Henry clapped him on the shoulder.

"All right, you old nursemaid! I'll smother myself with that cursed smelly goose grease tonight. It'll not do much for those clean sheets, though."

"Sheets can be washed, sir, and come up as good as new." He paused. "Will you not see the physician, sir?"

"No! I will not! You know as well as I that he'll only bleed me or clap some filthy poultice on my chest. Don't fret so, man. 'Tis only a weakness from that fever I had as a youngster. Don't make any more of it than it is, and don't let me catch you dropping hints to His Lordship or Master Quentin about physicians. Understand?"

Matthew bowed and stood back as Henry walked along the passageway. It was true that Master Henry's bouts of sweating fever were not of long duration. Perhaps he was making too much of it, as his young master had said, but those specks of blood on the soiled sheet were not imagination!

Henry descended to the great hall, and his gaze searched out Judith. The escort of gentlemen that Quentin had brought with him had lost no time in making themselves known to the slender, dark-haired beauty in the fetching blue gown. But their attentions were respectful. Even without the deference due to Lord Tarrant, Henry hazarded a guess that Quentin's presence must place a powerful curb on their tongues. They were all his brother's company. He knew them well, and none would risk dismissal from the king's elite, captained by Quentin.

Judith was smiling, he noted as he approached, but her smile was polite and not the merry one he knew. He thought back swiftly. There had been little time between the sound of arrival and the coming of Quentin to his bedchamber. Hardly time to give pleasant welcome to a guest, and no time at all to greet with affection one's betrothed. Quentin had not expected Judith to be at Tarrant Castle. Had he done the unforgivable and revealed his surprise in a look of dismay?

Henry reached Judith's side. The glance she turned on him was remote, as if she had withdrawn into a citadel of pride. It confirmed his suspicions. Damn Quentin for a cold, unfeeling man! Could he not appreciate a young girl's own apprehension on meeting the man who was shortly to become her lord and master? Five years ago he had been cold and distant, she had said. Time had apparently not changed his attitude, but Henry determined to find excuse for Quentin.

"Judith—" he began, but Lord Tarrant had noted his entrance.

"Ah, Henry. Where is Quentin? We are ready to go to table."

"I left him sleeping, sir. He begs to be excused until he has taken a few hours' rest, but we shall see him at dinner." He glanced at Judith. "Quentin is always at his worst when he lacks sleep. No one gets a civil word out of him, just dark stares and inattention. Wouldn't you agree, Father?"

He stared fixedly at Lord Tarrant, who recognized the appeal and came back smoothly. "Just so, Henry. It is always the way with Quentin. Did I not remark upon it, my dear? And of course he has been used to seeking out his brother at the first opportunity. They have ever been close."

The situation was helped by a fair youngster who remarked diffidently, "Had I half of Captain Tarrant's endurance, I would have collapsed long since. He rode through the night from Oxford to London, then had an audience with His Majesty before setting out at dawn to ride here. He could not be prevailed upon to delay this journey, my lord, for he declared it was of utmost importance."

Murmurs of agreement ran through his comrades, and an older man smiled in Judith's direction. "But now the reason for such impatience is apparent to us all."

Henry glanced cautiously at his father, who returned the look impassively, both aware that the reason voiced was untrue. Quentin had not known of Judith's presence, and if Lord Tarrant looked upon his visit as a mark of filial affection, he would soon learn his mistake. On the other hand, Quentin might come to recognize the foolishness of his words to Henry. It was to be hoped that softer reflection would change his mind.

"Then let us eat, gentlemen," Lord Tarrant announced. "After meat, you may amuse yourselves as you will. The hunting is good in these parts, and the archery butts are in the meadow. The quintain in the courtyard is at your disposal, should you feel the need to unhorse each other!"

There was a general laugh as the men took up the subject of tilting and spoke ruefully of the buffets received by their slowness in avoiding the swinging arm of the tilt.

Judith, seated beside Henry, would have preferred to eat alone and not in company with these exuberant men. The chill of Quentin's greeting was still with her. He had not even pretended a warmth for the girl he was to marry next month. Even a tired man could offer courteous words of welcome, but not so Quentin, it seemed. She turned to Henry and found his gaze upon her.

He smiled. "Forgive him, Judith."

She raised her brows. "Forgive him? What makes you think he is in need of forgiveness?"

"Quentin is foremost a soldier. The king's business weighs heavy on his mind, and knowing him as I do, I would guess that his greeting was somewhat absent-minded."

"A charitable way of putting it, Henry," Judith remarked dryly.

"You took him by surprise, but you will see a different man at dinner. Take my word." He prayed he was speaking the truth and Quentin would be back in his senses by then.

Judith's contribution to the general conversation was little, in spite of Henry's comforting presence beside her. She was glad when the meal ended and she could go to her bedchamber. Perhaps Henry's words must be accepted. A man as exhausted as he had described would have small desire to observe the niceties of the meeting, especially as it was unexpected. She felt a little comforted by the thought—but only a little. You will find a different man at dinner, Henry had said. Her thoughts were touched by wry humor. A very different man altogether seemed preferable!

Henry Tarrant also made for his bedchamber. He must be there when Quentin woke. If the fancy was still on his brother, he needed to reason with him before Quentin sought an interview with their father. Lord Tarrant would never accept the scheme, and Quentin was too like his sire for the meeting to end without harsh words on both sides.

It was late afternoon when Quentin woke. He came to full consciousness with the immediacy of a soldier. He lay motionless, his eyes slitted, his gaze veiled by dark lashes.

Henry was sitting on the window seat, immersed in a book, and Quentin lay still, regarding his brother. He had been too involved in his own schemes earlier to take the time for an assessment of his brother. Was he

well? The sunlight fell across the page Henry turned, and
Quentin noted the long, slender fingers. His gaze rose to
his face. A little thinner than before? Pale, certainly, but
Henry had always been pale. But now in the clarity of
the sun, Quentin observed the fine lines around the eyes
and lips. That confounded fever had taken its toll, and
none of the physicians had known its cause or had the
ability to cure him.

It came to him that if Lord Tarrant agreed to his suggestion, Henry could have the happiness he deserved
before it was too late. He loved Judith, and the girl had
seen much more of Henry than himself over the years.
She could well be in favor of the reversal of roles. Only
God knew the span of life allotted to the professional
soldier or a man weakened by a fever contracted in
youth. The girl's fortune, so important in Lord Tarrant's
reckoning, would remain in the family, whichever
brother married the wench.

His thoughts paused for a moment on the girl. She had
grown up prettily, he could not deny it. The child he
remembered was now a woman, a slender, dark-haired
creature with delicate coloring and blue eyes. Those
eyes had been as cool as her manner, and the few words
she had spoken had been delivered calmly, as if to a
casual caller and not to the man she expected to marry.
For some reason, that thought piqued him. Most girls in
her position would have smiled and fluttered prettily,
lowering their lashes in a show of maidenly modesty,
however false, in acknowledgment of the coming union.
In his experience, female behavior varied little. A show
of reluctant modesty, then the inevitable surrender. Of
course, he reminded himself, the women in his life had
not expected marriage. Would Judith prove a cold wife?
Hopefully it need not come to that, so he would have no
way of knowing.

Henry glanced over as he stirred. He closed the book,
smoothing down its leather binding, and placed it carefully on the bookshelf. He rose and walked to the bed,

looking down on Quentin with a smile.

"Are you rested, brother? If so, I suggest you remove your filthy boots from my bed so that Matthew can lay on fresh sheets. I would as soon not sleep in your dust and grime."

Quentin grinned and swung his booted feet over the side. he sat up, running his fingers through tousled black hair. "Quite recovered, Henry. Thanks for the loan of your bed. I'd repay the favor, save that mine is usually in a tent or under a tree in the open."

Henry laughed. "Thank you for nothing. You will understand if I decline your kind offer and hold to my own bed."

"What time is it? Did I sleep long? I must see Father."

"For pity's sake, Quentin, you can't approach him unshaven and in your riding clothes. I'll send Matthew for hot water and shaving gear."

Quentin regarded his brother in mild surprise. "You're right. I've barely been out of these clothes for the past three days."

"I would never have guessed it," said Henry solemnly, and Quentin grinned up at him. "But now that you mention it," Henry went on, "I must confess my bed-chamber has rapidly acquired an aroma akin to a stable."

"You may lay that charge on Coeur de Lion, but I'll take your advice and present myself to His Lordship in formal attire."

"You'll see him at dinner. Why bother beforehand?"

"You know why, Henry."

"Sleep on it, Quentin, I beg of you."

"I have already slept on it. Ever since Richard announced his intention." He stared into Henry's troubled face. "What would you have me say to Richard? 'My apologies, Sire, for neglecting my duty, but your senior captain has a marriage to attend. Would your majesty hold off the battle for a few weeks?'"

"But this is important—"

"So is my presence by Richard's side. Don't you understand, Henry? My oath and fealty are to the king. His word is my law. I must obey. If Father won't agree, then the wedding must wait and chance my survival."

His expression was so hard and determined that Henry acknowledged defeat. He gave a crooked smile. "Go, then, and beard the lion on your own doorstep. I'll give odds you get clawed."

3

Quentin Tarrant strode down the corridor to his father's apartments. The long dark tunic, plainly cut and lacking ornament, accentuated his height, and his black hair looked thicker for the vigorous washing it had undergone. From his own little-used wardrobe at Tarrant, he had selected a fresh shirt and breeches, discarding the heavy riding boots in favor of a pair of soft black kid.

He was frowning. His dark brows marked an almost straight line across his tanned forehead. It had all seemed so simple, but Henry's words had made him realize that Lord Tarrant could well have strong objections. But he must seek to counter every one. No force on earth was going to prevent him from boarding that ship by Richard's side.

His fingers moved without awareness to grip the haft of his dagger at his belt. He rounded the corner, and the duty guard outside Lord Tarrant's room came sharply to attention. He noted uneasily the hand clenched on the dagger, and his own fingers held firmer to his pike shaft. Quentin in his soft boots made little sound, and his swift approach carried with it an aura of danger, heightened by the dark, frowning face. The guard swung his pike across the doorway, blocking entry.

Quentin halted abruptly, staring at the man from eyes that had become cold slits.

"What the devil are you doing? What accursed insolence is this? Stand aside."

"Yes, sir. I'm sorry, sir, it was just—I mean I thought—

your dagger, sir."

"My dagger?" Quentin glanced down and realized the intensity of his grip. He relaxed and removed his hand. "Ah, yes. Plain habit, that's all. His Lordship has nothing to fear from me, but I commend your caution. Now, may I pass?"

He raised his brows in question and the guard hurriedly withdrew the pike, red-faced and shocked by his own effrontery in barring the way of His Lordship's elder son.

"Your—your pardon, Captain," he stammered.

"You have it, man." A rare smile touched Quentin's hard face. "I would that some of my own men were as alert as you." He gave a nod and passed into his father's room, leaving the guard sweating with mixed relief and gratification at the captain's words.

"Well, Quentin?" His Lordship said, his gaze on the servant who was easing a soft leather evening boot onto his master's foot. "Your message was brief but had the ring of urgency in it. What must you see me about that cannot wait?"

Quentin glanced at the servant. "I can wait until you are properly attired, sir. There is not that much urgency."

"Very well." Lord Tarrant rose to his feet, eying his son shrewdly. "With the situation changed, I agree that we must talk."

"Sir?" Quentin's brows came together. How could his father know what he wished to discuss?

"The circumstances of Mistress Bradley's arrival with your own random visit makes cause for review, wouldn't you say? I dare say our thoughts run parallel on that score."

"Grant me the privilege of a private interview, my lord, and I shall enlighten you as to my thoughts." Quentin swung about and strode to the window, where he stood gazing out, his hands linked together behind his back.

Lord Tarrant regarded the stiff back of his son with surprise and wondered at the formal tone. The boy was impatient, he decided. The sight of his betrothed, grown into a pretty young woman, was enough to give any hot-blooded man the urge to turn a betrothal into a marriage without delay.

"The chain and ring, Edward, then you may go."

"Yes, my lord." The servant produced the heavy gold chain and slipped it over his master's head, then held out the jeweled ring before bowing himself out of the room.

"Now, Quentin. We are quite alone, and I applaud your desire for privacy. No need to give the servants cause for tittle-tattle. I take it you are here on the matter of your marriage to Mistress Bradley?"

Quentin turned from the window. "Yes, my lord."

"Then let us talk freely and without formality. In my opinion, that pretty child has grown into a beautiful woman, slender but well-proportioned enough to bear you fine children. Well-versed and comely, though even had she been plain her fortune must have commended her." He smiled into his son's impassive face. "Though one must acknowledge that a pretty girl in one's bed makes the task of planting the seed more pleasant."

Quentin remained silent and Lord Tarrant's gaze sharpened. A spasm of irritation hardened his voice. "God's bones, boy, do I talk into the wind? For a man on the verge of wedding a pretty young heiress, I have seen more enthusiasm on the face of a man awaiting execution!"

"I beg your pardon, sir," Quentin said stiffly. "Mistress Bradley may be all that you desire in a daughter-in-law and a suitable bride for any man, but I have to inform you that King Richard has declared his intention of going to war with Philip Augustus."

Lord Tarrant's expression relaxed and he reseated himself, leaning back in the chair.

"And being Richard, he will seek the first opportunity

to sail. I take your point, Quentin. The king will expect you and your company to be with him." He rubbed his chin and regarded Quentin thoughtfully. "The wedding date is set for mid-May. It is not possible for the family to gather earlier, for its members are widely scattered." He narrowed his eyes to gaze up at Quentin and a smile curled his lips. "I see now the reason for your gravity. Fortune has favored us, Quentin. With the fair Judith already under our roof, there is naught to be done but bring the ceremony forward. The family will understand. Having set eyes on the lass, you are impatient to make her yours before Richard calls you to duty, eh?"

Quentin drew in a deep breath. "No, my lord. I have no feelings one way or the other. The girl and I are strangers, and in fairness I believe the marriage should be delayed until this business with France is settled."

Lord Tarrant's smile died. "Delayed, you say! Are you out of your senses, boy? Do you suppose you lead a charmed life? You are a soldier going into battle. What if you are killed? We risk both you and the wealth of the Bradleys."

"There is always Henry, sir," Quentin said carefully. "He has a fondness for the girl and will be my heir should I not survive."

"Henry?" Lord Tarrant dismissed him with a wave of the hand and a scornful tone. "Henry has a weakness and is unlikely to breed fine sons on the girl." He rose to his feet and stared frowning at Quentin. "Do you suggest we delay to see how the battle turns, awaiting news of your survival or death and keeping the girl here? How many years will the conflict last, tell me that! And how many years does Henry have if his weakness increases, tell me that! The betrothal contract stipulated the Tarrant heir, and you, Quentin, are my heir. There is no disputing that fact. I shall put things in hand for a speedy ceremony. There is no more to say on the subject and I refuse to discuss it further. Have I made myself clear?"

Quentin bowed. "With the utmost clarity, my lord." He swung sharply on his heel and strode to the door. He was through and halfway down the corridor, his steps long and lithe, almost before the man on duty was aware of his reappearance.

On his way back to Henry's room, Quentin cursed softly and fluently in a variety of languages, unaware of the servants who flattened themselves against the walls to give wide berth to this soldier son whose pace was furious and expression menacing.

Henry had no need to ask how the interview had gone. Quentin flung himself down onto a stool and glowered at his brother. Henry smiled faintly.

"A speedy ceremony, I would guess. Don't bother to acquaint me with Father's remarks on my own lack of suitability. I have lived for years on the glorious exploits of your valor and virility. Though the fever I endure was not of my doing, I have suffered its consequences by thoughtless comparisons. Father is proud of you, Quentin, and knows the Tarrant line will continue in your union with a healthy girl. His confidence in my ability to sire a child is therefore limited, though I could argue that fact. In Father's reckoning, it would be foolhardy to mate a healthy mare with an ailing stallion. Far better to have her covered by a stallion of known repute." He grinned as Quentin's brows rose in question. "Don't stare so, brother. 'Tis not a monastery we live in here. The world and its gossip passes through, and as a soldier and man of twenty-three years you'll not be telling me you took the oath of celibacy! Our father would be shocked if he thought so."

Quentin laughed, and his expression lightened. "I'll not pretend that, but if he looks for any Tarrant like-nesses across the shire as proof of my ability, he'll search in vain. I left no bastards, to my knowledge."

Henry nodded. "A few disappointed village girls, I'll warrant, but none has approached the estate to claim paternity of you."

"Shame on you, Henry," Quentin said, grinning. "You make me sound like some lusty old Norman baron, scouring the countryside for unspoiled maidens, willing or not. I assure you that none was despoiled by me."

"And none unwilling, I'd guess," said Henry mildly, glad that Quentin's first furious anger had lessened and he might listen to reason without an upsurge of fury. He took a stool beside his brother. "I think the fact must be faced, Quentin, that Father will never be swayed by any argument of yours, or even mine, should I be foolish enough to approach him. You have no alternative but to honor the betrothal contract." Quentin's face darkened, and Henry went on quickly. "Would it not be best to obey and marry Judith as soon as it can be arranged? That would please Father and secure her fortune, and, who knows, you could well be leaving her with child when you join Richard."

Quentin looked at Henry curiously. "That sounds like the reasoned advice of a disinterested party, but you love the girl. How can you urge me to this course so calmly?"

Henry shrugged. "There is no other course that Father will accept, nor, if you are honest, is there one for you. If this impatience to go with Richard was not eating you up, I feel you would look upon Judith differently, but at least, as your wife, she will be under the family's protection, as she will also be should misfortune make her a widow." He smiled into Quentin's somber face and spoke lightly. "And don't imagine my advice is entirely disinterested, brother. I shall have Judith's company in your absence which I should be denied if you remain obdurate." He rose. "Come, Quentin, the meal will be ready."

Quentin rose too, his expression thoughtful. "You're a good fellow, Henry. I doubt I'd be so generous in your place."

"Then you can repay my generosity by being pleasant to your future wife. I promised to show her a different man after you had rested. Don't prove me a liar, for pity's sake." Although his tone was light, his gaze was intent.

Quentin smiled. "On my honor, I'll act the perfect gentleman tonight if it will please you. The girl shall not lack compliment or pretty word, though they trip falsely from my tongue. Her wits will sink under my onslaught of flattery."

Henry heard the cynical note in Quentin's voice and reacted with a hint of mockery in his own. "Beware, brother, for Mistress Bradley may prove a stronger swimmer than you suppose."

They descended to the hall and found the company already assembled. For a moment they paused under the archway and Quentin's gaze took in the scene. Of his betrothed he could see no sign. He was about to remark on her absence to Henry when a close group of his own company changed position giving him a clear view of a slender figure in a vivid scarlet gown. The long, hanging sleeves were edged with silver-thread braid, and the pure sheen of pearls glistened about her neck, partly obscured by the fall of dark hair under the short veil. He studied her a moment longer. She was, no doubt, as ravishing as Henry had described, but for a man with no heart for marriage, she could well have rivaled Helen of Troy and he would remain unmoved.

Heads turned to observe the entry of the Tarrant brothers. The knot of men from Quentin's company loosened and moved back a pace from Mistress Bradley, eying the tanned face and cold eyes of their captain with a wariness learned of painful experience. Though Captain Tarrant was, without doubt, an excellent commander, it was always wise to judge his mood and temper before putting oneself in his way.

Judith noticed the slackening of attention and turned to seek its cause. There was Henry, tall and slender, but appearing quite pale in contrast with the dark face of the hard-eyed man beside him.

Her pulses quickened but she gave no sign of any agitation of mind. It was inevitable that Quentin should take his seat beside Lord Tarrant and equally inevitable that her own stool should be placed next to his, later at table.

She saw him raise a dark brow and make some smiling remark to his brother. Henry nodded solemnly. He followed more leisurely Quentin's long strides across the stone-flagged floor. Rushes flew under Quentin's boots, and the swing of the long tunic flung them wider.

"Good evening, Mistress Bradley." Quentin stood before her, bowing. "May I offer a belated welcome to Tarrant Castle? Forgive my lack of courtesy this fore-noon, but I had much on my mind and your presence here came as a surprise to me."

"A surprise, sir?" murmured Judith, a faint smile touching her lips. "I would have supposed it more of a shock."

Quentin looked down on her from narrowed gray eyes. "Why should you suppose me shocked, Mistress? Call it surprise that I was confronted so unexpectedly by the girl to whom I have been betrothed these ten years?" His gaze moved slowly over her, from the dark hair to the tips of her slippers, rising again to travel over the slim waist and firm breasts, coming at last to rest on her face. "You have spent these past years growing into a very beautiful woman, Mistress Bradley."

Judith felt a surge of anger at being observed so closely. "My teeth are good too," she remarked caustically, "should you wish to examine them. An important point when considering the merits of a filly, wouldn't you say?"

Quentin's face hardened. "You despise compliments, Mistress?"

"When accompanied by the close inspection one would normally associate with the buying of a horse, yes."

So Henry had been right. "Perhaps I am more used to

buying horses than flattering young ladies," Quentin remarked lazily, observing the hostility in her eyes with a flicker of amusement. "Since you choose to find insult in my compliment, I will offer no more." He gave a careless shrug. "As we are destined to be man and wife, it is as well that we may dispense with the charade of blissful reunion. I doubt you have spared me a thought these ten years past, and for my part, I admit to the same." He paused, his eyes cool and cynical. "Does honesty insult you, Mistress Bradley?"

"I welcome it, sir," answered Judith, her gaze as cool as his. "A pretense of love would be tedious to us both since we have met so little. Speak rather of the duty our parents have laid upon us."

Quentin regarded her in silence for a moment. Her words had been mild enough, but from that flash of temper she had shown earlier, he suspected that Mistress Bradley had more than a little spirit and certainly a mind of her own. She was not in a flutter at his nearness and performed no coquettish tricks to win his favor. Was she so unmoved by the impending vision of the marital bed? The women he had known had been only too eager to drag him thither. But Mistres Bradley was a lady. Should that make a difference? His spirits rose to the challenge. Since he had to marry the girl, he could embark on his own personal Crusade, breaking down her resistance until she clung to him with desire and wept bitter tears when he left her for Richard.

Judith was puzzled by the tight smile that hovered on his lips. His gaze was intent and strangely unnerving. Her sigh of relief was almost audible as Henry appeared at Quentin's shoulder.

Henry met Judith's warm smile and glanced at his brother. Quentin was smiling, too, and the glow in his eyes encouraged Henry to believe that his advice had been taken. Why kick against fate when the prize was Judith?

"To table, gentlemen," called Lord Tarrant, and Judith

found herself seated between the brothers. Thankfully Quentin was caught up in the male conversation and spared her little attention, but intermittently she found his gaze on her and his look seemed to hold speculation. She was conscious of the strong, masculine body so close to hers, the hard shoulder that occasionally brushed her own. The fingers that curled round the wine goblet were slender but sinewy and deeply tanned. Her heart gave a lurch as she speculated on her future as bride and chattel of this cold-eyed man. Quentin Tarrant had learned his trade in a hard school and survived the rigors of King Richard's Crusade. Was there any gentleness in a professional soldier? How different from Henry he was, she reflected, and how her heart would have rejoiced had she been betrothed to him instead. Quentin's voice broke in on her thoughts.

"Your tongue stays silent, Mistress Bradley. I'll warrant you are not so short on words when it pleases you. Do you find the company and conversation of soldiers not to your taste?"

Judith felt the color rise at the jibing note in his voice. She stared into the gray eyes, no longer cold but warmed, she supposed, by wine.

"Since the conversation is on a subject beyond my understanding, it would be foolish of me to voice any views. As to the company of soldiers—" she allowed a hint of mockery to creep into her voice. "You must acknowledge that my experience in that field is less than nothing. Pray ask that question elsewhere."

Quentin held her gaze for a moment. His smile was unpleasant. "Perhaps you will be better able to answer the question yourself in shorter time than you think."

"Is there meaning to that remark?" asked Judith coldly. "Or does the wine speak for you?"

"Not the wine, lady, but my respected sire. He has not spoken to you yet?" He set down the goblet and accepted a fingerbowl from a page. As he wiped his hands on the napkin, he looked at Judith, and his eyes were hard and cool again. "It seems the task is left to me, and believe me, Mistress Bradley, I take no pleasure from it."

The servants were clearing the tables and bringing in fresh flagons of wine.

Quentin rose, taking Judith's hand and drawing her to her feet. "Come, I will escort you to your maid." He glanced at Henry. "It seems I must acquaint Mistress Bradley with His Lordship's decision." There was a pause as the eyes of the brothers met. Judith was surprised to see a softening of expression on Quentin's hard face. "Should you hold back your prayers for my safety, brother, it may yet be."

Henry smiled faintly. "The first I cannot do and the rest lies in God's keeping." He turned and was gone swiftly from the hall.

Judith's gaze followed him, a slight frown between her brows. She looked at Quentin, who was also gazing after his brother.

"Henry looks ill," she said. "Is there nothing we can do?"

He brought his gaze down to hers. "We?"

"You must allow me to be concerned over the health of your brother, sir," she replied stiffly. "I have a great fondness for Henry and would help if it were in my power."

"It is not within the power of either of us, though I would to God things had fallen out differently. Since the power rests with our lord father, we must obey, but acceptance is less easy."

"You speak in riddles, sir. I fail to follow the connection."

"Then I must make all things clear to you." He took her elbow in a firm grasp, and his steps were so long that Judith had difficulty in keeping her feet.

"Is all this hurry really necessary?" she asked breathlessly and a little angrily.

His laugh was harsh and short-lived.

"Hurry? Our lord father believes it highly necessary."
They had reached the archway, and Quentin's hold
moved to her wrist and tightened. "But only for the
noblest reasons and the good of the family, you understand." He came to a halt at the foot of the stairs where
Lucy waited. "Go you ahead, girl, I have need to
enlighten your mistress on a few points."

Lucy glanced at Judith for guidance, then jumped as
Quentin's voice came harshly. "Now, girl. Do you hear?"

The maid cast the frowning face a terrified look and
fled up the stairs.

Judith glared at Quentin and wrenched her wrist free.
"I dislike being dragged along like some disobedient
page about to be whipped. I can happily dispense with
your escort, for it appears you have some mental
disturbance that causes you grave displeasure. Let me
not add to your state of vexation."

Quentin expelled a long breath. He looked at her. She
saw a tall, looming figure, dark of hair and tunic, his face
shadowed as he stood with his back turned against the
flickering cressets.

"God in heaven, Mistress Bradley, you are the center
and total of my vexation!" Quentin said with such force
that Judith stared up at him blankly.

He moved and the light fell upon his face. His expression was plain, no longer angry, but held a coldness that
chilled her.

"My lord father has decided that we celebrate our
union within the week," he stated baldly.

"What?" Judith gasped. "But the marriage date is set
for mid-May! Why should Lord Tarrant seek to bring it
forward?"

"You may well ask, Mistress." Quentin's smile was
thin. "Does the bee delay, leaving to chance that the
honey may be gathered by another? Is there such a
thing as a king bee, I wonder?"

"I have no idea, sir, but I wish you would make
yourself clear." Judith spoke sharply, her temper rising

under his quizzical look. "Give me plain answer, not riddle, for this change of plan. There is surely some reason for it."

"Indeed there is. My father would have us safely wed in case King Richard summons me beforetimes. He plans to sail for France, sooner or later, to dispute with Philip Augustus. The date is yet unclear, but Father is a man of foresight."

"And not unmindful of the fortune I trail," Judith said dryly. "In which case, for His Lordship, the sooner is better than the later." She stared up into Quentin's face. "And you, sir, I would hazard a guess, might infinitely prefer the later, or yet again, not at all. I understand now your vexation, and in that we accord together."

Quentin's dark brows rose. "You have no wish to marry me?"

"Do I have a choice?" Judith asked. "We were contracted as children. Even so, I dislike this sudden hurry to exchange vows."

Quentin leaned a shoulder on the stone walling. "You haven't answered my question. You may speak with honesty. Were the choice yours, would you marry me?"

"No, I would not. Neither sooner nor later."

"And why not, pray?" Quentin's voice echoed his astonishment. He found himself more than a little taken aback by the blunt words. "I am the Tarrant heir with a fortune to equal yours. Nor am I considered ill-favored by women. There are young ladies aplenty who would not despise the position were it offered."

"In what capacity, sir?" Judith spoke sweetly. "As the future Lady Tarrant or the occupant of your bed?"

Quentin jerked himself upright. "Either position would attract many," he snapped.

"Do not number me amongst the many, sir. The first would be entitlement on the marriage, but the second holds no appeal since we are strangers and have yet to hit upon common ground."

"Common ground? Is wife and mother not enough?"

"You may think you know women, sir, but like most men, you know them not at all."

"Save that they are obedient and bear healthy sons—I speak now of wives only—what else is there to know?"

Judith's eyes took on a mocking glint. "If you need to ask that question, sir, I fear you are past redemption."

Quentin glowered down at her. "You have a sharp tongue, Mistress. I dislike that in a woman."

Judith was moved to amusement by his glare. "It seems that honesty insults you, sir. You bade me speak so, yet my remarks have set you in a fury. Since the thought of marriage appeals to neither of us, I consider your anger unjustified." She tilted her head and smiled into the dark face. "Or is it that you believe my honesty casts slur upon your manhood? Not so, sir, for I know nothing of it, save what you yourself have intimated."

She was so right that Quentin's teeth gritted together. He felt his color deepen and spoke harshly through tight lips.

"Quite so, Mistress, but you will soon know in fact not from hearsay. I shall take pleasure in discovering just what does appeal to you."

"Your anger is most revealing." Judith said in a flat voice. "And I thank you for the warning. I can expect no kindness at your hands, for you are too full of pride to consider the feelings of another. Now, if you will stand aside, sir, I will wish you good night."

Quentin remained still, his eyes on the face that gazed up at him solemnly. Pride? Was he full of pride and had no care for others? It was nonsense, of course. He cared for his father and Henry. Also for the men under his command. He cared for Richard as friend as well as king. It was the girl's own pride that was hurt by his reluctance to wed her. Like all females, she was expert at the barbed word.

"You wrong me, Mistress. I care deeply for many, and especially for Henry whose health is of great concern to me."

In the flickering light, he saw the girl's face soften. "One could hardly know Henry without caring for him."

Quentin nodded. "So you care for my brother, and fate has made him the second-born Tarrant. Would you have been content, had he been our father's heir?"

Judith looked away. "Of course, but since he is not, I see no profit in discussing the matter." She looked back at Quentin. "It is you I must marry, God help me."

"Exactly, Mistress, but failing divine help, you would do well to remember that my hand can be heavy. I will tolerate no maundering, lovesick girl in my bed." His voice hardened and the gray eyes became bleak. "You are a child and know nothing of men, but you shall become a woman when I leave, make no mistake about that!"

Judith stood very still and her clear eyes met the hard stare. "I have been schooled in the duties of a wife, sir."

"Then your tutor was lax in the schooling of your tongue. It seems to run too free, in my opinion."

Judith stiffened. "Since my mother oversaw my education, you cast slur on her name and memory. I fully understand my future role without this show of arrogance to remind me."

The blue eyes locked in anger with the gray ones. It was Quentin who broke the silence.

"'Fore God, we're as ill-matched as a pair of fighting cats! For a girl on the threshold of marriage to a man she patently abhors, you're mighty calm, Mistress."

Judith's smile was slight. "One must bow to the inevitable to retain dignity."

Quentin's temper rose. He reached out and took her chin in a firm grasp. "Dignity? By God, Mistress, I don't look for dignity but some small spark of emotion. Is that beyond you?"

Judith raised her brows and regarded him steadily. He read the cool question in her eyes, and frustration snapped his control. She should be taught that marriage to Quentin Tarrant was not to be entered into so lightly and mockingly. His hands dropped to her shoulders and he pulled her roughly toward him.

"Emotion, Mistress," he snarled, "like this."

One hand rose to the back of her neck, forcing her face forward. The gray eyes blazed into hers for a moment, then the lips came down fiercely closing the mouth that had opened on a gasp.

4

The kiss was no gentle affair, no light brushing of the lips
in salute. This was the kiss of a man well-versed in the art
of arousing passion. As female, Judith knew this instinctively, but was child enough to be unsteadied and
frightened by his fervor. Yet the woman in her
recognized the sensual male, and as woman her body
responded. His lips and hands caressed and coaxed her
into melting softness until a strange languor spread like
fire through her body. Then her failing mind registered
the fact that Quentin's own body had not relaxed, that
these caresses were deliberate moves to gauge her
reactions and put the lie to her coolness. Anger and
frustration, not passion, drove him, and as her brain
acknowledged the truth, she began to fight back. A tiny
spark of anger flamed into life, giving her the strength to
stiffen her body and clench her hands by her sides until
the pain of fingernails biting into her palms steadied her.

Her strength was unequal to his, and she could do
nothing but remain quiescent until he chose to release
her. She willed her mind to scorn his base attack.

Quentin's arms slackened and he gazed into Judith's
face. The skin was flushed and her eyes glittered darkly.
The body under his hands was rigid. He released her
and drew back. The blue eyes regarded him dispassionately. He watched her thoughtfully. Was there
nothing to her but a sharp tongue? What was it that
Henry saw and loved? Pretty enough, but no fire in her.
He shrugged.

"As I suspected, Mistress. Your fiery tongue serves only to conceal cold ashes, but they are not to my taste. Farida, my little Saracen maid, held fire in her very soul." He shrugged again. "It seems she has spoiled my taste for others."

Judith forced a thin smile. "Since you expect only obedience, I fail to see why my dutiful behavior displeases you. Perhaps," she added with the ghost of a mocking smile, "you have been so long in the field that you are accustomed to being received by ladies of a different temperament."

Quentin stared down from gray eyes that seemed to hold sardonic amusement.

"For a girl who claims no knowledge of a soldier's life, you are pretty sharp with your observations, Mistress."

Judith considered him gravely. With his dark good looks, his lithe but powerful body, and the appeal of a gold coin, or perhaps none was necessary, she imagined that the camp followers must be eager for his passion. Oh, yes, she had no doubt that his passion could be explosive, but only in his own interests, and they lay at the moment in the desire to go with King Richard to France.

Suddenly, she wanted to end this confrontation. Her head had begun to ache and she felt the need to be alone, to come to terms with this twist of fate that had brought the fact of marriage so much closer. She must go before her mind broke at the thought.

"Do I have your leave to retire?"

Quentin was struck by the paleness of Judith's face. The blue eyes seemed brighter by contrast and held a strange luminosity, a sheen that might have been held-back tears, if he had thought she was capable of such softness.

He bowed and stood back. "Of course." He found that he, too, was tired and had no wish to prolong this interview. The girl was now acquainted with His Lordship's wish. He turned and strolled back into the hall.

When Judith reached her bedchamber she found that Lucy had her mistress's bedgown and slippers warming by the fire. She moved unobtrusively and held her tongue while helping Judith undress. The pallor and shadowed eyes of her mistress warned her to offer silent comfort only. That fierce man who had ordered her away was Master Quentin, her mistress's betrothed. She repressed a shiver as she slid a fur-edged dressing gown over the slim, pale shoulders. She loved her mistress but would not, at that moment, have changed places with her for a sack of gold pieces.

Judith slept badly and woke unrefreshed in the morning. She wished there had been a Lady Tarrant or some female of her class to talk with, for she felt uncomfortable in this household of men. The news that Quentin had imparted to her last night had come as a shock, and her reaction was to avoid his company and that of his sire until she could face them with her composure recovered.

And so she spent the day in the solar, a pleasant room overlooking the broad sweep of garden. The embroidery frame was set up, and as she stitched, Lucy sat at her feet sorting the pile of colored wools. She sent Lucy away at midday, refusing her offer to return with food.

Judith's needle moved slower and slower, until finally she sighed and put aside the work. It was no good sitting here and letting misery take possession of her mind. There was no appeal anywhere. The Tarrants must side with Quentin, for who knew when the king's summons would arrive?

As the hour for the evening meal approached, Judith came to a decision. Quentin might think her spirits over-thrown by the impending marriage and his actions in the hall last night, but she was not yet his wife and the obedience he demanded was not yet his either. Tonight he would see a strikingly dressed girl, bejeweled and

composed, not the silent, pale girl who had left him to
escape to her bedchamber.

Lucy stood back as Judith surveyed herself in the
polished steel. Her tunic was of finest wool, a brilliant
amber with wide hanging sleeves, the edges stitched
about with gold thread. A heavy gold and ruby necklace
fell to her waist, meeting the woven gold thread of her
girdle. Her short veil of bronze gauze was held in place
by a fillet of tiny rubies set in gold. Bronze-colored kid
slippers peeped from beneath the folds of the tunic.

Judith caught Lucy's glance through the steel. "Well?"
she asked.

"You look magnificent, Mistress," breathed Lucy. "I
have never seen you look so—so—"

Judity raised an eyebrow in question.

"So—so challenging," the girl said.

Judith smiled. It was a good description of the way she
felt. She would challenge Quentin on his own ground and
make him accept that she was a woman in her own
right and not to be browbeaten into submission—at
least, she compromised, not until their vows were
exchanged. Even then, he should find it a task more
difficult than he supposed.

She entered the great hall with a determined step, her
head high. She scanned the assembly quickly, and her
bravado suffered its first setback. Quentin was not there
and neither was Henry. But Lord Tarrant and his
gentlemen were, and they must suffice for the moment.

As they took their places and the meal progressed,
Judith's composure cracked a little.

"Your sons are absent, my lord. Is aught amiss?"

"Why no, my dear." Lord Tarrant beamed upon her
with an admiring glance at the ruby necklace. "Quentin
has ridden out on the king's business. He will join us at
wine, he says."

"And Henry?"

Lord Tarrant gazed round absently. "He does not
always join us."

Judith nodded. "I see." But her spirits sank a little, for she would have retired when the wine flagons were brought in. It didn't matter in the least, she told herself. She cared nothing for Quentin's opinion. It had merely been a gesture on her part. She felt herself flush as she recalled the interlude in the hall. Just for that she had wanted him to see her, unmoved and indifferent.

She turned with an effort to the gentlemen round her, and they smiled and talked eagerly, vying for her attention. It was a most enjoyable feeling to be admired and deferred to, she admitted. It seemed not to be Quentin's style of address, but tonight, in his absence, she would take advantage of the situation.

He had not come by the time the meal ended, and Judith rose, bidding good night to Lord Tarrant and his gentlemen. She went up the castle stairs in a light-hearted mood like a cat, she told herself in amusement, that has been indulged into purring complacency.

Her slippered feet tapped along the stone corridor toward her bedchamber, and the smile was still on her lips as she passed the open door, hardly conscious of the glow of candlelight within. A hard voice seemed to reach out to her.

"Ah, Mistress Bradley."

Judith stopped abruptly, her dark hair swinging as she stared into the room.

Quentin stood by a table in breeches and unbuttoned linen shirt. His face was flushed and his dark hair fell forward over his brow. His hand held a goblet of wine.

She had a vague impression of a large-proportioned room sparsely furnished, as one might suppose for a man who occupied it so rarely. There was little clue to his character here. A wide bed, thinly covered, a window chest, a stool, and the side table on which the flagon of wine rested.

Judith looked at him, feeling her own color rise at the shock of seeing him, but she schooled her expression to blankness. "Sir?"

His gaze ranged over her and he smiled. "You are looking mighty fetching, Mistress. For whose benefit, may I ask?"

"My own," Judith replied cooly.

"I trust the gentlemen below were properly appreciative." He drank from the goblet and smiled. "Forgive me for not being there to add my own appreciation. I trust Henry made up for my lack."

"Henry was not there either." She saw Quentin's hand hold still on the uplifted goblet.

"Not there?" Judith saw the slight frown on his forehead, but his voice came smoothly. "I will not detain you, Mistress."

He drained the wine from the goblet, and the movement parted the open shirt front fractionally. Judith's eyes caught sight of the fine gold chain about his neck and the flash of green fire.

Quentin saw the direction of her gaze, and his fingers slid the chain into view. On his palm lay a heart-shaped emerald. Judith blinked. The stone took on all the dancing flame from the wall cressets. She had never seen such a large and splendid emerald before. A mounting of gold followed the contours of its upper edge, and the fine chain threaded the loop set in the dip of its shoulders.

"How magnificent," she breathed. "One might guess it was a gift from some Eastern potentate to his favored lady." She raised her gaze and found him watching her.

"Your guess is exactly right, Mistress."

She glanced at the emerald, then slanted a look at him. "I cannot imagine that you came upon it by chance. Did you have to fight this sultan or emir for possession?"

"No. As you rightly guessed, it had been given to his favorite concubine."

"And you took possession from the lady?"

"Let us say she preferred me to her master and, in return for her freedom, made me a gift of this stone. A young Saracen beauty, a dancer, snatched from her

family by slave traders to fill the harem of the prince."
He looked at the emerald reflectively. "She had a similar
fire within her. I was almost sorry to restore Farida to
her family. Where else in the world can one meet such
fire in a woman, save in the East?"

"I understand that some of the Crusaders stayed out
there and took Eastern wives. Why didn't you do the
same if the girl meant so much to you?"

He gave her a surprised look. "And give up my home
and heritage? No woman is worth that much, however
tempting the prospect." He gazed musingly at the stone.
Then his eyes met hers. "I wear it always to remind me
that such fire is possible in a woman, Mistress, for I fear I
shall not be content with cold ashes."

Judith flushed. "If your allusion is to me, sir, why then
you must allow that I have not the experience of your
concubine. Our training is somewhat different."

"Then I must teach you the arts of pleasing your lord,
just as Farida was taught. You will find it most
instructive."

"How kind," said Judith. "But you must forgive a wife
who lacks the background of the harem."

Quentin smiled sourly at the dry note in Judith's voice.
"You may now retire, Mistress, and reflect on that fast-
approaching wedding night."

Judith turned on her heel and swept out of the
bedchamber. How dare he bring her down to the level
of a prince's concubine? Let him find his fire in the arms
of the professional purveyors of such things. Did he
really expect his wife to behave like a camp follower?
Was he serious, or had his words sprung from anger at
being forced into a marriage sooner than he wished? But
that was hardly her fault. She liked it no better than he
did.

Lucy was awaiting her, and the undressing was
conducted in silence. She climbed into bed and buried
her head in the pillow. Her last coherent thought was of
the Saracen stone, that great flashing jewel of green fire.

In her dream it came to life, moving to the sound of some strange music and swaying between two perfectly formed breasts of golden brown. In the shadows sat Quentin Tarrant, his eyes on both jewel and breasts. The face of the dancer was blurred as if glimpsed through veiling, but the impression was of black hair and eyes, long-fingered hands moving provocatively over face and body.

Judith woke with a start. It was past dawn and the thin shafts of sunlight through the grilled window lit the room and glinted on brass and silverware. She blinked. The sun was in her eyes and she turned, frowning. It must have been the first fingering of sunlight on her eyelids that had evoked such a barbaric dream. A Saracen girl, dancing almost naked, with the prince's gift flashing between her breasts, was how it might have been. Dancing for Quentin? How else had the stone come into his possession? He could not have been in the harem.

She shrugged away the dream and rose. It was a lovely day, a day for riding out. Would Henry ride with her? It could well prove their last chance for a private conversation. Since he was a Tarrant, she supposed he knew of the altered arrangements. He had not been at supper. Was he ill or merely tired? She must find out.

Clad in boots and the wide-skirted tunic she wore for riding, she descended the stairs. A turn of the steps and Judith narrowly avoided the hurrying figure of Henry's body servant. The man stopped abruptly. The smile died on Judith's face as she observed the towels and steaming water in the bowl. Not unusual in themselves, but the gray face that lifted to hers told a different story.

"What is it, Matthew? Your master is ill?"

"Why, no, Mistress. 'Tis no more than the usual touch of fever. Master Henry bade me fetch more water, that's all." His tone was flat, his face without expression.

Judith nodded and stood aside. She would get no more from Matthew, she knew that very well. His devotion to Henry was absolute, and if the fever troubled Henry in the night, no one would ever learn of it from Matthew. Henry himself never spoke of it, but there were times during the years she had known him when he gasped for breath and his frame had shaken as if with the ague. At those times he had gone swiftly to his bedchamber, appearing later with some wry comment on the inclemency of the English weather.

. Damn Quentin, Judith thought savagely, for being so strong and healthy, avoiding whatever childhood fever had caught Henry in its grip. An uncharitable thought, but Henry was far dearer to her than his arrogant, domineering brother. How unfair life was, she reflected, swinging down the last step and coming face to face with the object of her rancor.

"And where might you be going?" asked Quentin in a hard voice.

Judith stared up at him in surprise. "Since I am dressed for riding, that is what I intend to do. Why? Am I a prisoner in your father's house?"

He seemed not to hear her. His gaze was on the upper curve of the stone stairway. He held silent for a moment as if his question had been out of habit and her response immaterial.

"I had thought," she ventured, "that Henry might ride with me."

His gaze came down to hers. "Henry?"

"Henry. Your brother," she said flatly. "Had you forgotten?"

Quentin's look sharpened. "Go to the hall and wait. Don't leave the castle." Then he passed her, his long strides taking him up the steps three at a time. "I'll let you know," he threw over his shoulder.

Judith stared after him blankly. What was the matter with the man? Why should she need his permission to go riding? Even so, she moved into the hall to await Henry should he be inclined to ride.

Quentin reappeared within a short time. Judith watched him apprehensively as he approached. He was dressed for riding. Despite the heavy leather boots, his step was soft.

"Are you ready?" he asked.

"Where is Henry?" she countered. "I expected Henry."

"I fear you must content yourself with me, Mistress." He gave her a quizzical look. "If 'content' is the right word."

She ignored the opening. "Is Henry ill?"

"No," he said evenly. "Why should you think so?"

"I saw Matthew. He looked worried, and so did you when we met before."

"Matthew fusses like a hen over a chick. I followed to convince myself that there was nothing amiss."

"And you found nothing?"

Quentin shrugged. "Nothing unusual. A restless night, that's all. Henry has many of them. The fever passes quickly, he tells me, but leaves him tired. He sends his apologies and bids me escort you instead." He smiled, but there was little warmth in his smile. "That is, unless you have changed your mind about riding."

Judith shook her head. "There is not the least need for you to put yourself out. I can go with a groom quite happily."

"I'm sure of it, Mistress, but His Lordship would rather you are escorted by a member of the family."

"In case I run away?" Judith could not resist saying.

Quentin gave a short laugh. "That might well have something to do with it." The gray eyes looked keenly into hers. "And would you?"

Judith shrugged. "Where would I go? I have no family, and besides, I should always wonder—" She broke off and turned away.

Quentin's hand on her shoulder brought her round. "Wonder what?" he demanded. "How it would be as my wife and bedmate?"

She stared at him coldly. "No. I should wonder constantly how Henry fared. Does that disappoint you?

After all, you have told me already what I am to expect as your wife. It is hardly a source of wonderment."

For a long moment he regarded her. "Then I must seek to make it so. No girl can be as truly cold and passionless as you would have me believe of you."

"I am not always so. It depends upon the company."

"I see. You are fond of Henry because he demands nothing. As a husband he would be gentle and considerate, expecting no more than is offered him in affection. Is that what you want, Mistress? A serene and placid life built on mutual fondness?" He raised a hand as she opened her mouth. "Don't pretend that you love Henry with some wild passion, for I would recognize the falsity of the statement, yet I judge you capable of passion. Is your sharp tongue a defense against any that seek to fire that hidden spark?"

Judith felt her cheeks flush but her voice was steady. "You are wandering in a world of fantasy, sir. Go back to your Saracen maid if you search for passion, since I fear you will not find it in a marriage with me." Her eyes darkened with resentment as she looked into his confident smile. "We are bound by duty, and if there is no liking, how then is passion possible?"

"The two do not necessarily go hand in hand. Love and hatred have passion in common and the blood runs hot either way. It will be interesting to learn which emotion is dominant in your blood."

"I find you arrogant and quite insufferable," Judith snapped. "I have never met a man with such a high opinion of his own worth."

Quentin laughed suddenly, and his gray eyes seemed to look down on her with amused approval. Judith felt her senses rock for a moment, then steady as she realized he had been goading her.

"Despicable, too," she muttered.

"Your tongue is refreshing, Mistress. Not amiable, but refreshing, like plunging into a cold river at the conclusion of a heated battle. But a man may grow tired of cold rivers and seek warm, scented waters by his own hearth and be in the right to demand them." He held her gaze for a few seconds. "Shall we ride, now?" he finished, mildly.

Judith turned without a word, and they moved to the entrance of the great hall. On the steps she paused, fastening her cloak and looking down at the waiting horses. She began to descend, but Quentin remained where he was. She glanced back at him, but his gaze was far above her head and he was narrowing his eyes against the sun.

Judith heard it then. A faint humming in the distance and the farway note of a horn. A hunting party? The noise drummed more distinctly now. Horses' hooves coming closer, a vast concourse of riders heading toward Tarrant Castle. Judith mounted the steps, to stand beside Quentin.

"What is it? Who comes?"

He shook his head and continued to gaze into the distance. Faces began to appear behind the iron grills of the rooms as servants peered out. A clatter of boots and Lord Tarrant stood beside his son.

"What do you see, Quentin? I can see nothing but the dust rising, but they're heading this way, I'm certain."

"Yes, they're turning into the valley road and it leads nowhere but here. Have the men stand to, my lord, and alert my own company."

Lord Tarrant turned, answering the command in Quentin's voice. He had barely taken two steps when Quentin spoke again, and this time his voice held amazement.

"Wait! I can see the banner they carry. 'Fore God, Father, it's the royal standard." He looked sideways at Lord Tarrant, then his gaze returned to the distant view. "By the Saints, Father, King Richard of England is upon us. What brings him this far from London?"

5

As the outriders and heralds drew nearer, Judith recognized the badge of the Plantagenets on the breasts of their surcoats. Beyond, riding in the midst of his armored knights came the tall handsome man they called Coeur de Lion. As he reached the drawbridge, he drew off his helmet, and the sun caught and turned his hair into golden fire. A big, powerful man, he still had the slim, hard body of a boy but tempered by the experiences of thirty-seven years.

He was in the courtyard, flinging himself from the saddle and bounding up the steps, his blue-gray eyes alight and alive.

Lord Tarrant and Quentin bowed. Judith had withdrawn into the shadowed hallway.

"My lord King," said Lord Tarrant. "I am honored by this visit. Please enter and discard your armor. I will have food and drink brought immediately, then order all chambers to be prepared."

Richard inclined his head graciously and followed Lord Tarrant, taking Quentin's arm as he passed.

"Do not concern yourself with bedchambers, my lord, for this visit is fleeting, but wine and food will be welcome." He glanced back toward his knights. "No ale for the men. Meat and water only. Keep them on standby, for this business will take but an hour at most."

Judith saw the puzzlement on Lord Tarrant's face, but His Lordship made no comment. The three men passed her without a glance. She caught a last glimpse of

Quentin. He was smiling into the king's face, and his eyes were as alight and alive as those of the Plantagenet. Why had King Richard come? What purpose was in this brief visit? She shook her head and returned to her apartment. It was not her concern. The king looked happy, so no disaster had befallen England, that much was sure. As she turned into her own room she glanced down the corridor. Perhaps Henry would be at the midday meal. A poor night he had had, according to Quentin. She would see him later when he was rested.

King Richard stood in the hall while his esquires removed his armor, gathering all up and withdrawing with bows.

"Let us be private, my lord," he said, soft-voiced. "A side room without hangings. Mean it may be, howsoever it lacks ears."

"As Your Grace wishes." Lord Tarrant turned to a small room off the hall. It boasted only tables and stools, being used as a repository for an assortment of weapons and pieces of armor. He bowed the king, his hand still on Quentin's arm, into the room.

"I will instruct that you be served here, Your Grace," said Lord Tarrant as he moved outward.

"Yourself too, my lord, for I need your acquiescence in this."

Lord Tarrant stared. "My sword is yours, Your Grace, and by that token my allegiance in all your dealings is assured."

Richard smiled warmly. "If Tarrant be true, I am indeed well pleased." The frank smile, the golden gaze that rested now on Lord Tarrant's face had won for Richard many friends. Men were dazzled by the personality of this Plantagenet and went to the brink and beyond in his cause. Women adored him and men served him proudly, but only a few were aware of the cold streak of cruelty that ran in his veins. It was unwise to oppose the Plantagenet. He could change in an instant.

But today Richard was in good humor. After wine was served, the three men drew stools to the table. Quentin had said nothing, studying the face of his king. Under the open gaze of the king there was controlled excitement, an air of taut expectation that Quentin knew well. It was always so on battle eve with Richard. Battle eve? Was he ready to cross swords with Philip Augustus, then? But what acquiescence did he seek from Lord Tarrant?

Richard spoke. "The time has come, my lords. I can no longer endure the occupation of my lands by that wily French fox. The treasury is nigh exhausted, but men have given generously to my just cause."

Quentin nodded gravely. "Your Grace is well served by loyal subjects." He was well aware that all gifts of money to this fiery and imperious king had not come from generous hearts but rather by extortion and fear of reprisal. But it mattered little save to surprise Quentin by its speedy accumulation.

"Nothing is left undone," went on the king. "The country is roused, and the army now gathers south of London." He gave Quentin an approving nod. "You have done well. Coming here I passed many troops on their way south. We shall attack from strength and hurl that dog from my lands." He rose abruptly to his feet, holding his goblet aloft. "Let us drink to victory before we ride."

The Tarrants came to their feet, and three goblets touched rims.

Richard drank deeply and turned his glowing gaze on Lord Tarrant. "I know that your son arrived but lately, my lord, but I have great need of him now. Will you think ill of me if I carry him off forthwith? For that I ask pardon and beg your acquiescence."

Lord Tarrant's brows rose. "But Your Grace—a few days surely—" He broke off, his voice so full of stunned amazement that Richard frowned, his eyes narrowing dangerously.

"Your son is my senior captain of horse, my lord. Would you keep him beside you while his king rides into battle? The Tarrants have ever been loyal to the crown."

"Indeed, Sire." Lord Tarrant had recovered his composure. "And will be so for all time. May I ask when you sail, Your Grace?"

"The weather promises good, and should we reach the coast in force by Mayday we will embark on the second day of that month, for the tides will be right to carry us swiftly across to Normandy."

Lord Tarrant looked down at the table. Quentin's gaze rested on the king, and he felt a glow of anticipation build up in him at the thought of going into battle once more at Richard's side.

Richard was regarding Lord Tarrant thoughtfully. "Speak your mind, my lord. Your support is less than wholehearted. Do you have reason for this hesitation in parting with your son so reluctantly?"

Lord Tarrant raised his eyes. "A domestic matter, Sire. Quentin has been betrothed these ten years. The marriage was set for mid-May, but the girl is already under my roof, due to the death of her surviving parent. I had hoped the ceremony might be performed before you summoned my heir. If you carry him away now, I fear he will lose the Bradley girl to another."

"Bradley? A Dorset family, I recall. A knight of my own sire." At Lord Tarrant's nod he smiled and went on. "A goodly fortune, I believe." He rubbed his chin, looking at Quentin with raised brows. "And what say you, my captain of horse? Have you no opinion on this matter? It is your sire who acquaints me with this marriage plan. Does he also court the girl and sing your love songs, too? Why do you hold silent? Is the girl—and her fortune —of so little account that you overlook the mentioning of it?"

Quentin's color deepened at the laughing note in Richard's voice.

"My first duty is to you, Sire," he returned stiffly. "Wherever you go, my sword is beside you. All else must wait."

Richard sobered and regarded them both in silence for a moment. "There is no time to lose," he said. "My regret is deep, my lord, but chance has it this way. What is to be done? I cannot, in truth, order the wench to hold fast to this betrothal if the groom appears not at the appointed time. Yet, if he apears not and is still of this world, the bond may be forfeit and the girl free to marry elsewhere."

"And undoubtedly would," said Quentin in a sardonic voice.

The two older men turned to stare at him.

"Would she, indeed?" the king murmured, pulling his lower lip thoughtfully. "By your tone, my friend, it is not a match that commends itself to you. Is the wench so uncomely that only the betrothal contract compels you in honor to take her?"

Quentin's mind dwelt briefly on Judith. "She is comely enough, Your Grace," he said gruffly. "Run wild, I'd guess, and unrestrained by doting parents. A sharp, answering tongue that needs schooling, but that would come, given time." He shrugged dismissively.

"But time there is not," murmured the king. "Neither for marriage nor for the taming of this wild Bradley wench."

There was a moment of silence, then Richard spoke again. "Is it not fact that my Lord Tarrant has fathered two sons? Does your second, my lord, have too few years for marriage?"

Lord Tarrant stared, appalled, at the king. "Henry, Sire? He has but two years less than Quentin, yet is not my heir as the contract stipulates. Besides—"he paused.

" 'Besides—'?" the king prompted. "There is maybe some flaw in his character which ill fits him for marriage? I will not believe you sired an idiot, my lord!"

"Never that, Your Grace, but Henry is unsuitable for

marriage."

Quentin struck in angrily, glowering at his father. "Henry has brains enough for two and though his health is not as he would wish it, he is as other men in wenching." He stared a challenge at his father. "Lustier men than he have proved impotent and weaker men have bred many on the bodies of healthy wives!"

"Softly, softly, Quentin," the king advised, amused and intrigued by Quentin's hot defense of his brother. "My Lord Tarrant is wise to think first of his continuing line and choose the stronger son. But even were your brother as apt in wenching as you say, the fact remains that you are the elder. The girl was promised the heir of Tarrant and would hardly be content with less."

"My brother, Henry, is mine own heir, Sire. I would gladly renounce all claim on title and estate in his favor."

Lord Tarrant's voice came strongly in fury. "You would renounce your birthright, turn your back on the title and become landless, all in favor of a weakling brother? You expect my agreement to that? By the Rood, I'll have none of it, boy!"

"Should I die in this campaign, my lord," Quentin said grimly, trying to control his flaring anger, "your weakling son will inherit my style and properties with or without your concurrence! And may I remind Your Lordship that I am long past boyhood," he finished through gritted teeth.

The gray eyes of father and son locked together for a full minute in mutual anger. They were so alike in temper that stalemate threatened. Lord Tarrant was the first to break away. His sigh was deep with disappointment, but victory was conceded, for he knew that Quentin would never withdraw. However, he made one last effort.

"And should you return, what then? Have you thought thus far?"

"I will revoke nothing I have put my hand to. Henry will be, as always, my well-loved brother, and nothing shall be taken from him. As I live, I swear it. May His Grace bear witness to my words."

Richard nodded. "I will do so if His Lordship is content."

Lord Tarrant's thick brows drew together in sudden suspicion. He stared darkly at Quentin.

"The interview you sought with me last night should have given me clue to your intent. Knowing of His Grace's arrival today, you had only to bide your time till he came to your aid. With your reluctant air and talk of Henry, I was a fool not to see the ground being prepared."

Quentin's gaze was as dark as his father's. His words came stiffly.

"Acquit me, my lord, of deliberate deceit. I knew His Grace was impatient for Normandy, but I had no fore-knowledge of his visit. The proposal I put to you last night was dictated by my own feelings of heart and mind. You turned your face from it, and I accepted my duty to the girl, however reluctantly. But now my duty to His Grace outranks all other. Believe me, my lord, there was no conspiracy. You have my word on that." His eyes narrowed suddenly. "Is my word still good, or am I no longer your son?"

"You are my son till death," Lord Tarrant spoke harshly. "That you cannot renounce."

"Nor wish to, my lord," said Quentin in a gentle tone. "That honor and respect will never be renounced, but to the other I must hold fast."

Lord Tarrant was in no way content, but in the face of Quentin's obduracy and determination to go with his king, he could do nothing. He rose, his features schooled to calmness. "Then I will send for my clerk to draw up this deed of renunciation." His gaze rested on his elder son. "God's teeth, Quentin! You are a landless vagabond and by your own hand."

"Not so, my lord," said Richard, rising and laying a hand on Lord Tarrant's arm. "Have my esquire bring

here my sword. On this very spot of renunciation, I will
knight my well-loved captain of horse. He shall be Sir
Quentin from this moment. Grieve not, my lord, that he
will be a landless knight, for I have long meant to bestow
on him the manor of Fairmile in the county of Kent. It is
in the royal keeping since its owner died unwed and
without kin of his name. Small, yes, compared with
Tarrant lands, but your son will not lack favor in his
service to the Crown. Let me once win back my lands in
France and there will be many vacant honors to be
shared."

"Your Grace is benevolent," Lord Tarrant said,
bowing. He left the room with more spring in his step,
mollified somewhat by the king's quick action.

Richard turned to find Quentin's gray eyes regarding
him somberly. "It was not necessary, Your Grace. I serve
without reward or—"

"Bribe?" Richard suggested, a slight smile lighting his
eyes. He reached over the table to clap Quentin on the
shoulder. "Do I not know it well, man?" he demanded.
"If bribe you call it, it was not for your sake. Your father
is a proud man. It would break his heart to think his
firstborn landless and a commoner. Would you deny me
generosity to your sire? Further advancement for you,
my friend, must be hard won, and so I tell you." He
grinned, and Quentin returned the grin with a relaxing of
his hard expression.

Both deeds were done, the knighting of Quentin
Tarrant and the deed of renunciation composed and
signed by father and son with the king of England as
witness, together with the cleric who had drafted the
deed.

The small party moved from the side room to find
food and wine spread on the long trestle in the hall.

Quentin's own company were there assembled,
having been apprised of the situation by the king's
esquire. They were to join the royal train and head
south, his majesty having come himself to fetch their

leader. While they ate and drank with the royal party, the courtyard was abustle with horses, esquires, and pages, all making ready for the signal to depart. So high in favor, it seemed, was Captain Tarrant that Coeur de Lion had made him knight within the walls of his father's castle in gratitude for the speedy assembly of his fighting force.'

The meal, which had been called for earlier than usual in view of the king's wish for speed, was almost over and the hall thinning of company as men left to make their final preparation, when Quentin remembered Henry. 'Fore God, he could not leave without acquainting his brother of the changed position. Better himself than Lord Tarrant, who would not hide his scorn and anger. He set down his goblet and rose.

"I beg you will excuse me, Your Grace. I must have word with my brother before we ride." He glanced at the king, but Richard was staring down the hall, the wine goblet held in an arrested position.

"By the Saints, Quentin, are you mad?"

Quentin frowned and turned his gaze in the same direction as Richard. Coming into the hall, staring about at the stream of men, some going and some hurrying through the hall, was Henry with Judith on his arm.

"Sire?" asked Quentin, perplexed.

Richard cast him a golden glance from those distinctive Plantagenet eyes.

"Mad, I said, if that be the Bradley wench." At Quentin's nod, he went on, "To forswear the beauty of that female alone would tax the strongest man, but to renounce all else in favor of another can scarce be believed! You said naught of her beauty and grace, my friend. You would have none of it, do you say?"

"I told Your Grace she was comely enough," Quentin said grudgingly.

"An understatement, indeed. And from the likeness to you, though less robust, your brother Henry escorts her."

"Yes, Sire."

"And both unaware of events."

"Indeed, Sire, and I beg you will allow me to reach my brother before His Lordship does. My words will fall gentle on his ears."

"And what of her ears, Quentin? Do you not owe gentleness there too?"

"Why—why yes, Sire. I will deal courteously with Mistress Bradley in the matter. I'd best take them both apart from this scene."

"Then bring them to me afterward," Richard commanded, a spark of humor lighting his eyes. "If the wench lays you low with a joint-stool and names you jilt and betrayer of maidens, I will accept all blame on your behalf."

Quentin bowed and strode away from the trestle to intercept the two newcomers. God's death, he thought savagely, to be thought mad by three men in the space of two days filled him with irritation. What did they all see in the wench that they thought him fool to reject her? He was unaware that his dark brows had formed a black bar above eyes that glittered as gray as the sea on a dull and wintry day.

Judith and Henry had halted and were staring at the tall, dark-tuniced, thigh-booted man coming toward them, grim-jawed and frowning. Judith held herself stiffly, her expression composed. Only her fingers tightened a little on Henry's arm.

Henry was fighting his own battle. Though he had passed a restless night and still felt weak from the coughing fits that left him exhausted, he had determined to show himself on hearing of the king's arrival. Brushing aside Matthew's anxiety, he had washed and dressed with care. Tarrant should show two sons when the monarch came a-visiting.

In the hallway, he had come upon Judith, hesitating and wondering.

"Well met, Mistress," Henry said, smiling. "Two late-comers together. It seems the meal was put forward to convenience our good King Richard, but none thought to warn you and me of it. What a company of guests. It will be luck indeed if we find a dish unemptied!"

Judith smiled at Henry's gaiety, grateful for his support at this moment. She was even more glad as they observed the purposeful approach of Quentin. He looked, she thought, like a man bearing down upon his enemy. Though he held no weapon, his very expression seemed threatening. He came close, and Henry spoke lightly but with mild reproof in his voice.

"God save us, Quentin, you come at full tilt as if prepared to fell us with one blow. Abate that fiery look, brother, for neither one of us deserves your wrath. What is amiss, pray?"

Quentin stopped abruptly, his scowl even blacker. "Wrath, you say? Why should you suppose me angered?"

"I beg you will enlighten us on that score," Henry said patiently. "You bear down like a thunder cloud and nothing is amiss?"

"There is naught amiss. On the contrary, the king comes opportunely, though our good sire has cause to question it." His tone was sardonic, and his gaze flickered briefly over Judith. "Come both of you into the sidechamber. We need no witnesses to what I tell you." Quentin turned on his heel and strode to the chamber where the events earlier had taken place.

Judith glanced uneasily at Henry as they followed. "Your brother looks most dark for a man with nothing amiss. What face does he show when in true anger, I wonder?"

Henry smiled at her. "One you will never see, I am convinced. His nature is hot, but there is no viciousness in it."

Quentin shut the door behind them and indicated the stools. "Sit down, Henry." He glanced as if by afterthought at Judith. "You, too, Mistress. Forgive my lack of manner, but there is much to do before we depart."

"Depart?" queried Henry. "What talk is this? You have been here scarce two days. What of Mistress Bradley and your wedding plans?"

"As to the wedding, why, Mistress Bradley may revert to the original date appointed in mid-May if she chooses, though our father may wish it sooner in any case."

"Will you talk plain, man?" Henry said, his own dark brows frowning. "The lady deserves the courtesy of plain speech."

Quentin recalled the king's words and nodded, seating himself on the third stool. "I beg pardon, Mistress. I will speak plain. I am for war with the king and we sail, please God, on May second. His Grace has commanded my company this day."

Henry stared. "Do you say there will be no wedding between you?"

Quentin looked at Judith. "Neither sooner nor later, Mistress." There was the hint of a smile on his lips. "Your own words, if you recall."

Judith's blue eyes met the gray ones calmly. "An opportune visit indeed, by your own words, sir, and one I will not dispute."

Henry was still frowning. "You spoke of our father. He cannot like this, Quentin. He set great store on the marriage between Mistress Bradley and yourself. What of the betrothal contract? That surely is binding?"

"Ah, yes, the betrothal contract. It is binding between Judith Bradley and the heir to Tarrant. I am no longer that heir. I have set my hand this day to a deed renouncing all rights and claim to that estate. You, my dear Henry, became the Tarrant heir from that moment."

"I?" Henry looked aghast. "Are you crazy? Our father has never agreed to this!"

"A trifle reluctantly, I admit, but His Grace has a powerful persuading tongue."

"Aided by your own word, I would guess," Henry said sharply.

"As you say, brother," Quentin agreed. He looked at Judith. "You are not throwing hysterics, Mistress—nor even a joint-stool! I think we are as one in this business."

Judith nodded, wordlessly. All she felt was a great relief that this hard, strange man was not to be her lawful lord and master. Her relief was so heady that she did not fully realize the implication of Quentin's renunciation.

"So—so I am free to marry whomever I choose?" she asked.

Quentin smiled. It was not an unkindly smile. "Hardly that, Mistress. The only firm stipulation in our betrothal contract is that you wed the heir of Tarrant. By reason of my renunciation of the title, there beside you, Mistress, sits the heir of Tarrant, my brother, Henry!"

6

Henry came to his feet so swiftly that the stool beneath him overturned. His face had lost all color, but the gray Tarrant eyes blazed down on Quentin.

"You have done this outrageous thing with the connivance of that royal upholder of chivalry and conduct? How dare you suppose I would accept with a glad heart what is not mine by birth? I will have none of it, Quentin, do you hear?"

"I hear you, brother, but the thing is done and naught will undo it," Quentin's voice was strong and implacable.

"And what of the lady you have wronged? This is callous treatment, indeed! You set her aside at the king's bidding, renouncing your own part in the betrothal contract, yet declare she is still bound to Tarrant. Ah, no, Quentin, it will not do. Your name may not be writ into the contract, but only your death will persuade me to don your mantle of heir-apparent."

Quentin rose and laid the palms of his hands on the oak table. "This is no day to debate morality or indulge in high-flown sentiments. I have not the time for either. You echo our father when you suspect connivance with Richard, but on my oath it is not so. I had no fore-knowledge of his coming."

"But welcomed it, nevertheless," Henry said on a bitter note.

The color flared in Quentin's cheeks. "Quite so!" he snapped. "You know I was not of a mind to marry, but, leaving my reluctance aside, do you see Mistress Bradley making great ado? She holds quiet and is content, I vow."

The dark figure turned, and Quentin looked down on Judith with an intensity that brought the color to her own face. She nodded wordlessly and stared at the table top.

Henry was still glowering at Quentin. "You may have made it impossible for me to deny this role thrust upon me, but I will not hold to the contract in your stead. I laid my hand to no document, so Mistress Bradley is free, by my word, to choose elsewhere. Not even Richard himself can dispute that I have some right in this matter."

"Do as you wish," Quentin said angrily. "Take the wench or leave her. It is all one to me." He broke off, his face changing, anger dying swiftly. He stared at his brother.

Henry's knuckles were white on the table top, his complexion suddenly ashen. A harsh, gasping cough tore through him, violent and unsteadying, as if a giant hand had grasped and shaken him. Slowly his body sagged forward, lungs laboring for air.

"Wine," Quentin said to Judith and was round the table in time to prevent Henry's collapse. He lowered his brother to a stool as Judith poured wine hurriedly from the flagon used earlier in the side chamber. Quentin took the half-filled goblet from her hand, and as Henry's spasm subsided, presented the rim to his brother's lips. Henry drank deeply. His face became flushed and droplets of perspiration sheened his skin.

After a few moments his breathing quietened and he smiled weakly into the two anxious faces staring at him.

"Damn you, Quentin," he said mildly. " 'Tis anger that robs me of breath, and 'fore God you made me angry." He looked at Judith. "Forgive me, Mistress. This accursed fever shows me in poor light and fills me with shame that you should be witness."

Judith shook her head, smiling, and took his hand in

hers. She knelt beside his stool. "There is nothing to forgive. I am no stranger to illness. My dear mother suffered such spasms for many a month. I nursed her and learned much of herbal remedies from village women. By your leave, I will tend to the growing of special herbs when we are married."

In the silence they heard quite clearly the king's voice calling on his knights to assemble the men. Henry's hand had jerked in Judith's, but she held it fast, smiling.

"That is—" she said gently "—if you will take me to wife."

The glow in Henry's eyes touched her deeply. His voice came huskily. "Though honor and delight it would be, you are free to make your own choice. Did I not swear it?"

"Indeed, Henry, and I honor you for those words, but my choice is made. Will you send me from Tarrant and deny me my wish?"

Henry's hand turned and clasped Judith's tightly. They both looked up as Quentin stirred.

"I must go to the king," he said in a subdued voice. He laid a hand on Henry's shoulder. "Forgive me, Henry, for causing you distress. I deserve your censure, but give me your blessing and let us part as true and loving brothers."

Henry raised his free hand and Quentin gripped it.

"Go with God, Quentin, and may He smile on your endeavors. Come back safe to Tarrant and I will be even more blessed."

Quentin glanced at Judith. "Take good care of him, Mistress. I have but one brother, whose courage and strength are greater than mine, and I love him the dearer for these things." He stepped to the doorway. "I will send Matthew to you, Henry."

His brother swung round on the stool. "Would you have me led to my bed like a beardless youth to be cosseted and swaddled by that old hen-mother for the sake of a coughing fit? And in front of the king, too?

Don't shame me on this happiest of all my days, I beseech you."

Quentin nodded. "Then I leave you in God's care."

Judith rose. "And in mine, sir," she commented quietly. "Henry shall lack for nothing that is within my power to give him. God speed you, sir."

With her hand still in Henry's, Judith smiled across the room.

Quentin's fingers were arrested for a moment on the door latch as he looked back at the girl. Her smile was dazzling, and although he knew it for relief and happiness, his gaze was held for a long moment by the vivid, glowing face. He would have awakened to that face on his pillow next month. Now, he had given her over to Henry, along with his heritage. A flicker of some emotion touched him briefly and was gone without conscious interpretation. Just a pretty face with body to match, he concluded. There were many such in the world, moving in pattern but never entering the heart of it. Only Richard Plantagenet was the heart of his world, the sole passion of his existence. Quentin nodded and raised the latch.

Richard was waiting for him, already armored and girded with weapons. He grinned as Quentin strode forward.

"You emerge unbloodied, Sir Quentin, so your late betrothed did not belabor you with her joint-stool?" He glanced past Quentin toward the side chamber. "They do not come out. Is the lady then prostrate with grief and your brother wiping her pretty eyes and congratulating himself on his good fortune?"

"No, Sire," said Quentin flatly. "Quite the reverse. My brother was angered and denounced me heartily for a scoundrel." A smile twisted his lips. "It was in truth the lady who congratulated herself on evading our union!"

Richard's brows rose. "Indeed? The Mistress Bradley bears no love for the Tarrants, then?"

Quentin's smile grew into a wry grin. "Not this Tarrant,

Sire, but she gladly takes Henry in my stead."

"Ah, I see," Richard murmured, stroking his chin. "There, it seems, lies the true fondness. Since we are not to be named as a pair of black-hearted villains, we may ride away without curses being flung in our wake." He slanted a bright look at Quentin. "A fair maid to renounce for my sake. Now the deed is done, do you not feel a shred of remorse for the thing, or a hint of envy that your beauteous Mistress Bradley will be bedded by another?"

Quentin regarded the king thoughtfully. "Neither, I think. My brother is well-deserving and the girl is content." But as he said the words, he recalled the moment of stillness by the door as he stared into Judith's smile. Neither remorse nor envy, he decided. He could neither begrudge nor deny their happiness. Vanity? Perhaps that was it, a mere flick on his male pride that a girl should turn from himself to another with such ill-concealed joy. She had called him proud on that other occasion, he remembered, frowning.

"There will be others, Sir Quentin," said Richard on a laugh as they clattered into the courtyard.

"Aye, many others, Sire, and a deal more willing," answered Quentin, swinging into his saddle. He smiled back at Richard, then cast an experienced eye over his own company. Alert, well-armored, they formed up behind him, falling into place with well-drilled efficiency. Mistress Judith Bradley was already fading from his thoughts as he awaited the king's signal to ride. He was for Normandy now and the contest with Philip Augustus. No wife lay behind him, no ties of body or mind to distract his brain from his duty to Richard Plantagenet. In this he must be single-minded, and he thanked God that he was.

7

When Lord Quentin returned to his apartments after seeing King Richard and Quentin depart, he found Henry pacing the antechamber. For a moment His Lordship paused, unseen, and regarded his son thoughtfully. Henry paced with hands clasped behind him, his tread as long and lithe as Quentin's. The dark frown on his face was not unlike that look of Quentin's when he, too, had sought audience. But there the likeness ended, for Henry was slimmer, almost to the point of gauntness, and his cheeks were hollowed by ill health.

God's teeth, thought Lord Tarrant in a spasm of irritation. Why must the king be so hasty in settling accounts with France? What could a week or two matter in bringing the dispute to a head? One week or less was all they needed to arrange things here, to bind the heiress to Quentin and plant the seed of future Tarrants. He had no doubt that his lusty firstborn was man enough to leave his lady convinced of his virility.

His eyes narrowed on the pacing figure. He had no such confidence in Henry, but ill luck and the king's need of Quentin had forced him into this position, and what could he do but accept the substitution? Pray God the boy would not disappoint him.

Henry heard the sigh and swung round. Lord Tarrant forced a smile, but Henry still frowned.

"Well, my boy," said his sire. "It seems that you have become my heir and are therefore entitled to all that it means. Is it not wondrous what kings may decree to suit their own ends?'' He could not hide the slight bitterness in his words.

Henry watched his father without expression, and his voice was neutral. "Lacking Quentin's consent, the decree would have had no meaning. Since he must have it so, we have no choice, but the position is not one I sought and I will take no delight or advantage from it."

Lord Tarrant moved past him and seated himself in his large carved chair, drawing toward him a jug of wine and a goblet. He poured wine, then glanced up at Henry, his son's words registering in his mind.

"You will have the advantage of a pretty young heiress. Does that not add sweetness to your position, should it need it? I foresee no trouble from the Bradley girl, for you are my heir and the betrothal contract remains the same in content."

"The position of your heir I can accept, but I need time to reflect on the other matter."

Lord Tarrant was conscious of a flicker of alarm. Was Henry proposing to adopt some righteous attitude and stand against the marriage? He sipped his wine slowly, watching Henry over the rim of the silver goblet. He held his irritation in check, deciding on a reasoned approach.

"Do you have a distaste for the girl, my son?" At Henry's shake of the head, he continued in the same mild tone. "It has always been my belief that you dealt well together."

"Indeed we do, and I have a great fondness for Mistress Bradley."

"Then what in God's name stops you from marrying the wench?" Despite his efforts, Lord Tarrant could not hold back the caustic note from his voice. "It is your plain duty to bring this girl into the family. Good God, boy, the betrothal has been arranged these many years. It cannot be broken without dishonor. Surely the girl expects it? Has she voiced some protest to you?"

"No, my lord." Henry stood very erect and still, his

dark gaze fixed on his father's reddening face. "Mistress Bradley has spoken of being well content with the new arrangement. It is I who doubt the wisdom of it."

"You?" Lord Tarrant set down his goblet carefully, giving himself a moment to gather his thoughts. Henry's words seemed to be echoing his own doubts, but just as he had put those doubts behind him, so must Henry. This marriage must take place. Whether she bred or not, the Bradley fortune must be brought into the Tarrant family.

He resumed his mild tone. "Your doubts do you credit, my son, but think of Mistress Bradley's position if you refuse this marriage. How could I keep her here under my protection? She has no other kin, so where would she go? It would be kindness to continue our protection, and how better than by marriage? She is willing, you say? Then put aside all thoughts of yourself and seek only the happiness of Mistress Bradley. Does that count for nothing?"

"To me it counts a great deal, Father, and that is why I hesitate."

"I fail to understand your reasoning."

Henry smiled and there was an unusual touch of cynicism in that smile. "I think you understand me very well, Father. This defection of Quentin's has shaken your confidence in the continuance of the Tarrant line."

"What nonsense is this?" Lord Tarrant spoke angrily. "Are you not man enough to breed sons on that young, healthy girl? You are my son, and the Tarrants were ever fruitful." He stared hard into Henry's face. "Don't prove me wrong and put the lie to Quentin's commendation."

He cursed his impetuous tongue as Henry's face tightened. The gray eyes looking down on him were reminiscent of Quentin's. Hell's teeth, the boy was proving more difficult than he had anticipated.

"Come, Henry, and take a glass of wine to settle accounts, I meant only that Quentin upheld my own judged opinion that neither of my sons were worthless in the marriage bed." His laugh sounded hollow, even to himself.

Henry had not moved, only his pallor had increased. "I suspected as much. You allowed Quentin to quieten your doubts, not for my sake nor even the Mistress Bradley's sake, but for that damned fortune." He turned abruptly on his heel and made for the door.

"Henry!" The roar of Lord Tarrant followed him. "You will do as you are bidden, for Quentin's sake and that betrothal contract. It is the least you can do for the honor of your name, do you hear?"

Henry paused at the door and glanced over his shoulder. His voice was calm, but there was a note in it his sire had never heard before. "Indeed, Father, I hear you most plainly. I shall do precisely as you ask, retaining only the right to choose the marriage date." Then he was gone and Lord Tarrant was left, staring fixedly at the heavy oak door.

He leaned back and poured himself another glass of wine. A frown drew his brows together. By the Rood, he had mishandled that interview, he thought sourly. Henry had surprised him by proving himself no malleable boy, overjoyed by his good fortune in being handed the Bradley girl. Lord Tarrant had seen them together and observed their easy companionship. His own attitude had been benign, for he knew that Henry would never seek to usurp his brother's position. Why, in God's name, was he proving difficult when the matter was so simple? His frown deepened. Henry was no longer in the shadow of his brother. Henry was his heir, and the future of the Tarrants depended on him.

Henry strode along the corridor to his own apartments. Color touched his cheeks, contrasting sharply with his pale skin. His step was firmly controlled, his back erect, but his harsh shallow breaths betrayed his agitation of mind. Pray God he reach his bedchamber before being overtaken by the weakness that was destroying his body. It should not humiliate him, here in the corridor, and his mind battled and won that fight for supremacy.

Once inside his own chamber, he sank wearily onto his bed, covering his eyes with long white fingers. Though events had combined to give him his heart's desire, was it truly wise to marry Judith? Only Matthew was party to the knowledge of his master's condition, the more frequent attacks of breathless pain, the sweating sleeplessness of long, dark nights. Quentin he had convinced by a deprecating allusion to the inconvenience of these spasmodic bouts. Lord Tarrant deplored his son's weakness, and, as a healthy man himself, rarely asked how he was. But Henry knew that his condition was deteriorating. Was it fair to bind an enchanting and healthy girl to a man of delicate and declining health? Not fair, perhaps, but could he stand firm against Judith's own willingness and the demands of his sire? He knew he could not deny either of them, nor did he want to, for the unattainable was now within his grasp. Judith, so long betrothed to Quentin, was by wondrous circumstance to become his own wife. He lay back on the bed and closed his eyes.

Henry slept a little, and dreamed that Judith stood before him, smiling, her gown of white lace shining in the sunlight. Her hands were outstretched, and as he moved to take them, he saw her expression change to horror, for his hands were red with blood. Then he was down on his knees, and the grass was wet and very cold. He reached to catch her skirts, but they were suddenly and shockingly streaked with blood. He knew that the blood was his but could do nothing to stop the scarlet fingers rising on the once pure-white lace. He looked up in despair, seeking the wide, blue eyes but finding such a terrible emptiness in them that he dropped his gaze in horror. But still the blood came, and his breath was torn from him in a long groan.

Henry woke, hearing the groan ring in his own head.

Perspiration soaked him and he gasped for air, the
choking sensation receding a little. He turned on the
bed, face down, and lay like a man exhausted by
physical exercise. For a long time he lacked the strength
to move, even the will to try.

Matthew entered the bedchamber as silently as he
always did. He congratulated himself on his quick
reaction that morning on seeing Master Quentin's face
earlier before the turn in the steps had hidden him from
view. Those brief words with Mistress Bradley had prevented his master's brother from arriving at an incon-
venient time. A clean sheet tossed hurriedly over the
bed had hidden the bloodstained evidence of Master
Henry's dreadful attack. The swift donning of a fresh
robe, a moment with a damp towel, and Master Henry
had been seated by the window as his brother burst in.

Matthew, his hands shaking, had half hidden himself in
the depths of the clothes press, apparently engrossed in
selecting day attire for his charge. Master Quentin might
be most fearsome in the battlefield, but Mastery Henry
fought a harder battle and did it with incredible courage.
Only he, Matthew, was privy to that unequal battle.

And now, as he glanced about the room, he was
surprised to see Master Henry lying motionless on the
bed. He approached, soft footed, and looked down. He
was appalled by the ravaged face and the deathly pallor
of the skin. For the space of a heartbeat, he thought the
battle lost, but he steadied himself as he noted the pulse
throbbing in Henry's neck. He retreated as silently as he
had come.

Along the corridor, Judith Bradley sat in the window
alcove, her eyes brilliantly blue as she smiled at the girl
kneeling by her feet.

"So, Master Quentin is gone with the king," Lucy said,
"And you will not marry him, Mistress?"

Judith nodded and linked her hands about her knees.
"I feel quite light-headed with relief, Lucy. A dark cloud

has lifted from my mind. I shall marry Master Henry with delight and not the dread I felt for Master Quentin. Is it not the strangest thing that I should thank the king for taking away my betrothed?" She gave a gasp of delight, and Lucy smiled.

"Master Quentin is very handsome, Mistress. The kitchen girls say he is known as a fierce lover, though none can claim he looks their way. 'Tis just talk."

Judith gave a tiny shiver and turned to gaze out of the window. Henry was gentle and kind. They had much in common, and Henry would not seek to dominate as Quentin had done. Her deep fondess for Henry made her want to care for him and minister to the ills of his body. With her help, he should get well again, please God, and there was no longer any Quentin to question her actions.

"Do not speak to me again of Master Quentin, Lucy. It is Master Henry who concerns us now."

"Yes, Mistress." Lucy sat in silence, reflecting on the ways of the gentry. Master Henry was a kind young gentleman, considerate to his servants and fiercely championed by his body servant, Matthew, but Master Quentin was a strong, lusty man who, from all accounts, albeit hearsay, was such a one to set a maid afire and burst her heart with longing. And yet her mistress turned from the one to the other with such relief. Had she, Lucy, been given the choice— She jumped as Judith spoke.

"Stop dreaming, girl, and bring out my yellow velvet. Then fetch hot water for my toilet. We shall dine quietly tonight, for the hall will be bare of company."

8

A week had passed since King Richard had ridden from
Tarrant with the former betrothed of Judith by his side. It
was the third week in April and the weather had turned
from fair to changeable. Sudden showers and chill winds
had whipped the tapestries in the great hall and con-
vulsed the candle flames so that they burned unevenly,
sending tongues of smoke into the faces of the diners at
table.

Judith accepted these inconveniences as normal, but
to Henry they were a source of agonizing irritation. The
chill crept into his bones, and the urge to cough in the
smoky atmosphere was overpowering. He forced his
mind and body into obedience, and it was on these
occasions that the appalling dream came back to him.
Scarlet blood on white lace. He fought his battle more
constantly and fiercely than before and achieved a
measure of success, for Judith smiled on him and talked
of the future. He was conscious of his father's gaze and
knew that his sire was fast losing patience. A date for the
marriage must be stated, and very soon.

Lord Tarrant intercepted his younger son at the
threshold. "A word, Henry," and he led his son a little
apart, then turned to face him. "You have kept your
distance from me this last week, Henry. I gave you leave
to set the marriage date, and you have given me no
word yet. Will you dally all summer without securing
your bride? What am I to make of it? Do you keep me in
suspense for private reasons, or does the maid hesitate

and stand by the arranged date? I have the right to know." He waited, hands on hips, his feet planted firmly apart. There was a flush on his face and his eyes were intent, the beginning of a frown marring his tanned brow.

"Tomorrow," Henry said. "Tomorrow you will know my intentions. You have my word on it, Father." He smiled.

Lord Tarrant stepped back, his face expressing mingled relief and irritation. "Very well. You have made your point in keeping me waiting, but I forgive you for it. I will expect news tomorrow."

Henry was still smiling. "You shall have it without fail, and I think you for your forgiveness, Father."

Judith was waiting for Henry, and they walked up the steps together. Outside Judith's bedchamber they paused, and Henry lifted her hands and kissed them. "Dearest Judith. You have given me the happiest week of my life." His gray eyes looked down, full of love, and Judith, on impulse, stood on tiptoe and kissed the fine skin of his cheek.

"The arbiter of the heavens has not chosen to bless the day with sunshine," she said, smiling. "But there will be many more and better weeks to come." She regarded him keenly. His face had flushed under her kiss and the gray eyes were bright. "Good night, dear Henry, and God give you a peaceful night. I see kind, loyal Matthew by your door, impatient to take you away from me."

Henry smiled. "Good night, my dear, and let us meet next in dreams." He bowed and walked down the corridor and through the door that Matthew held open for him.

The dawn came brightly with the true promise of spring in the air. It was warm, even at that hour, and the heavy wind of the past few days had blown itself out. A breeze ruffled the treetops and the sky was blue. Henry

Tarrant stood by the grilled window and looked for a long moment across the acreage of his family home. When Matthew entered with wine and oatcakes, he paused in surprise before laying down the tray.

"Why, Master Henry. You're up and dressed." He ran his eye over his master's short frieze tunic, the breeches and high riding boots. "Do you ride out so early, sir?"

Henry smiled and moved to the table. "I do, Matthew. I slept most soundly and, as you see, the bed covers are barely disturbed."

"Thank God for that, Master." Matthew stared closely into the thin, pale face. The ravages of illness were still apparent, but there was a different look about his master, a relaxation, almost a serenity in the steady gray eyes.

"Do you remember, Matthew, the spinney you took me to as a boy, the precise spot where I killed my first buck?"

Matthew remembered and smiled. "Aye, Master Henry. A rare struggle you had to bring the brute down and fierce as a young cub when I offered to help. He took you deep into the trees, but you wouldn't give up for he had your barb in him." He glanced curiously at his master. "'Tis all of ten years ago. What brings that to mind, sir?"

"I've a thought to go again, that's all. The day is fair and the distance not far. Have my horse saddled, if you please."

Matthew glanced at the bright morning, then he bowed. "With your permission, sir, I'll have two horses saddled."

Henry hesitated, and Matthew went on swiftly. "I'm not so old that I've forgotten how to ride, Master. It will not be too taxing for my old bones, I assure you."

Henry laughed. "You're a devious rogue, Matthew. 'Tis naught but an excuse to keep me in your sight, but come if it will make you happy."

They rode out of Tarrant Castle while only the kitchens

were astir, and if the guards in the gatehouse were surprised to see the young master pass on his bay gelding so early in the day, they gave no hint but saluted smartly, for this was the heir and the next lord.

The gelding was impatient and fretted at the steady canter his rider forced on him, but Henry held back his mount's urge to gallop. His strength was taxed sufficiently in controlling this leisurely pace.

They came out of the valley below Tarrant and began to ascend the hillside. Beyond the hills was the sea, and running parallel to the cliffs was the spinney where, in the robust health of his childhood, he had hunted and killed that first buck.

Henry felt the trickle of perspiration down his spine as they breasted the hill. His face and hands were damp, but he gritted his teeth in a determined effort to reach the spinney. Mother of God, he thought savagely, I have less strength than a puling infant. Was it God or Satan's work that offered him his heart's desire, then racked him in body and mind in an attempt to dissuade him down that sweet road?

He was breathing heavily as they reined in by the spinney. The sun on the horizon irradiated the sea as if it were afire, and the gray silken folds of slow-moving water glittered like some jeweled serpent. He and Matthew dismounted and sank to the still wet grass to regain their breath. The horses moved into the shadow of the trees and began cropping the grass.

"There'll be no buck here, Master," commented Matthew, "not these days. The lords or the peasants have driven them from this refuge."

Henry nodded and rose. He removed his tunic, dropping it at his feet, and wiped his forehead of perspiration. The white shirt clung to his body, and he plucked it away from his damp skin.

"Stay with the horses, Matthew. I shall walk to the headland and let the breeze dry out my shirt."

"Not too far, Master Henry, for a sea wind can be

monstrous cold and it'll not do to get yourself chilled."

Henry turned on him fiercely, a glitter of anger in the gray eyes. "God in heaven, am I a child to be harried by its nursery woman?" He stopped, and the glitter left his eyes. "Forgive me, Matthew." He passed a weary hand across his brow. "I spoke in anger, not aimed at you, old friend, but the cursed fate that has ruined my life." He held out his hand to Matthew, who knelt to take it. He kissed the long fingers. "Your pardon, Master."

Henry raised him up and let his hands lie for a moment on Matthew's shoulders. He was so familiar with his body servant that he had failed to note the toll taken on that sturdy, middle-aged man. The lines were deep on cheeks and forehead, and the hair had thinned and was streaked with gray.

"I am the one to ask pardon, good Matthew, for those gray hairs your care of me has earned you. It is a poor reward for one so loyal and true."

He dropped his hands and turned away, shading his eyes to stare at the sea. The tide was ebbing, leaving the rocks below the headland like chipped crystal. He turned his back on the spinney, Matthew, and the grazing horses and moved along the earth track. Spindly, surf-sprayed grass crunched under his boots, and the wind was brisker here. He walked slowly, and his steps took him higher, toward the cliff from which the sea had receded.

At the summit he paused, breathing deeply. The wind whipped his hair and dried the sweat-soaked shirt. The sea had changed color, the deep gray giving place to green and beginning to reflect the blue of the heavens. For a long time he stared out to sea. Quentin and King Richard would soon be crossing that wide channel of water, taking an army to fight the French king.

His gaze came slowly back to land, the furrowed sand where crabs dwelt and the streamers of seaweed left behind. From the shore the rocky, boulder-strewn wall that was the cliff began to rise to the turf under his feet.

It was like standing stop the highest turret of Tarrant Castle. His Lordship had demanded an answer of him today. He should have it.

Henry glanced down to where Matthew lay relaxed, so far below. His servant lay on his elbow, chewing a blade of grass, but his gaze was on his master.

Henry smiled and raised a hand in salute, then stepped forward into space.

9

Sir Ranulf Gann rode through the driving rain to Tarrant.
Swirling mist and the incessant upflung spray from his
mount's hooves barred the castle from his view until he
was almost upon it. The massive walls streamed with
water, and the once bright banner curled wetly round its
staff. Sir Ranulf slowed his pace and considered what lay
ahead of him. His stomach muscles tightened and he
swallowed hard. Two horses had almost foundered
beneath him, and his brief halts had not included sleep
or a change of clothes.

He checked the leather pouch by his knee. It was safe.
The two letters within were to be handed personally to
the Lord of Tarrant, and one of them was sealed by
royal cipher. Yesterday, in the early evening, he had
been summoned to the lodgings of Sir Quentin Tarrant
on the outskirts of Dover. His startled glance had taken
in the tall, flame-haired man who stood with a hand on
Sir Quentin's shoulder, before he dropped on one knee
to salute his sovereign lord. Then he had looked at Sir
Quentin Tarrant and what he saw brought his heart into
his throat. Deep-sunken eyes stared from a face whose
skin was drawn as tightly as on a skull. The black stubble
of an unshaven chin enhanced the pallor of that skin.
The quill clenched in the right hand snapped with a
report in the heavy silence that made Sir Ranulf jump.
The king's fingers bit into the shoulder beneath his hand,
and Sir Quentin flung the quill from him.

Quentin Tarrant rose and buckled the strap of the

pouch lying on the table before him. He glanced at the king. "His Lordship will be grateful that Your Majesty expresses sympathy on his loss." He pushed back the black hair with a weary gesture. "The death of my brother is the most cruel hurt I have yet known. God rest his soul, he was most dear to me."

Richard nodded. "We must redress the wrong I forced on your sire or God will surely frown on our venture. It would not be just, otherwise."

Quentin straightened his shoulders and beckoned Sir Ranulf forward. "I wish you to ride to Tarrant Castle with all speed and deliver this packet to my father. You know the direction?"

"Yes, sir. I know the road well. Do I wait for the return of message from His Lordship?"

For the first time a little color entered Sir Quentin's face, and the harsh voice softened. "I cannot say, but I will hope for a word." He looked into the earnest young face of his very junior officer. "If Lord Tarrant asks a service of you, will you obey in my name?"

Sir Ranulf drew himself to attention. "Of course, sir. I will consider it a privilege and an order from you." He looked from Quentin to the king, and they both heard the uncertainty in his voice. "I shall be back for the sailing two days hence, will I not, sir?"

"If you leave at first light and discharge your duties with all speed, then I see no problem."

"Very good, sir." He bowed and glanced at the king.

"You have our leave to retire, Sir Ranulf," said Richard. "Remember that you ride in my name too, and conduct yourself well, for you go to a house of mourning."

Sir Ranulf Gann held his horse to a walking pace as he approached the gatehouse. He peered up at the gray walls, sheened by running water. The great gates were closed and there was no sound from within. He could hear nothing but the sigh of the wind and the staccato beat of raindrops. The heavens were adding their own grief to that which lay in the castle. He shivered, as much from superstitious awe as from cold and weariness.

He jumped as a challenge rang out. He peered through the curtain of rain and distinguished a helmeted face through the iron grill of the gate. "In the name of His Majesty, King Richard of England, I seek audience with my lord of Tarrant," he shouted, flinging back his cloak to reveal the badge of the Plantagenet.

The face disappeared. The grating sound of iron on wood followed, then the great door opened. He urged his tired mount forward and passed into the courtyard. Figures surrounded him, and the spluttering wall torches glinted on steel, but a groom held the horse's head while he dismounted. Another figure led him up the steps, while another divested him of weapon and sodden cloak. He stared round then, noting the absence of lighted candles, and the soft, almost furtive tread of servants going about their business. A man passed him silently, heading toward the dim pool of light by the hearth. A murmur of voices, then Sir Ranulf saw movement in the heavy carved chair half-turned away.

"Let him come forward," a voice said, and Sir Ranulf strode across the hall at the servant's beckoning.

He looked into a face so like his captain's that he bowed, knowing this to be the lord himself. The same haunted expression and dulled gray eyes stared up. The man sat, his neck hunched into broad shoulders, strong hands hanging limp.

Sir Ranulf was conscious of the steam rising from his sodden tunic as he fumbled to detach the purse from his belt. He handed the sealed packet to Lord Tarrant, who scanned the superscripture quickly. He looked up, and the gray eyes had lost their dullness. "My son's own hand," he exclaimed. "They have not yet sailed?"

"No, my lord. I come from Dover and am ordered to be at your service by my captain and the king himself."

"Your name, sir," came the sharp enquiry, the voice

strengthened.

"Sir Ranulf Gann, my lord."

"Then, Sir Ranulf, you may withdraw and refresh yourself while I read the messages you have brought." He turned to his steward. "Bring more candles, man."

Sir Ranulf bowed himself away as Lord Tarrant's strong fingers broke the seal on his son's letter.

Judith sat at the window of her bedchamber, gazing listlessly at the rain-drenched countryside. Her eyes were swollen with weeping, and she had not left her bedchamber since Henry had been lowered into the crypt of the Tarrant chapel. Henry, who was to have become her husband, was dead, his broken body brought back to Tarrant by men of the estate who wept openly, for Henry had always been their favorite.

Judith had knelt beside Lord Tarrant as the castle's own chaplain had committed Henry's body to the ground and his soul into the keeping of God. When it was over, Lord Tarrant had looked into Judith's white face, his own gray and lined. She had half-raised a hand to lay on his in a gesture of comfort, but the movement was stilled by his words.

"Is my house accursed, Mistress? Two sons I had, and you betrothed to both in turn. One already claimed by death and the other gone to face that same prospect. Does my line end here?" He swept an arm about the chapel. "My ancestors lie below, but not a one gave up his soul without leaving witness to his coming and a likeness on his departure." His eyes had rested on her accusingly. "Was it too much to ask? My generosity to you both has cost me dear." He had turned on his heel and strode from the chapel, leaving Judith trembling and stricken.

His words had been unfair. Instead of them drawing together in grief, he had laid the blame upon her. Truly she had been betrothed to both his sons, but not even Lord Tarrant himself had prevented King Richard from taking Quentin, and Henry she would have married happily had not death intervened.

"You must eat, Mistress," said Lucy, who had come to stand beside the window. "You have scarce touched a thing for days. Why do you not go down to join his lordship in the hall?"

Judith shook her head. "No. My lord does not favor my presence. We hold to our grief separately."

"But, Mistress, you are growing pale and thin. Your gowns will hang loose and—"

Judith turned on her with a flash of temper. "Let me be, Lucy. For whom do I need to look comely? Lord Tarrant rebukes me for lack of Tarrant seed in my body and holds my maidenhood as insult. What would you have me say in reply?"

She turned her back and resumed her listless gaze out of the window. Lucy sighed and picked up the tray with its untouched food and carried it below to the kitchen. She entered on a buzz of comment and noticed a sodden frieze cloak spread before the hearth. Leather riding boots stood to one side.

"Who comes?" she asked a hurrying manservant.

He shrugged. "A king's knight, I hear, but on what mission I know not."

Lord Tarrant laid aside the two letters and stared into the fire, feeling hope and strength return to him. Thank God his messenger had found Quentin before he sailed. All hope would have died otherwise. Lord Tarrant looked again at his son's letter. The heavy quill strokes had, in places, pierced the parchment, indicating the horror and grief he felt on learning of Henry's deathfall. The letter had gone on to acknowledge his sire's claim that he now revert to his previous position as heir of Tarrant and accept the terms attached to it.

Lord Tarrant's left hand unclenched, and he stared down into the green fire of the Saracen emerald, the fine gold chain curled beneath. A token of my obedience, Quentin had written, and the parchment was deeply scored at that point. Lord Tarrant guessed at the effort it had taken to part Quentin from his beloved stone, and he smiled grimly. By the living God, if proof were needed of his son's adherence to filial duty, this was the evidence of it. The Bradley fortune was saved, but the line of Tarrant still waited for its certainty of continuance until Quentin's return. He rose, calling his steward.

When Lucy returned to the bedchamber, she found her mistress pacing the floor. There was color in her face, and the tone of her voice was decisive as she spoke.

"I have determined to leave this place, Lucy, and return to Bradley. The manor is still in my keeping, and I would as soon be there as here. I refuse to be treated with indifference, nay even dislike, by Lord Tarrant." Her blue eyes regarded Lucy with the hardness of sapphire. "He dealt with me kindly for the sake of what I brought, but since defection and death have robbed me of husband, I am of no further worth to him." She paused for breath, and Lucy saw the pulse beat strongly in her slender neck. "Arrange for my boxes to be brought, if you please."

Lucy curtseyed. "Yes, Mistress," and turned toward the door. Before she reached it, a knock on the panel sounded from the corridor. Lucy opened the door and was faced by Lord Tarrant's steward. The maid allowed him entry, and he bowed low to Judith.

"His Lordship begs the pleasure of your company at dinner, Mistress."

Judith stared at him. A hot refusal rose to her lips, but she restrained the words. Almost a week had passed, and Lord Tarrant's disregard of her presence had been painful and bitter. Why now did he want her company? Why now at the moment when she had decided to end her stay at Tarrant Castle? Since she was neither wife nor betrothed, her life was her own. She toyed with the idea of declining the invitation, then changed her mind. It would give her opportunity to inform him of her decision.

"Very well. Inform his lordship that I shall be present at table."

The steward bowed and retired.

Later, as Judith descended to the great hall, she paused to look about her in surprise. Candles glowed everywhere, the hearth was a beacon of burning logs, and servants moved swiftly about the trestles, setting pewter plates and goblets of silver in line before them. It was as if a great banquet were planned.

She turned to Lucy, raising her brows in question. "What is this? Has a party arrived? I heard no sound of horses in the courtyard."

Lucy remembered the rain-soaked cloak. "One horseman only that I know of, Mistress. They told me in the kitchen that he was a king's knight."

"A king's knight? The king is in Dover and sails shortly for France, I understand, so this cannot be in his honor, nor surely for a lone knight." She shrugged and moved further into the hall, her gaze seeking a sign of Lord Tarrant. She blinked as she saw him. He approached, a magnificent figure in long embroidered tunic, the waist caught in by a broad jeweled belt. His hands were out-stretched, and his smile so affable that Judith could scarcely believe him to be the same man who had scorched her with his glance in the chapel. She watched him warily and timed his approach, dropping to a curtsey and avoiding the necessity of taking his hands.

Only then did she see the man who followed closely. He was a stranger, young and round-faced, but she observed the fatigued look about his eyes and the slight twitch of a cheek muscle. The king's knight? Perhaps, but she had no time to speculate further, for Lord Tarrant was presenting him.

"Sir Raulf Gann—Mistress Bradley," and Judith felt

Lord Tarrant's hand under her elbow, guiding her to the table.

"Sir Ranulf has ridden from Dover," went on Lord Tarrant, casting the young man a beaming smile. "He brings messages and great news from that port."

"Great news?" queried Judith, refusing to be warmed by His Lordship's apparent high humor. "Has the king of France surrendered already and the army not yet shipped?"

Lord Tarrant gave her a sharp look, although his smile remained, but to Judith's surprise the young face of Sir Ranulf had turned a dark red and his shoulders shifted uncomfortably under his tunic.

"Both Quentin and His Majesty send condolences." Lord Tarrant lowered his voice suitably.

"That was kind," said Judith. "I trust His Majesty is well, Sir Ranulf?"

The boy met her gaze. "Very well, Mistress." He looked away, and Judith sensed his embarrassment. "And of course, Sir Quentin," she added as if on an afterthought.

It pleased her to note the tightening of Lord Tarrant's lips, but he said no word while the meat was being served. The meal reached its conclusion in silence, and Judith herself was the first to speak.

"I am glad of this opportunity to see you, my lord, for I have news of my own. I have not been honored by your company since my betrothed husband was laid to rest, I can only thank you for this meeting."

Lord Tarrant's smile became tolerant. "As we both seem to be great with news, Mistress, I suggest we adjourn to the solar. We will be private there."

Judith wondered at his smile as they made their way up the castle stairs. Had there been a hint of amusement lurking beneath his blandness, as if her own news was of little account against his own? The arrival of this young knight had somehow restored her to favor, and she distrusted the motive that had placed her there. What was Lord Tarrant planning? He no longer had any claim upon her, and she was free to pursue her own life.

Lord Tarrant positioned himself before the wide hearth, clasping his hands behind him. "Be seated, Mistress, and you may also take a stool, Sir Ranulf. I know that you have been in the saddle for many hours and will be so again before dawn."

Judith sat, spreading her skirts about her, and glanced at Sir Ranulf. The young man looked haggard with weariness, but his gaze was fixed on Lord Tarrant and he held himself stiffly. He did not return her glance.

"I will come to the point swiftly, Mistress Bradley," Lord Tarrant said. "For you will need time to prepare yourself, and we have little of that if Sir Ranulf is to sail on the Mayday tide." He paused, and Judith watched him closely, a cobweb of fear beginning to touch her with delicate strands.

"My son has not failed me, Mistress, and I thank God that my message reached him in time. Overwrought as he was by the news of Henry's death, he yet remembered his duty to the house of Tarrant."

The gray eyes, bright and triumphant, stared down into Judith's. "Since I have but one son left in life, that son is my heir. All contract to the contrary is now revoked."

Judith rose to her feet slowly, feeling the gossamer threads tighten into steel mesh and close about her. Her hand flew to her throat, and for a moment she swayed, staring at Lord Tarrant from a face grown pale.

"So, Mistress Bradley, we revert to the original position and hold to the contract of betrothal."

Judith forced herself to speak. "How can you do this, my lord, when your son is on the point of departure and lies, even now, in Dover? He cannot return in so short a time."

"Exactly, Mistress. I believe I have already mentioned our lack of time, but Sir Ranulf is here, beside you."

Judith turned to the silent young man. "I fail to see Sir

Ranulf's connection with this matter."

"His presence is most essential, Mistress. He stands as proxy for my son and will act in his name at the wedding ceremony."

"I have no wish—" began Judith, but Lord Tarrant's brilliant gray eyes had turned into cold stone.

"You have no choice, my dear, but to fulfill the terms of the contract laid down by our two families. That bond of honor cannot be set aside lightly, and since King Richard himself knighted my son within these very walls, you will become Lady Tarrant in my lifetime. Does not that add to your stature?"

Judith's knees weakened under her, and she sank back onto the stool, staring mutely but unseeingly at Lord Tarrant.

"And this, my dear daughter-in-law to be, is the proof of Quentin's fealty to his house."

Judith felt his fingers at her throat, then a heavy cold weight lay upon her breast.

"When the war is over, my son will return to claim his token and his bride, you may rest easy on that score."

Judith's gaze cleared, and she found herself staring down into the smoldering depths of the emerald, given in love by a Saracen concubine to the man she was once again pledged to marry.

Part II

10

It was six years since Henry Tarrant's death and Judith Bradley's proxy marriage to Quentin Tarrant, once more his father's heir. The Saracen emerald, presented to her by Lord Tarrant in his moment of triumph, lay unworn in her jewel box. She hated it, for it linked her with the arrogant, mocking man who had sought to rouse her dormant senses with practiced ease. She also remembered with shame her body's frightening response. Frightening because there was no tenderness in Quentin. He had used her with the calculation of a puppet master, and with as little feeling. It was despicable and shameful, mere play-acting on his part. Realization had numbed and frozen her body into unyielding stiffness. Cold ashes, he had said with uncaring brutality, and she had hated him from that moment for his lack of understanding. Should a child of tender years and gentle upbringing be expected to show the passion of a well-versed Saracen concubine?

Judith sighed as she gazed from the window onto the frosted garden. The winter had been hard, but life was slowly returning to the landscape. A drift of snowdrops below her window heralded the return of spring in the new year of 1200. So much had changed and been swept away in the last year. King Richard was dead, struck down by an arrow as he laid siege to the castle of Chaluz in Poitou. He had lingered, then expired in his own tent, surrounded by the noblest of his realm.

While the country mourned the passing of the beloved

Coeur de Lion, Prince John, younger brother of Richard and youngest son of Henry the Second, sped home from Normandy to claim the crown of England. They called him usurper, for the crown belonged rightly to the young Prince Arthur, son of John's elder brother, Geoffrey, but such was John's speed of action and the support of his friends that few believed he would not gain the prize he had coveted for so long. The crowning had taken place last May, and now King John was in full command of his country and subjects.

Judith put aside her embroidery and lay back in the armchair. Lucy, seated on a stool by her side, looked up and smiled.

"I will light the candles, my lady, for the light is too gray to set a stitch in its proper place."

Judith nodded absently and glanced out of the window again. So long ago she had looked upon Henry's face and thought happily of her wedding day. Now he lay with his ancestors. Her mind dwelt on Matthew, that devoted body servant. He too was gone, his body found below the headland, much as Henry's had been. They said he had taken his own life, and knowing the single-minded love he bore his master, Judith did not doubt it.

As Lucy lighted the candles, Judith's thoughts turned to Lord Tarrant. Since Richard's death he had fretted with impatience for the coming of Quentin and the culmination of his long-held hopes. As month followed month, Lord Tarrant's agitation showed itself. He became moody and short-tempered. Still there was no word from Quentin, and the messengers despatched to France returned empty-handed. None could find Sir Quentin Tarrant. Men came home to rebuild their lives disrupted by five years of war, but none could ease the mind of Lord Tarrant.

"In God's name!" he roared at his luckless household. "A king's friend and a knight does not disappear from the face of the earth! He was not with the king when he died. That has been established by those who were.

None laid eyes on him after the siege began, but, by the Rood, I should feel it in my heart had he perished."

Despite the posting of notices and promise of great reward for knowledge of the whereabouts of his son, none came forward.

Time passed, and Lord Tarrant's despair etched deep lines on his face. Judith watched him with sympathy, noting the sagging shoulders and graying hair. She watched but did not seek to comfort him. His eyes were baleful when they rested on her, and she was increasingly aware of his simmering resentment.

Toward the end of March, Lord Tarrant was summonded to Westminster by King John. He returned after three weeks, and Judith received a summons to attend him in his apartments.

"Take care, Mistress," Lucy warned her. "I liked not the expression on His Lordship's face when he came into the hall."

Judith stared into the troubled face. "Then—then he failed to learn any more of the fate of his son," she said slowly. "God have pity on him."

"And you, too, Mistress," Lucy muttered. "though 'tis none of your doing, fate has robbed him of two sons and left no Tarrant seed behind."

Judith shivered, remembering Lord Tarrant's words at Henry's committal in the crypt. If Quentin was truly lost, then the Tarrant line was at an end.

When the guard allowed her to enter his lord's antechamber, Judith was composed, her step firm and her chin high. She glanced about the room, noting the comfortable furnishings and rich ornaments. Then the inner door opened, framing Lord Tarrant as he paused on the threshold. Judith flinched inwardly despite her proud resolve, as she met the hostile gaze. He stared at her in brooding silence for a long moment, his thick brows drawn together, before a curt movement of his hand directed her to a stool. She curtseyed quickly and seated herself, glad of the stool's support. Lord Tarrant began to pace the floor, his hands clasped behind him, and she glimpsed the whitened knuckles as he turned again and again. She sat quite still, waiting to learn his reason for summoning her.

At last he paused and fixed her with a hard gray stare. "It seems the royal coffers are empty, due to the demands of His late Majesty and the excesses of war." He paused. "Therefore, our new king requires the filling of them." He took another agitated turn about the room, and Judith waited, silently. Lord Tarrant came to rest before her stool, and she gazed up into the dark face.

"Further, His newly crowned Majesty is taking to himself the properties of those nobles who perished on the battlefield." He drew in a deep, gasping breath, and Judith saw the pain in his eyes. "Since my son has not returned, King John has presumed him dead, and his name and estates have been added to the official list he caused to be drawn up."

"I am sorry, my lord," whispered Judith. "Is it not too soon to renounce hope?"

Lord Tarrant continued as if she had not spoken. "The king desires the revenues of Bradley and those of Fairmile, the estate in Kent, which King Richard conferred on my son when he received his knighthood." His mouth twisted into a grim smile. "And you, Mistress, are now officially widowed."

Judith bent her head to avoid the probing eyes, her fingers locked tightly together. "I had hoped," she murmured huskily, "that Your Lordship would allow me to retire to one of those two properties, since my presence does not please you, but now—" She shook her head sadly.

"But now, Mistress, you will have a new home by courtesy of the king, for he has taken you into wardship."

Judith looked up questioningly. "What does that mean, my lord?"

"Think you that our good King John will be forgetful of any rich, young widow?" He stared at her broodingly as a dull flush suffused his face. He said, through gritted teeth, "He demands a full accounting of your fortune and decrees that it shall be in total as it was on the day you set foot under my roof." He spun away from her, unable to hide his angry resentment.

"For what purpose does the king do this thing, my lord?" Judith asked in a toneless voice.

The color left her face as Lord Tarrant turned and she read the contempt in his eyes.

"What years do you have now, Mistress? Two and twenty, I believe, yet your simplicity is that of a child. To grasp a throne, whether lawful or not, a man needs friends to help set that crown upon his head. Such friends had King John, and to them he is indebted. Why think you he seizes estates and revenues? Does a man toil and fight for love of virtue itself? Disabuse your mind, Mistress. The reckoning is here for our good King John."

Judith stared at him confusedly. "But this wardship the king has taken of me, my lord, what does it mean?"

Lord Tarrant gave a short bark of laughter, but there was no humor in the voice that spoke with deadly clarity.

"It means, Mistress, that having taken you into ward, His Majesty now holds you in his reckoning against demands for recompense. You are no more than a pawn in the game of kings."

"Do you tell me, my lord, that I may be used to pay off some debtor of His Majesty?"

Lord Tarrant shrugged indifferently. "I tell you nothing. His alone will be the decision now that you are pronounced widow."

Judith's pallor increased, and she could not have risen from the stool had she wanted to.

"You made no protest, my lord? I am Lady Tarrant and your daughter-in-law." Her voice was scarcely a whisper, but Lord Tarrant heard the words and his lips curved in a smile that mocked her plea for his support.

"Daughter-in-law, yes, but mother to my grand-children, no. For that I am content for His Majesty to assume wardship of you and your accursed fortune."

Judith's strength returned with her growing anger. She rose slowly. "I do not deserve your enmity, my lord. How can you hold me to blame for the failure of your line? I did not take Quentin to war, nor did I conspire in the death of Henry. Given time, a marriage to either would have brought forth a child to inherit the honors of Tarrant. Do I need forgiveness for something I had no part in?"

Her voice had risen, and she saw an answering blaze of temper in the hard gray eyes. He stabbed an accusing finger toward her.

"Did I not see for myself by the castle stair the eager arms of my son reach out to you? He was afire with passion, yet you stood mute and unresponsive, so that he turned away in disgust."

Judith's face flamed with the memory of Quentin's fierce kiss so long ago. Lord Tarrant reached out and gripped her arm painfully.

"Quentin would not have waited for the vows had you shown a like fever."

Judith stared up in horror. Lord Tarrant had witnessed the embrace but mistaken its meaning. Her horror gave way to coldness.

"It would have pleased you, then, my lord, to have your son seduce me on our first meeting, like some kitchen maid waylaid in the pantry?"

"It would have ensured an heir," Lord Tarrant growled and dropped her arm abruptly.

"Conceived in dishonor upon the body of an unwed girl," Judith returned, low-voiced. "Such a course would have brought shame on us both."

"A quick marriage would have wiped away the stain. It was what I suggested to Quentin anyway."

For the first time Judith smiled, and there was a bitter twist to her mouth. "But Quentin would have none of it, I surmise. You deceive yourself, my lord, and seek to lay the blame on me. Not even you foresaw King Richard's coming. It is pointless to argue from hindsight. Both you and I, my lord, were but pawns in the game your son and King Richard played. Your son did not want a wife. Only Henry's death and your desperate message forced his hand. Of that I am certain, my lord." She turned away and moved to the door. Her voice was very calm as she gazed back. "Now that we have the truth of it and well understand one another, I am willing to obey the command of His Majesty." She left the room and softly closed the door behind her.

Now that she understood Lord Tarrant's twisted logic and his reasons for holding her in constant dislike, Judith was eager to quit Tarrant Castle. Six years of somber living had dulled her wits, the monotony broken only by the changing seasons. She was a widow, it was true, but a maiden still, and though her years were two and twenty, she rebelled against the idea of settling into staid maturity. From Bradley to Tarrant was all of life she had known. Could the future be less exciting? What did it matter if King John sought to direct her destiny? When Henry died, her own expectation of happiness died too. Lord Tarrant might grieve for Quentin, but for Judith, the only grief she felt was for Henry.

11

Judith, Lady Tarrant, ignored the gusting April wind and clutched the wooden rail of the ship, straining her eyes until they blurred with tears, as the cliffs of Dover dissolved into the haze. Calais and a new future lay ahead, but her thoughts were so wretched that she could almost wish the little ship would founder as it beat into the wind, leaving all she loved behind.

For now she was truly alone. Lord Tarrant, in a last gesture of spite, had dismissed Lucy from her service and banished her from Tarrant. The servant girl had been returned to her family in Dorset under guard. Judith was escorted to London where she had a brief interview with King John. She recalled with clarity the vulpine face with its sallow complexion, the bright, clever eyes that assessed her as she curtseyed before him. Though he was less than forty years old, self-indulgence and crude sensuality marred his features. He was said to have great charm, but he showed no sign of it when it clashed with self-interest.

Once more she found herself wed by proxy, this time to a Baron of Vallone.

She clung to the ship's rail, heedless of the spray from the choppy sea as she remembered the smile on the sensual mouth.

"Twice betrothed, now widowed, my lady, yet a maid still. That should please the Baron de Gras, for he pays a high price for you."

She had not understood her position until later when

the term "disparaged bride" had been whispered about
the palace. Girls like herself, well-born and rich but
lacking the protection of family, were being disparaged
by the king in his endless search for wealth. Sold to the
highest bidder whatever his rank, a valuable pawn to be
used and moved by royal whim. To protest was useless,
Judith had learned, since King John's fines for non-
compliance were iniquitous. The country grew restless
under the weight of royal taxes, old or newly invented
by the king. Even the ancient tax law of scutage, paid in
lieu of military service, was demanded by King John
before and not after a campaign as was usual. By his
new ruling, the king was assured of the payment
whether or not he embarked on a campaign. Unlike his
brother Richard, John was not fierce in defense of his
lands beyond the Channel, and the French king eyed
those lands with covetous eyes.

But England and the growing unpopularity of its king
were far from Judith's mind as she reluctantly released
her hold on the ship's rail. She turned her listless gaze to
the companionway ladder where her new servants
stood waiting. She had disliked them on sight. The
woman, Maria, was tall and heavy-breasted, black hair
pulled severely back and braided about her head.
Broad-featured with bold black eyes, she had performed
her duties impassively, making no attempt to befriend
her mistress. Every move Judith made was watched,
either by the woman, Maria, or her equally silent
husband. He too was tall, but narrow-faced, like a fox,
Judith thought. A fox and a vixen, set to watch a cooped
chicken should it attempt an escape. Goods bought and
paid for must be carefully supervised to be delivered in
prime condition to their new owner. She meant no more
to this couple than that, Judith told herself wryly. She
had asked once about the baron and what kind of a man
he was, but Maria and Luigi had both shrugged, and the
woman had said in heavily accented French, "We were
hired only to fetch you. We do not know the Seigneur."

and she had left Judith to her doubts and fears.

She knew nothing of this man who had become her husband save that unrest within his domain had impelled him to remain and deal personally with the troubles. She had gained that much from the proxy who had left immediately to return on a faster ship to his master. The proxy had been nothing more than a German mercenary. Her new servants were Italian. What was the baron? He ruled a small mountainous province, she knew, in the south. French, German, or Italian, she had no idea, for he had never set foot in England. Only King John knew him, and she was the payment for his indebtedness.

In the small cabin Judith occupied alone, her baggage filled half the space. The woman—she must try to think of her as Maria—and her husband were in a tiny cabin to one side. They had been helpful in piling the bags, but Judith had the cold feeling that their show of interest was excessive.

The woman's hands had caressed the corded jewel box a shade longer than was necessary, and Judith had not liked the curiously sly look cast at her as the woman laid it down.

Judith dismissed the woman from her cabin and lay on the hard cot bolted to the bulwarks. She tried to dismiss her past as briefly as she had dismissed Maria, but it was impossible. Her mother, Henry, and Lucy had all loved her, but all were gone now. Those she had loved were lost to her, and only the memory of them could carry her through the next state of her life. Memories of happier times, and her own courage. She would need all that and more, for once inside the mountain fastness of Vallone and the property of its baron, there could be no escape. The motion of the ship lulled her into an uneasy sleep.

She came awake to a violent jerk that almost threw her from the cot. Still dazed by sleep, she clung to a deck beam to avoid being hurled across the cabin.

Darkness was all around her, and the timbers creaked and shuddered about her as if being struck with blows from some giant hammer. Canvas cracked whip-sharp, and the world seemed rent apart by the lash and howl of wind and sea. Thudding feet overhead told her that seamen were fighting the elements in defense of their ship and the lives of those on board.

Judith listened intently to the shouted orders. The words were spun away by the wind, but urgency was clearly in the voices, and a rising edge of panic, she decided. Rather more was happening, it seemed, than a mere storm at sea, but her servants had not come to rouse her. She slid her legs over the cot edge and heard the splash as her riding boots met water. Outstretched fingers, groping for support, touched the vessel's vibrating sides, and the shock of icy water wreathing through her fingers brought her fully awake and aware of her peril if the ship foundered. Below decks was no place to be trapped. Her earlier thought that she would care little if the ship foundered was forgotten. It was not in her character to submit without a fight, and she staggered toward her baggage, taking advantage of every handhold. She had not undressed and required only her cloak and jewel box. If nothing else could be saved, so be it, but without her jewels she would be penniless in a foreign country. Her lips twisted wryly. Even this unknown baron could hardly be expected to honor the proxy marriage if she presented herself little short of a pauper.

She found her cloak and swung it about her shoulders, tying the ribbons quickly as she fought for balance. She clutched the jewel box to her breast and listened again, though it was difficult to hear anything above the wind's howl.

A sharp crack overhead, then a scream that blended and was swept away on the wind startled her, but in that moment the ship spun wildly and she was hurled onto her baggage. The ship was not answering to any control but leapt and whirled like a young colt freed from all restraint.

Judith pulled herself to her feet and made an effort to reach the cabin door, but as she grasped the handle, the hull of the ship rose and hurled its length across a hard, unyielding surface that clawed and grated the timbers. The vessel screamed its protest like the death roar of a slaughtered bull. The jar of settling timbers and the abrupt cessation of forward movement threw Judith back once more onto her baggage. The wind still howled, but the stillness above decks was uncanny.

Judith scrambled to her feet, a touch of panic in her movements. How long before the sea burst through the bulwarks and flooded this cabin? In the passageway she paused. The cabin door opposite hers was open, but no one was there. She turned and began to climb the companionway.

Once on deck, she stared about her, seeing tangled cordage and baulks of timber littering the wet planking. Seamen staggered about in dazed silence. The ship's mainmast lay across the vessel, its canvas sails dipping into the creaming waters. Looming to one side of the ship was craggy rock, and Judith guessed that the storm had driven them into shallow water where the hull had been caught by a jutting reef.

Her gaze fell on Maria and Luigi. They were cowering together beneath the hatch cover under an oily tarpaulin, and Judith noted that the man's face was as white as his wife's. She turned from them with disdain. Fine servants they were! Had they been too fearful to venture below and seek to protect her? What tale would they have told to the baron had she drowned in the cabin?

She approached the ship's master, who was ordering his men to hack away the remains of the splintered mainmast. He glanced up at Judith's approach and touched his forehead in salute.

"Madame. You have suffered no hurt?"

Judith shook her head. "I am afraid it is your ship that has suffered, Monsieur. What happened? We seem to have run aground."

"Indeed, Madame, and I give thanks that we were almost upon Calais when the rudder cable snapped. Without control, the wind drove us on the rocks. Now we are, perhaps, six or seven miles down the coast from Calais. You may disembark by boat with your baggage and servants." He raised an eyebrow and glanced with derision at the two still cowering servants. "Italians!" Had she not been there, Judith was convinced that the master would have spat over the side. He shrugged. "They are not a seafaring people, Madame, unlike the French and your own countrymen." He smiled, and Judith responded, liking this tough little Frenchman. "There is a small village, Madame, and a clean hostelry where you can rest the night. I will send my boy to guide you."

"I thank you, Monsieur. I shall remember your kindness and your bravery." She held out her hand, and the little captain took it in a leathery grip and she felt the hard lips touch her fingers swiftly.

He smiled into her face. "You were being received, perhaps, in Calais?"

"Yes, indeed. I was told that an escort awaited my coming."

The master nodded. "The landlord of L'Hirondelle will send a messenger to Calais to summon your escort. Where do you head for, Madame?"

"Vallone, Monsieur."

The smile was gone, and Judith felt that a shutter had fallen between them. There was a moment of complete stillness before the Frenchman bowed stiffly and turned away. The blood seemed to cool in Judith's veins and she shivered. "Monsieur," she called, her voice barely above a whisper. "You know this place?"

He glanced back, and she noticed that his fingers were hooked into a crucifix round his throat. "You go as a stranger, Madame?" he asked. At Judith's nod, his eyes softened. "May God go with you, my lady." Then he turned and strode away.

Judith was aware of Maria beside her. She eyed the woman coldly. "See that my baggage is put into the boat."

"Yes, Madame, at once." The woman flushed at her tone, but there was a defiant gleam in the bold eyes. "What a storm, Madame. We feared for all our lives."

Judith included Luigi in her cold stare. "So I noticed. Now, if you can bring yourselves to go below, do as I ask. I assume it is quite safe."

She caught the angry glint in the man's eye before he swung away without a word. Judith waited by the rail, her arms clasping her jewel box beneath her cloak, as she stared across the short stretch of sea. A village of sorts was visible in the rising moonlight, a small cluster of cottages, most of them dark, but one showed candle-light. L'Hirondelle, she assumed. A clean inn, the master had said, a place where she could rest before the escort arrived.

"Madame, your jewel box! I cannot find it!" Marie's voice came breathlessly. She peered anxiously over the rail and shuddered. "Down there, maybe, and floating away! Mother of God, perhaps split apart. You should have given it to me for safe keeping, Madame. Luigi will be most furious! What am I to do?" Her tone was almost accusing.

Judith looked at her curiously. "What has Luigi to do with my jewel box?"

Maria pulled herself together and pushed back her greasy hair with a shaking hand, but Judith noticed the sheen of perspiration on her face despite the chill air. "It is for your own sake, Madame," she muttered.

"Then you are both stupid, Maria!" Judith said sharply. "I have the jewel box with me. Did you think I would chance it below when I came on deck?"

The woman's face shone with relief. "Thank God it is

safe."

"You could have ascertained its safety earlier, had you thought to ascertain my own as well."

"Forgive me, Madame. I would have come, but the storm—" She shrugged expressively. "But I can take it now. It is too heavy for you, and I will keep it most carefully—"

Judith cut her short. "Attend to the baggage. I am well able to carry my own jewel box." She felt a rising distrust of both Maria and her husband. Neither had come to her cabin during the voyage. Was her own well-being of less value than the contents of her jewel box? She resolved in that moment to keep the box in her own possession, allowing no other to lay hands on it.

She recalled Lord Tarrant's reluctance to part with the jewels that were hers by right of being Lady Tarrant. She had not wanted them herself, but King John had commanded it on pain of sequestration of all Tarrant property. That final scene with His Lordship had been soured by hostility on his part and deep hurt on hers. His disregard for her unknown future was proof enough that he had held her to blame for the loss of two sons and the lack of a Tarrant heir. It was unjust, but a proud man humbled was not concerned with compassion.

"Your baggage is loaded, Madame la Baronne."

Judith started and looked down into the upturned face of Maria, who was squatting in the boat. Luigi hovered by her side, ready to help her down. Judith shook off his hand and stepped over the rough planking that two seamen held steady. Seated in the boat, her jewel box on her knees, she glanced up at the battered little ship. The master was watching her. She smiled and raised a hand in farewell. The master drew himself up and saluted, his heart touched by the lost, lonely look in those expressive blue eyes. Madame la Baronne was she, and bound for Vallone. May God protect the lovely English lady. He found his fingers reaching for the crucifix again.

It took only a little time for the rowing boat to reach the pebbly beach. The seamen splashed through the shallows, hauling the boat up the shingle. Judith stepped out, accepting the calloused hand proffered by one of the seamen. Drawing her cloak tightly about her, she made for the lighted inn, leaving the two servants to collect her baggage. As the sailing master had said, it was small but passably clean, and she ordered two rooms to be put at her disposal. She realized her hunger as the rich aroma of baked meat reached her. It was many hours since she had eaten.

The landlord directed her to a small bedchamber and promised to bring hot water and food. As he left, Maria and Luigi came in with her bags. They both looked wet and ill-tempered. Judith stared at them without expression. If she was allowed any say in Vallone, her choice of servants would not be this craven couple, she decided.

The woman glanced over to where Judith sat on the bed. Her gaze faltered a little as she met the cold stare, but she forced a smile and approached. Her curtsey was ungainly, and Judith realized that it was the first time the woman had made the gesture.

"All your baggage is here, Madame. I will help you disrobe and prepare you for the night."

As she came closer, Judith smelled the rank sweat on the woman's body. The pulled-back hair was greasy and her hands unclean. Judith's disgust must have shown on her face, for the woman stopped, her face reddening.

"I need no help," Judith said. "The landlord is bringing hot water so that I may wash before I eat. I suggest you do the same. Your shelter could not have been over-clean." She turned away and walked to the window, loosening the neckbands of her cloak. Her heart was beating uncomfortably. Perhaps to show such open contempt was not wise, since they were to be her companions on the road to Vallone, but her anger had been too high to restrain. Was her tongue too sharp, as Quentin had said all those years ago? She must learn to guard her speech and walk warily until she knew what manner of man was her new husband, this Baron Ivo de Gras.

Judith did not see either of her servants again until morning. The sun rose on a cloudless sky, and from her window Judith could see the little wooden ship balanced on a causeway of rock. Even when the high tide lifted her off, there would be much work needed on her ravaged timbers before she attempted another Channel crossing.

A tap on the door and Judith turned to see Maria, who watched her warily as Judith ran her eyes over the woman's attire. There was an improvement, to be sure, for a kerchief covered the greasy head and her hands were cleaner, but as she looked at her, Judith mourned the absence of Lucy. Not even that one familiar face had Lord Tarrant allowed her. How could he have been so cruel? Only Henry, of all the Tarrant men, had possessed a heart that was neither flint-hard nor vindictive. Those last few words of Lord Tarrant's still had the power to hurt her.

"You leave my house as you came, Mistress, save that you are old and have stolen my heirlooms and my heirs. My home is barren and the poorer for your coming. Such hopes I had, and all gone as the passing of the wind. Your coldness and self-interest daunted one son, and frivolous delay drained life from the other." His fierce glare had stilled her protests. "Take comfort in the Tarrant jewels, for I shall allow you nothing else. Your maid returns to Dorset. Would that I could return you likewise and put back time, but Tarrant shall be cleansed of all trace, even so."

Judith raised her chin and forced back the threatening tears at the bitter memory.

"What is it?" she inquired wearily.

"Madame, there was a message from Calais." Maria hurried on as Judith's brows rose. "He came while you slept, and I would not allow you to be wakened for so little a thing." She spread her hands, and her smile was ingratiating. "It was a reply to Luigi's message of last night, telling the escort of our accident."

"I heard neither messenger," Judith pointed out.

"Ah, no, Madame, for Luigi ordered silence. Madame la Baronne must rest undisturbed, he insisted."

"What time, then, does the escort arrive?"

"It does not, Madame. Since we must pass through Calais to join the road to Vallone, the leader orders that we proceed there as soon as possible." She shrugged. "These Vallonese, Madame, are hard men. They care little for the inconvenience to you. Luigi has gone out to find horses."

"In this small village?"

"It will be difficult, Madame, but Luigi will bring the best he can hire."

Judith nodded. "Very well, Maria. Have my baggage taken down, then inform me when all is ready."

The woman smiled and turned to the door. Judith looked after her, a little surprised by that smile. It seemed one of genuine pleasure and what else? Relief that her mistress had not been angry at the discourtesy shown her by the escort's leader, who should have come immediately to this village? But Maria herself had not shown overmuch courtesy up to now. It was inconceivable for her to resent it in others on Judith's behalf.

As she waited, she paced the small bedchamber, considering the facts. She had heard no messenger leaving the inn, nor had she heard the arrival of another one. Was there reason to doubt Maria's word? These Vallonese are hard men, Maria had said. But were they hard and inconsiderate enough to show discourtesy to the new bride of their lord, the Baron de Gras? That seemed hardly likely.

Judith stopped her pacing and stood with her back to the hearth with its neat pile of chopped logs, made ready for the evening's fire lighting. Her baggage had been taken down and now stood assembled in the small porch of L'Hirondelle. All that remained was her jewel box, set on the bed with her cloak tossed beside it. She thought of Maria's smile and her sly interest in the box, the despair of the woman when she supposed it had been washed overboard. Luigi will be most furious, she had said. And her sweating relief at hearing of its safety seemed to indicate that it held a higher place in Maria's concern than the safety of Judith herself.

Judith frowned at her jewel box. Its contents must be safeguarded. Perhaps they were more important to the baron than she was herself, and Maria knew it too. A small tight smile touched her lips. She knew of only one way to ensure their safety. Her thoughts winged back to a candlelit room where a man had raised a goblet to his lips, his throat and upper chest exposed by the movement.

It was a lesson unrecognized until this moment, and the one single thing for which she need thank her late, unlamented husband, Sir Quentin Tarrant. She crossed the floor swiftly and bent over the jewel box.

12

Judith stood in the courtyard of the inn and surveyed the three horses Luigi had procured. Her brows rose and she looked at the man.

"They are the best I could find, Madame," he said with a sullen note in his voice. "We will not need them for long."

"I am glad to hear it," Judith murmured. "Never have I seen such decrepit beasts." She eyed the mule that carried her baggage. "Pray God they do not expire from old age before we clear the village." She stood for a moment in frowning silence, then her sharp upward glance caught Luigi's intent stare. His stance was as taut as a bowstring, and even Maria beside him was staring from brilliant black eyes.

Judith's thoughts hovered uneasily. The very air seemed charged with expectancy like that of spectators waiting for a tableau to unfold. It was only a few miles to Calais, but the journey had to be undertaken in company with two people she both disliked and distrusted.

"Allow me, Madame." Luigi bent and cupped his hands beneath the stirrups of one droop-headed horse. "Forgive this cattle, Madame, but the lord of Vallone is not a patient master."

Judith accepted his reasoning and the gesture, placing her boot between his palms. There was no point in delaying their departure. A few hours in the saddle, even this worn, ungroomed one, was freedom of a sort, perhaps the last she would know.

Their progress was slow, for Judith did not urge her mount forward out of pity for the poor, ill-fed creature. Once outside the village, Luigi turned to follow a track on higher ground, away from the coast road.

"A shorter route through the hills, Madame," he explained. "It will be kinder on the legs of these beasts. Besides, the main road is potholed and I dare not risk a broken leg to delay us further and risk the Seigneur's anger."

The horses plodded slowly, the land rising all the time. Judith glimpsed forests and pastureland, but the ground roughened into stone-strewn wildness with sparse grass and barren trees. As they crested yet one more rise, Judith reined in her horse. Its breath was soughing through its lungs, and she seriously doubted that it could ever reach Calais.

"What is it, Madame?" Maria had glanced back over her shoulder.

"Rest your horses, for pity's sake," Judith called and looked behind at Luigi. "We have scarce covered four miles, yet the beasts are foundering." She looked ahead, seeing only tracts of rough land, hill after hill rising and falling like the swell of the sea. On a distant hill stood a small stone building half hidden by trees, but the curving track they followed veered away and ascended even higher.

Luigi drew level. "See that stone crest on the hill yonder, Madame? Beyond there the path falls and Calais lies below. Come, the horses are rested. There is no time to delay." He twitched the reins from Judith's fingers, flung them over the horse's head, and set off at a swift canter to the stone-crested hill.

Judith gasped in astonishment at his action and clung to the saddle pommel. "Luigi! How dare you! Release my horse at once!"

He made no answer but kicked his heels savagely into the sides of his mount.

Maria was now behind her, and Judith heard a throaty

laugh, then the horse jerked forward as Maria's switch cracked sharply on its haunches. Judith turned in fury and saw the openly hostile gaze of Maria. The switch snaked forward again and Judith felt the sharp stab of pain as it cut into her cheek. She swayed in the saddle with the shock of it, and the hand she instinctively raised was red as blood trickled through her fingers.

Maria's laugh came again, high and triumphant. "Oh, Madame, are you hurt?" she mocked. "Madame la Baronne, did I hurt your pretty face?" She raised the switch again, but Judith deflected it with an upraised arm. Maria's face was ugly with fury. "For your cold English contempt, I beat you, Madame la Baronne. I am of the hot blood and like not to be looked on with scorn. Soon, you will not look from eyes of ice but beg me to be kind."

"You are mad and a fool as well," retorted Judith, fending off the wild blows and gasping with the effort to keep her swaying seat in the saddle. "The baron will seek you out and punish you for this outrage."

They were at the top of the crest now, and Luigi had halted. He directed an angry stream of words at Maria, and her wild laughter faded but her gaze on Judith was vicious.

"Get down," he ordered Judith, and her protest died as he pulled her roughly from the saddle. He looked at the slash on her cheek and frowned at his wife, but she shrugged, tossing her head.

"You have been attacked—" he said flatly.

"That is a very obvious remark," said Judith, but Luigi continued in the same flat voice.

"—By brigands in these hills. It is dangerous to travel without strong escort hereabouts. Strangers are robbed and killed every day. One more would cause little comment."

Judith stared into the bright black eyes, hardly believing what she heard. Luigi smiled unpleasantly, and Maria gave a giggle that was not far from hysteria. "All the time, Madame. Robbed and killed." Her gaze strayed to the jewel box strapped to Judith's saddle.

"You speak of the Seigneur, the Baron de Gras," Luigi continued. "He will know nothing, save that you did not arrive. Will he leave his rebellious country to search the whole of France for you? We were hired to escort you, yes, but by a cousin of mine in Vallone. The Seigneur ordered it, but we are strangers to him."

Judith drew in her breath slowly and fought down her panic. In this vast landscape the three of them stood alone. They were unknown to the baron and the escort, just as she was. They were not natives of Vallone but Italians. On good horses they could travel to Italy and with her jewels begin a new and wealthy life.

She glanced at Maria. "I understand now your interest in my jewel box. Had I let you care for it on the ship, I fear that I might have conveniently been washed overboard in the storm. Had I left it in your charge last night, I don't doubt I would have wakened alone this morning."

"You would not have wakened at all, Madame," Maria said.

Judith paused to let her heart slow its clamor. She wondered vaguely if its hammering were audible.

"Do you seek my life as well as my jewels?"

"It is safer," Luigi said simply. "A silent tongue cannot speak." He gestured to Maria. "Get the box."

The woman unstrapped the jewel box with trembling fingers. She began to unknot the cords.

"Strap it on your horse," Luigi ordered sharply. "This is no time to gloat over its contents. There will be time enough to try them on when we are safe."

Maria tossed her head and threw him an angry look but obeyed.

Judith clutched her cloak about her. Only a lazy breeze whispered through the trees, but her body felt as cold as if an icy wind swept through her. Where in God's name were they? Far enough from civilization to be undisturbed by any passing traveler. A shorter route? Undoubtedly a lie, and they were deep inland at some desolate spot where the likelihood of her body being discovered was remote.

"Move," said Luigi, and Judith started, her gaze dropping in sick fascination to the slim, glittering blade in his hand. She looked up into the empty eyes.

"No wonder I heard no messengers, for there were none, neither coming nor going. As for your short route to Calais—" She shrugged, and the contempt on her face was vivid. "Liars and murderers both! You sicken me and your very presence fouls the air. May you burn in hellfire, for your souls will be blackened beyond all redemption for this deed."

She turned and began to mount the rocky path Luigi had indicated. He followed closely, and Judith stared about her as if memorizing the place where her unmarked grave would be. At the stone crest she paused and looked down. Calais did not lie below as Luigi had promised, nor had she expected it to. Below lay a stunted forest, sinewy roots clinging for life to a rocky ravine. As if a mountain had been split in two by some giant hand, the rocks spread wide and the stunted forest was denied a glimpse of sunlight by its over-hanging cliffs. The air that rose was dank and foul, its soil unwarmed by sun and ignored by cleansing wind. Judith's fingers tightened on the cloth of her cloak. It was a long way down.

Luigi's boots scraped on the rock behind her. She whirled and moved sideways along the lip of the chasm. He smiled and moved toward her. She knew it was hopeless to run, hampered by her cloak and heavy skirt. He was tall and long-legged, the chase would be short. She faced him, her chin high.

"Scum," she said clearly. "Gutter filth. Damn your soul to eternity!"

Then the knife flashed in the sunlight. She heard the tear of cloth as it speared through her cloak. The point jarred as if caught on some obstruction, but the blade edge sliced deep into her breast, then Luigi righted the knife and drove home the point. She was already falling from the first savage attack and knew only the explosion of pain, the searing agony that raked her mind. Before all sight faded she looked into the whirling darkness of the pit. The rocks rose to embrace the limp body that writhed and twisted, glanced off stone and tree in macabre dance before coming to rest in the deep silty earth that was the chasm's floor.

13

It was the dog that brought Judith back to the real world. A flicker of consciousness recognized the animal smell and identified the rough wet tongue across her cheek. She pushed away the bristly muzzle, but the dog, as if playing a game, swept her cheek again and emitted a soft, contented rumble deep in his throat. Judith's hand dropped to the loamy earth. She had no strength to quell the dog. It retreated a pace, gave an encouraging bark, and returned to its task.

Judith's mind floated in and out of darkness, but the unflagging attention of the dog was the irritant that brought her slowly to consciousness. She was aware of the cold striking up through her body, but her limbs would not answer to remedy the situation. The wet tongue ceased its ministrations, and she felt the heavy body subside outstretched beside her, his muzzle tucked under her chin.

"Go away," she thought she heard herself say, but the dog nudged closer and whined. After a moment, or an hour, she had no idea, the warmth of the animal came to her, and she began to experience the easing of stiffened muscles.

Very slowly, as her consciousness gained strength and coherence, she remembered the chasm and the start of that terrifying fall. Maria's almost hysterical excitement as she handled the jewel box, and Luigi's flat cold stare as he raised the stiletto. She shivered and the dog whined. What if they came back? How long had it been?

If Maria's impatience to open the box had prevailed, they would certainly come back, and this time make quite sure of her death.

Her body was warmer now. She tried to turn on her side, but a searing pain in her breast took all sound from her scream. But she had to move, get away before they came back. Her mind swam dizzily with pain and exertion, but fear drove her on. Her limbs were like those of a puppet, but she forced herself into a kneeling position, resting heavily on the dog while she gasped for air. Unsteadily she staggered upright, and the dog rose too as if sensing her dilemma. He was large though gaunt, and despite the ridged back under her hands, he was strong.

"Whoever you are, my friend," she said, her voice sounding cracked and strained, "I give thanks to God for His mercy in directing your steps."

The dog flailed a long tail, and Judith saw that he was black from muzzle to tail, his hair roughened and dusty. The eyes that regarded her were yellow. She laid a hand on his head and his tongue lolled, rough and pink. Judith raised her head and stared up at the sides of the chasm. She was surprised to see that light still showed above this dank and gloomy place. She glanced down into the yellow eyes.

"We must ascend from this pit, my friend. 'Tis no place for either of us."

Before attempting the climb, Judith knew that she must attend to the stab wound. The breast of her tunic was soaked in blood, and any exertion might open the wound further. Her fingers fumbled with the cloak fastening. Beneath it hung the large Saracen emerald. Its fire was dulled by streaks of red that still lay moist on its surface. The stiletto point, aimed for her heart, had rasped across the stone, and the deathblow Luigi planned was deflected. The blade had continued its course but with less ferocity. The cut was deep and diagonal, but not a killing blow. She knew from her weakness that she had lost blood, but, God willing, her injury would not prove mortal. A torn piece of under-garment, wadded into a pad and strapped across her breast, was the best she could do.

She glanced down at the dog, his head now resting between his paws as he lay waiting. The yellow eyes were fixed on her face.

"Black hound of Satan I might have termed you else-where, my friend, but my deliverance deserves better. I shall call you Angel until I learn to the contrary."

The dog seemed to cock a quizzical eyebrow at the name, then he yawned and rose, turning toward the thickness of trees. Judith followed him slowly. It was unlikely that the dog had come by the route she had taken, and she was content to follow him.

It was a painful progress, and Judith gasped as her boots jarred on stone and tree root. Apart from the throbbing wound of her breast, every bone in her body seemed to have made contact with some hard surface. Her whole frame was one vast ache, and her cheek stung from the lash of Maria's switch. Several times she found herself on her knees without knowing how she came to be there, but each time her wandering gaze soon fell on a black outline from which glowed yellow eyes.

"Have patience, Angel." Her words came muttered and incoherent, even to her own ears. "I have but two legs and they not obedient to my will."

During a later pause, she forced her swimming gaze ahead. The yellow eyes were not regarding her. The dog was gone. Panic swept through her. "Angel!" Her voice came high and scarcely more than a croak. "For the love of God, don't leave me. There is no one and nothing without you. Help me, I beg!"

Distantly she heard the full-throated bark of a dog. Where was he? The barking combined with a roaring in her head and the sound spun round the pit, soaring through the air like a great wave of beating wings. She screamed, a high, shrill scream of terror as the sound mounted to her brain and tore all reasoning apart. The black, whirling tide lifted her and threw her into a howling vortex. Then she was tossed into black, endless space.

Judith lay still, and in the comings and goings of her mind, she imagined herself on a bed with a coarse lavender-scented sheet drawn up to her chin. She feld mildly surprised that her body was no longer chilled. Her bones still ached and the knife wound in her breast throbbed, but the rough wad of torn underskirt was gone. Her hand rose to draw back the sheet, but the effort seemed unimportant and she let her fingers drop over the edge of the bed. She tensed as a wet muzzle nudged her fingers. Of course, the dog. Turning her head sideways, she looked into the yellow eyes.

"Angel," she murmured, and at the sound of her voice he whined and a small figure she had not noticed before crossed the room to stand by her bed.

"Well, Mistress," a soft female voice said. "You are of this world once more."

Judith half-feared that Maria's face was the one bending toward her, but it was the face of a stranger, dark-garbed and with a lined face framed by a white cowl.

They stared at each other for a long moment, then the woman smiled. "Your color is better, my dear, and I give thanks to God for His guidance in directing my small skills." She placed a cool hand on Judith's brow. "Do not tire yourself with questions, my dear, for I will answer all those I see in your eyes. I am Sister Ulrica and this is the Convent of Saint Theresa near Marquise, some twelve miles beyond Calais."

"How—" began Judith, but Sister Ulrica finished the question for her.

"How did you come here? Two days ago, our old gardener—a poor peasant who digs for us, and though he is old, we are older yet and cannot do it ourselves—"

her eyes twinkled as she shrugged in acceptance. "He came from selling our produce in the market and found the cart track barred by this dog of yours, barking so fearsome and thrashing in and out of bushes. Poor frightened Rene." She gave a chuckle, then sobered. "Ah, I must not laugh at another's expense. Rene is a good, kind soul and when he understood the dog's actions, he followed him and came upon you, lying as one dead. Indeed, Rene was convinced of it, but he lifted you into the mule cart and brought you hither for Christian burial."

Judith smiled into the bright face. "Without good Rene and Angel here, I would have found my burial place where I fell." A shudder ran through her and Sister Ulrica looked anxious.

"Forgive me for tiring you. I should curb my tongue, as Reverend Mother bids me daily."

Judith reached out a hand and clasped the thin, old one. "No, please do not be distressed. I am grateful for your care and happy to know how I came here." She paused. "Has anyone inquired for me?"

"No, my dear, though 'tis strange, now I think on it, for one of your rank. Where were you bound when you had your—your accident?"

"It was no accident, Sister Ulrica, and I had no choice in my direction."

The nun regarded her gravely, then nodded. "You were attacked, I think, for only a knife could inflict that wound on your breast." She nodded again. "And you were left for dead below the rocks. Such banditry is not uncommon after a war." She rose, birdlike and brisk. "Now you must rest, my dear." She turned, but a new thought brought her round again. "You were attacked, without doubt, but why did these robbers not take your jewels?" She indicated the leather pouch on the bedside chest. "The bag was still strapped to your girdle. The green pendant has been washed of blood and placed within. It seems the stone deflected the blow and thus saved your life." Then she was gone before Judith could say anything more. She closed her eyes and relaxed into the softness of the bed. She felt a wet tongue lick her hand.

"Good Angel," she murmured and drifted into sleep, visualizing Maria's fury when she opened the jewel box, only to find in it an equal weight of firewood.

It was another two days before Sister Ulrica allowed Judith to leave her bed. She professed herself well pleased with the fast-healing wound on Judith's breast. The numerous bruises across her body were fading, and the scoremarks of twig and bramble were barely noticeable. Angel was her constant companion, save when the nuns took him for food and exercise. He tolerated these interruptions, but on his return he came to stand by Judith's chair, subjecting her to such scrutiny as might be expected from a mother to an ailing child. When satisfied, he would stretch out at her feet, unmoving but for the cock of a yellow eye when Sister Ulrica came in.

"A most faithful dog you have, my dear," she pronounced with a smile. "I confess to surprise that he allowed any attacker to come close."

"But he is not my dog, Sister. I met him only after the attack. He came like an angel to my rescue, but from where, I do not know."

Sister Ulrica shook her head in wonderment. "A well-deserved name you have given him. He is unknown to us, as he apparently was to old Rene."

"Then I shall keep him if he chooses to stay with me."

They both looked at Angel, who yawned, sighed deeply, and rolled over settling his lean length at Judith's feet.

"Would you say he accepts my offer?" asked Judith of Sister Ulrica.

The nun's eyes twinkled. "I sincerely hope so, for he eats largely and some of our frailer sisters fear for their balance when he is around."

* * *

It was toward evening on the fourth day when Judith heard the latch of her small bedchamber being lifted. Angel raised his head then allowed it to fall between his paws as a small, robed figure entered. Sister Ulrica had warned Judith to expect a visit from the Mother Superior. Judith found herself looking into an incredibly aged face, the transparent skin cobwebbed with fine lines. The soft brown eyes held an expression of total serenity. Her smile was gentle, and the thin white hands clasping the crucifix at her waist were at peace.

"Good evening, Reverend Mother," Judith said, rising to her feet.

"Be seated, my child," said a calm voice. "Since your arrival amongst us, you have been under the care of Sister Ulrica, for she is our Nursing Sister. Now that you are well enough to leave us, I would assure myself of your well-being. Sister Ulrica is troubled and has confided her fears to me. Will you not do the same, my child?"

"Yes, Reverend Mother." Judith stared dully across the chamber. "You have been so kind to me that you deserve an explanation of my presence."

"Not deserve, my child, but ask humbly for your own sake."

"Forgive me." Judith bowed her head. "My destination is Vallone. I was wed by proxy to the Baron de Gras. It is to that province that I am bound in obedience." She raised her gaze as she spoke and found that the brown eyes, though faded, were watching her shrewdly.

"Alone? Where is your escort? What became of your attendants?"

"To the best of my knowledge, my escort still waits in Calais unless they have since learned of the storm that blew the ship off course and wrecked her near Wissant. As to my two attendants—" she spoke bitterly. "They and not robbers lured me to that desolate place with the sole intention of robbing me and disposing of my body."

"But you were not robbed."

Judith shook her head. "The woman's interest in my jewel box made me uneasy. I transferred my jewels to a pouch and wore the emerald as I had seen my husband do. It seems his beloved Saracen Stone saved my life."

"Where is your husband now?"

"Sir Quentin Tarrant. He is dead, with all those who fought by King Richard's side. I am English, Reverend Mother." She was not aware of the defiant note in her voice, but the old nun smiled.

"And I am Spanish, my dear, so it matters nothing to us. When kings lead armies against each other, our only concern is to care for the injured, whatever their place of birth."

"Of course, forgive me."

"These servants of yours," went on the Mother Superior. "What will be their reaction when they discover their mistake?"

"I imagine they will return to that place and search."

"Would they be an Italian couple, by any chance?"

Judith stared into the gentle face. "Indeed they were! Maria and Luigi Velardi by name, but how could you know of them?"

"Old Rene came this afternoon. He said he was questioned by two such people. He told them he had carried the body of a lady to this convent. He is as yet unaware of your recovery, and I thought it wiser to leave him in ignorance."

Judith and the Mother Superior sat in silence for a long moment, their eyes on each other. At last Judith spoke.

"Then they will come here, pretending distress, and seek to carry my effects away, wouldn't you say?"

"Precisely. And not to their master in Vallone, I would guess." She paused, considering. "You have been with us for four days now. It seems unlikely that the escort sent by Baron de Gras remained idly in Calais. If the

master of your ship has not already gone to Calais, the
news of a shipwreck will by this time have reached them.
The men of the escort will search for you, beginning at
the point where you came ashore.''

At Judith's nod, the Mother Superior continued.
''Though this house is isolated, it is not inaccessible.
Before long they will be asking questions in Marquise,
our nearest town.''

''And should the Velardis arrive first?''

The Mother Superior rose and moved to the door.
With her hand on the latch, she glanced back at Judith.

''You may safely leave the Velardis to me, Lady
Tarrant. I am not Spanish for nothing!''

Judith was left with the impression that the Mother
Superior's countless years of devotional studies had not
entirely quenched the innate pride of the Spaniard. She
thought of the Velardis. While they hesitated, the men of
Vallone were drawing closer. Were they stupid enough
to imagine that the escort still waited in Calais? Greed
must surely bring them here, and very soon. But she was
no longer alone, and the feeling was good. If the
Velardis dared force their way into the convent, Angel,
who had elected himself her protector, would give them
pause, for he was, she admitted, a fearsome, black-
jowled, shaggy brute, but how true and loving he had
proved.

The morning of the fifth day dawned bright and clear,
the sunrise a pageant of gold and pearl-streaked
excellence. The countryside, dew-sparkling and vivid,
was warmed by a gentle breeze, and Judith was tempted
to walk the enclosed lawns behind the main chapel. Her
only garments, save the soft woollen robe Sister Ulrica
had lent her, were still those she had worn from Dover.
The tears in the fabric she had stitched, but the blood-
stains were visible, despite all efforts to remove them.
So, dressed in these, she ventured into the gardens,
hoping to come across old Rene and express her

gratitude. Angel padded behind her, pausing occasionally to investigate some interesting bush. Old Rene was not about, and Judith strolled the environs of the convent, coming at last to the small courtyard fronting the arched entrance porch to the convent.

It was Angel who saw the man first. A low, rumbling growl swelled in his throat, and Judith felt the pressure of his flanks on her side. Between her and the entrance porch, a man was pacing, chin down and hands clasped behind him. At Angel's growl he turned, and Judith saw that he was in soldier's garb, sword and dagger buckled about his waist. He stood quite still, regarding both her and the dog. Angel rumbled on, though he did not move, and the man stood silent and watchful. He was tall, his head covered by a velvet cap, a neat beard framing the lean, tanned face. He was not Luigi, and Judith's caught breath was released in a sigh of relief.

They might have stood regarding each other until sundown had not the entrance door opened and a nun peered out. She saw only the man and stood aside.

"Reverend Mother will see you now, sir."

The man nodded and stepped through the porch without another glance at Judith. The door closed, and Judith laid a hand on Angel's head.

"Come. We will return to our chamber the way we came."

It was half an hour later when Sister Ulrica appeared.

"The Reverend Mother asks if you will join her in the hall, my dear. She has a visitor who, being of the opposite sex, cannot be allowed further into our house." Her face creased into a smile of mischief. "A very presentable gentleman, I would note, if I had not put such thoughts behind me these many years."

Judith smiled, though her heart had begun to beat rapidly. The soldierly bearing she had noted could only mean that her brief sojourn in the convent was over. The Mother Superior would not send for her unless she had assured herself that this man was of the escort sent to

Calais. She rose and followed Sister Ulrica to the hall.

The Mother Superior was seated in a high-backed wooden chair, her hands folded in her lap. The man stood with his back to the window, silently watching Judith's approach as she crossed to the chair.

"You sent for me, Reverend Mother."

"Yes, my child. This gentleman is Capitaine de Foret. He leads the party sent by Baron de Gras to escort you to Vallone. His credentials are quite in order, for he consulted our Lord Bishop who gave him our direction."

"I see," said Judith flatly. She glanced at the man, who had stepped forward. His head was uncovered, his hair dark and cropped short. Running down one side of his face, from temple to ear, was a healed scar. A fearful blow it must have been, she found herself thinking, for the hair grown above his temple was white. A streak of white in the dark hair, a memento of battle, she supposed. "Then I will prepare myself to accompany you, sir."

The man bowed. "Madame la Baronne," he said in a low voice. "You may be assured of my complete protection on your journey to Vallone. Reverend Mother has told me of your ordeal." His voice seemed to harden and deepen. "The Velardis will be sought out, never fear. What they stole from you will be returned."

"What they stole was not what they wanted, but I should welcome the return of my baggage. I possess only what you see, sir. Excuse me." She turned and was almost through an inner door when hooves were heard in the courtyard. She paused and Capitaine de Foret took three long strides toward the grilled window.

"A man and a woman with horses and a pack mule," he snapped. He glanced at Judith through suddenly narrowed eyes. "Into the shadows, Madame, if you please. If this be the Velardis, we shall hear their version of events."

Judith stepped through the doorway, and Capitaine de Foret took a position beside the Mother Superior's chair. Sister Ulrica answered her superior's nod of consent and hurried to open the outer door.

Judith, watching from the shadows, tensed as a breathless and tearful Maria came into the hall, followed by Luigi. Their clothes were torn and both were disheveled. Maria's step faltered as she saw the soldier by the Mother Superior's chair, but she rallied swiftly and sank to her knees.

"Reverend Mother, forgive this intrusion, but we learned from an old peasant that he had lately delivered the body of a lady into your care. We are distraught with fear that it may be our mistress, a lady our lord bid us accompany from England." Tears rolled down Maria's face. "Oh, pray God it is not she who lies dead!"

"Who was your mistress, and which lord do you serve?" asked the Mother Superior.

Maria's head drooped. "Ah, Reverend Mother, you say 'was.' Is our lady, Madame la Baronne de Gras, indeed dead? Pray you let me look on the dead face of this lady to be sure. The lord of Vallone will be heartsore. Such tragedy!"

Capitaine de Foret spoke for the first time. "And should the lady already be consigned to the earth, what then? How can you prove that it was she?"

"Her possessions, sir. I will instantly recognize Madame's clothing and trinkets." She cast a look of desolation at the Mother Superior. "It will be little consolation to our lord, but he has the right to demand them."

Luigi was looking at the soldier. "Sir. Since you appear to take interest in our tragic affairs, may I ask who you are? Could you but lately have come from Calais?"

"Indeed, I have," returned the capitaine. "I am Leon de Foret, leader of the escort appointed by the Baron de Gras. It seems we come to this house on the same mission. Tell me, Monsieur—er—?"

"Velardi, sir. Luigi Velardi and this is my wife, Maria."

"Ah, yes. Perhaps you had better explain to me what

befell you after leaving L'Hirondelle in Wissant. I have the story so far."

"We were attacked, sir, by a band of ruffians and—"

"A moment, if you please. Where were you attacked precisely?" The capitaine's voice was smooth, but there was a hard edge to it and Luigi lost a little color.

"Why, in the hills, sir. These bandits lie in wait for travelers."

The capitaine frowned. "Hills? What hills lie between Wissant and Calais?"

Luigi swallowed audibly. "I—I am a stranger in these parts, sir. I fear we mistook the road and were directed wrongly. We found ourselves in hill country."

"How many men attacked you?"

Luigi shrugged. "Six or seven, sir. I was too busy trying to protect the women to count their number. Does it matter? We suffered grievously enough without counting heads." The sullen note in his voice caused the capitaine to eye him sharply.

"Apart from torn clothes, you seem to have taken no hurt in defense of Madame la Baronne."

"Luigi was struck senseless, sir," put in Maria quickly. "I too was hurled to the ground. Madame had disappeared when we recovered. We searched and searched, but in vain. No trace of her could we find save this." From under her torn cloak she produced the jewel box and threw back its lid. "See, good sir and Reverend Mother. Empty! The jewels taken by robbers and Madame tossed aside when they realized their prize. We thought the brigands had carried her off before we met the old peasant." Maria rose to her feet and faced the capitaine. "Now that you know the truth of it, may we be permitted to see the dead lady, or at least confirm by her possessions that Madame has perished?"

"A fair question, Mistress Velardi. You may see the lady."

He glanced toward the shadowed archway, and Judith stepped forward into the full light of the hall.

Maria's face drained of all color. The wooden jewel box dropped from her hands, to bounce and clatter on the stone-flagged floor. Without a sound she fell into a dead faint at the feet of the Mother Superior.

14

Luigi was the first to move. He swung around and leapt for the entrance with the speed of a panic-stricken hare. The hiss of a blade leaving its scabbard drew Judith's gaze to the soldier. Before the weapon was clear of its sheath, the Mother Superior was on her feet.

"No!" she said, and the clear, resonant voice compelled attention. There was no doubting the heritage of Spain in the authoritative voice. "No instrument of destruction shall be bared in the sanctity of this house. I forbid it!"

Such was the dignity displayed in the small upright figure that none sought to dispute the order. The capitaine's hand dropped from his sword hilt and the blade returned to the scabbard. Luigi had paused in his headlong flight and stood with his back to the door. His eyes stayed wide with fear, sweat trickling from his brow, but he focused on the Mother Superior as if his life now rested in her hands. Maria was beginning to stir, but no one moved to assist her as she came to her knees. Her gaze wandered vaguely for a moment, then realization dawned and she dropped her face into her hands and began to weep.

"Tears will avail you nothing, Maria Velardi," said the capitaine. "The reckoning will be paid in Vallone." He walked toward the door. Luigi shrank away, but the capitaine did not look at him. Instead, he beckoned. Feet crunched on gravel, and the doorway was darkened by the shapes of armed men.

Maria screamed faintly as she was hoisted to her feet. In silence, both she and Luigi allowed their wrists to be bound in front of them, and in silence they were taken from the hall. Neither had looked at Judith nor made plea to the Mother Superior. The matter no longer lay in their hands. The sin was against Vallone, and its representative had every right to take charge.

Judith glanced curiously at the baron's man. About thirty years old, she judged, but the stern lines on his face, together with the streak of white hair, might put him older. His movements were swift and economical, lithe as a cat—or a Tarrant. A soldier's stride and the hard-eyed indifference to anything but duty. Yet he had respected the words of the Mother Superior. Judith glanced quickly at that lady, who had resumed her seat. The skin of her face was like parchment and her blue-veined hands were clasped so tightly together that the knuckles shone ivory-white.

Judith caught Sister Ulrica's eye. An imperceptible nod united them, and they moved to the Mother Superior's side. Between them, and with no visible appearance of support, they escorted her from the hall.

Judith returned to find the capitaine, hands once more clasped behind him, gazing out of the window. He turned at her approach and bowed. Now that she was closer to him, she saw that the scar above his left cheek had drawn up the skin so that the brow held a permanently quizzical tilt. That look was greatly at variance with the cold gray eyes. Never had she seen such cold eyes. Not even Lord Tarrant at his most hostile looked from eyes that were flat and granite-gray.

"Madame?" he said politely and quite tonelessly.

Judith realized that she had been staring at him. She turned quickly to hide her flush of embarrassment.

"I—I would be obliged if you could arrange to have my baggage brought inside, Monsieur. As I said, I have only this garment to my name. I would be rid of it most heartily, for it has suffered much."

He nodded. "I will attend to it, Madame." His gaze moved over her, then paused on her breast. "That stain, Madame, and the great tear around it. The fabric is cut clean."

"A knife is expected to cut cleanly, Capitaine."

The gray eyes rose to hers and for a fleeting second they held a terrible light. "You were stabbed? Mother Superior spoke of a savage attack but avoided a detailed description."

"The details are now irrelevant, sir. I survived, as you see, and would prefer not to recount the episode again. My life was saved by Angel and preserved by Sister Ulrica."

"Angel?" The brows rose, the one higher than the other.

Judith smiled. "You met Angel in the courtyard, before you received audience with Reverend Mother."

His lips gave the faintest smile. "That great black brute of a dog? And you call him Angel?"

"Outside of these walls, he is my only friend and will have my protection from any that seek to part us. I hope that is understood, Capitaine de Foret?"

"Of course, Madame. My own aim is your protection. You may fear nothing on our journey to Vallone while I lead the escort. My duty to Baron de Gras is absolute."

"Quite, Monsieur, but there is no third party in Angel's allegiance to me. He has proven his loyalty."

"I take your point, Madame, and heed your warning."

Was there a note of mockery in his voice, Judith wondered? She shrugged mentally. After her experience with the Velardis, she had no cause to trust in words only. Let this man prove himself her protector as Angel had done without thought of self. From her small knowledge of men, she knew that their minds were devious, their moves calculated with cold self-interest. Only Henry had been different. But she must not think of Henry. He was of sweet memory, long ago.

"How far is it to Vallone?" she asked.

"Two weeks' journey, perhaps, if all goes well,
Madame. Be prepared to leave at first light, if you
please." He bowed stiffly and strode from the hall into
the courtyard.

Judith gazed after him. Two weeks? Thank God she
had Angel with her as companion. She sensed that this
capitaine was not overkeen on playing escort to a
woman. There had seemed a strange antipathy in his
bearing toward her. From the scarred evidence of his
face, he preferred the battlefield to the task of dancing
attendance on his master's bride.

She returned to her bedchamber. Angel rose from the
flagstone and fixed her with a reproachful eye. She was
glad now that she had thought to shut the door on him.
It would not have helped if he had somehow sensed that
the Velardis were enemies. She knelt and hugged him.

"Be my friend always, dear Angel, for God knows I
shall stand in sore need, once we have left this
sanctuary."

Angel's wet tongue was answer enough, and she
pushed him away, laughing at her sudden descent to
gloom.

The sun was climbing the hilltops, creating deep and
mysterious caves of shadow, touching the dew-
drenched land with crystalline fingers, when the escort
of Madame de Baronne de Gras moved out of the courtyard fronting the Convent of Saint Theresa. Judith,
dressed in a moss-green riding tunic, a fine fur-trimmed
cloak about her shoulders, took a last look at the small
house of religion. Farewells had been said in private,
gratitude expressed and blessings received. She had left
a richly jeweled chain as a mark of thanks for their care
and shelter. Now, with Angel loping alongside the fine
bay mare, the party began the long journey to Vallone.

During the first day's ride, Judith had time to observe
her companions. Five soldiers and the capitaine made
up her escort. The soldiers were all swarthy and hard-

faced, strong-looking men who rode easily in the saddle but lacked the grace of that long-ago company of men who had come to Tarrant with Quentin. Leon de Foret was less swarthy, his looks finer, as if he came from better stock. Even so, she was glad of the company of Angel. Lacking a maid, she was forced to rely entirely on the capitaine to arrange her care and accommodations.

But in this, Leon de Foret was quite competent. When they turned into an inn yard at sunset, Judith found herself provided with a clean chamber and an obliging landlord whose wife brought hot water and attended her needs. The troopers were housed in a barn with the horses, but to Judith's surprise the capitaine sat down at table with her, neither asking permission nor appearing to notice her slight stiffening. She relaxed almost immediately, her quick mind accepting that it would be foolish to alienate this man. He was to be her companion for many days, and of the handful of soldiers, he had the most pretensions to gentility. Besides, she could question him about the baron and what she might expect in Vallone.

The task proved more difficult than she had expected. The capitaine did not seek to engage her in conversation. Her ventured question on the country to which she traveled was met by a blank stare, then a brief apology that his mind was elsewhere. He excused himself the moment the meal was finished, stating that he must attend to his men. Judith had been vaguely aware of noise drifting from the direction of the barn. A short time after the capitaine's departure, the noise ceased.

The day's ride had taxed Judith more than she would have expected. She was glad to lean back on the settle by the hearth and let her body relax after the capitaine had left. Sister Ulrica had warned her that her strength would not return immediately, and she had been proved right. But what ailed Judith was more a condition of mind, weakened by her experiences. She found herself wondering if she could trust the men of the escort, even

Capitaine de Foret. The Velardis had been sent by the
baron and very soon proved their disloyalty. No, it was
a ridiculous comparison. The Velardis were not bound
in service to the baron as were these soldiers, and yet
she found herself recalling with a shiver the cold hard
faces of the Velardis.

She closed her eyes and the warmth of the fire carried
her along on a drift of memory. An English spring, the
gardens of Tarrant Castle, the sensitive face of Henry
regarding her with tenderness. The joy of that betrothal,
then the tragedy of his death. He was falling—falling into
a rocky pit, and she was beside him, reaching
desperately for his hand. Together they were falling,
tossed apart, then brought closer by the fates that flung
them down. Henry was still smiling but drifting away as
she sought despairingly to close the gap between them.
But he was receding, away and away until she saw him
only faintly. Then he was gone.

Judith's head moved in anguish on the settle back. Her
eyelids fluttered half-open, her mind dazed. A shadow
stood before her, a tall, dark shape with Henry's face
and lithe body.

"Henry!" she said, her hands reaching out. "You
came—" Her voice faltered as her mind cleared.

The man before her was real enough but he was not
Henry. How could he be? Henry had been these six
years at rest in the Tarrant Chapel. She looked at Leon
de Foret, who was regarding her fixedly.

"A dream, Capitaine, that is all. Do not be alarmed, I
am not subject to fits of madness." She noted that he
carried a flagon and two goblets. "Ah, I see that you
expect company. I will retire in that event."

"No company, Madame, save your own," he replied.
"The ride has taxed you today, though I made it shorter
—on the orders of Sister Ulrica."

Judith stared into the gray eyes and saw for the first
time a glint of genuine amusement. She smiled and
accepted the glass he offered.

"Indeed, for so small and gentle a lady, Sister Ulrica has remarkable powers of persuasion. Reverend Mother too, as you found out yourself, sir!"

He nodded. "My sword has never before been halted in such manner, but the lady was right. My anger near drove me to sacrilege." He paused, watching her. "Who is Henry?"

The question came so abruptly that Judith was startled and her fingers trembled on the goblet. She felt again the pain and loss of her dream.

"I was betrothed to Henry Tarrant, once," she replied shortly.

"Your dead husband?"

Judith shook her head. "No. Our betrothal lasted until—" She stopped, biting her lip, remembering. She sipped from the goblet, then looked at him from over its rim. "I would rather not discuss it, sir. It serves no purpose now."

"I am sorry to upset you, Madame, but I understood from the baron that you are a widow, a Lady Tarrant."

Judith set down her goblet and regarded him from a smoldering blue gaze. "And so I am, sir, if you will have the truth of it. I was married to his brother, the heir, in much the same way that I married your baron." She rose, forcing de Foret to rise also. Her eyes had lost their fierceness and were now shadowed by tiredness, but her voice was steady. "If you have done with catechism, sir, I will bid you good night. I am sure the baron has been fully apprised of my circumstances."

Leon de Foret bowed but said nothing more as Judith left the room.

Judith was refreshed by her long sleep, and as exercise and rest followed each other over the next few days with regularity, her health was restored and her mind cleared. She began to enjoy the adventure of travel, passing through small French villages, sending her horse to splash through a stream or putting him to a hedge. The Vallone capitaine stayed by her side, his gaze watchful despite all her attempts to outstrip him. He rode too well for that, she admitted. She glanced at him once and flushed as she caught the mocking glint in his eye. He knows, she thought, and he is enjoying the thwarting of me, damn him.

"Take care, Madame," he called over his shoulder as he let his horse surge forward into a powerful gallop. "The baron will not thank me to deliver you in worse condition than the Velardis left you, by my fault or your own."

And damn the baron too, muttered Judith to herself as she realized that, far from outstripping the capitaine, he had been holding back his mount to equal the speed of hers.

She saw him circle the positioned riders, paying special attention to the leading trooper who had the duty of forward scout. She was surprised to see him wheel away suddenly, horse and rider streaking over the countryside like one being. The bow looped over his shoulder was in his hands, an arrow notched while in full flight, the horse guided by knee alone. The goosefeather quill blurred in the light, and she could not see its point until it met and buried itself in the heavy neck of a fleeing buck. The aim must have been true, for the buck faltered in mid-gallop, its knees bucking beneath it. She could almost hear the thump as the body collapsed and lay still.

The troopers shouted their approval, and Judith had to admit that it was a skilled piece of marksmanship. When the capitaine returned to her side, he seemed scarcely out of breath. He did not look at her but scanned the land ahead. "An hour maybe, Madame, before we reach a night's lodgings."

Judith glanced back to where the buck lay as they rode on. "What of the animal, sir?"

"The men will go back and collect it. The Velardis can prepare and cook it. What remains will be left with the innkeeper. He will be glad of fresh meat.''

''Congratulations, Capitaine. That was well done.''

He looked at her then and she saw the ghost of a smile on his lips. ''Thank you, Madame. You flatter me. Is it not done so in your country, with the bow?''

''Yes. With the bow or the spear, but it still requires skill.''

''The English do this well?''

''Indeed they do. My late husband—'' Her mouth twisted. ''According to his father, he did everything with skill. Unlike his brother, Henry.''

The gray eyes rested on her searchingly. ''Ah yes, your Henry, the one you loved.'' Judith opened her mouth, but Leon de Foret went on. ''But his brother, your husband, was one you viewed with contempt and could never have loved.''

''I did not say that—'' she began hotly, but he laughed, his eyes bright and mocking.

''You said it, Madame, but without words. I should feel sorry for that poor husband of yours, were he not dead, for your tongue could take the skin off him.''

Judith glared furiously at him. ''Sorry for him! How you men stand together in your self-conceit, blind to anything save your own ambitions.''

''And what was his ambition, Madame?'' The capitaine was still smiling as if listening to the babbling of a child.

''To go to war with his king!'' she snapped. ''Forsake and betray all else when Richard raised a finger.''

Leon shrugged. ''That is duty, Madame, and inescapable. You speak of betrayal. Did his duty to his king rouse you to hatred and a betrayal on your own part?''

''I do not understand you, sir.''

''Your own betrayal with his brother, perhaps? You speak of Henry in your dreams, yet your husband risked and lost his life for his king. Did you give thought to him in your dalliance?''

Judith eyes glittered with anger. ''How dare you speak

so of me? You, a soldier of Vallone! Do you stand so
high with the baron that you can insult me with
impunity?"

She wheeled her horse away and urged it into a headlong gallop toward the tiny habitation she saw in the
distance. God's teeth, what insolence the man had! Who
was he to judge her? A paid servant of the ruler of a tiny
mountainous province, peopled by dark, swarthy, and
no doubt villainous people. And she was going into that
province, God help her. She remembered suddenly the
face of the ship's master as she had pronounced her
destination. That involuntary reaching for his crucifix.
Holy Mother, what kind of a life was she bound for? And
now she had broken her earlier resolve to keep this man,
if not as her friend, at least an ally.

She dismounted outside the inn and glanced back at
the fast-approaching party. She would apologize for her
outburst. Not humbly, of course, for he was only a
soldier, but with dignity, and hope that he would be well-
born enough to accept it.

As she changed out of her riding clothes, Judith considered the bearded Capitaine de Foret. Before the
battle that had scarred his face and set the white streak
in his hair, he might have been a handsome man. In a
way, he still was, with the fine gray eyes that could
brighten with mockery or grow cold with fury. Lines of
suffering were commonplace amongst soldiers, yet with
him they seemed to add an air of distinction. Had he
been courtier instead of soldier, he would have been
equally at home, she sensed. What kind of a court did
the baron rule over, she wondered? Was there a place
for an English lady?

She descended the stairs an hour later and
encountered the man she had been considering. She
stopped and looked at him, both with amazement and
trepidation. The rough soldier's garb was gone. He was
attired in a short tunic and breeches of fine black cloth,
white linen at neck and wrist, jewel-hilted dagger

strapped to the fine leather belt. His beard and hair had been trimmed. He heard her step and glanced toward her. His gray eyes expressed nothing.

"Well, Capitaine," she found herself saying. "Do you hold court tonight for some reason? You are so grand that I should respond and offer you a curtsey. Do I look upon courtier as well as soldier?"

To her relief he smiled. "Why no, Madame. I make no claim to favor or kinship with Baron de Gras. I rise on my merits, if such they be. Even a poor adventurer may be allowed fine clothes if he has the price of them. The occasion, Madame, if it can be named so, is some village celebration, a local tradition, and we have come aptly upon a feast day. Our buck has received a hearty welcome. It would be churlish to deny the villagers the pleasure of roasting the beast out of doors." He extended an arm. "Allow me to escort you to this scene of great rejoicing. Since we have completed half of our journey, I fancy the men will take full opportunity of all offers that come their way and I will allow them this night of—er—freedom."

Judith glanced up into the calm face as they reached the outskirts of a small field. "Freedom, you call it? I hope the village elders will not call it something else when the festivities are over. Your troops have a wild look about them."

"Have no fear, Madame. I have already consulted with the elders and their priest, and my orders to the men under my command have been most explicit. There will be no trouble."

The torso of the buck was already turning on the spit over a large fire that threw out sparks and hissing grease. Judith watched the village women hurrying about with wooden platters and great baskets of bread. The elders, with the priest in their midst, were seated on stools beyond range of the heat. Casks of ale had already been broached, and the noise of shouts and laughter filled the air.

The scent of roast venison seemed to be a signal blown along the breeze to summon yet more people to the feast. Small, grimy children hopped beside the blazing logs, attempting to snatch a strip of cooked flesh, while goodwives threatened them with long wooden spoons. Every strong boy and urchin lent a hand at the task of turning the spit, under the watchful eye of the red-faced landlord.

A little apart and far enough to avoid errant sparks and the capering children, stood a bench and two stools. To this spot Capitaine de Foret led Judith. As if at a signal, an inn servant appeared, carrying a tray with a flagon of wine and two goblets.

"Spanish wine, Madame. I trust it is to the taste of a lady of the court of King John?"

"Thank you, Capitaine. In truth, my time at the court of King John was very brief."

De Foret smiled, and in the fading light his eyes were touched by the glow of the fire.

"In truth, Madame, a great deal of experience may be gained in quite short a time."

"A riddle, Capitaine? I cannot vouch for any but myself, and I was not a true court lady."

"But a lady of experience, nevertheless."

"Not at all, Capitaine."

"Two betrothals and one married state, Madame?" He laughed and raised his goblet to her. "I would consider that a fair count of experience. Come, Madame, you are no shy maiden, though you may play the role to please the baron."

"You mistake the matter, sir," Judith began stiffly, but as she looked into the gray eyes she was jolted to see that they were regarding her cynically. She felt the anger rise in her again, the anger she had resolved to hold down.

"Since you hold such a poor opinion of women, sir, I would suppose that your own experience has fallen short of expectation. Do not be at pains to lay the blame so heavily on the female, sir, for the fault may lie within you, though 'twould be heresy to admit it!'' Her anger had passed and she smiled into the dark face, her eyes taking on a mocking light to match his own. ''Was ever man born that did not strut in self-conceit, a cock on his dunghill, giving voice to his own prowess? And yet you scorn the drab but seek to attach the same vices to respectable women in the name of experience and hold yourselves thwarted when they have it not. Has life left you so unfavored, sir, that you seek a scapegoat?''

''Your pardon, Madame. As a humble soldier of Vallone, I am apt to forget my place and thus earn your censure.''

Judith looked at him closely and caught the reflected gleam of the fire on white teeth. ''Humble, I would doubt strongly, sir, but even so, you are unlike the troopers you lead. Are they, or you, Vallonese?''

''They, Madame. They are mountain people who rose to the baron when he annexed Vallone.''

''Annexed Vallone? In whose name?''

''His own.'' The tone of de Foret was casual.

''Then he holds it by conquest and not heritage. What happened to the hereditary rulers, if such there were?''

''Exiled, some two years ago. The Duke of Vallone was said to be corrupt. Oppression spawned revolution and de Gras emerged as leader. I doubt he was a baron then, but a new ruler must give himself a title to distinguish himself from other men.'' He looked down into Judith's intent face. ''Letters patent have been granted by France, Madame, so have no fear that your title will be empty.''

He poured more wine into the goblets and watched Judith thoughtfully. He noted that she had grown very pale. In the flickering firelight, he saw clearly the wide blue eyes staring straight ahead, fixed and unblinking. He remained silent, contemplating the fine curve of her cheek, the slender neck beneath the fall of dark hair. He wondered what thoughts were passing behind that blue stare. When, at last, she turned toward him, he felt a sense of shock. The gaze was dulled and desolate, the look of a woman in the extremity of hopelessness.

"Madame?" he asked, a note of alarm in his voice. "What ails you?"

"Disparaged, by God, but I did not dream by how much. The king knew full well." A sudden fierce light flashed in her eyes. "God's teeth, sir! Even King Richard in his greed for fighting money did not debase Crown Wards in this manner."

De Foret saw the eyes glaze. The warning was sufficient, and his arms reached out to catch the limp body as it fell.

15

Judith was vaguely aware of strong arms lifting and
carrying her away from the bright light of the fire,
through shadowed places and fading voices, into the
darkness of a room. She was lying on her bed and
someone was shielding a candle flame from her eyes.
She opened them slowly, seeing only fingers protecting
the light, then the candlestick was set on a window
chest.

Leon de Foret looked down at her. "You fainted,
Madame, but your departure was unobserved."

Angel had thrust his heavy body between them and
his yellow eyes also looked into hers. She had heard the
warning growl, though seemingly from a distance as
they entered, but at the sound of the capitaine's voice,
Angel had relaxed. Of all the company, he allowed only
the capitaine to approach his mistress.

To avoid striking terror into the hearts of the
assembled villagers, Angel had been shut into Judith's
room. His reproachful gaze told her that he thought it
was unfair to lock him in, but she was forgiven.

Judith touched his face, then raised her eyes to the
capitaine. "Thank you, sir," she murmured, though her
lips felt stiff. "It must have been the heat. Please do not
deny yourself the enjoyment of the feast. You may
safely leave me here."

Instead of obeying, de Foret pulled up a stool to her
bedside and sat down. "It was not the heat, Madame.
We both know that. You fainted from shock, and I wish

to know why. This talk of Crown Wards and disparagement—what does it mean?"

Judith turned her head from him. "It is my shame only. Is it not enough that I bear it alone? What reason do I have for revealing it to you, save to give sharper point to your jibes on the foolishness of women?"

De Foret frowned. "I never reckoned you a fool, Madame. Only a lady of courage and experience would accept the future you intend." He paused. "It seems that my own words were the cause of your collapse. Why should that be? You accepted the baron in marriage, knowing that he ruled a small, mountainous province. You could not have expected a court such as the one you left, surely?"

Judith moved her head restlessly. "I did not chose this future, sir. The decision was made for me by King John when he presumed my widowhood."

"If a husband was your aim, Madame, why did King John not find you one amongst the English gentlemen?"

"I imagine your baron's bid was higher than that of any other. Your master paid highly for an English lady, I was told." She could not disguise the bitterness in her voice. "Did he buy me with the exiled duke's plate and jewelry? As you serve the baron, you will be party to this knowledge, of course."

Leon de Foret sat very still. "I will not believe that of him. He dealt most leniently with the duke, allowing him and his household safe passage into France." The gray eyes sharpened coldly on hers. "The country also believes that in return for some service he rendered, your king promised him a bride. How, then, could you be bought, as you claim? Vallone is poor and the taxes heavy, but the baron shares the people's poverty. Only by such measures can the country be brought to prosperity."

Judith smiled. "You sound like a bishop, Capitaine, preaching economy to his flock while indulging in a life of luxury."

Leon de Foret rose to his feet. The gray eyes that stared down were glacial. "I find your remarks as the wife of the baron most unseemly. May I remind you, Madame, that you are bound in duty to your husband."

Judith's smile was equally cold. "With you to remind me, Capitaine, how could I forget, either the baron or the King of England? I will perform my duties, never fear, but I confess to a certain shock on being allied with a self-ennobled mountain fighter when I expected to be received into some house of minor nobility at the very least."

De Foret made no answer but strode soft-footed to the door. Judith's gaze followed him, and as he lifted a hand to the latch, the tall, lithe figure, half-shadowed in the gloom, might have been Henry's, the dark hair and slim body, so dearly loved and lost to her. She must have made some sound of distress, for de Foret turned.

"What is it?" he said sharply.

Judith shook her head, feeling the pain of loss. "For a second you reminded me of Henry. It was a fleeting impression only."

De Foret smiled coldly. "And where was this gallant Henry of yours when King John was deciding your fate?"

Judith stared back at him, angry with herself for revealing her emotion. "Henry is dead. He has been dead these six years and was so before I married his brother. So, Capitaine de Foret, you may rule out any act of dalliance on my part while my husband risked his life at the side of his king." She turned her back on him and pulled up the coverlet, closing her eyes.

Leon de Foret's steps took him wide of the fire where eager hands were already plucking at the scorched meats, and he paced the perimeter of the field where the light blended into darkness. He walked almost without seeing, his mind on the girl in the tavern bed-chamber. Deep in the bushes, a trooper's face appeared; recognizing his capitaine's dark mood, he hushed the giggling drab beside him. He was not alone in the bushes with his companion. The soldiers of Vallone were making the most of this rare opportunity to feast and take their pleasures.

De Foret was so sunk in thought that he never noticed the coquettish advances of a village girl, nor did he see a drunken trooper weave an unsteady path to the bushes, half-supported by a buxom female. Had he seen, he would not have cared. The men were entitled to their wenches, though he would not have joined them, for he preferred a clean, untainted body whenever he felt the need.

But tonight he was pondering Madame la Baronne's words. She had to be lying when she spoke of being bought. But why would she be here if King John had not ordered it? In Calais they had talked of the English King, his debauchery and self-interest, his greed for money to spend on his favorites. The graybeards had shaken their heads and prophesied ruin for England, for John cared nothing for the provinces of Europe that his brother, Richard, had so nobly won in conquest and died to retain.

What was that word she had used just before her collapse? Disparaged? Brought down to shame. She had not known of the baron's adoption of a title. She was well-born, a lady of rank. Had the king been so desperate for money that he took into ward all gently born females, maidens or widows, to hold them for sale? Could a king debase himself and his subjects so? If all they said of John was true, then as an income, it was most profitable.

He thought of de Gras. Could the baron have deceived his followers, deciding on a dynasty with a well-born bride to further that aim? A ruling family that would prove as harsh and corrupt as the one it replaced? Could a conqueror remain true to the ideals of liberty and freedom?

He thought of himself, he, Leon de Foret, a wanderer

with a sword for hire. Where did he call home? It was so long ago. There had been no life of ease for him, always fighting, riding into battle, dealing death to the enemy. He fingered the scar high on his cheek. Almost a mortal blow, had not the man who delivered it died first. In Poitou that was, and he could no longer remember the master he had served. He stopped his pacing and stared into the fire. The nightmare of that battle was one he had finally conquered, driving it deeper and deeper into the recesses of his mind. It lay dormant. Dormant, but not dead, vanquished but stirring from time to time to disturb his nights. Now he probed those hidden depths as gently as he had touched his scar.

With the coming of night, the battle had flowed over and away. The dead man lay across him, pinning him to the ground, the bloody sword cold on his face. De Foret had known himself powerless to move the body aside, so he had lain where he fell, the blood of both men mingling together and the lifeblood of the living man slowly ebbing away with every beat of the heart. Then the murmured voices had roused him, the glow of lanterns coming closer. There was always carrion that followed the kill, despatching the wounded and looting the bodies. By their very furtiveness, he sensed they were not monks, and he watched indifferently as the lights weaved through the trees, crossing and recrossing but following the swathe of destruction wrought by battle. What would it be? A quick dagger thrust or a casual slicing of the throat as if he were a felled stag? His mind jerked into motion. God's teeth! He was not prepared to lie supine and wait for the butcher like some dumb animal. The rejection of this fate had given strength to his slashed arms, and the task of throwing off the heavy body brought the hot sweat surging to warm, stiffened muscles.

He never recalled how he reached the covering bushes. Blood had dried on his face and tunic, and he lay as a bloodied corpse until moonlight revealed other companions, all truly dead.

His stomach had revolted at the stench of blood, and he slipped off the ruined tunic that had stiffened with another man's blood. It was cold. His sword-slashed body ached with it. Groping fingers touched cloth, thick and coarse. His need for warmth was greater than any dead man's, and he rolled a corpse from its tunic. Then the mist had closed on his mind and darkness had come. He remembered vividly the darkness. It had been full of fire and devils. A skull-thin face had peered at him, retreated, then peered again. Satan was waiting to claim his soul, and he lacked the strength to raise a hand to cross himself. Pain and the stench of decay were everywhere, and time was the limbo of purgatory.

De Foret jerked himself back to the present and watched the Velardi couple, ragged and gaunt, being taunted by his own troopers who demanded that the Italians serve them from bended knee. De Foret turned from the dwindling fire and resumed his pacing. Just so had those fires of hell dwindled into candles and the devils into gray-habited men. The face of Satan had softened into a lined face beneath a cowl.

"You are safe, my son," the old voice had said. "God has rekindled the spark we feared had failed. In time your strength will return, and Vallone will see you again. What are you called, my son? I am named Ignatious; Father Ignatius."

A name thrust into de Foret's mind. He uttered it. The priest nodded and de Foret slept.

When he left the monastery, he went in company with others, all soldiers gathered by the monks from the battlefield, as was the custom. Under the healing hands of the priests, it mattered little that friend or foe lay side by side on the straw pallets. All were the children of God. Before he left, de Foret had glimpsed his own reflection in the silver of the chalice. It was the face of a stranger. Hollow-cheeked and with a newly healed scar curving upward to a flash of white hair streaking the black.

" 'Fore God, Father, I know not that man. Why does he wear my body and speak with my voice?"

Father Ignatius had smiled. "You will learn to trust him, my son, have no fear. He is Leon, for you told me so yourself. Leon—" he smiled and spread his hands as if sharing a joke. "To us you are Leon. Leon de Foret. It is a good name."

Capitaine de Foret drew in a deep breath and moved toward the inn. The memories were old now and the re-examining of the nightmare had lessened its power to torment his dreams.

Sunrise was an hour old when Capitaine de Foret left the inn and made his way to the barn. He surveyed his heavy-eyed troopers with derision.

"Since you took your ease last night and indulged in the delights of the flesh, I will extend our travel today to make up for lost time." He grinned as someone gave a low moan. "You have proved your worth as men to females hereabouts. Now prove your worth as soldiers to me. You have an hour to saddle up." He glanced about him. "Where are the prisoners?"

"Outside, Capitaine, with Farino keeping an eye on them."

De Foret nodded and crossed to the stables where he found the youngest of his troopers lethargically engaged in feeding the horses. He raised bloodshot eyes to the capitaine and executed a shambling salute.

"Wake up, Marco," said de Foret crisply. "We ride in an hour." He regarded the dreamy-eyed youngster in amusement. "Please remove the daisy chain before we ride, won't you?"

The youth blinked and looked down at his chest. He removed the daisy chain reverently, then lifted a scarlet face. "A—a girl gave it to me," he said.

"Of course. I didn't suppose you got it from a village elder!"

The boy smiled, and de Foret recognized the expression. He grinned. "For pity's sake, don't tell me

you're in love again. God's teeth, lad, you've been that
at every halt, and you a bare seventeen. Do you aim to
repopulate the earth?''

He left the stable, still grinning, and did not notice the
sullen gaze of the Velardis following him, but Farino did,
and merely out of habit with prisoners, he struck Maria
an open-handed blow, then brought his fist round and
hit Luigi on the side of the head. Farino was tired after
the night's excesses and even more tired of being
responsible for the prisoners. Had the decision been his,
the pair would have hung from the nearest tree as soon
as they had left the convent. Prisoners were useless and
had to be fed and watched. The baron had said that in
the early days of the rising, long before this de Foret had
come to Vallone and been appointed capitaine of
troops. A pity de Foret had influence with the baron,
who had been a man after Farino's own heart, a fierce
peasant who had taken reprisals on all those who had
followed the duke. It had been to his taste before, but
now the baron—or Ivo, the ironsmith as he had been—
wanted respectability. Farino spat in the dust. It had
been better when men ran in fear and spoke of Vallone
in terror-struck tones. He spat again and kicked the
prisoners to their feet.

Both Judith and de Foret were silent as they rode out
that morning. Judith was angered by her own weakness
last night. How stupid to confide in this man, a soldier
and servant of Baron de Gras. His loyalty lay in Vallone
with the self-styled baron. His sworn task was to deliver
her into the hands of Vallone's ruler.

As they rode, Judith came to terms with what she had
learned from de Foret. She, Lady Tarrant, the well-born
Judith Bradley, was bound in marriage to a peasant of
God-knew-what ancestry. To lead a country into revolt
against its hereditary rulers showed him to be brave and
strong. What else was to his credit? The desire to have a
lady wife? She repressed a shiver as she recalled the
little French ship's master's face when she stated her

destination. The revolution was over, but what had it left in its wake? A freed people did not return at once to quiet and lawful pursuits. The oppression of years was invariably followed by the vengeance of the oppressed. Was the baron strong enough to contain his people in peace?

She glanced over her shoulder and met the eye of a trooper, a large man who held the leading reins of the Velardis' horses. He was a coarse-featured man of brutal aspect, a Vallonese. She glanced past him to the prisoners. In spite of her dislike of them, she was shocked by their appearance. Plump Maria was now almost as gaunt as her husband. Her dark, greasy hair was filth-streaked, and grime covered her like a second skin. Her clothes were torn and even more stained than when they had left the convent. Luigi's thin face was almost skull-like, his black eyes full of fear.

She looked ahead again. The Velardis had shown her no pity. Why should she have the slightest sympathy with their plight? And yet she did, for it was obvious they were half-starved and ill-treated. Angel, loping along at full stretch, was treated royally compared with the Velardis.

By late afternoon they had reached a small wayside inn. Judith slid from the saddle and, preceded by Angel, who considered this his right as her guardian, entered the timbered building.

Capitaine de Foret was waiting for her as she descended the stairs into the tiny room set with benches and stools. A log fire burned, and the aroma of cooked food gathered over the years met her, but the accommodation was clean. She saw that de Foret, although still in riding clothes, had washed and brushed his tunic. He bowed, and she smiled her thanks as he pulled out a stool for her. It was no use being at odds with this man, she decided. If he believed in the qualities of his master, then the baron must surely have something to commend him. Leon de Foret had intelligence.

There was no look of the brute about him. That reminded her of the Velardis and their guard.

"I know the Velardis are criminals, Capitaine, but I doubt they will reach Vallone to answer for their crime unless you improve their conditions. They appear to have spent every night since we left the convent, under hedges or in ditches, with barely enough food to keep them alive."

De Foret's gray eyes regarded her steadily. "As to the hedges, Madame, your surmise is correct. The men refuse to share their quarters with criminals. I cannot force them. Farino, the trooper I appointed to guard them and see to their wants, assures me of the adequacy of their food. The appetite is inclined to diminish, Madame, when faced with even closer retribution. Admittedly, it is not of the quality served to you. Would you have me direct that they be served the same?"

Judith looked down at the well-cooked food before her, then raised her gaze to meet his. There was a glint in them that might have been cynicism. She felt herself flush and tried, but failed, to hold back an angry retort.

"I would have them treated a little better than animals, sir. It may be the custom of your people to degrade prisoners, but I feel they are suffering unduly. A little humanity would not come amiss."

Capitaine de Foret gave a short laugh. "And do your people, Madame, forgive would-be murderers so easily? Do you, yourself, forget that they left you for dead in some wilderness? Is that scar on your breast not constant reminder of their evil action? Show softness, Madame, and they will call it stupidity."

Judith looked into the scarred face. The gray eyes were cold and hostile. "Is that a lesson you learned, Capitaine? How came you by your own scar? Did a moment of softness betray you into stupidity and thus kill all compassion?" She stopped, appalled by her own clumsiness and the flash of anguish that came and went in his eyes. "I did not mean—"

He had risen, his face tight and pale. "A battle, Madame, with bravery and honor on both sides, not by the hand of a slinking cur. And compassion came at battle's end." He turned and strode from the room, leaving Judith full of angry self-criticism. She was a fine one to talk of stupidity. Her first dislike of the Velardis should have warned her that they were not to be trusted, and yet she had gone into the wild countryside with them, instead of insisting that the escort be summoned to L'Hirondelle. And now she was defending that very couple against the man who had sought her out and offered his protection. It had been unforgivable of her to comment on his battle wound. Now they must be further constrained than before. She stared into the fire for a long time after he had gone, then sighed and rose.

Her foot was on the lowest step of the stairs when she heard the scream. It was high and piercing, the cry of a woman in pain. Maria? There was no other woman here. She whirled from the stairs and began to run toward the sound.

Outside, the twilight was settling into darkness. Apart from the inn, the only lights came from torches by the barn and horse lines. She rounded the corner of the barn and her steps halted abruptly. Her hand reached out to the barn for support, her fingers gripping the rough wooden pole.

Maria was kneeling on the hard-packed earth, her face in her hands, her black hair hanging in thick greasy tails about her shoulders. She was weeping, great gasping sobs shaking her thin shoulders. Luigi stood by, arms pinioned by two soldiers. The rest of the men stood in a half-circle, their eyes fixed on the man who stood with his back to Judith.

She felt a sickness rise in her. He had no need to turn, for she knew he was de Foret. As Maria bowed over her hands, still sobbing, Judith saw the back of her dress. It was torn, and blood welled like long red fingers from shoulders to waist. Judith stared in sick horror. It was like a scene from hell, highlighted by the blazing torches to one side and the fiery splendor of the dying sun on the other. A tableau of immobile figures, the only sound being Maria's weeping.

But Judith's gaze was held by the horsewhip clenched in the capitaine's hand. The narrow leather tail lay curled on the ground, stained with the same red that trickled down Maria's back. Judith gave a long, shuddering gasp, turned with hair flying to run back to the privacy of her bedchamber, where physical sickness engulfed her.

16

During the next day's ride, Judith kept her gaze straight ahead and did not look at Leon de Foret. She could not bring herself to speak to him after witnessing his brutal treatment of Maria Velardi. Had she met his eye, her contempt would have shown too clearly, and had she spoken to him, she could not have trusted herself to stay calm. She glanced over her shoulder and saw the woman's white, strained face. The torn dress was gone, Judith noticed with surprise. Maria wore a coarse-fibered tunic, probably begged from the inn landlord, for it hung loosely.

Judith's gaze moved to their escort. It was not the brutish-faced man who had led them previously. This guard was a youth who might have been termed fresh-faced had not hard living and probably debauchery etched lines around his mouth and shadowed his eyes. Judith's one glimpse of Leon de Foret that morning had shown her a tight-lipped, hard-eyed face of granite. In spite of her indignation, she knew that she dared not voice her protest after his cynical rejection of her plea on behalf of the Velardis last night. If the whipping was his answer, what might he have in mind for her, after that insult she had delivered so hotly?

Much to her relief, de Foret did not keep station beside her as he had done on previous days but ranged his horse wide, first in the van, then dropping behind to keep the party close together. He seemed a tireless rider, grim-faced and silent. There was no banter

between the troopers as on other days. A wary
avoidance of the capitaine's eye held them quiet. Judith
found their attitude a little puzzling. Could hardened
soldiers who had lived through revolution and bloody
battle be shocked by the whipping of a woman
prisoner?

De Foret finally gave the order to halt as they came up
to a plain, timbered building. Judith saw with astonishment that the young soldier was assisting Maria to
alight. Had she been right? Were the troopers as
offended as she was by the whipping?

Judith turned in her saddle to find the capitaine by her
stirrup. Refusing his help, she descended, giving him a
cold glance as she passed into the inn. It could hardly be
described as luxurious; in fact, now that she thought of
it, their accommodation had deteriorated since leaving
the convent. Vallone came closer each day, and the land
grew poorer and more hilly. Soon they would reach the
mountains and begin the last phase of their journey. A
few days more, perhaps. Her heart sank at the thought.

The innkeeper showed her into a bedchamber that
was barely more than a garret under the eaves. She
glanced round at the stained walls and crude furnishing.
She knew it must be the best room the inn could offer,
for Leon de Foret had assured her that night stops had
been arranged to the best of his ability, but he could not
promise much comfort since the road to Vallone was
little traveled. She shivered as the implication of the
phrase struck her. A little-traveled road or a well-
avoided one? Was Vallone, since the revolution, a
fortified province, ruled for and by peasants, with a
peasant baron at their head? A land that welcomed no
other but their own kind? What, in God's name, had King
John sentenced her to?

A knock on the door startled her. It was the landlord.
His bow was obsequious, his gaze flickering over her as
if unwilling to meet her eyes. He muttered about food
being ready and took himself off as if he shared her mis-

givings.

She was descending the rough-hewn wooden stairs when she realized that de Foret would be her sole companion for the meal. How could she face him with her disgust so apparent? She knew that she could not hide her feelings. It would be better if she ate in her bedchamber and avoided the man. The landlord came from the kitchen, carrying a flagon and mugs. As he moved into the side room, she followed and made her request. He set down the flagon and looked at her, then his gaze rose and she saw fear in his eyes. As she turned, he hurried past her and she found herself staring at Leon de Foret.

His expression was quite unreadable, but there were deep shadows under his eyes.

"You are unwell, Madame?"

"I am perfectly well," she said quickly. "But a little tired."

"Then hot food and the comfort of a fire will benefit you. I will not guarantee the quality of the wine. This is a poor place."

"I know."

"Yet you prefer to eat in a damp, shabby bedchamber. Why?"

Judith felt herself flush, but she kept her gaze steady. "What I prefer is no concern of yours. You have no right to question me. Now, if you will excuse me—"

Instead of moving out of her way, he stepped forward and shut the door behind him. He leaned against it and folded his arms. Judith stared at him, then her anger came.

"Stand aside, if you please." Her voice was low but furious.

"I do not please, Madame. Not until I have had an explanation from you."

"An explanation! How dare you, of all people, demand an explanation from me? I am not your helpless prisoner. Get out of my way, damn you!"

The black brows drew together as if in genuine puzzlement. "First, you will tell me in what way I have offended you."

"Offended me?" She caught her breath on a sharp gasp. "Speak rather of offense to another which I had the misfortune to witness. For myself, I hold you in contempt. It seems I was wrong to rate your position of capitaine as a sign of higher breeding. You are as base as the men you lead!"

His shoulders left the door and he was upon her as swiftly as a springing beast. Hard fingers gripped her wrist and she gasped at the pain.

"You will explain that remark, Madame, before you leave this room." He towered over her, as lean and dangerous as a leopard. Her heart jumped painfully, but she forced herself to defiance.

"And if I do not choose, sir, what then?" Judith asked unsteadily. "You will have me whipped? Or better still, whip me yourself!"

He released her wrist. "You were there?"

"Yes. It seems I was wrong to plead for the prisoners. You only increased their suffering."

"Ah, I understand now." His eyes were still hard, but he had stepped back a pace. "It was a pity you did not arrive sooner, Madame, then you would not have jumped to the wrong conclusion. Sit down and take a goblet of wine."

"I will not—"

"Yes you will, Madame, or I shall bar the door and prevent you from leaving."

Judith saw that he meant it and sat down, ignoring the wine he poured. She had begun to shake from reaction and held out her hands to the fire, avoiding the need to look at him.

He made an exclamation of disgust. "Refuse the wine, by all means. It is fearsome stuff." He sat down on a stool opposite her. "Now, Madame, you shall be informed of the true events. Farino, the trooper I appointed as guardian of the prisoners, betrayed my trust. He has been punished."

At her startled glance, he nodded. "Yes, Madame, by the same method he used on the Velardi woman. You were right to point out their condition. I had neglected it myself. Farino has a cruel streak. I should have remembered. It amused him to deprive them of food and physically abuse them. He demanded the woman submit to him in other ways. The whipping was her punishment for refusal. I arrived at the wrong moment for Farino." He gave her a tired smile and rose, moving to the door. "Now, you may retire, Madame. I will arrange for food to be sent to your bedchamber."

Judith did not move. She stared into the fire, feeling shamed and foolish. She had put her own interpretation on what she saw and it was wrong. She looked toward him. He waited, his eyes empty of emotion. She smiled. "As you say, Capitaine, a fire is most beneficial, and I am hungry. Is the wine really fearsome?"

For a moment he stared in silence, then a smile twitched his lips. "Most fearsome, Madame." His smile grew, and it was neither mocking nor cynical. It was one of pleasure, unanticipated and beyond expectation. He moved to the wine flagon and picked it up. "That rogue of a landlord will have better, I swear. He shall fetch of his best for Madame la Baronne."

He was back in a few moments with a fresh flagon. He smiled at her. "When I mentioned Vallone, he suddenly recollected a fine French wine he had put by for the last Feast Day and somehow forgotten."

Judith felt a flicker of fear touch her spine. "Does he then go in fear of Vallone?"

De Foret handed her a goblet and sat down. "He has no need now, for Vallone is calm. We are but twenty miles away, and at the start of the revolt, I imagine this road was used by those who fled and those who pursued."

"Were you not there when the peasants revolted?"

"No. I was pursuing my trade elsewhere."

Judith thought back to the night of the village feast. "You said the troopers were men of Vallone, Capitaine, but you were not. Where, then, is your place of birth?"

"I am a mercanary, Madame, a wandering soldier without home or ties."

"I see, but even a wanderer can claim some birthplace."

De Foret smiled. "I claim no place, and in return, no place claims me."

Judith frowned. "What does that mean? Did your country disown you?"

De Foret laughed. "Not that I heard of, but then, a mercenary hears nothing but the sound of battle. It is, after all, what he is paid for."

"I shall not pry into your past, sir."

"I have no past, Madame. It went in the mist of time. I have only a future. When I have completed this duty to the baron, I shall take my sword elsewhere."

Judith stared at him and her heart skipped a beat. "You intend to leave Vallone and the baron's service?"

"He has no need of me now. He has assumed all authority. There is no reason for me to remain."

Judith stared into the fire, feeling a chill creep over her. De Foret was not a Vallonese. He had a perfect right to go where he wished, but in spite of everything, she had come to rely on him. He was proposing to leave her with a peasant husband in that land of peasants. Even the baron was a stranger, and she knew nothing about their customs, nor even if they spoke the same language she did.

"Must you leave Vallone, Capitaine?" She looked at him from very blue eyes and was unaware of the fear that showed. "I go as a stranger, and an ignorant one, at that."

De Foret leaned forward and took her hand. It lay cold in his. He had never expected to be touched by female distress, but this girl, for all her pride and hot tongue,

stirred some chord in his heart. She had beauty and
breeding. He could envy the baron that much. But there
was more, and it hit him like a blow to the heart. He
envied the baron for possession of this girl, this dark-
haried, blue-eyed beauty whom the baron would bed as
casually as he took a serving girl. How could he stay and
accept that? He halted his thoughts and looked at the
girl, still staring at him.

"Madame, you have nothing to fear, though the baron
is, admittedly, of peasant stock. You have been married
before. Is it so hard to take another in his place?"

Judith dropped her gaze and withdrew her hand.
"Perhaps not, had there really been another. Forgive
me, Capitaine. It is the expected foolishness of the
young maid, and as my father-in-law pointed out in his
desire to be rid of me, I am old, being two and twenty
years." She gave him a wry smile.

The landlord's entrance with food halted the conversation, and they ate in silence. De Foret spoke first.

"Do you tell me, Madame, that your marriage was not
a true one?"

"We were never man and wife in the true sense." She
smiled. "My husband was such as you—a man who lived
to fight. We were betrothed as children, but when his
king called, he happily consigned me to his brother,
Henry. I would have been content, but Henry died.
Since my Lord Tarrant was set on acquiring my fortune,
my first betrothed was compelled to obey his sire,
though it was on the eve of his sailing for France." She
raised her brows in self-mockery. "So, you see,
Capitaine, I am well experienced in marriage, albeit by
proxy."

De Foret was frowning down at his food as if trying to
recall something. Then he looked up. "I believe you said
that you were *presumed* a widow, Madame, by King John.
Does that mean your husband's body was not
recovered?"

Judith nodded. "It was a great grief to Lord Tarrant to

know that Quentin was lying in an unmarked grave in Poitou."

"Ah yes, Poitou. I too, was there. Where the English fought the French. Did not your King Richard die there too?"

"Yes, but he now lies at Fontevrault. His grave is known."

"You have my sympathy, Madame, in your loss, yet I am curious. You speak of great grief to your husband's sire. Was it not grief to you also?"

"Quentin and I were barely acquainted. We met little during our early betrothal. It would be false to claim that I felt true grief when he died. For Henry, yes, but not for Quentin." She set down her goblet. "I believe I will retire now. I confess to weariness. You rode us very hard today, Capitaine."

Leon preceded her to the door. She smiled up into his face. "Thank you for your understanding, Capitaine, and for your forgiveness of my stupidity. I would wish us to part in friendship."

Leon took her offered hand and carried it to his lips. "Always, Madame." Then he bent forward and kissed her gently on the mouth.

Judith felt the tenderness of his touch and her eyes misted. She gave him a tremulous smile. For a moment she felt a wild urge to fling herself into his arms and beg to be taken anywhere but Vallone. Then her mind steadied as she realized the futility. Even had he not been in the service of de Gras, he was a mercenary, a traveling soldier. Her plea could only cause embarrassment.

It was not until she reached the privacy of her bedchamber that it struck her that Madame la Baronne de Gras had not resisted, nor even disliked, being kissed by a servant of her husband.

As they rode steadily toward Vallone, the land grew even rougher. Their path became more circuitous as they were compelled to avoid rockfalls and areas of marshy ground. Leon de Foret rode by her side, and Angel's tireless lope kept pace with her horse. The day had turned dull, and thunderheads wreathed the distant mountains, making the peaks appear to float free, like the ridged backbone of some serpentine creature.

The party rode in silence, the swarthy faces of the troopers expressionless. Judith saw the large, rough-faced man, Farino, who had been the Velardis' guard, riding flank, and by the stiff way he sat his horse, she knew he had been well whipped. Her gaze passed over the Italian couple. They were cleaner, their looks less haunted though still gaunt faced. Judith returned her gaze to the front as the ground rose. She needed to guide her horse carefully over this rock-strewn surface.

Leon de Foret had moved ahead to join the leading trooper, and the two were halted on the crest of a small hill when the rest of the party reached them. Judith drew rein beside de Foret and regarded the view. From this crest, she saw the sweep of a narrow valley which curved at either end and disappeared to completely encircle a high, rocky position. On its high eminence stood a castle. Arrow slit walls and high iron gates proclaimed it a stronghold. No sign of life could be seen, but above the battlemented tower a banner curled and spun on its staff.

Judith stared at the quarterings on the banner. Green and yellow like Tarrant, but the colors lay on gray, not azure. The castle itself was not dissimilar to Tarrant. She turned with a smile to Leon de Foret. His gaze was fixed on the banner, and there was a rigidity about his posture that alarmed Judith. She was about to ask if the lord of this place was enemy to Vallone, when de Foret's murmur halted her words.

"Green and yellow," he said, as if to himself. "I once knew such, but not this. There is flaw somewhere." His gaze moved over the ground and his brows knitted. "Not this—but 'tis gone now." He roused himself and saw Judith. He smiled and the darkness was gone from his face.

"Ah, Madame. Did you ever see such a strong-built place that glowers so dark as to put fear into men's hearts before they set foot within?"

"What is this place?" asked Judith.

"A prison, I am told, Madame, where the duke sent the more troublesome of his subjects. It was fitting that he and his household should be sent there by the baron. They were lodged in the same conditions as the duke's former prisioners, they say, while they awaited the escort that took them into exile."

"Where are they now?"

De Foret shrugged. "In France, I believe, Madame, save for the duke's heir, Count Alberto. He was away from Vallone during the revolt. I imagine he is now with his family." He glanced up at the lowering sky. "Come, Madame, let us not linger. The storms are swift and heavy in these parts, and I must find you shelter before this one breaks."

He called to his men and they circled the grim prison, keeping to the ridge until the ground leveled and the shallow valley was left far behind. Judith, glancing over her shoulder, took her last look at the relic of the duke's fierce rule. How many persons had entered there, never to see the light of day again? As de Foret had said, it was fitting that the duke should view the conditions for himself as a prisoner of the baron. She visualized, with a shudder, the treatment he might have received from the victorious peasants before he had gone into exile. She thought of the baron who had been generous in victory, allowing the hereditary ruler his life and property. That was what de Foret had said, although he had not been there at the time. Would a poor peasantry allow the family to go into exile, retaining their valuables? If it was true, then how had the baron accumulated sufficient wealth to satisfy King John in the matter of a wife? If de Foret's assumption was mere fabrication by the baron, and he had retained the duke's wealth, what else might he have exacted? Revenge was a powerful motive when servant overthrew master. The picture of that brooding prison was still in her mind. Had the duke really left it? She tried to shake the dark thoughts away. Whatever was the truth of it, it was history now, and she had no right to question it. Bondage was drawing closer day by day. It was that thought that had thrown her into such a somber and fanciful mood.

De Foret came alongside as the first drops of rain began to fall. He glanced into her face and smiled gently.

"Let not the sight of that prison distress you, Madame, for it is far behind now. My men assure me that it is quite empty. Though the banner still flies, it is of no consequence since the duke has gone."

A raindrop splashed on Judith's cheek. "How far to shelter?" She returned de Foret's smile.

"About two miles." One dark brow rose in its familiar exaggerated quirk, and the white teeth flashed her a challenging grin. Judith found her spirits soaring, and she laughed aloud. With a quick movement she kneed her horse into a gallop. As his stride lengthened, Judith lay forward over his neck, narrowing her eyes against the wind. She thought she heard a laugh from behind, then the sound of thudding hooves made her urge her mount into a wild, exhilarating, headlong flight. She had no expectation of outriding de Foret, but she needed the fierce excitement of this ride to purge her mind of all thought.

A distant cluster of buildings began to shape themselves into cottages, and a rough track of hard-packed earth formed under the flying hooves. A cottage, larger than the others, proclaimed itself an inn by the bush hung over the lintel, and to this Judith headed. De Foret had still not overtaken her, and she could only guess that he was allowing her the victory to dispel the sight of the prison fortress.

When she drew rein outside the inn, she was flushed and breathing quickly. She watched him approach, riding his horse at what seemed a leisurely pace, but the animal's long, rangy stride was deceptive. She knew he could have outpaced her had he wished.

He slid from the saddle and reached up to help her dismount. He stood with his hands still about her waist as he smiled down into the sparkling eyes.

"So, Madame, it is not only English men who ride like the wind."

"You could have passed me by, Capitaine, had you wished, I am sure. Why did you not do so?"

He dropped his hands from her waist, but the smile was now in his eyes as well as on his lips. "Less fatiguing, Madame. Had I ridden ahead, I should needs crane my neck to observe you, whereas from behind, I could admire your skill and suffer no such inconvenience. Besides—" he paused. "Even the most skillful rider may take a toss, and I needed to be in a position to reach you quickly."

"Oh." Judith could not make up her mind whether to laugh or scowl, but de Foret took the decision out of her hands by leading her into the inn and calling for the landlord to show himself.

Judith's breathing had slowed, but she was vividly aware of de Foret's hand on her arm, the touch of his shoulder, and most of all those smiling gray eyes. She would never have believed that those hard gray eyes could soften so, and she was strangely moved by their warmth.

The full storm broke as they were eating, and the first crash of thunder startled Judith. De Foret's hand reached out, then halted, and he turned the movement into a pretense of refilling his wine goblet. His intention had been to lay his hand on hers in a gesture of comfort, but the action had been dictated by his heart and not his head. He must be careful. She was the baron's wife. She belonged to another man, and the tender regard growing in him had to be quenched. Both his tongue and his actions must be curbed. He was aware of his duty, just as she was, and the closeness they had achieved so suddenly since last night must not be wrecked by thoughtless familiarity on his part.

Judith had not noticed his movement, nor seen any change in his manner, but she felt a warmth that pleased her. Thunder still rumbled across the heavens, and lightning lit the room intermittently, dulling the candles by comparison. The rain beat down steadily and seemed in no mood to cease, even by the time the meal ended and Judith was bidding de Foret good night.

The capitaine frowned as he listened to the heavy drumming. He looked at Judith.

"We have a river to cross before we reach the main track to the city. The rains come early. We shall be delayed if the river is in flood."

"That will be a shame," Judith said, trying to keep her voice flat. "Good night, sir."

She went up the stairs, smiling. Let it rain forever, she thought, if it meant their arrival in the city was delayed. De Foret might be eager to discharge his duty to the baron, but she was not at all discontent to have the capitaine's company for longer than expected.

In spite of the continuing violence of the storm, Judith fell asleep quickly. She had never ridden so constantly in her life before, but the exercise had strengthened her body, and her muscles no longer protested. She would always bear the scar on her breast of Luigi's vicious attack, but the bruises were healed, as were the flesh wounds dealt by rocks and trees.

For the first few hours Judith slept deeply, but the ceaseless cacophony of the storm began to intrude, forming a wild background to her dreams. The prison fortress was there, a dark and sinister place but so like Tarrant Castle that it became inhabited by Tarrants. But still the banner flew the colors she had seen, lacking the azure field of the Sussex stronghold. Figures passed

across her mind. There was Lucy, dear Lucy who had
been dismissed. Why was she back at Tarrant? Yet she
knew it was not Tarrant, although the lord himself was
on the steps, glowering down at her.

Her body moved restlessly on the bed. There should
have been another face. Where was he? She tried to call
to the smiling Lucy, but no one heard. They moved
about without seeing her. How could they, for this was
not Tarrant, so why were they here? A presence at her
shoulder brought her about slowly. A dark, lean face
was regarding her sadly. Henry? But Henry was dead,
and the face was like, but unlike. The courtyard was
suddenly full of people, horses and riders. A tall man,
flame-haired, raised a hand in salute. But Richard, Coeur
de Lion, was dead too. There was yet another face and
another voice. Her hands pressed to her ears, for it was
another of the dead. But the face looked into hers and
she recognized it. Quentin? How could the dead be part
of the living? He was with Henry, and his name was
inscribed on the tablet above the empty vault. Henry
was there in body, but not Quentin.

The face came closer, and her dream body recoiled.
The figure was Quentin's but the face was not. Quentin
was never bearded. The gray eyes were the same but
the face was older. A violent crash of thunder sent the
picture scattering into fragments.

Judith fought her way to consciousness in the pitch-
dark bedchamber. She was sweat-soaked and trembling.
The dream was receding, but one vivid fragment
remained. The bearded man with the streak of white in
the thick black hair above his temple wore the face of
Quentin.

17

Judith slid from the bed and fumbled with the tinderbox. When the candle was lit, she climbed back into the bed and pulled the coverlet about her shoulders. It was a dream. It had to be a dream. Quentin was dead, though his body had never been found. But Leon de Foret? He had fought in Poitou also, but as a mercenary for the French, she had supposed. She drew up her knees and sat huddled on the bed, trying to calm her mind. It was too ridiculous, a mere coincidence that without his beard and the streak of white hair, Leon de Foret should have borne a striking resemblance to Quentin Tarrant. The gray eyes were there, and the lithe stride that had reminded her of Henry. Quentin also had that Tarrant stride. She frowned as she recalled her questions to de Foret of his birthplace. He claimed none, he had said, and his past was lost in the mists of time. She had accepted that he preferred to keep his past secret. Perhaps that was the way of mercenaries. Her thoughts moved to their first view of that Vallonese prison fortress. De Foret's fixed stare at the banner and the murmur, "There is flaw somewhere." The flaw had been in the gray field, the only difference between that banner and Tarrant's, but how could de Foret know that unless he had seen Tarrant Castle? France had its castles, too. The one he recalled could have been anywhere.

She shook her head in tired confusion. It was impossible. If Quentin had survived Poitou, nothing

would have prevented him from from returning to
England. It was inconceivable that he could have
become a mercenary and adopted a new name. For
what purpose?

She lay down and drew the coverlet over her. It was a
dream, a nightmare brought on by the storm and her
own vivid imagination. Tomorrow she would look upon
Leon de Foret and find no likeness whatever to Quentin.

Judith was not the only sleeper in the inn that night for
whom the storm had created a background for dreams.
Leon de Foret lay on his bed in the small room opposite
Judith's. He was awake, but his wakening had not been a
jolt into consciousness as Judith's had been. The scratch
of flint, then the narrow rim of light under Madame's
door had alerted him. A soldier's instinct for the
unexpected or unusual had honed his reactions and
kept him alive more times than he could count. The door
of his bedchamber was slightly ajar, a precaution he had
adopted since Madame la Baronne's life was in his trust.
He listened, but no sound came. The dog, Angel, was
with her, and it would have been a mad or desperate
thief who braved that defense. He smiled in the dark.
Angel! What a name to call that fearsome black brute.
Yet the dog had saved Madame's life and was fiercely
loyal to her. His own presence was tolerated, but he
knew himself watched by those yellow eyes. One
threatening move against Madame and the dog would
be at his throat. He smiled again, and his thoughts
drifted to recall the dream the sound had interrupted.

In the usual manner of dreams, the greater part had
faded, leaving only disjointed memories, yet he knew
that the prison fortress had figured somewhere. The old
ducal banner flying over the unfamiliar landscape had
evoked a memory that still eluded him. The face of
Madame, the sapphire eyes and long black hair, were all
part of his dream, but he lacked the connecting link.
Since they were both strangers to that place, and

strangers to each other, no link was logical. He listened to the rain, and his mind reverted to the immediate future and the river they must cross. Would the rain never cease? He fell asleep.

They woke to a dark, sodden morning. The storm had gone, but the clouds hung menacingly, like brooding gods daring any mortal to show defiance in the face of their power. Judith and de Foret met in the small dining room to break their fast. They were each aware of the subtle change in their relationship, though neither was prepared to advance it. Judith had convinced herself of the ridiculous nature of her dream, but even so, she could not help but regard de Foret closely. A similarity of height and build, that was all. Many men had dark hair and gray eyes, just as many men were soldiers. In a small company like this, it was inevitable that she and de Foret should be thrown together. But there was nothing inevitable, she told herself, about the warm glow she felt in his presence! She had to remind herself that a husband awaited her coming and de Foret was pledged to deliver her to the baron.

At the meal's end, de Foret rose. "If the rain holds off until we reach the river, it should be possible to ford it and reach the city." The gray eyes regarded her for what seemed a long moment, then he nodded. "Yes, we had best make haste, Madame. I will attend to the men." He turned and was gone from the room.

Judith sat very still, wondering about that long look. Did he feel that haste was prudent because she was another man's wife and he wished to be rid of her? Or because they had shared a kiss which might have developed into something else? Whatever his reasoning, she knew he was right. De Foret must be put from her mind. The longer they spent together, the harder it would be. She rose as the clatter of hooves came louder.

Outside, Judith looked at the sky. The clouds were still

heavy, but the sun was making a brave effort to recover
its hold on the day. De Foret waited by her stirrup, and
she rested a hand on his shoulder as he helped her
mount. As he handed her the reins, their eyes met
without expression. He mounted his own horse and
glanced behind, checking the troopers, the Velardis,
and the baggage mule. Then he raised a hand and they
moved off.

At first the wet ground sucked at the hooves of the
horses and progress was slow, but as the track hardened
into stone-packed earth, they moved more swiftly. By
midday the river was sighted, overhung by tendrils of
mist. Judith looked beyond the river and saw only rock
and rising ground, a winding track flattened by horses
and wagons. She stared at it miserably. The road to the
city. The road that would take her to an unknown future
in the heart of these mountains that were dark and gray,
mist-wreathed and forbidding. From there, there was no
escape.

She glanced sideways at de Foret. He was frowning,
his dark brows drawn together. Judith's heart lurched.
Such was a look that Quentin had worn when he told her
of his father's insistence on an early marriage. That same
hard profile as that shown her by Lord Tarrant when he
rebuked her for lack of child. But Quentin had never
smiled gently as de Foret had done—but what use to
think of either? She checked her thoughts savagely. All
was lost to her save the peasant baron of Vallone.

They came to the river bank and halted their horses.
The gray water tumbled and swirled past them, carrying
dead branches and weeds into the swift-running current
at its center. Tied to a stout post at the water's edge was
a broad, flat-bottomed barge, a long pole lying inside.
The troopers gathered about de Foret as he issued
orders, then he turned his gaze to where Judith sat her
mount.

"The water is rough, Madame, but the horses can
swim across." He smiled slightly. "They will not care to

stand in the barge, and it would be foolhardy to expect them to. The baggage mule, in Marco's charge, and the prisoners can be poled across by the strongest trooper, Farino. You will be safe in their company until we join you with the horses."

Judith looked at the barge. It seemed stout enough, but she had a strong disinclination to travel with the Velardis and a packmule.

"Thank you, Capitaine, but I too will swim my horse across. I would not wish to be beside the mule if he should suddenly take a dislike to his mode of travel."

"The Velardis will control him, if only for their own safety."

"Even so, sir, I will do well enough with Angel beside me. He would expect to accompany me in the barge, and that might not be to the liking of the mule."

"Ah yes, Madame, you have a valid point there. I had overlooked your protector." His smile was brief but warm. "Such faithful friends must not be ignored, for there are few around."

While the troopers held the barge steady, the protesting mule was dragged aboard by the burly Farino and the young boy, Marco, who had taken over Farino's duties in guarding the prisoners. They, Luigi and Maria, were ordered into the barge. The boy gripped the animal's halter and braced his legs to take the swing of the barge.

As Farino dug in the pole, the troopers released their hold on the barge. For a moment the reedy mud retained control, but Farino's powerful arms broke its grasp and the barge moved forward to be taken into the choppy water. The Velardis squatted low, one on each side of the mule, who lifted his head and disclaimed with an ear-splitting clarity his opinion of events. He began to move restlessly, causing the barge to sway.

The party on the near bank watched closely as Farino poled the barge through the choppy water. Soon he would enter the center current. He turned his head as they watched and snarled an order to the Velardis. The sense of his words was lost in the noise of the rushing waters, but Maria and Luigi moved with reluctance from their crouching positions and clutched the baggage packs, pressing their heads and shoulders into the flanks of the mule. Marco clung fast to the halter, defying the tossing head and determined efforts of the animal to hurl him away.

Farino plunged the long pole in deeply as the barge gained midstream. Here the current was swift, and his task was not aided by the restless mule. Red-faced, the bulging muscles of his body drawing the cloth of his tunic tight across back and shoulders, Farino worked the barge with what appeared to be tireless strokes.

The barge broke free of the current and swung into calmer water. Beyond, at the chosen landing place, muddy banks of reeds swayed and dipped, as if reaching out to beckon them shoreward. The movement of the barge was easier, but the mule was unappeased and continued his stamping, with the Velardis clinging on, white-faced.

De Foret turned to the three remaining troopers. "Into the water now. Make for that tree downstream of Farino's landing. Should the barge break free of its mooring before they unload, save the mule. The rest can swim."

The three troopers saluted and urged their mounts through the knee-high reeds. They splashed through the shallows, then plunged into the river. The horses threshed into furious activity, shoulders rising and falling as they swam.

De Foret looked at Judith. "Well, Madame? You have proved your worth as a horsewoman on land. Shall you now invade Neptune's domain and ride the water?"

Judith nodded and unfastened the neckbands of her cloak, draping it before her on the saddle.

"Since we have no wings to fly, I see no alternative. May the gods of the river grant us safe passage."

They pushed through the reeds and the shallows, then as the horses sank to their haunches in the cold water, de Foret laughed at Judith's gasp of shock. The water surged over their knees and thighs, and the spray flung up by the plunging forelegs and tossing manes soon had them soaked. Judith shook the water from her eyes and fixed her gaze on the opposite bank. The troopers were fighting the midstream current but were in control of their animals. Judith nodded to herself. She had come to know her own mount and believed him capable of carrying her safely. Angel was swimming as easily as if he were loping along on land. De Foret was on her other side, and between them she felt quite secure.

They were approaching midstream now. Blinking through the spray, Judith saw that the three troopers were almost in the far shallows. Farino was negotiating the barge into the reeds, she noted, then ducked her head as the drenching spray made sight impossible.

Farino was in a foul mood. He was convinced that the capitaine had given him the job of poling the barge as an extra punishment. He knew himself to be the strongest man in the troop, but it was a strength he preferred to use for his own ends. He might have felt more honor if Madame la Baronne had been his passenger, but being told to carry two whining prisoners and a godforsaken stupid mule was the height of indignity. Marco had been no help. He'd had trouble keeping his own balance with that son of Satan to control. He looked back at the two Italians, his face menacing.

"Wait till I get you two ashore, you hopeless gutter rubbish. You'll feel my boot in your ribs before you can scream for the capitaine. And you—" he glowered at the cowering Maria. "I'll show you how I treat drabs who spurn me. You'll do well to say yes this time!"

The mutterings thrown over his shoulder had not interfered with the rhythm of his strokes, and now his pole hit mud and he eased the barge into the shallows. Rushes

swept alongside as the barge steadied. Farino squinted
at the thick post driven into the wooden structure that
served as a landing stage. Marco tightened his grip on
the mule's halter and thanked God the beast had not
overturned them. The sooner he got himself and the
mule onto dry land, the happier he would be.

Farino drove the barge pole upright into the mud and
held it with one hand.

"Come here, you," he ordered Luigi. "Pick up this
mooring rope." As Luigi hesitated, Farino roared in
exasperation. "Can I hold the barge from swinging and
throw a line as well?"

Luigi obeyed, picking up the thick mooring rope. At
Farino's jerk of the head, he made a feeble attempt to
throw the line with a curving motion. It fell into the water
and Farino cursed.

"Dolt. Idiot. Hold the pole, then, and God help you if
you let go." He shouldered Luigi aside and drew in the
sodden rope. He flung it in a shower of spray to encircle
the post. As he grasped the end, the mule bucked and
Maria screamed.

"Get that damned creature off, Marco," shouted
Farino. "Here, Velardi. Help me hang on this rope until
that fiend is ashore. We will secure it later. Help Marco,
woman! Put your shoulder under the brute's backside
and heave."

The mule was creating too much confusion for Farino
to risk more than hold the rope and encircle the post
with a massive arm.

The mule, so disenchanted with his passage over the
water, was now objecting to being forced off the barge.
With Marco cursing and dragging at the halter and Maria
thrusting from behind, the mule eyed the grassy bank
and finally capitulated. It gathered itself together and
leapt. Maria sprawled in the bottom of the barge, and
Marco fell back into the reeds but retained his hold on
the halter. He scrambled up and cuffed the beast, then
led him away from the barge. Farino was grinning as he

pulled on the rope. He did not see Maria glide up behind him, for Luigi blocked his view. He felt a movement at his belt, but he turned too late to ward off the blade that rose and hissed down, burying itself deep in his back.

The dagger of Farino had become his own death weapon. His arm slid from the post and his heavy body sagged over the side of the barge. Luigi bent and caught the trooper's feet, flinging the body over the side. He snatched up the long pole and jabbed vicously. Farino's body rolled and spun, then the current caught him and whirled the slack body along its path, as casually as if it had been just one more dead branch.

Marco, struggling with the mule, turned at the sound of Maria's shrill laugh. He dropped the halter and began to run, his boots squelching in the mud. He staggered and fell against the mule, then regained his feet. Freed now from all restraint, the mule turned his back on Marco, hunched his hindquarters, and kicked out. The flying hooves took Marco at waist level, sending him hurtling forward, a spinning bundle of arms and legs. He fell into the reeds, sending up a shower of muddy water. His face rose first, dripping water and weed. His shocked stare was fixed on the barge and the figure of Luigi, poling strongly out of the shallows.

Judith and de Foret were in midstream, well below the jetty. Judith wiped the spray from her face and threw de Foret a laughing look. He smiled, then the amusement was wiped away as he stared intently up river toward the barge. Judith blinked away the droplets of water and followed his stare. At first she could see nothing wrong, but a flurry of water beside her showed that de Foret was aware of some danger and was urging his mount into greater activity. She saw him rise in the stirrups and shout to the three troopers who were across and leading their dripping horses ashore. They were laughing together, but one glanced back and saw de Foret pointing an arm. All three flung themselves back into the saddle and forced their mounts into the river. But the horses were tired, their progress sluggish, and de Foret knew that the approaching barge must pass them before they could reach midstream again. Only he and Madame were close enough. If Luigi poled cleverly, he could send the barge circling about them and swing into the current downstream. He drew his sword, holding it aloft in his right hand.

Judith caught up with de Foret. "You cannot stop them," she gasped. "It is madness to try."

De Foret did not look at her. His eyes were on the barge, his face grim. "They have murdered Farino. There will be no mercy now." He glanced at her. "Move away, Madame. Head for the bank. I must try to stop them."

Luigi had seen the three troopers edge into the water again. To avoid them, he must swing across current to the far side, well ahead of the two figures in midstream. Once he was past them and into calmer water, the way would be clear to pole downstream and rejoin the rushing water, following the late Farino's example.

He was judging the distance before he needed to swing across, when Maria tugged his sleeve. She pointed toward the two riders ahead.

"See, my husband. The capitaine bares his sword. He may try to damage the boat if he fails to injure us."

"Be still, woman. I shall turn away at the right moment and put much water between us."

"I have a better idea," Maria said, her eyes gleaming with malice. "They are in midstream and the current is with us. Send the barge like an arrow and strike him down. Let him go where that Farino went." Luigi hesitated, but Maria hurried on, her voice gaining strength. "Let him live and we will find ourselves pursued by the capitaine wherever we go. Will he not seek vengeance for the blow I struck Farino? It was seen by all, my husband. He will not be content to hold us prisoner again. We shall hang from the nearest tree if he

catches us. What have we to lose now? We have only
our lives, since the baronne tricked us over her jewels.
There will be another Farino to kick us. Now, Luigi, now,
before it is too late!"

Luigi nodded and his eyes narrowed. They were
upstream of the couple in the water, broadside on. He
put his weight on the pole, bringing the barge round
sharply until the blunt prow was in line with the
swimming horses. Then he worked the pole fiercely until
the barge caught the full current and surged forward,
heading directly toward de Foret.

The barge scythed through the water with alarming
speed, seeming to grow in enormity as the current kept
it on course. De Foret saw the face of Maria, teeth bared
in a cruel grin, her eyes like points of brilliant light as the
barge sped toward him. Luigi had not encircled them
as he had anticipated. His intent was to run him down, to
hurl the full weight of the wooden barge against the
unprotected bodies of horse and rider. It was
impossible for him to avoid the impact, for a swimming
horse was no match against the speeding barge. Luigi
handled the pole like an expert, de Foret's mind noted
dispassionately, as proved by the slight adjustment in
direction, the feather touch of the pole to the water. De
Foret watched the answering move of the prow. It did
not point directly at him anymore. The blood seemed to
leave his heart as he realized the true intention.
Madame was a bare few feet away from him. Luigi was
in position to cut between them, striking both with the
force of a battering ram.

Maria's hand was already raised, Farino's dagger
gripped tightly. Her eyes were not on him but on
Madame. A slashing downward thrust at the precise
moment when Madame's body cannoned off the barge,
and she would have achieved the same objective as
when they had attacked her before.

Almost without thought, de Foret jerked the reins of
his horse, bringing the beast into a tight half-circle. He

dug in his heels with a savagery he rarely used on horses.

Now he was in Madame's wake as she plunged shoreward. He was also broadside to the barge and urging his horse forward to create a barrier between her and the barge. His horse was strong, he knew, but could he reach her in time? The barge was close, then it was towering over him like the wall of a barn. The jerking head of his horse was level with the flanks of Madame's horse.

''Ride!'' he yelled, and raised his sword and twisted in the saddle. There was no time left. The bow wave rose over him. He slashed with his sword but was blinded by water, not seeing any target. Maria's scream merged with the stunning impact on his body and the squeal of terrified horses. His sword was jarred from his hand and pain engulfed him. His feet no longer pressed on stirrups, for he was rising to the agony of a stunning blow on the back of the head, a blow that seemed to split his skull, sending out fragments of brilliant light that soared and hovered, then slowly dimmed as they fell until only darkness was left.

18

Judith screamed as the barge struck the haunches of her horse. The force of the impact swung the animal about and slammed them both against the wooden side. The breath left her body as her shoulder struck, and through the mist of pain and drenching water, Maria's face looked down. She was so close. It was the face of evil, and the blood-stained dagger was its instrument. Shrill laughter merged with the scream of the injured horse, and the blade flashed toward Judith's face. She ducked instinctively, and the blade cut into the haunches of her horse. It reared, panic-stricken, unseating Judith and flinging her into the water.

Then the barge was past and the pale sun lit up the spreading ripples of blood. When the troopers reached the scene, they found de Foret's horse floating, legs stiffened in death. The horse of Madame la Baronne climbed up the bank, but of the two riders there was no sign. The troopers' own horses were blown, and it was quickly decided they must return to shore lest their mounts become too weak for their own safety.

It was a somber party that assembled at the jetty. Three troopers, young Marco, and the baggage mule, four survivors from the party of seven. Farino was unimportant, they agreed, for he had not been liked, but how in God's name could they continue into the city and face the baron? Who would tell him that the English bride he expected so eagerly was lost? The lady they had sworn to protect and deliver safely was drowned.

There was no capitaine to blame for the disaster, either. Two of the older men, who had been with the baron during the revolt, shook their heads, remembering the terrible vengeance he had meted out on those who incurred his displeasure. Displeased would be too mild a word for what had happened here. The baron's fury would fall on their heads, and those heads would be adorning the city gates atop pikestaffs.

"What shall we do?" breathed Marco, his eyes full of fear.

"We sleep and rest the horses," grunted the trooper who had taken charge. "Tomorrow we recross the river. For myself—" he shrugged. "I take off the badge of Vallone and head north. I will find a living in the service of some other lord. You may do as you please. Vallone will not see me again."

Marco nodded. "And the mule?"

The old trooper laughed. "Let it go its way, too. Its packs are full of woman's things. What use are they? You cannot sell them without questions being asked. Save yourselves and disappear. If the baron comes searching, he will find one dead horse cast ashore somewhere, and maybe three bodies."

"Could Madame and the capitaine have escaped?" Marco ventured.

"Could any have lived through that battering? There was much blood on the water. If they were not dead, then the current took them under." He grinned sourly. "Go and seach if you will. Explain all to the baron—if you get time before he has the hide off you."

Marco shivered, but persisted. "The baron has brought freedom and fair trial. He would not—"

The old trooper interrupted harshly. "Would he not? Go ask the old duke about such things." He jerked his head in the direction they had come before reaching the river. "His bones lie in the old fortress!" Marco's mouth opened, but closed as the trooper snarled, "Hold your tongue, boy, and rest yourself. You are a child in your innocence. Words and actions do not always run the course together."

In silence, the troopers shuffled away to curl up under the bushes. Marco did the same.

Judith was certain she was drowning as her body spun wildly in the current and she had no sense of direction. Her lungs were bursting and the pain in her chest was intense. Weeds brushed her face and broken wood scratched and whirled about her. A sturdy sapling, many-branched and with thorny twigs, caught at her hair, and she grasped it, trying to throw it off. But the twigs held fast and her fingers could only reach the narrow trunk. She gripped it as firmly as she could, but the cold was in her bones and her senses were going. Her failing mind registered patchy lightness among the spread branches, but it made no sense though it grew in size with brighter shafts of light darting down. The branches dazzled and shimmered with flying diamonds that hurt her eyes with their half-closed swollen lids. Then the weight on her chest was lifted and she choked out river water as her head broke surface. Choking and gasping, she breathed and retched until her head stopped swimming. The sapling trunk was still gripped in frozen fingers, and it whirled her on and on, but Holy Mother, she was alive and breathing air!

She clung to the sapling and shook back the long black hair plastering her face. Trees and bushes fled past on either bank, and there was no sound save the rushing water. Craning her neck, she looked behind. Not a soul in sight. Only the gray river pursued. Ahead there was nothing, no sign of the barge with its treacherous Velardis aboard.

Leon? Her heart jumped as she remembered the sudden closeness of him behind her, his desperate yell for her to ride. He had deliberately put himself in the way of the barge, taking its full force in an effort to shield her. Dear God, he could never have survived that

impact. Tears ran down her wet cheeks. Was it her fate
to be robbed of everyone she held dear? She thought of
that dark face with the quizzical brow under the white
streak of hair, the gray eyes that had warmed as his lips
had touched hers. How she could have loved him, but
for the baron who stood between them. The baron! She
raised her head and peered along the water. If the
troopers reported her drowned—what then? Could she
stay in hiding and make her way back to England? The
baron would not mourn, for they were strangers. Her
lips twisted wryly. Perhaps he would demand another
wife from King John.

The sapling jerked and she almost lost her grip. It
veered sharply, swinging away from the center of the
river. She peered ahead and saw a rocky, bush-strewn
finger of land protruding into the water. Its tip was a
jagged hump of rock against which the current flung
itself, only to be rebuffed and sent slinking around its
base. Judith eyed the rock uneasily as the current swept
her toward it. That was an impact she had no wish to
test. She glanced quickly along the spit of land. Broken
water, more green than gray, so the bed of the river
shelved landward. It was a chance she had to take or be
pounded by the rock.

She had freed her hair and tunic from the sapling
twigs, and now as she careened toward the rock, she
flung herself away from the sapling and struck out with
flailing arms, hoping to be carried to the spit of land.
She saw the slim tree strike and fly into the air before
disappearing over the rock, then she dog-paddled
furiously. Her knee grazed some obstruction and she
floundered, sinking. Her foot caught some object and
she fell face down, her scream choked off as her head
went under water. Scrabbling fingers found pebbles and
sand. She clawed her way up, and her feet found
bottom.

For a moment she stood swaying, gasping in the sweet
air, then she pulled herself up onto the tongue of land

and lay motionless, her mind and body freed from the fight with the river. Cold and the reaction from shock set her shuddering, and she climbed unsteadily to her feet. She twisted her long hair into a rope and squeezed out water, then attempted to do the same with her tunic.

Birds calls rang out from the trees, but there was no sign of smoke nor sight of anything else living. There must be shelter somewhere, some cottage or habitation, but which way and how far? She began to move along the land spit. Bushes grew to the water's edge and were thick and coarse. One seemingly impenetrable bush forced her into the water, and as she tried to regain land again, her boots kicked something that moved. She recoiled with a sharp cry. What in God's name was that? A movement in the bushes, a slithering sound, then a rasping cough that cracked the silence and shook the leaves with its harshness.

Judith held her breath, not daring to move. She could not pass that bush without creating noise on the pebbles. When the thing, whatever it was, quietened, she could pass, she thought. Then her heart almost stopped and her mind reeled into disbelief. She was staring down at a booted foot!

Heedless of the reaching twigs, she pushed her way through. He lay on his back, staring out of a scratched and mud-stained face. Under the wet black hair, the gray eyes were vague.

Judith dropped to her knees. "Capitaine, thank God you are alive."

The gray eyes moved over her and the vagueness faded. "Madame? Are you here, or do I dream?"

"I am here," Judith said and bent to kiss him.

He pulled himself up on one elbow. "I believe you." He reached out and drew her head toward his, and his lips were firm and warm. Then he regarded her closely. "Are you hurt?"

Judith shook her head, smiling, and pushed back her damp hair. "A little bruised, that is all."

De Foret rose, drawing her to her feet. He stared about. "How came we here? I have no memory of it."

"We were both unhorsed by the barge and swept into the current. We owe our lives to this strip of land. See, where it juts from the land, like a breakwater."

"Flung forth by the gods of the water to arrest our passage, I shall evermore believe. They have been kind to us, Madame, though a little rough in the doing. We are together. I would have been in torment otherwise."

"For the baron's sake?"

"No, for my own." He rested his hands on her shoulders and looked down into the pale, strained face. His arms drew her close, and Judith laid her cheek on his chest. " 'Fore God, for myself," he murmured. "I had no thought for the baron."

"Nor I," said Judith. Then the cold gripped her and she shuddered.

"We must find shelter," Leon said, putting her away from him. "The night will be cold and our bodies freeze in these wet clothes."

"Do you know where we are?"

"In Vallone territory, surely, but where precisely, I have no idea. There must be farms or villages hereabouts. Let us make a start before the night catches us in the open."

They moved slowly off the strip of land, their steps unsteady but gaining in strength as their muscles warmed to the exercise. Through a copse and across rough fields they went, searching the horizon for signs of smoke or grazing cattle to signify some habitation. The land rose gently, then fell again into endless valley and hill, but the scrub was wild and not laid to pasture or tilled field.

Judith stopped, gasping, her body swaying with weariness. Leon was stumbling, too, and it was obvious to both that habitation was sparse in this part of Vallone.

"Not even a track," he said, frowning. He looked at her white face. "Rest, Madame. You have done well, though God knows, we may have been walking in circles.''

Judith sank to the coarse grass and rested her aching back against a tree. Her damp clothes felt even colder as the breeze cooled. The sky was dark, the little sun that had shone that day was hidden by clouds. Another storm, her mind asked tiredly? Leon sank down beside her, and they regarded the barren landscape in silence.

Judith spread her fingers over the grass, ruffling the weed heads. Her gaze wandered absently, then she stiffened. Leon felt the movement and was on his feet instantly, his hand falling to his dagger.

"What is it? What did you see?" His eyes scanned the bushes around them.

"Not up there, Capitaine, down here. Look, do you see the goat droppings?"

He stared down as if she had become delirious in fever. "Goat droppings?"

"Follow them with your eyes," she insisted. "See how the earth is hardened, though the coarse grass springs back."

He dropped to one knee and followed the direction of her pointing finger.

"Of course," he said. "A goat track must lead to or from a village. If not a village, then a goatherd's shelter."

Judith scrambled to her feet. "One way or the other, we must find something."

They began to follow the goat track quickly while daylight held. Once darkness fell, the task would be hopeless. They must reach shelter before then.

The track wound without purpose, the goats seemingly unconcerned as to direction unless checked. They rested at the base of a small hill, casting about for sight of a village, but there was none.

Leon stared at the hill. The track seemed to end here, but the grass was thicker, the droppings could be hidden. He took Judith's arm.

"From that crest, we shall get a better view. We must

climb there."

Judith nodded. Another hill, another valley, what did it matter? They were lost. But she plodded beside Leon, her head bent, her gaze on the grass. She would have staggered on had not Leon halted her.

"Look!" he said, and his voice was triumphant. He put an arm about her shoulders and pointed.

She looked across at the small, stone-built hut. It stood alone, tucked into a fold of rock, its door sagging, a neglected air about it.

"Come," said Leon. "A poor enough place, but a shelter for the night."

As if to add point to his words, the rain began to fall. They staggered, half-running, to the goatherd's shack, and Leon pushed open the door. A single room without a window; to one side a rough hearth of stone pieces had been formed. Above the hearth there was a hole in the roof. A powerful odor of goat pervaded the atmosphere.

Leon grinned at her. "Without doubt the home of a goat herder." He glanced round. "A fellow with foresight, too." He crossed to the pile of broken branches stacked in the corner. "I'll get a fire going, Madame. See if you can find any further evidence of the fellow's foresight, like food or drink. He may have stayed here for days in good weather."

Judith probed into the dark corners and unearthed a small cooking pot and a stone jug, half full of wine. Something wrapped in canvas caught her eye. It was tucked into a crack in the uneven stone. It was wet and limp, but the odor corresponded with the smell of the hut. Goat meat, she hazarded a guess.

"Indeed a man of foresight," she said, with a smile toward Leon, who was using his flint on the dry twigs. "I believe there is a blanket, too. Ah yes, and a goatskin jerkin. What more could one ask?"

She tipped the goat meat into the pot and added wine. The twigs caught light and Leon fed the fire with broken branches. Judith advanced with the pot. Leon took it from her and settled it firmly in the center of the hearth, then sat back on his heels.

"When the goatherd arrives tomorrow, I shall fill his hands with gold pieces, for though he is unaware of it yet, he has saved our lives."

Judith knelt by the fire, and as the heat built up, steam began to rise from her tunic.

Leon rose, walked to the corner, and returned with the blanket and jerkin. "You must take off your clothes, Madame, and spread them to dry. We cannot sleep in their dampness without risking some fever." He removed his own tattered tunic and began to unfasten his shirt.

He paused as Judith did not move from her kneeling position.

"Madame," he said gently. "You have my word of honor that I do not spring upon defenseless females with uncontrollable lust. Besides—" He slanted a mocking look at her. "I have seen many a naked woman. It is no new experience for me."

Judith flushed and rose. "I don't doubt it, sir," she began angrily, then caught his smile and laughed. "Very well, sir. You have made your point. It is sense."

She unstrapped her belt with its hanging pouch. "Though I am once more without change of garment, my jewels are safe." As de Foret's brows rose, she smiled. "I learned that lesson early. My jewels go where I go."

"A very wise lady. By the way, Madame, what is your given name? In our present situation, the formality of Madame and Capitaine seems slightly ridiculous. I am called Leon, but you know that."

"I am Judith. I was born Judith Bradley. The rest you know." She kicked off her boots, then drew the damp, clinging tunic over her head. The long, white shift clung to her body, and she stripped it off and picked up the blanket, wrapping it about her nakedness. With one arm freed from the blanket, she used her shift to rub her hair and wipe the mud from her face.

Through the veil of her hair, she stole a look at Leon,
standing with his back to her at the other side of the fire.
He was naked and, like herself, was using his damp
undergarments to dry his hair and remove the stains
from his face. Broad-shouldered and narrow of waist, his
hips met strong, well-shaped legs. Heavy bruising was
already beginning to purple his skin, but there were old
scars too, sword slashes, she guessed. He bent, picked
up the jerkin, and slipped his arms through the
sleeveless garment. A belt of goatskin secured the waist.
It had been made for a broad but shorter figure, and the
hem reached barely below Leon's knees.

As he turned, Judith lowered her gaze and shook out
her hair, running her fingers through it. Her heart was
beating fast, for she knew that Leon de Foret had come
to mean a great deal to her. What she had felt for Henry
and his gentle ways was not at all like the feeling she had
for this man. Gentle he could be, she knew that, but
what set her heart beating and her blood racing was not
mere affection but something strange and savage, a
primitive calling of blood to blood, like a she-wolf
acknowledging the existence of her mate, the
nonexistence of others.

Judith thrust back the hair out of her eyes, raised her
chin, and smiled up at Leon. He was looking down at
her, and the gray eyes were wide with shock.

Judith's smile faltered and died. She dragged the
blanket close, feeling the warmth leave her in a wave of
chill confusion.

"What is it? Why are you staring at me like that?" she
whispered, then realized that his eyes were not level
with hers but were fixed on her breast. Her hand went
up instinctively, her fingers closing on the emerald
pendant.

"That stone!" Leon said in a harsh voice. "How in
God's name did you come by the Saracen Stone?"

19

Judith's eyes widened, her own shock equal to his, for the question had been asked in English! The man with the face of Quentin! The dream was back in her mind again. Holy Mother, it was true! But how could this man be Quentin Tarrant? Yet he knew the emerald and the name that Quentin had called it. She breathed in deeply and began to speak.

"It came to me from my husband, Sir Quentin Tarrant. It was brought by the proxy." She lifted the stone clear of the blanket. "He sent it as proof of our bond of marriage." She had answered the question in English, but de Foret appeared not to be aware of the change of language. He sat down across from her and took a twig, giving the contents of the pot a stir. He laid the twig down carefully and looked at her.

"A pretty bauble. I must have seen its like somewhere."

"It's like, Capitaine?" Judith raised her brows. "Another, bearing the same name?"

Leon frowned. "Perhaps I met your late husband in Poitou." He shrugged. "I met many soldiers. I don't remember them all."

Judith kept her voice steady. "Then you must have served in the Holy Land, too."

"No. Why? I see no connection."

"This stone never went to Poitou. It has been in my keeping these six years. Quentin brought it back from Palestine. It was given to him by a Saracen girl during

209

King Richard's crusade. Hence, its name."

Leon shrugged again. "Then I cannot think of explanation."

"There is one other you have not considered."

"Then tell me of it."

"That you are, in truth, Sir Quentin Tarrant, and for reasons best known to yourself, masquerade as Leon de Foret."

He stared in shocked surprise. "Impossible! I am Leon de Foret."

"If you say so, Capitaine." Judith spoke wearily. "You are a Frenchman, with a French name, but you speak the English tongue with perfection."

She saw the awareness strike him. "By the Rood, I had not realized it." His eyes held bafflement. "How can I be Tarrant and you not know it? Surely a wife would recognize a husband."

"A 'husband' I saw for only two days, six years ago? A man may alter out of all recognition in that time, and a soldier even more so."

Leon remembered his reflection in the silver chalice as he had stood beside Father Ignatius in the monastery. He even recalled his own words. " 'Fore God, Father, I know not that man." Yet he was Leon de Foret—the old priest had said so.

"Madame—Judith," he said. "We are cold and tired. The mind plays tricks in such conditions. Let us eat and take a little wine. Tomorrow, all questions will be answered or find themselves irrelevant."

A wanderer on the river bank might have been forgiven his terror on witnessing a strange river monster with long, wolflike snout and ridged back, both shiny and phosphorescent in the pale moonlight. The creature was swimming steadily toward the tongue of land jutting out from the bank. There it staggered ashore and fell panting, lacking even the energy to shake off the water. A few minutes later it crawled into the bushes.

Angel fell asleep. He moaned softly in his dreams, feeling again the pain of a threshing hoof striking his head, his struggle to the bank, then the blurred picture of bodies in the water. Then they were gone, rising and falling, until only horses and shouting men were left.

He had risen and loped along the bank in pursuit, but the pain slowed him down and he was clumsy. Clumsy enough to get entangled in a tree root that flung him sideways into the river. He had swum then with failing strength, and found his paws scrabbling on rock. It was dark and he could not find her. Later, when the pain was gone, he would search her out.

Judith woke first in the cool light of dawn. Pale fingers of sun probed the cracks in the door, and the sky was visible through the hole in the roof. She lay still for a moment, cocooned in the blanket, seeing the figure of Leon beyond the hearth. She heard his soft breathing and eased herself from the blanket. The fire was out, but her clothes were dry. She dressed quickly, hoping he would not awake just yet. Last night, in their weariness, it had not mattered that he might have seen her naked, but today was different and the goatherd might surprise them.

As she built up the fire again, she pondered their conversation. Was he Leon or Quentin? If Leon—how did he know of the Saracen Stone if he had not served in the Holy Land? If Quentin—why would he be escorting his own wife to the bed of another in a bigamous marriage while insisting that he was Leon de Foret? She shook her head in puzzlement. There were no answers, only questions. Was her dream the truth, or was truth a dream? She placed the pot with the remains of the goat meat onto the fire and went to the door.

The grass was still damp, but the rain had stopped and the sun was rising in golden splendor, promising a warm day. The land was still empty, not even a cowbell or a sight of the goatherd. She moved round the hut, but the

view was no different. In which direction lay the city of
the baron? Would Leon force her to take that road? She
returned to the doorway and found him awake. They
drank wine and ate the remains of the meat. When they
had finished, Judith looked at Leon as he stared into the
fire.

"What now, Leon?"

He started and looked up. "I was thinking of that
prison fortress we passed. There was something familiar
about it, yet I had not passed that way before. Did it
mean anything to you?"

Judith nodded. "Yes. Its design was similar to Tarrant
Castle in England, though the countryside of Sussex is
soft and green."

"Was anything else different? The banner, perhaps?"

"Yes, the banner had two colors that were Tarrant's."

"And the flaw I sensed—was it in the gray field?" His
gaze was fixed intently on her.

"Yes, the Tarrant field was blue."

He seemed to relax. "Blue. Yes, I have seen that
banner." He shook his head. "It must have been carried
in Poitou. I can think of nowhere else that I might have
seen it."

"Save Tarrant itself."

"I am not Tarrant."

"Yet you frowned at the land about the fortress, as if
surprised by its rocky surface, where you would have
expected the softness of grass. Can you deny it?"

"I cannot deny it, for you are right, yet what does it
prove?"

"Nothing, by itself." She stared into the fire, thinking,
then looked up. "You told me once that you claimed no
country and no country claimed you, but every man has
a birthplace. You are not so old that you have forgotten
it, surely? Disregard it, if you will, but Leon de Foret was
born of woman and not placed on earth in full-grown
manhood." She smiled. "We all begin at the beginning.
There is no evading that." She rose and walked to the

door. "The sun is well-risen, but I see no goats. Without the goatboy we have no direction."

Leon put on his breeches and boots, tucking the torn shirt into the waistband. He regarded the tattered tunic, then tossed it into a corner. He checked that the dagger was in his belt and went to join Judith in the doorway.

"Let the fire go out. We shall not need it until tonight. The goatherd may have chosen another grazing ground today and we shall need food later. And water," he added. "If we're to cook anything I can catch."

"You will need the pot," Judith said. "Shall I come, too?"

"No. Stay here in case the goatboy arrives. He will give you direction."

"To where?" Judith asked. "Will you force me to the baron against my will?"

Leon hesitated. "It is my duty." He looked down at her gravely. "And for you, Madame, it is your wifely duty."

"Duty, duty," Judith mocked. "You are equal to Quentin in that respect. Duty to King Richard, then duty to his father and the house of Tarrant. Duty above all, and woman must accept her role as pawn in the interests of men. One day it will not be so, Capitaine, and a woman will have the right to give her love to the man of her choice." Her voice choked and she swung away from him, but he caught her shoulders and held her close.

"Judith, dear Judith, do not be angered. Were I not pledged in duty to de Gras, it could be no different. You are lawful wife to the baron. You are bound in duty the same as I. Should we both forswear our vows and run like criminals?"

"We should be together," murmured Judith.

He put a hand under her chin and looked into her eyes. "Have I not thought of that, too? You have become most dear to me, but our future cannot be linked. You are Madame la Baronne and I am a mercenary. I can give you nothing."

"But as Quentin Tarrant—" she began, but he placed a finger on her lips.

"I am Leon de Foret, no other. A likeness is no proof. Would you have me step into a dead man's shoes, pretend to a masquerade I know to be false? No, my dear. We could not live in such dishonor."

He turned and looked across the countryside. "Had I my bow and sword, the task would be easier, but my dagger flies true. A rabbit, perhaps?" He smiled and took the cooking pot from her. "I'll be back before dusk."

Then he was gone, striding away to disappear over the bush crest they had surmounted yesterday. Judith sighed and turned back into the hut.

By mid-afternoon, Leon had caught nothing. He found no spoor of deer or wild pig. Even the rabbits were elusive, but he came upon a spring of water that gurgled into a narrow stream. He drank and rested, eying the small copse beyond the stream. He leaned his back against a tree and thought of Judith. Behind his closed eyelids, he saw her face again, and knew that he loved her, but how could a man reared in the tradition of duty betray a trust? The sun lay warm on his face, and his thoughts wandered to the strange shock he had felt on seeing the emerald last night. The Saracen Stone, given to Quentin Tarrant in the Holy Land. He saw it again in memory and visualized the golden-skinned beauty, Farida. The sun blazed down and horses kicked sand as they stormed into the town with its minarets and fleeing white-robed figures. Leon opened his eyes and felt the sweat break out on him. He frowned. It was not that warm here, not that intense golden sunshine of his daydream. Nor was there sand beneath him. It was imagination, a vivid picture, yet he named the Saracen girl, Farida. Judith had not spoken the name, he was convinced of it. How then did he know it? Farida and the Saracen Stone had no connection with Leon de Foret.

He rose and crossed the stream to the copse. He moved silently, casting about for tracks. The larger animals seemed to have fled this area or been taken already, he decided. The copse was quiet, save for the sudden whirring of a partridge that flew noisily out of a bush almost at his feet. He threw the dagger with swift expertise and the bird dropped in mid-flight. Retrieving his dagger, he sheathed it, picked up the partridge, and took a step back to the stream before another sound halted him. He listened. Transferring the partridge to his left hand, he drew out the dagger again and moved toward the sound. On the edge of the copse, he paused. The unmistakable odor of goats reached him, then he saw the herd grazing in a valley. Was this the same herd whose refuge, about two miles distant, they had used? He looked for the goatherd and found him seated on a rock, his back to the copse. The first sight of another human being. He must know where the city lay.

Leon crossed the stretch of land. His step on the grass was silent, then he kicked a stone. The goatherd wheeled about. He rose, his eyes wild with fear. From the rock he leapt, as nimble as one of his own goats, and broke into a run that took Leon by surprise.

"Stop!" he yelled, but the goatherd raced on in seeming terror.

Leon dropped the partridge and set off in pursuit. "Hell's teeth," he muttered angrily. "What ails the fellow? Off like some damned flushed partridge on first sight of me!" He increased his long stride and began to shorten the distance between them.

The man glanced back and his eyes seemed to roll in terror, then he missed his footing and sprawled, rolling down the slope. Leon was upon him before he could scramble to his knees. He caught him firmly by the back of his collar and shook him.

"Hold still, man," he growled. "Why do you run off as if the devil were after you?"

The goatherd stayed on his knees and clasped his

hands together. "Mercy, Master," he gasped, and the sweat poured off him. "I have nothing but my goats."

Leon held him off, recoiling from the smell of goat and sweat. "I don't want your damned goats. All I want is an answer to my question."

"Everything was taken by the soldiers, Master. My daughter, too. I am a poor man. I swear on the grave of my wife that I never bore arms for him." Tears coursed down his face, and Leon frowned in puzzlement.

"You make no sense, man. I accuse you of nothing. But, for whom did you not bear arms?"

"Baron de Gras, Master. See—" he raised his right hand. There were three fingers missing. "How could I hold a weapon like this? Believe me, Master, for God's pity."

"I believe you, man, but why did you run? I meant you no harm. I am lost and seek direction, that is all. Which way to the city?"

The goatherd looked at him uneasily. "The city, Master? All the baron's men are inside, and Count Alberto's army besieges it. You wear no badge, Master, but you are a fine gentleman. How is it that you are lost?"

Leon stared into the weathered face of the goatherd. "Do you tell me the country has risen to Count Alberto?"

"Yes, Master, save that he calls himself Duke of Vallone, for his father is dead in the fortress and went not into exile. For that, he swears he will have the head of Baron de Gras."

20

The horseman wiped his brow with a lace-edged and heavily perfumed handkerchief. He tucked it into his sleeve and looked about him. One cursed hill looked like another, and he was no seasoned campaigner. He should not have sent his men on without him, but that innkeeper's daughter had been a saucy wench. He cantered his horse up a gentle rise to a clump of bushes and reined in. From there he obtained a better view, but he cursed the empty landscape. Where the devil had his fellow got to? He looked down the incline and saw a small stone building. A shepherd's hut or some such, he decided and turned his horse's head toward it. Some peasant fellow might give him direction.

Judith stood in the shadowed doorway, watching the rider. As he came closer, she noted the velvet suit and the jewel-hilted sword strapped about his waist. His wide-brimmed hat bore a plume, held there by a pin of diamonds. As he reached the hut, she stepped forward and looked into his face. It was long-nosed with full lips, and the expression in his brown eyes was cold. He stared down on her, then brought his handkerchief into play again, eying her with distaste.

"Goatwoman," he said. "Direct me to the city." He pressed the handkerchief to his nose. "God in heaven, what a stench!"

Judith felt herself flush. She had grown accustomed to the smell of goats but knew that it clung to her, and with the soiled clothes and disordered hair, she must look

every inch the person he took her for. She decided it
would be wise to play the part, for he looked dangerous.

"I know not the way," she said, looking at the ground.

The man sighed and swung his riding whip idly against
his boot. "Have soldiers passed this way?"

Judith shook her head. "No one."

"Where is your man? Inside?"

"No. Hunting, but I expect him any minute."

He looked past her into the hut. "An isolated spot," he
mused. "An ideal hiding place for rebels. Stand aside,
woman. I had best make sure you've none skulking back
there."

He swung down from his saddle, and Judith stared at
him in astonishment.

"Rebels? What rebels do you mean?"

"Followers of that upstart peasant who styles himself
baron."

Judith gasped. "Do you mean the Baron de Gras?"

"Aye, woman. That filthy clod of dung."

Judith stumbled aside as he shouldered his way past
her. "And who are you, sir?"

"An officer in the army of Vallone. The Duke has come
to claim his birthright and cast the usurper down."

He glanced around the inside of the hut. He had
known it was empty, of course, for he was not a man
given to heroics. But he could claim to have searched
out rebels when he reached the duke's side. He was
about to return to his horse when he saw the tunic in the
corner. The badge of the peasant ruler was on its sleeve.
He shot a quick, nervous look around. No other room or
hidden alcove that might shelter a desperate rebel. They
had all fled, of course. His courage returned. He picked
up the tattered garment between thumb and forefinger
and stormed outside. He thrust the garment under
Judith's nose.

"No rebels, woman?" he snarled. "Then who owns
this? Your man? Hunting, indeed! More like he sighted
me coming and fled from the wrath I should deliver."

Judith looked from the tunic to the man's own velvet jacket, to the badge she had not noticed amidst his other splendor. A cockade of green, yellow, and gray silk was pinned to his sleeve.

The man dropped the tunic to the ground. He stared down his long nose. "Well, do you have nothing to say? Your man has fled and left you alone, isn't that it? We deal harshly with traitors, woman, but I am a humane man where wenches are concerned, so will be lenient to you." He walked over to his horse and drew out the long riding whip. "A few stripes on your back will teach you where loyalty lies."

He stood, running the leather thong through his fingers, and his eyes were bright.

Judith's own eyes widened in horror. "You would not dare—" she began, but knew that he would, and take delight in the doing. Another Farino, she thought wildly, but of the opposing force.

"If this is your way," she shouted, fury boiling up inside her, " 'tis no wonder the peasants rose against you."

His teeth showed in a smile as he cracked the whip with deliberation. He advanced, and Judith retreated, moving sideways from the open doorway. No shelter in there, she would be trapped. The whip snaked forward, and Judith raised her arms. The leather thong wrapped round her wrist, and the man pulled back. Judith was jerked forward and fell sprawling in the dust. She heard him laugh, then the next stroke scythed through the air, slicing tunic and flesh like a knife. Judith screamed as red-hot agony engulfed her, filling her mind with intolerable pain.

On the hill's crest, deep in the concealing bushes, two yellow eyes blinked open. The ears pricked at the sound of that scream. That was a voice he knew. The horseman had passed him earlier, but he had stayed quiet, for the scent of him was not familiar. But this was the one he had been searching for, and she was in danger. Angel rose, stiff-legged, the fur on his back rising. He came out of the bushes silently, a long black shape that moved down the slope with deceptive speed.

The horse glimpsed him first from the corner of his eye. His eyes rolled and his head tossed in alarm. He swung away, moving restlessly. The man flicked his whip irritably, and the tip caught the horse sharply on its haunches. He bounded away with a shrill whinny.

The whip rose again, but its downward sweep was never completed. Angel rose in a powerful leap, his speed and aim flying true as an arrow. Angel's jaws fastened on the whip handle. The man's yell was of pure terror as the whip was torn from his grasp. He fell back, his eyes bulging as the creature made for the woman, struggling to her knees.

Judith's arms rose instinctively to protect herself, but through the pain and tears she felt the rough wet tongue and heard the deep-throated rumbling.

"Angel, Angel," Judith choked. "I thought you drowned. Oh, thank God." She hugged him to her.

The man had recovered his wits. A dog, a damned ugly brute of a dog, that was all, but his heart still pounded and he was drenched with sweat. Fear made him angry, and anger made him vindictive. This peasant wench should not be left to laugh or babble about his fearful scream. She must die, she and that hound of hell must be left as rotting corpses as proof of his vengeful passing. She was a rebel. The tunic proved it. He moved softly and reached to grasp the whip the dog had dropped. He straightened. Now he was master again. He toyed with the idea of using his beautiful sword but rejected it. The whip would provide better sport.

Judith heard him coming and looked up. For a moment she had forgotten him in her joy at reunion with Angel. She read the purpose on his face and scrambled up quickly, thrusting Angel away.

"Go, Angel, go!"

The dog sensed the urgency in her tone and turned,

his teeth bared in a snarl. The whip flashed down, and
Angel's snarl turned into a yelp of pain. Then he moved
out of range and circled the man, legs bent, his belly
brushing the dust. The yellow glare of his eyes never left
the face of the wielder of the whip. The man felt fear
begin to rise in him. The dog must be dealt with first. It
was a dangerous brute. But where was the woman? He
shot a quick look over his shoulder and his heart almost
stopped. She was not there! Was there some weapon in
the hut? He realized now that he should have used his
sword. This damned circling to keep the brute in view
was making him dizzy. Could he draw his sword, or
would the dog spring as he wrestled it from its clipped
scabbard?

Leon de Foret, on his way back to the goatherd's
shack, had the partridge slung over his shoulder, and
the cooking pot was full of water. News of the baron's
fall had surprised but not dismayed him. He felt only
anger that de Gras had lied and deceived him about the
old duke. Judith had been right. How else could the
baron pay a fortune to King John for a lady bride save by
annexing the treasure of the house of Vallone? The
young Count Alberto had moved swiftly. If his army
stood already at the gates of the city, there had been
little resistance. A rising to the count, or duke as he now
was, seemed to indicate that the Vallonese were not
without loyalty to the hereditary rulers. If the young
duke had learned anything from recent history, he
would do well to put those lessons into practice when
the country was quiet again. He thought of his own
position, a lone soldier, far outside the city. Since the
baron had dishonored his promise to allow the old duke
into exile, he, Leon de Foret, no longer considered
himself bound to the baron. He thought of Judith and
felt a sense of elation. She could not go to the city now.
It would be far too dangerous, and if the duke carried
out his threat, Judith would again find herself a widow.

It was then that he heard the scream. High and pain-ridden, like that of Maria Velardi when Farino had whipped her. The sweat broke out on Leon's face. He dropped the cooking pot, hurled the partridge away from him, and began to run in long, bounding strides that tore up the distance. God in heaven, what was happening? A whip cracked sharply, he heard the yelp and snarl of an animal. A horse, barely observed, grazed nervously, ears pricking at every sound. Leon raced on, then came to a skidding halt as he reached the goatherd's hut.

Judith, her tunic almost ripped off her shoulders, was gripping a stout piece of firewood in both hands. A velvet-suited man whirled about like some insane being. His fine jacket was blotched with sweat. And there was Angel, darting and snarling. The sight of Judith's strained white face drove Leon into fury.

"Hold there, fellow!" he roared at the top of his voice. "What in God's name are you about? Drop that cursed whip and stand back or I'll spit you like the damned poltroon you are."

There was a moment of dead silence. Angel stopped snarling, and Judith lowered her weary arms. The man swung round and stared at Leon.

"Judith," Leon said in English, "call off Angel." He strode toward the man, his face dark with anger. He reached out a hand and gathered the velvet jacket in one fist. With the other he took the whip and tossed it away. He dragged the man up by his jacket and glared into his face. "Explain," he snarled in French.

"Let me go. I demand it," the man said, but his voice was reedy with fear.

"Certainly," said Leon. "You have a bad smell," and he threw him aside. The man staggered and fell to his knees in the dust. He eyed the tall, menacing figure warily, then climbed to his feet, retreating a few paces and pulling his jacket straight.

"I'm waiting," Leon said, and his fingers caressed the

hilt of his dagger.

The man slid a glance past him. His horse was too far away for him to run for it. He pulled out his lace-edged handkerchief and wiped his brow.

"I—I was teaching this goatwoman the penalty for harboring rebels," he said, regaining his hauteur. "Then she set that damned hound on me." He drew himself up. "I am a French vicomte, soldier, and friend of the Duke of Vallone." The brown eyes held a vindictive light. "I shall see that you are punished for this, you rebel goatherd. Now fetch my horse." He was not prepared for the blow Leon dealt him on the side of the head, and he went down again.

He met Leon's icy gaze and flinched.

"The lady you call goatwoman is my wife. I am Sir Quentin Tarrant, an English gentleman and friend of kings. What is a petty vicomte in comparison. You insult my wife and therefore me."

The man lost color. "But the goat hut—"

"Do you see only what you expect to see?" snapped Leon. "A goat hut is a shelter from a storm as much as a fine castle. God knows why anyone chooses to travel in this benighted country, since it is full of peasants and court fops." He turned to look at the horse. "What price did you pay for that piece of horseflesh? Or did it come free with your fine clothes?" The sneer in his voice brought a flush to the Frenchman's face.

"A fine horse, that," he grated. "Worth five gold pieces of any man's money."

Leon opened the pouch at his waist. He took the man's hand and dropped five gold pieces into it. "Good day to you, Vicomte. You will find the city in that direction." He pointed. "A mere five miles away."

The man looked at the gold pieces, then raised his gaze. "Five miles? I don't want your money—"

"You have it in your hand," Leon said coldly. "The bargain has been struck. What is five miles to a soldier of the Duke of Vallone? I have walked fifty for my king."

He took the man's arm firmly. "I will escort you part way. I have a partridge to retrieve."

When Leon returned, he was leading the horse, the partridge tossed over the saddle and the cooking pot, full of water, in his free hand. Judith had built up the fire, and Leon set the pot on the sticks before turning to her. He took her gently in his arms and kissed the pale face.

"Take off your tunic, my darling, and I will bathe your back. The vicomte's saddlebag yielded salves and cloths, but I doubt he envisaged them to heal wounds. More likely to keep his skin soft. A fellow like that stays well back when there is fighting to be done."

"Will he not come back and try to take his horse?" Judith asked wearily as she bared her back.

"Not if he has any sense," Leon replied, his voice hardening as he examined the line of cut flesh. "I would kill him for this alone. And with Angel standing guard, he wouldn't dare."

He bathed the wound, smoothed on salve with gentle fingers, and bound the vicomte's clean linen about her body. Then he wrapped her in the blanket and sat outside the door, plucking the partridge. Angel sat beside him, turning his head occasionally to sniff suspiciously at the salve Leon had smoothed into his cut flank.

Judith dozed, to be awakened by the aroma of wine-cooked partridge. She smiled up at Leon stirring the pot.

"You told the Vicomte that you were Quentin Tarrant. It is so, and you know it now?"

Leon shook his head. "I said it to impress, but I am not he, and yet—" He looked over the pot at her. "I rested in the heat today and felt myself in a place of Arabs. Was the Saracen girl named Farida?"

"Yes," Judith said slowly. "You knew it, but not from me. I did not speak her name."

He nodded. "When I served the baron, there was nothing of familiarity in Vallone to make me imagine I was other than what I supposed. With you, it is like the unrolling of an illuminated manuscript. Each part reveals a picture that finds echo in my senses."

Judith's gaze was soft and shining. "You are Quentin. I know it."

Leon smiled at her. "You tell me so, and I would like to believe it, for that would make you my wife and the bond with the baron unlawful. But not until my mind is convinced and I truly feel a Tarrant, will I discard Leon de Foret, for he has served me well."

They ate the partridge with their fingers, and Angel received an equal share. Then Leon rose. "We must leave this place now. The Frenchman may have fallen in with his companions. If that be so, he will return full of new valor."

Judith slipped on her tunic, and Leon shrugged his shoulders into the goatskin tunic. The old blanket he laid before the saddle of the horse, then returned inside to stamp out the fire. In the rough crack where Judith had found the goat meat, he placed two gold pieces to compensate the goatherd for the loss of tunic and blanket.

Judith sat before Leon as they rode over the crest of the hill. His arms held her steady, and she relaxed in the warmth of his body. Angel loped alongside, his yellow eyes bright, his heart at peace for he had found her again.

21

They traveled slowly over rough country throughout the next day, away from the city and on a parallel course with the river. The invasion of Vallone, if sufficiently mounted, would have come by river route, Leon guessed, the duke's forces massing on disembarkation to march on the city. All the main tracks would be choked with men and horses, foot soldiers and supply wagons. It was essential that he and Judith travel the rough places and wooded ground. He could not guess at the strength of the duke's army, but he knew that the peasant army of the baron would fight with the utmost ferocity to hold what they had won. Many had suffered under the old duke's harsh rule. To rebel meant torture and death. Better to die in battle than accept the yoke of slavery again.

How would it end, Leon mused, as he called a halt under a thick stand of beech trees. In bloodshed on a mighty scale if the young duke took after his father. Unless he abolished the previous harsh laws, and sent messengers throughout the land to convince the peasantry of his good intent, Vallone would not come to peace.

Leon swung himself down from the saddle and helped Judith dismount. He held her for a moment, looking into her face. Shadows lay under her eyes and she held her shoulders stiffly, but her gaze was steady.

"I will dress your wound again, then you must rest." He led her to a small grassy knoll, set between thick bushes. The night was dry and warm, dusk thickening the shadows cast by the tall beeches. "At first light, Angel and I must hunt," he said. "No fire or meat tonight until I have discovered our position. I doubt either army will come this way until the battle for the city is decided."

Though he spoke confidently, he was aware of his lack of knowledge as to the disposition of any forces.

Angel backed away as the aroma of the salve came to him. He sank onto the grass, his muzzle resting on his paws, and watched as Leon dressed his mistress's back. When the task was done and Judith wrapped in the blanket, Leon looked round, but Angel had merged into the darkness. Leon chuckled and Judith smiled, her eyelids drooping.

"He will heal without the salve, for he is a creature of the wild, a primitive." She yawned and closed her eyes, curling into the blanket, the stench of goat mingling with the scent of grass and mossy earth.

Leon rose and unsaddled the horse, leading it apart, then haltered the animal to a nearby tree. A corn-fed beast without a doubt, but tonight the lush grass must suffice. Angel was not in sight when Leon stretched himself out near Judith. He was, as she had said, a primitive, a seeker of dark places, an observer unobserved. He would be close, Leon knew, every instinct alert though his body slept.

Dawn came with curling mist and birdcall. A pale band of gold edged the horizon, but the hills of Vallone lay still in purple shadow. Leon rose, stretching, and looked down on the girl curled in her blanket like a kitten. Though her face was grimed, her hair a matted tangle, her face held the serene beauty of a sleeping child. She stirred, and he turned away guiltily, striding into the trees, knowing that he desired her but could not in honor, take advantage of her position. He was her guardian and—he whirled, reaching for his dagger, but only the long black shape of Angel stepped soft-footed from the bushes. The dog cocked his head, long pink tongue lolling in a grin. Leon smiled grimly and reflected ruefully that here was the lady's true guardian.

"Today, my friend," said Leon, his fingers scratching the rough hair over the dog's eyes, "we hunt and I will train you in the ways of a hunting dog."

He bent and pulled up a handful of dew-drenched grass, wiping his face and hands. On the ground lay a short length of broken branch. He lifted and tossed it hard from him.

"Fetch," he ordered.

Angel looked at him, hearing the command in his voice. As if some dim memory was stirred in his brain, he gave a throaty bark and hurled himself in pursuit of the stick. The sun rose fully as Leon worked the dog by simple commands to seek, hide, and stalk, moving and stopping on command.

Judith joined them, having, like Leon, endeavored to cleanse herself with wet grass. "Angel seems to be enjoying your lessons," she commented.

Leon nodded. "I'll swear he's no stranger to command. Perhaps some shepherd once owned him, or maybe some land-owning soldier who returned not from a campaign."

He looked at Judith whispering praises into Angel's ear and grinned. "Save your praises until he has caught us a hare or partridge. Then you may laud him to the skies."

They moved on, keeping to rough and wooded ground. Leon paused occasionally to select young saplings, testing their pliancy carefully.

"I need a bow," he explained, and Judith remembered his skill on the journey when he had brought down the stag which had led to the village feast.

"Then you'd best catch something feathered if you intend to make arrows," she said, and her heart warmed as he gave her a slow smile.

Holy Mother, thought Judith, as the warmth of her feelings spread throughout her body, making her tremble. How I could love this man with a passion undreamt of and entirely unexpected. Whoever and whatever he was, he would remain in her heart until death. Even death seemed unimportant if they met it together. She shook away the morbid thought, but it hovered, for they were between opposing armies.

Angel coursed a hare in the late afternoon, and as they moved deep into the forest they found remains of some predatory animal's night-time activity. Leon pounced on a scattering of feathers about the fragile bones of a bird. They risked a fire and roasted the skinned hare on an improvised spit. It was their first meal since leaving the goatherd's hut and was the more delicious because of their hunger.

Angel gnawed the bones while Leon set about making arrows. From the skin of the hare, he fashioned a bowstring, securing it by thongs to the supple sapling. Judith watched, her back comfortably against a tree.

"How far are we from the river?" she asked.

Leon glanced up. "I shall find out tonight. You will be safe with Angel while I'm gone."

Judith felt a cold touch of fear and drew up her knees, cradlng them with her arms. "Will it not be dangerous?"

He shrugged. "There is a narrow ford maybe a mile down stream. I need to know the strength of its defense and who holds it."

"Why did we not use that ford to enter Vallone?"

"Because it loops close to the French border and beyond is an encampment of Vallonese exiles who harass the borderlands. It would not have been wise to pass that way with you, for the baron's bride would have made a fine hostage."

"Would the baron have heeded that, I wonder?" Judith murmured, her tone bitter. "An inconvenience, perhaps, but he could have sent for another bride."

Leon looked at her sharply, his eyes hardening, then he sighed. "I fear you may have the truth of it. I thought him a man of honor, but now I know that belief to be false. Neither the old duke nor his treasure left Vallone. The freedom fighter has turned into a despot. He enslaves his people in much the same manner as the old duke. It is civil war again." He rose and tested the bow, then laid it aside, bending over the task of sharpening the handful of saplings into fine points.

Judith kept her fear hidden as Leon made preparations to leave. As he moved, the dwindling firelight played on his face, making dark pits of his eyes and highlighting the cruel scar. A tall, hard-faced man moving silently with an aura of danger. She wanted to beg him to be careful but held back the words. Of course he would be careful, he was a fighting man used to the conditions of warfare. She tried hard to dispel the fear that he might not come back and she would be lost in a terrifying wilderness. But she smiled as he stood before her, his hand on the horse's bridle.

"I'd best take this fellow along and seek for fodder. He is used to better than grass."

Judith nodded, not trusting herself to speak, and Leon glanced at Angel. "Guard," he commanded, and the dog sat back on his haunches, yellow eyes fixed on the man's face. Then Leon swung into the saddle and the darkness closed about him.

The night was silent, yet filled with small sounds, the rustle of a leaf, the snap of a twig, and Judith peopled it with creeping figures and stealthy predators. Angel stayed quietly by her side, and she knew her fears were groundless. It was imagination and the absence of Leon that made her start at every sound. The fire died, and she rolled into her blanket. Angel was on guard. The warmth of his body relaxed her, and her mind drifted into sleep.

When she woke, the sky was lighter, the stars paling. Angel was gone. She sat up in panic, then her gaze fell on the curled-up figure a few feet away. Her breath left her, almost in a sob of relief, for the figure was unmistakably that of Leon. Beyond him she saw the outline of the horse and heard the rhythmic crunching of jaws. She moved carefully, pulling herself over the damp grass until she was close to Leon. Staring down into his face, she was aware of a great tenderness. His dark hair was shaggy, his beard untrimmed, and he seemed akin to a desperado, dangerous, scarred, and filthy. Who on earth would believe him an English Milord, especially if the stench of goat reached out first? She was in no better position herself, she reflected, for she carried the same aroma in her own person. Dear God, how were they going to get back to civilization? Strangely, the thought did not disturb her greatly. They were together, and time would solve all problems. She found herself looking into gray eyes and started.

"Oh! I did not know you were awake." She backed away, flushing, as if caught in some flagrant indiscretion.

He smiled. "I woke the instant you moved." He sat up. "Is anything wrong?"

"No, I was relieved to see you and wondered if you'd been hurt. Are you all right?"

"Perfectly." He stretched and scratched his beard, wrinkling his nose. "By my faith, I smell like a herd of goats. Keep your distance, Madame."

Judith laughed and sank back on her heels. "I, too, am a member of that same herd. Haven't you noticed?"

"I am too overpowered by my own filth to detect it on others. However, it is our best protection for a while."

Judith nodded toward the horse. "I see you found fodder."

"I stole it, to be exact. As I thought, the ford is guarded by the duke's men, but they guard it laxly with only two sentries. It was no problem to reach the horse lines. There's a wagon of fodder there."

"Can we cross, do you think, without being discovered?"

Leon shook his head. "Not that easy. They patrol the bridge they have thrown over and the far landbank where the barges are moored."

"Is there no other place to cross?"

"No. This is the wrong season for the river is full and the current strong. The snows in the high peaks have melted, and the streams to the river are in high spate. There is no other crossing of safety."

"Then do we wait until the battle is resolved?"

He laughed softly. "Months, maybe years? The Vallonese will not be subdued easily. They have long memories. No, my lady, we must forget the ford and move deeper into the countryside."

"So close," Judith murmured, sighing.

"Close and alive," Leon said. "They have swords and pikes. I cannot vanquish a score of men with my puny bow and saplings arrows." He rose, looking down on her with a sardonic twist to his brow. "Did you expect it of me, Madame la Baronne?"

Judith rose quickly, staring at him. "I would not have you risk your life for any reason, and please do not refer to me by that name. It is as false as the man himself." She narrowed her eyes against the rising sun. "Is your allegiance still to de Gras after what you have learned of him?"

"Only by his death shall I be freed of the duty he laid upon me. That duty is to safeguard the person of a lady of rank. I shall fulfill that duty to the best of my ability."

Judith pushed back her matted hair. "A lady of rank!" she exclaimed with a smile. "Who would believe it, seeing me in this state?"

Leon did not smile. He looked thoughtful. "The bridgehead guards must have an officer in charge. He could be convinced by your manner and speech that you had strayed unwittingly into Vallone territory."

Judith stared aghast into the lean, dark face. "Are you suggesting that I walk to the ford and trust in Providence that I will be treated respectfully while seeking interview with their officer? Holy Mother, they would jeer me for a drab and treat me as such before I got near to any officer!"

"No," he said quietly. "They would not mistreat you. I would see to that."

There was a brief silence as Judith frowned up at him. "If it were known that you served the baron, your life would be forfeit," she said on a strangled gasp. "It is madness! I will have no part in it!"

"You would be safe," he insisted, taking her arm. "Rid of this goat stench, given food, and escorted into France. They could not doubt you, for you are assuredly not Vallonese and there are no ladies of rank left in this country."

"And will you be safe?" Judith asked angrily. "Shall I ride light-heartedly into France while your body hangs from the nearest tree in a traitor's death? I would as soon be twice-grimed and smell yet more foul." She shook off his hand and swung away, running deeper into the trees, unaware of the tears of anguish coursing down her cheeks.

She ran until her breath came gasping, then stopped, leaning her forehead against a tree trunk. Until a wet muzzle thrust itself into her hand, she had been unaware of Angel's pursuit. He whined, staring up from yellow eyes. His brow seemed to wrinkle with worry, and he whined again, sitting heavily on his haunches, his gaze never leaving her face.

A twig cracked, and there was Leon, too. Judith turned, fixing him with a defiant stare. "No!" she said firmly. "And you have no power to force me."

"I know," he said mildly and came closer. With the back of his hand he brushed the tears from her cheeks. "That's better. Your face is much cleaner." His lips curved into a smile. "A barred effect, but a definite improvement." He stood smiling at her. "Come, let us eat cold hare before we move on."

"To the countryside?" She stood, unmoving, with her back to the tree.

"Of course. Where else?" He lifted an arm toward her. "My hand on it."

Judith relaxed, stepping forward. She took the proffered hand. Leon's fingers closed about hers.

They moved westward, keeping a crest between themselves and the river. When the rough line of rock petered out, Leon scouted ahead, crawling on his stomach if necessary, to discover what lay beyond the next crest. Judith sat the horse, ready to move forward at Leon's signal. The eyes of girl and dog never left the dark shape in the distance.

In such manner they moved deep into the countryside on a course between city and river. The land was barren, the soil thin and uncultivated. Goat tracks there were in plenty, and it seemed to Judith that a man's wealth must be counted in the number of goats he possessed, for the infertile soil could only support such creatures. Where were the cornfields, the orchards, the dairy cows, such as were abundant in England? The only lush grass was in the woods, nourished by dew and leaf mold.

Later that day, Angel flushed a grouse and Leon brought it down with an arrow. A small overhang of rock diffused the smoke from their fire as the bird roasted on a spit. Leon had discovered a higher, more broken crest of rock, and it was here they made camp. Judith turned the spit and put her thoughts on the land to Leon.

He nodded. "Goats mainly and a few oxen. The valley surrounding the city is more fertile and crops do well. By tradition—and force—it is farmed by the rulers, the produce sold in the markets at a price fixed by the Council of Nobles. Those who could not pay the price starved, for all was held by the duke. The baron sought to change that. A lesser council of peasants with knowledge of the land yield was proposed, so that men should not starve if the crops were poor." He shrugged. "The duke would not hear of it and declared the baron traitor with a price on his head. He should have considered it, for a starving peasantry makes a dangerous enemy."

"Was the baron true to his promises?"

"I believed he was, but power can turn a man's nature. A tyrant, well-born or peasant, comes to the same thing. A man can starve equally, whoever rules."

Judith asked no more questions, but knelt, turning the spit occasionally. She did not care who won the battle for Vallone, save only where it concerned Leon de Foret.

Leon took his direction by stars and sun as they traveled on. The weather became colder, and rain threatened. Dark clouds built overhead, and even the animals lurked in cover, making the problem of food difficult. Angel became skilled and swift in his craft, obeying Leon's every gesture and word with the instincts of a born hunting dog, but even he was hard-pressed since little game presented itself. The reason became obvious when a storm broke. Thunder rumbled across the mountains, and lightning struck savagely across the sky, the late afternoon darkening into a semblance of night. Rain hurled itself in torrents onto the land, creating quagmires on soil that had been iron-hard only hours before.

As thunder crashed overhead, the horse trembled, tossing a nervous head, eyes rolling. Judith slipped from the saddle and grasped the reins securely, trying to soothe the horse. Without Leon's hand on the bridle, the horse would have bolted, for its movements became erratic in its efforts to shake off the restraining hands.

The rain, cold and slanting, struck into their faces like needle points, and visibility was no more than a few yards. Leon shouted something, but the wind tore away his words and Judith could only follow the direction of his pointing finger through drenched and narrowed eyes. At first she saw nothing, then a faint gray outline penetrated her swimming vision. A building of sorts, perhaps another goatherd's hut, she surmised.

The horse became even more fretful as mud sucked at its hooves. The wet mane flung showers of water on them both as the horse twisted and turned to avoid the slashing rain. Half-blinded by the spray, they staggered on until a stone wall reared out of the gloom before them.

Judith unwound the wet reins from her hand and rubbed her numbed fingers. Leon led the still protesting horse round the corner of the building, seeking an entrance. A large wooden door confronted them. To one side was built a rough wooden shelter. Leon stopped moving. Judith reached him and looked where he looked. Her breath came in a gasp. Under the shelter roof were haltered six horses, unsaddled but in healthy condition. Whose horses? They, too, were moving restlessly as thunder still cracked overhead. Their own horse gave a shrill neigh as if recognizing old comrades. Leon jerked its head about, and the look on his face gave Judith warning that all was not well.

"Go—" he began, but the shrill cry of the horse had been heard. The wooden door crashed open and six men spilled out of the barn, swords raised. With the hand out of sight of the circling figures, Leon flicked his fingers in a gesture of dismissal, and from the corner of her eye Judith glimpsed the black, sleek shape of Angel slinking into the gloom.

The men wore uniforms, stained and wet, which were unfamiliar to Judith.

"Horse thieves," a man stated baldly.

Leon shook his head. "Not so. Count them."

"All there, sir," a soldier reported. "That one is extra."

The officer in charge looked at the horse, then ran his gaze over Leon and Judith. He eyed them for a moment, sucking his teeth. "A fine horse, that. Where did you get it? Stole it, perhaps?"

"Damn your insolence!" Leon barked so suddenly that the man took a step backward. "I bought the brute. Now have done with questions and tell your men to put up their swords. Would you have us stand in the rain all night while you babble on? We came for shelter, not conversation. Allow my lady and me into this hovel at once. As you see, I have no sword, nor do I plan to cut you down." He handed the reins of the horse to a nearby soldier. "Stable and feed the brute, if you please."

The bemused soldier obeyed the note of command in Leon's voice without question. Leon took Judith's arm and strode forward, the soldiers parting for them in silence.

The stone-walled barn proved dry and smelled strongly of garlic and animal fodder. Judith felt almost glad that they had come through a rainstorm, for the goat smell had been partly washed from them and did not overpower the smell of the barn. She noted the sleeve-badges, some device surmounted by a coronet. The duke's men, of course. Would they both hang now? She shrugged mentally. At the moment she was too wet and hungry to concern herself with what might happen. The soldiers had followed them into the barn, and the door was closed. Leon stood in the center of the earth floor surveying the men, dark face expressionless, eyes hard.

"Who commands here?" he snapped.

The man who had called him horse thief spoke. "I am in charge until the commander returns."

"Returns?" Leon frowned. "Is he marching on the city, then? Why are you not with him? There seems little enough in this area to warrant the stationing of half a dozen fighting men!" His cold gaze passed over them. "You all appear uninjured." A hint of scorn edged his voice. "Do you hide like women to avoid the fight? You!" he stabbed a finger. "What is your rank?"

The senior man flushed darkly. "I am a sergeant in charge of these men. I have my orders." He eyed Leon with suspicion but spoke warily. "You ask many questions, Monsieur. What right do you have?"

His gaze faltered as Leon stared at him fixedly. "I will discuss that with your commander. Meanwhile, you will oblige me by building up that fire and putting a pot of something on it. And you will oblige me further by addressing me as sir, or milord, if you prefer.'' His face relaxed slightly into a faint smile. ''By the Rood, Sergeant, this is a devilish inhospitable country. Even the game has fled, and I think they've got the right of it.''

Some of the tension left the soldiers at this abrupt change of address. The sergeant permitted himself a grim smile.

''Aye, sir. 'Tis godforsaken, but the duke will bring it to rights.'' He turned and flung out commands. Grain sacks were dragged toward the hearth for seats, and as their wet clothes steamed, the aroma of cooking meat rose from the pot.

The soldiers were well provisioned, and in addition to the wooden bowls of stew presented to Leon and Judith, there were flat cakes of bread and cups of rough red wine.

Judith smiled at the sergeant and spoke for the first time. ''You have been most kind, Sergeant, and I fully understand your first hesitation.'' She laughed lightly and spread her hands. ''What a bedraggled vision I must appear, but there is no help for it since my villainous maid and manservant made off with my baggage, leaving me no change of clothes. They were not French, of course.'' She smiled mistily at the sergeant. ''This country is no place for a lady.''

''Indeed not, milady, but—er—how come you to be in it?'' He glanced cautiously at Leon, who did not raise his eyes from the stew.

''A mistake entirely, Sergeant. I was too trusting of my guide after being abandoned by my servants. I give thanks that my lord came swiftly, for I swear I believed myself in France. Perhaps your commander will help when he arrives.''

Leon looked up. ''When do you expect him, Sergeant?''

The man scratched his chin and looked baffled. ''I

don't rightly know, sir. We left him in a village some days ago. He was to catch up with the main troops next day, but we've see neither hair nor hide of him since. Our officer took on the main body and left us as escort should the commander show up."

Leon frowned. "A strange story, Sergeant. Where do you think he is? Captured, perhaps?"

The sergeant's smile was sour. "Too far in the rear for that, sir." He shrugged. "Maybe just lost his way."

There was a muffled laugh from one of the soldiers. "Another cozy tavern, more like."

The sergeant turned angrily. "There's no call for that! The duke gave him a command, and our duty is to obey."

Leon looked at the sergeant. "The duke gave him a command, you say. Is he not then a trained soldier?"

The sergeant stared into the fire morosely. "He's a friend of the duke's, sir, a noble."

"I see," said Leon slowly. "Have you searched for him?"

"Every day, sir. Until this storm drove us here. We'll search again when the weather clears."

The storm petered out as they slept, and the dawn broke on a bright, newly washed landscape. The soldiers emerged, stretching and scratching, to attend to the horses. Their own horse was fed with the others, and the company breakfasted on bread and cooked oatmeal. The sergeant sent out scouts as soon as they had eaten, and when the sun had fully risen, Leon began to saddle the horse. The sergeant stood by the barn door looking unhappy.

"If we don't find the commander soon," he muttered gloomily, "they'll have taken the city and it will all be over before we get a chance to fight."

Leon finished tightening the girth and glanced over his shoulder. "Have you seen action before, Sergeant?"

"Yes, sir, when we went against the English. A real

fighting man, their King Richard."

"He was indeed, God rest his soul." He touched his cheek lightly. "I got this at Poitou."

The sergeant eyed the scar admiringly. "Aye, I wondered where, sir, for though you're of the nobility, you've the air of a man who leads from the front." His face darkened as he stared over the empty countryside. "Please God we find our commander soon. 'Tis irksome to sit by while our comrades storm the city gates."

A faint sound drifted toward them, and both men stood listening, eyes narrowed against the sun, staring into the distance. The sound was repeated, faintly but seeming closer.

"Perhaps your prayer has been answered, Sergeant," Leon marked, and listened as the distant sound of hoofbeats came to them. "On the other hand, it could be a Vallonese patrol."

The sergeant jerked his head round, eyes widening. "God's love, you could be right, sir. I've sighted none, but that's not to say there couldn't be one."

He swung on the four remaining men. "Arm yourselves and mount up." He hesitated and glanced at Judith. "The lady, sir?"

"My responsibility, Sergeant. See to your own men."

The sergeant hurried away and Judith came closer to Leon. "Can you see who it is?"

"I don't think it's a patrol. Two horses and, yes, one man on foot." He grinned down at her. "Maybe their long-lost commander. He appears to have taken over one of the horses, for the man on foot was here last night."

He stared keenly as the figures approached. The smile died from his face and his jaw muscles tightened. "By the Saints, it can't be! Dear God, what ill luck!"

Judith grew cold at his tone. "Who is it? Someone who knows us?"

"Someone who knows us both, and the memory of our encounter will stir up painful memories."

Judith peered at the rider in the mud-splattered uniform, then caught her breath as the sun sparked on the jeweled hilt of a sword. One shoulder still held traces of a gold lace epaulette. The face was hard to define under its filth, but Judith knew beyond doubt that this man, the missing commander, was also the vicomte whose riding whip had scored her back.

22

The vicomte was in a furious temper. His small, bloodshot eyes fixed on the sergeant who had moved forward to help him dismount. He struck away the man's hand and glared at the converging soldiers.

"The duke shall hear of this," he growled. "Traitors all! I'll have you hanged for dereliction of duty."

The sergeant stiffened. "Our orders came from Capitaine Deauville, Excellency."

"And where is he, dolt? He is under my command. Send him to me, at once."

"I cannot, sir, for he has marched on the city, leaving myself and this escort to convey you there at the soonest possible moment." He stared, wooden-faced, over the vicomte's head. "The capitaine was insistent, for he said you would not wish to miss the battle."

"Did he now?" A little heat left the vicomte's face. "He is quite right, but it must be obvious even to you that I am in no state to march. Tomorrow, perhaps, when I have rested." He snapped his fingers at the soldiers. "Don't stand there like halfwits. Get me food and wine, clean linen and water. Enough to wash off this cursed filth."

The soldier looked at the sergeant, who cleared his throat nervously. "We have no extra clothing, sir, nor sufficient water—"

"God damn you, man!" snarled the vicomte. "There's a river full of water."

"Sir, it's twenty miles away—"

He was interrupted by a roar of displeasure. "Twenty miles? What is that to a soldier? Dear God, I have tramped that far and more round this cursed country-side already ever since—" His roving gaze fell upon Judith and Leon standing silently by the horses. His eyes bulged and his face suffused with blood. His mouth opened and closed, a strangled breath choking him. "There—there—" He pointed a shaking finger. "There's the man who stole my horse!"

Leon stepped forward as heads turned. "Not so, Excellency." He smiled pleasantly. "You mistake me for another. Your own sergeant's first words were 'horse thief.' " He smiled briefly at the embarrassed sergeant. " 'Tis an easy mistake to make when a man's apparel suggests him worthless. Your own state might well lead people to disbelieve your claim to owning a horse. Yet I would hazard a guess that your money belt contains enough gold pieces to give your appearance the lie."

"That is no concern of yours!" the vicomte flared, his eyes narrowing viciously. "You are a horse thief and I will have you hanged. Fetch rope, Sergeant, curse you!"

"Not so fast, Excellency." Leon spoke with an edge to his voice. "I paid five gold pieces for that brute. It was sold by a fellow that had no stomach for battle, a posturing fellow who called himself by some fancy name. An impostor, no doubt, for what soldier sells his horse? I cannot remember his name, but my lady may have better reason to recall it."

The vicomte's gaze moved past Leon and alighted on the slim figure beside the horse. He glowered, then remembered his treatment of her. His throat worked as he swallowed hard. He glared as his sergeant. "Get your commander food and wine, Sergeant. A man thinks better on a full stomach."

The sergeant saluted, grateful for the order, and soon the vicomte was seated on a grain sack by the fire, being served with hastily warmed stew. He ate noisily, his glance darting upward toward Leon, who sat on a grain sack opposite with Judith beside him. The soldiers stood in a group by the wall, except for a sentry outside. Leon watched the vicomte impassively. The man would not give up easily in his need for a victim on whom to vent his discomfort and rage. These soldiers were under his command. Unless the vicomte did not think better of his threat to hang them, they might end their journey here. Without a sword, he was defenseless to make a fight of it. Only one course remained. He must ensure that the vicomte did think better of his threat.

The vicomte put aside the bowl and stared across the fire. "Your name?" he demanded.

"Tarrant. This is Lady Tarrant by my side. And your name, sir?"

The Vicomte frowned. "The questions are mine. You will answer them truthfully."

Leon raised a sardonic brow. "By all means, if you so wish."

The Vicomte was torn between desire for vengeance and fear of Tarrant's revelations. "What are you doing in this country?" he asked in compromise.

"Trying to leave it."

"That is no answer. Are you Vallonese?"

"No. I seek only to get Lady Tarrant to safety. The duke's fight is not mine."

"Not yours? Every true Frenchman should be fighting this just war."

"My fighting days are over."

Hope stirred in the vicomte's breast. He had his soldiers about him. This man was no threat. "So a coward, eh? As well as a horse thief."

The sergeant interposed helpfully. "Monsieur was at Poitou, Excellency."

The vicomte turned on him. "Hold your tongue until I give you leave to speak." He looked at Leon again. "Poitou has no bearing on this hearing. How do you account for being in possession of my horse?"

Leon shrugged. "A horse is a horse. I bought it from a dressed-up puppy, as I told you. Perhaps your men would be more interested to hear how you came to be deprived of your own mount. Surely that is more to the point before deciding ownership of this brute. I am sure there is a valuable lesson to be learned from your experience."

Leon regarded the vicomte with a half-smile on his lips. The man was a fool, a self-indulgent incompetent, but he was the commander of these men. Leon's eyes were watchful, calculating their chances. Even the most stupid of men, driven into a corner, could turn and savage his tormentor. Since the vicomte could not admit the truth, he must be offered a way out of his dilemma, a way that would bring him no loss of dignity. On the contrary, decided Leon, it must be heroic and splendid.

The vicomte's lower lip jutted as he raised his eyes from the fire to stare into the dark face opposite. Leon leaned forward and his eyes scrutinized the vicomte's face. The man stared back, unable to decide his next move.

"You are wounded, sir," said Leon. "You made no mention, Excellency, but that is the way of the soldier. An ambush, perhaps? They showed you no mercy, the villains."

The vicomte lifted a hand slowly to his bruised cheek. His lips moved, but no sound came.

"You are lucky to escape with your life, sir, for I have met these desperate men myself," went on Leon. "A brave fight on your part, I don't doubt, for that sword you carry looks most handy." He shrugged. "The loss of a horse is a small thing compared to your life, and 'tis no wonder that a man in the aftermath of battle views a stranger with suspicion."

The vicomte's mind was struggling to make sense of the words. Villain? A brave fight? What was the fellow babbling about? Trying to cover up his own crime by talk of ambush and desperate men? He would soon show this thieving villain that lies would get him nowhere. When his men heard the truth of it, they would laugh the fellow to scorn.

But wait a minute. A flicker of caution touched his mind. The truth would not redound to his own credit. The idea of a battle appealed more, and the fool was offering him a most plausible story to account for the loss of his horse. No need for awkward questions. And he did bear the bruise where the scoundrel had struck him. He would have liked to hang the man, and woman too, but he was unsure of his men's obedience to hang two strangers out of hand, for they were obviously not Vallonese rebels. He found himself nodding. Glancing round at his troopers, he saw attentive faces, full of expectancy and, yes, he was convinced, admiration.

He lifted his chin, expanding his chest. His smile was almost benign. " 'Tis the lot of a soldier, Monsieur, and though no great battle, was in itself a small victory for the duke's cause." He glanced up at the sergeant. "You wondered at my absence, Sergeant, but an embattled man without his horse makes sore progress." He rose, his gaze sweeping the assembly. "Your commander has journeyed to join you, brushing aside the hazards and overcoming them all. Now I will rest, and tomorrow at first light we march on the city." He raised a clenched fist. "Tomorrow the city!" He lowered his arm, and his dark eyes fixed on Leon. "And you, Monsieur, will ride by my side." His fingers fluttered. "No, do not thank me for the honor, I command it. Guard the horses well, Sergeant, we can ill afford to lose any more."

The sergeant was baffled by the sudden good temper of his commander. Even the request for water was not repeated. He glanced curiously at the recumbent body of the vicomte, noting the smile on his lips under the small purpling bruise of his cheek. A battle wound?

More like a thump from a tavern wench who thought him too fancy, the sergeant reflected sourly as he left the building to double the guard on the horses.

He saw the monsieur and his lady strolling some distance away, and he frowned. From wanting to hang them both, the vicomte had been almost affable and now desired the man to ride by his side on the morrow. He made a gesture of impatience. More delay, but this time he would not let the vicomte out of his sight, however many taverns they passed.

Judith and Leon stood by a clump of thorn bushes, talking easily, or so it would appear to a casual observer. Angel lay concealed in the bushy depths, gnawing on the bones of a hare Leon had purloined from the unattended cooking pot.

"What are we to do now?" asked Judith. "The vicomte is making doubly sure of the horses."

"Yes. Curse the fellow for arriving when he did. Another hour and we would have been well away. There is nothing for it but to fall in with his plans." He smiled. "His Excellency is full of valor at present, but tomorrow his ardor will have cooled somewhat. I foresee delays on our progress into the battle area. We must take our chances when they show themselves." He broke off a small twig, and two yellow eyes glanced up alertly. The dog accepted the low-voiced commands, then Judith and Leon strolled back to the soldiers.

Dawn found the vicomte in less euphoric mood. He had washed from a leather bucket, but no amount of rubbing with dried hay could bring back the splendor of his uniform. But even that annoyance paled against the enormity of what lay ahead. The road to the city! His stomach lurched as he thought of that road. In a few hours' time, it would be filled with humanity. Fleeing peasants with the duke's army in pursuit, or, he quaked inwardly, ducal soldiers with vengeful Vallonese on their heels?

He looked down at his uniform with distaste. He could send men to the river and have the thing washed properly. It would mean a delay, of course.

He looked up, his mouth opening on the order. The sergeant stood erect before him.

"The men are ready, Excellency. Your horse is saddled and waiting. The monsieur and his lady share the pack mount. He requests that his own horse be offered to you, sir."

The vicomte closed his mouth and looked past the sergeant at the troopers. There was an air of excitement about them, he reflected sourly, as if they were bound for a Feast Day festival instead of bloody warfare. The mere thought of it made him sweat with terror. How could these ignorant louts understand the sensibilities of the nobly born? The sergeant was waiting. The vicomte urged his reluctant limbs into motion. He avoided all eyes as he was heaved into the saddle. He stared ahead in numbed silence, then started as the sergeant spoke.

"We await your signal to move, Excellency."

"Of course, of course. I was—er—planning my campaign," he muttered in unsteady tones. He raised an arm that shook only a little. "To the city, men."

"To the city!" they roared and fell in behind, the sergeant stationing himself a horse's length behind the vicomte.

They moved off at a walk, and the vicomte seemed content to retain that pace, but he became aware of muffled voices and restless stirrings behind.

The sergeant drew level. "Excellency. We must increase our speed or we shall not reach the city before nightfall. We are too few in number to make camp safely within sight of the city after night has fallen."

The vicomte looked at him. "We shall spend the night in a tavern or farmhouse, then approach the city at daybreak. Is that not a better plan then blundering on in darkness?"

"Yes, Excellency, save that taverns and farmhouses may well be in the hands of the rebels. It would be wiser to make swiftly for the city and join up with our comrades."

"You may be right, Sergeant, but the decision will be mine. We shall cut a swath of destruction through any who would bar our way and the dogs will flee before us. Look to your men, Sergeant, and have them follow me closely in order to obey my signals."

The sergeant saluted and dropped back, and the vicomte put his horse into a trot and then a gentle gallop.

The miles rolled away slowly, with frequent halts to enable the vicomte to refresh himself from the wineskin while staring toward the city, still invisible, with the concentrated frown of a commander pondering the disposition of his forces. The sergeant was by his elbow. He pointed.

"Over the next crest, Excellency, and the city will be in sight."

The vicomte stared at the horizon. Surely it was darker. Let that damned sun go down and he could, without loss of face, decide to halt for the night. He glanced about. There was no sign of life. Surely a barn or derelict farmhouse must present itself. A cowering peasant family would be no trouble to dislodge. Preferably one on this side of the crest. He frowned into the distance. It was darker, he was convinced of it.

The sergeant made an exclamation and the vicomte jumped.

"What is it, damn you?" He found his nerves tightening.

"Look, Excellency. A dark cloud over the city."

"Darkness? Of course it is darkness, for the night comes. We cannot proceed further."

"Not the darkness of night, Excellency, for the sun still shines. It is smoke. The city is afire."

They both stared as columns of smoke spiraled upward beyond the crest. From their position, they could see only the huge gray pall spreading wide, smearing the blue of the sky with its density.

"We must ride like the wind," muttered the sergeant.

"Ride? Into that?" The vicomte was appalled. "The peasants will surrender now that the duke has fired the city. It would be dangerous to risk the lives of my men at this point. No, Sergeant. We shall be needed to prevent the rebels escaping by this route."

The sergeant regarded him without expression. "As yet we know not which side fired the city, Excellency. If the rebels still hold sway, then our comrades are in desperate need of assistance."

The vicomte felt the sweat on his body turn cold. "We are only six, Sergeant."

"Enough to turn the scales in a savage skirmish. Do we ride on, Excellency?" His tone was flat, but the eyes were cold, and the vicomte shifted uncomfortably. He nodded. "To the crest only, where we may view the situation and plan accordingly."

The small troop moved on, and the vicomte's eyes flickered over the countryside. Dear God, there must be some shelter hereabouts. It was madness to ride into a burning city. Who knew where an enemy might lurk, waiting to release a storm of arrows on the soldiers riding below? His heart gave a great shuddering leap. There, in a fold below the topmost crag of the crest, lay a building of sorts, farmhouse or shepherd's hut he could not guess, but it would be some form of barricade between himself and the city.

He pointed it out to the sergeant. "There we will form our headquarters, Sergeant. A good vantage point with a view over the city and the countryside. Make haste to our new position."

* * *

Leon helped Judith dismount in the lee of the stone wall. He held her for a moment, pushing back her dark hair.

"I hoped to lag behind," he said softly, "but our brave commander was of the same mind." He glanced over her head toward the smoke. "God knows which side has the upper hand, but whatever the case, our position is not one I like."

Judith leaned against him tiredly. "Perhaps in full dark we may see a way to escape."

"I fear full dark will not come tonight. The fires will burn until daybreak."

The moved to enter the building, a low one-room cottage. The air of hasty departure showed itself in over-turned stools and dirty platters on the bench table. Leon caught up a stool and set it in the corner nearest the door, directing Judith to take its seat. He stood beside her, his arm resting lightly on her shoulder.

The vicomte slumped at the table, his face pale and sweat-streaked. The sergeant regarded him impassively for a few moments, then turned to the door. As he passed Leon, their eyes met and the sergeant's shoulders moved in a slight shrug. Leon detained him, speaking low-voiced.

"I would feel easier with a sword in my hand, Sergeant. So close to battle, a man feels naked without weapon. I must protect my own and, if needs be, yours too."

The sergeant's lips moved in a thin smile. "I have no doubt the need will arise. You say this war is none of your concern. Do you give me your word that His Excellency will suffer no hurt from you?"

"You have my word, Sergeant." He grinned suddenly. "As long as you dissuade him from hanging me for a horse thief. Now, that I really could not allow!"

The sergeant's lips twitched. "Aye, sir. I believe I can

guarantee that." He stepped outside and returned after a few moments bearing a scabbard and blade.

"My second blade, Monsieur. Well-traveled but still keen enough."

Leon hefted the sword, gauging its balance. The steel had been honed to a fine edge and the weight was less than Leon expected. He glanced into the sergeant's face. "Well-traveled, I believe, and well-used I have no doubt. Thank you, Sergeant."

They both turned as the vicomte spoke. "God's teeth, Sergeant! What do you mean by giving a sword to that villain? Disarm him at once! I command it!" He glared balefully from bloodshot eyes.

The sergeant stiffened to attention. "Since Monsieur has no part in this affair, he demands the right to protect his lady in the only shelter available. We cannot deny him that right, sir. If Your Excellency will accompany me to the crest, we may view the progress of the battle, and I will receive your orders." He stood to one side of the door and waited expectantly.

Leon slid the blade into its scabbard and buckled the belt about his waist. He moved to the other side of the door, and both men looked at the figure slumped by the table.

The vicomte's face looked paler, and moisture beaded his brow. "Now?" he croaked. "There is not sufficient light—" he stopped, remembering the fires.

"Bright as full day, Excellency," Leon said blandly. "It would not surprise me if you could count the corpses quite easily from the crest." As the vicomte dragged himself upright, Leon murmured encouragingly, "You may even get your own sword bloodied this night, if luck is with you."

The vicomte spared him a look of loathing and walked into the night without another word of protest. He had the look of a man on the way to his own execution.

Judith, watching from her corner, almost felt sorry for

him. As Leon turned toward her, she said, "Do not bait the man so readily, I beg of you. If the duke triumphs, the vicomte will be in a stronger position to enforce his will. He would happily see us hang."

Leon nodded. "I know, which is why I requested this sword. If the sergeant can persuade His Excellency to ride into battle, that is the moment we shall attempt our escape. The longer the battle, the better our chances while all is confusion."

"I wonder where Angel is."

"Close by, you may be sure."

Judith rose from the stool and moved to stand in the doorway. The setting sun glowed dully on the horizon, its glow masked by drifting smoke. She looked toward the rocky crest where the soldiers grouped, staring down. The vicomte was at the sergeant's shoulder, his body moving nervously.

"I would like to view the city," Judith said. "Had all gone as the baron planned, I would have been its first lady." She shivered. "And where would I have been now? If the ship had not wrecked and the Velardis been true, we should both have been in that city."

Leon put an arm about her shoulder. "Come. I will show you your first and last sight of the city before it is burned to the ground."

They left the shelter and followed the track upward. The light grew stronger, and the sound of destruction reached them. On the crest, to one side of the watching group, they stopped and gazed over the valley. Judith caught her breath as she stared into the inferno. The scene shimmered in a heat haze, woven through with towering columns of fire. Sparks from timbered dwellings hurled themselves skyward, and the rumble of falling masonry droned like distant thunder. It was impossible to divide the battling armies, for the smoke hung in a funereal pall over all, only gusting away as a building fell, but returning to join the uprush of stone dust. In the firelight, figures ran and fell, staggering blindly, and fell again. Groups formed and reformed, plunging headlong into alleys and leaping over obstructions. The ringing clash of metal, the roar of exploding timbers rendered the night hideous to the ear.

Her gaze was caught by a fleeing figure, ducking and crouching, making for the darkness outside the lighted torch that was the city. A plunging horse, nostrils splayed with terror, erupted from the smoke. The runner screamed once as a sword blade took him in the throat, lifting him off his feet and tossing him aside. The horseman's lips were drawn back in a fixed snarl, the firelight turning his eyes into rolling redness, then he was swallowed up in the smoke. The body of the man lay crumpled in death, the blood jetting brightly. What Judith had taken for toppled trees revealed themselves as more bodies when a gush of sparks put fire to a dried-out bush.

She suddenly felt very sick and sagged against Leon. ''Enough,'' he murmured. ''The city has received mortal wound this night.'' He took her arm and led her back down the track. They passed the grouped horses. Two soldiers were guarding them with drawn swords. Their eyes watched the crest, waiting for orders.

''How is it, sir?'' one asked.

''Like a scene from hell,'' answered Leon. ''There's no telling who'll take the victory.''

''We should be down there,'' his companion muttered.

''Tell that to His Excellency,'' said the first one in an undertone as Judith and Leon moved away.

Inside the cottage, Leon paced restlessly, his fingers gripping the sword hilt. ''The vicomte will hesitate all night, curse him, and the sergeant is bound to his side. If the duke comes victorious from the valley, only then will the vicomte act, and it will be too late for us. I am loath to kill the guards outside, but we must be away before the duke and vicomte come together.''

"We could leave on foot," Judith ventured, but Leon shook his head.

"They would hunt us down if they found us gone. That's all the excuse the vicomte needs to declare us traitor."

"Do you expect the duke to win?"

Leon halted and stared down at her broodingly. "With French weapons and well-taught troopers, yes. The men of de Gras are brave enough, but they are without skill and discipline. They will fight like a mob, which is little use against experienced soldiers provided by France." He glanced at the open doorway. "Come into the open. I dislike being surrounded by walls and have no desire to be trapped in here if the battle flows over this crest."

Judith followed him, and he turned away from the guarded horses to come upon the crest from a different direction. With reluctance, she stared down. The fires had spread and the smoke was thicker. Could there be more noise? She blinked through the curling wisps. The fight was spreading as Leon had feared. The valley floor below the incline to the city was darkened by movement, a restless flowing to and fro like wind-whipped bushes over a landscape. Yet these dark shapes were shot through with flashes of light as steel caught the firelight. Smoke-blackened faces, swift bloomings of crimson, flowering and fading below the surface, held her gaze in fascinated horror. Those were men, teeth bared in the bloodlust of battle, faces of fear and cruelty, blank faces as death claimed them.

Leon's arm was tight about her shoulder. "They're breaking for this crest." He looked toward the vicomte's group. They too had observed the movement. The sergeant's voice rang out, and the men spread wide. The vicomte remained still and made no move to draw his sword. He stood, a man trapped by fear.

The sergeant ran back to him, gripping his arm urgently, speaking words unheard. The vicomte started, then turned and in a stumbling run skidded down the track to the cottage.

Leon drew his sword and pulled Judith toward the track. "Stay near the horses," he hissed. "Don't go inside the cottage. Here." He pushed her into a shadowed crevice of rock. "Stay here under cover. If there's a chance to steal a horse, take it and head back the way we came."

"Without you?" she hissed back fiercely.

Fireglow glinted on his teeth as he gave her a soft grin. "If you could make it two horses, so much the better. I will find you, never fear. And Angel will surely find you first. Promise me you'll do it?"

Judith bit her lip, then sighed. "All right, I promise. What are you going to do?"

"Join the sergeant. I can do no less, but I'll fight a defensive battle only. I will not kill."

Judith stared into the space where he had been. She could see the horses clearly. She also saw the stumbling figure of the vicomte, his blade still sheathed. The fingers of one hand were spread wide on his chest and he swayed as if concealing a chest wound. The two guards looked at him wide-eyed as he gesticulated with his free hand. They ran to the crest, drawing their swords. The vicomte's hand dropped, and Judith saw him reach for the bridle of his horse. Did he intend to flee the fighting? Only a coward would do that. The same thought must have struck the vicomte, for his fingers released the bridle and he took a step toward the cottage. He paused and stared back to the crest, his heavy face full of indecision.

Hide yourself away, Judith urged him quietly. Go into the cottage, away from the horses. Dear God, give me the chance to steal two, she prayed silently. But the vicomte did not move.

Then it was too late for any decision. The crest of the hill was black with struggling figures. The thud and grunt of body meeting body, the ring of steel on steel, and the hoarse cries of pain made the air vibrate with sound.

Judith shrank back into the shadowed crevice. She was between the cottage and the fight and could not emerge in either direction without full brightness falling upon her. The vicomte fumbled the sword from its scabbard and held it out in front of him, his arm shaking.

The sergeant and his men were retreating slowly down the track, drawing their attackers forward, bunching them together. The peasant fighters, for they must be of the baron's army, Judith judged, were unaware of the sergeant's tactics, the encirclement of them by these better-trained soldiers. A small party only, it seemed, but now they were isolated from the main group still in the valley. As the flanks of the sergeant's men joined to complete the circle, the peasants realized their danger. They lashed out in panic confusion, but were cut down swiftly and cleanly.

The last man was falling to the sergeant's sword when the vicomte hurled himself forward, plunging his own blade into the dying man's body.

"So die all the duke's enemies!" he howled, then withdrew his dripping blade to hold it aloft, unaware, or perhaps very aware, of the blood running over his fingers and staining his tunic, and proclaiming him a man of action.

"Well done, Excellency," said the sergeant dryly and wiped his sweating forehead with the back of his hand.

A groan from the pile of bodies made the vicomte jump. He located the wounded man and brought up his sword to plunge it into his victim. "One villain lives," he mouthed.

"Hold, Excellency," the sergeant said quickly. "We need a prisoner."

"For what reason?" the vicomte demanded. "This scum deserves to die."

"Indeed, Excellency, but first we question him on the

state of the fighting.''

"Of course, of course. My nature is too eager for blood. Yes, yes, we will question him first, then despatch him. Take him to the cottage.''

Beyond the sprawled corpses, Judith caught sight of Leon, idly running his sword blade through a handful of thick moss. His gaze was half-turned to the crest when the vicomte spoke.

"Come, my lord stranger, and observe how we question such traitorous scum.'' He stood, hand on hip, as Leon strolled down the track, his air one of polite disinterest.

"Your prisoner and your glory, Excellency,'' he said, shrugging lightly.

"To be sure,'' the vicomte replied, his eyes on the blade Leon held loosely. "And since the battle is over, I command you to return that sword to the sergeant.''

Leon looked at him for a long moment, then laughed. "Over, Excellency? Dear God, that was a mere skirmish. The battle is yet to come.''

"What—what do you mean?'' the vicomte licked his lips.

"The city is neither won nor lost, not yet. The battle still rages. Can you not hear it?''

"Monsieur is right, Excellency. We do no good here while our comrades die below.''

"We guard the ridge,'' the vicomte snapped at the sergeant, who fell silent, having said all he dared.

It was Leon who put the question. "From what, Excellency?'' He touched the nearest body with the toe of his boot. "A few fleeing peasants taken by surprise?''

The vicomte looked at him coldly. "I will issue my orders when I have dealt with the prisoner. A commander does not risk his—his men's lives without all possible information. Set guards, Sergeant, while I am in the cottage.''

Leon followed him through the doorway, and Judith

came out of the crevice, seeing no point in concealment since a guard stood by the horses. She looked into the cottage.

The prisoner lay on a beaten-earth floor, blood from a shoulder thrust plastering his tunic. A scalp wound matted his hair. He was a mere youth, she observed, and very badly frightened. He stared up into the fierce face of the vicomte, who waved his bloodied sword in front of the wretch.

"You will tell us all you know, peasant. I want a truthful account of the battle, the number of men your false baron musters, the disposition of his soldiers, the fortifications and emplacements, in fact, everything."

The boy looked at him blankly. "I know not your words nor their meaning, lord."

"Then you will learn fast," growled the vicomte. "On your feet, scum! You address a nobleman of France. I will have you flogged if you defy me."

The boy lurched clumsily to his feet, holding his injured shoulder. His face was ashen, and drops of blood trickled down from the scalp wound. "I know naught of anything, lord. They took me from the land and put a sword in my hand. I am no true soldier." His eyes were desperate with appeal.

"Hah!" sneered the vicomte. "You attack my position and pretend ignorance. Your foul companions are dead, but you I will kill slowly if you persist in this stubbornness."

The sergeant had been watching the boy closely. "I think you will get nothing from this one, Excellency. He is but a common, untrained youth."

The vicomte stared at him through narrowed eyes. His expression was unpleasant. "So, you would instruct me in this matter? Is that so?"

"No, Excellency," said the sergeant carefully. "But this fellow has no rank. He would obey instructions only."

"Then you should have chosen better when they attacked. What good is a illiterate peasant?"

"We did not seek to attack you, lord," the boy quavered. "We knew naught of your position. We meant only to escape the battlefield."

"Running away? You admit to cowardice, then?" the vicomte's tone was scornful. "You know the penalty for cowardice in the field?"

The boy nodded dully. His eyes wandered restlessly over the faces about him. They rested on the tall, silent figure leaning on the door jamb. They held still, and a bewildered expression crossed his face.

Judith knew with appalling clarity what was about to happen. Her hand reached to the stone wall for support as a silent scream of protest welled up within her. Leon knew it too, and his fingers tightened on the still-unsheathed sword hilt.

The boy threw himself forward and dropped to his knees in front of Leon. "Forgive me, Capitaine. I was afraid and fled. We could not fight as you taught us. We belong to the land, not in your army." Tears ran down his face. "I deserve your punishment, Capitaine de Foret. God help me to face it now."

23

An instant of shock immobilized the men in the cottage —all save Leon, who had been expecting it since he had vaguely recognized the boy. In that instant he moved with the swift, silent passage of a nocturnal predator. He sidestepped the kneeling boy and locked his left arm about the vicomte's throat, pulling him backward, hard against his chest. The slender sword pointed at the sergeant, whose own sword was half-drawn.

"Release your grip, Sergeant, if you value the life of your commander. Attack me and he dies. Otherwise the word I gave you holds good."

The vicomte made a choking sound. "Do—do as he says, man."

The sergeant's blade dropped back into the scabbard. He spread his hands in surrender, but his eyes never left Leon's face. His expression was that of a man whose trust had been betrayed.

"Call in the horse guard," ordered Leon. The sergeant turned, but Leon cut in curtly, "I said call, not fetch."

The sergeant obeyed, and the guard came in, his face showing sudden alarm as he saw the situation.

"Into the far corner. You too, Sergeant. I could disarm you, but I will not. This is no place for a weaponless man."

"So you said before," the sergeant said dryly. "And I was fool to trust you."

"Not at all, Sergeant I also told you this conflict was not my concern."

The sergeant gave a harsh bark of laughter. "Does the boy lie, then?"

"No. He speaks the truth. I am no Vallonese but was hired to teach the rudiments of soldiering to a defensive force the baron wished to create. My terms were to instruct, not lead the province into battle. Its politics are not my concern."

"A defensive force against its true ruler, the duke? What kind of a man are you?"

"A deceived one, it seems, for I took the baron's word that the old duke was in exile. But I have a duty until death. His death or mine." He urged the vicomte nearer to the door. "Pray your young duke deals more kindly with his people than his father or Vallone will never know rest." He gestured to the boy. "Outside and mount up. You too, Judith. Head down the track."

They went, and Leon looked back at the sergeant. "You will understand that I must take all the horses to avoid pursuit, as I leave you armed for your own protection." He pushed the vicomte through the doorway. "Mount up."

As the man climbed clumsily into the saddle, Leon kicked the vicomte's dropped sword into a corner. He half-smiled at the sergeant.

"He will live to use it again, if only on dying men. Another walk will do him no harm. Meanwhile, you are in command, Sergeant. Make the most of it."

Outside, he swung into the saddle and slapped the two riderless horses on their rumps with the flat of his sword. They skittered off down the track and Leon followed swiftly, urging the vicomte on ahead of him. At the base of the crest Leon found Judith and the boy waiting. Judith's tense expression relaxed as Leon came into sight. She stared with distaste at the sweating vicomte.

"Must we take him?"

"Yes, we must, my dear. The brave vicomte is our permit to travel freely. The sergeant will make no move to pursue while we hold his gallant commander. If we run into the duke's men, our good friend here will order them from our path, will you not, Excellency?"

The vicomte licked his lips and shifted uncomfortably in the saddle.

"On the other hand, if we come upon the baron's men, they will be only too delighted to take him off our hands."

He smiled into the vicomte's stricken face.

"You would deliver me to—to the enemy? They would hang me."

"I suppose so," Leon said easily. "But then, it was the very thing you wanted to do to us."

"I did not mean it," the vicomte croaked. "I was suffering the aftermath of battle. You said so yourself."

"Battle?" Leon mocked. "Come now, Excellency. We both know what battle that was." His voice hardened. "Now hold your tongue and speak only when I bid it."

They galloped on in silence until they had put two miles between the crest and themselves, then Leon called a halt. The fiery cloud over the city was still visible. Leon beckoned the boy to him.

"What do they call you?"

"Gaston, sir. I am the—"

"Never mind that. You will lead us into the city by the west gate where the alleys are thick as rabbit warrens."

The boy's shoulders drooped. "There has been much fighting there, sir. The dwellings are mere rubble since the invaders passed through."

"So much the better. An attack from a ruined position will be unexpected. Lead on to the city, boy, when I give the word."

Judith felt her heart sink at the order. Into the city where only death and destruction reigned? What did Leon suppose a man and a boy could achieve? She looked at him searchingly, and he met her eyes, his own narrowed. Was there a warning in his gaze? Of what she could not fathom, but she decided to hold silent and trust him.

Leon turned to the vicomte. "Your time has come, Excellency. Dismount, if you please."

The vicomte's hands tightened on the reins. Sweat ran down his face. "Dis—dismount? You intend to kill me here?"

"Did you want to go to the city?" Leon queried.

The vicomte shuddered. "No, no, not the city!"

"Good, for I have no wish to burden myself with your useless body. Dismount."

The vicomte drove his heels into the horse's flanks savagely. The horse jerked and threw up its head, its teeth baring in a neigh of protest. Its haunches bunched to leap forward, but the sound was echoed by a low rumbling growl. The horse shied, almost throwing the vicomte from the saddle. Leon leaned forward and grasped the reins.

"What—what in the name of God was that?" the vicomte quavered.

Leon's grin held a wolfish quality. "An old friend of yours, Excellency, and another who may find forgiveness difficult." He snapped his fingers.

Yellow eyes showed first, then a lithe black shape materialized. The eyes looked up unwinking at the vicomte.

"Holy Mother of God," he whispered. "That hound of hell!"

"Have a care, Excellency," warned Leon. "He would like nothing better than to tear the throat out of you. Now, I tell you one more time to dismount. We have wasted enough time."

The vicomte lowered himself to the ground with great reluctance. His eyes had dulled and his shoulders were slumped.

"You can see the crest where your men are. It is out-lined plainly enough by the fire. It should not take you more than an hour to reach it."

The vicomte's head came up with a jerk. "You are releasing me?"

"I gave your sergeant my word on it. This time I am merciful, Excellency. Should we meet again in the city, I will kill you. Now go."

The vicomte backed away, his expression uncertain, then he turned and ran, casting frequent glances over his shoulder as if it might all be a trick. The sound of skidding boots and labored breathing gradually faded into the night.

"Lead on, Gaston."

The boy turned his horse without a word and they followed him in silence, the ground rising, rocky and grass-tufted. They rode wide of the city, high above the ridge that looked into the valley. The rocky crests here on the sound side of the city rose higher and stretched toward the mountains. The sun was almost gone, but the city still smoldered under its smoky pall. Leon ordered a halt at its highest point. He had watched the boy's swaying progress, the lessening of control as it slipped from boy to horse.

"Climb down, Gaston." he said. "Let us take a look at that shoulder of yours." He dropped lightly from his own saddle and looked up at the boy who had not moved. The young face was gray, the eyes almost unseeing. Leon reached up and lifted the boy down, laying him on a stretch of mossy grass. He straightened up, glancing toward Judith peering down from her saddle. He swept her into his arms and set her onto the grass beside the boy. "We rest for a while and attend to the boy. Can you manage his tunic while I investigate the contents of these saddlebags?"

When he returned to her side he was smiling. "I knew that sergeant was a good man. We have all manner of herbal salves here and linen strips for binding wounds. Potions for fever and even purges to rid blood of venom." He spread out the remedies on the grass and examined the boy's bared chest. "A loss of blood, certainly, but a high wound, thanks be to God. He does not bleed from the mouth."

They worked together, laying cloths plastered in salve on the wound, then lifted him into a sitting position to wind the linen about his body. The tunic was carefully replaced. Angel's nostrils twitched as he caught the scent of medication. He tensed, ready to leap away if hands were laid on him.

Judith sank back on her heels and looked at Leon. She felt tired and dispirited. "This boy is not fit to go back into battle. How can you think of entering the city? He will collapse of a certainty without rest and food." She paused. "As to rest and food, I too am in sore need of both."

"Oh, I do not intend to go into the city, by the west gate or any other."

"But you told the vicomte—"

"And he will tell the sergeant and any duke's man who comes his way. He will be eager for the city—when danger has passed—in order to search us out and complete his heart's desire, which is to hang us. Therefore, we shall not go south but north."

"And the baron?"

Leon's expression hardened. "I am obeying his last command to escort you into safety. My sword is my honor. I will not use it blindly without good reason and respect for the man it serves."

He rose abruptly and went to the horses. "These extra mounts will hold us up. I'll turn them free." He emptied the saddlebags, discovering a number of oatcakes and the vicomte's half-empty wineskin. He came back smiling, his expression no longer hard.

The boy was persuaded to drink a little wine and munch an oatcake. His eyes still held a haunted look, and his pallor alarmed Judith.

"No need for despondency, Gaston." Leon told him. "We go not to the city but to your home."

The boy stared his disbelief, swallowing the last of his oatcake with difficulty. He blinked rapidly, his eyes full of doubt and hope.

"Has there been fighting thereabouts?" Leon asked.

The answer tumbled out eagerly. "No, sir. The village is small and isolated, some ten miles to the north. I will take you, sir, for you saved my life."

"As to that, I would rather you did not speak of it. Say we are travelers seeking a night's lodging. Foreigners caught unaware by the fighting and came upon you by accident. 'Tis better to keep your village in ignorance in case questions are asked."

The boy nodded, thoughts of returning home lifting his spirits. A little color crept back into his cheeks, and his eyes lost their blankness.

Leon glanced at the sky. "It will be full dark soon with little moon to guide us on this rough terrain."

"I know the country well, Capitaine. I can lead you without trouble, even at night. I have spent many nights with the herd and less moon to guide me."

"The herd?" asked Judith faintly.

"Yes, my lady. My father has many goats, the largest herd in the village, at least fifteen," he finished on a note of pride.

"How—how splendid," Judith said, and refused to meet Leon's eyes for she knew they would be full of suppressed amusement. She noted from the corner of her eye the slight tremor of his shoulders in silent laughter as he bent over the saddlebags, collecting objects of use.

They mounted the three strongest-looking horses and turned the others loose. As Leon checked the girth strap of her own mount, he glanced up and she could not avoid his gaze. She tried to frown, but a muffled laugh escaped her. Leon grinned.

"There are worse things than the smell of goats, but do not ask me at precisely this moment what they are. Dear God, how I should welcome a swim in a river, a stream even, or a pond. Not to mention a change of clothes."

"Then pray do not. I beseech you, for I swear 'tis only the dirt holds my tunic together."

They moved off into the night, the boy leading, his countryman's instincts putting them on the right road although there was no visible track. Judith followed him and Leon rode behind, eyes and ears alert for sounds which should not be there. Angel ranged a parallel course, although nothing could be seen or heard of him, save a glint of yellow when a shaft of moonlight touched his eyes.

The way wound between rocks and pinnacles of stone, yet underfoot the ground was surprisingly soft. The boy seemed to know the easiest routes over moss and grass, saving the legs of their horses. They traveled at walking pace for nowhere was it safe to gallop on the winding track. As darkness grew deeper, a wind sprang up and Judith shivered, remembering heavier tunics and fur-trimmed cloaks in the saddlebags of the mule. Where was that mule now? And where, indeed, were the Velardis and the men of the escort? Thank God she had Leon. She no longer thought of him as Capitaine de Foret, nor even Quentin, although she still believed he was Tarrant. It mattered little one way or the other. He was the man of her heart.

They came to a plateau of land that stretched out into the distance. Faint stars pricked the night through the cloudy heavens. A light scattering of raindrops touched their faces.

Gaston turned in his saddle. Judith noted the clumsy movement and strained her eyes to his face but could only discern the pallid outline. He spoke in a hoarse whisper.

"A few miles only. The ground is firm. We can canter the horses, sir."

Leon drew level with Gaston. "How is the shoulder?"

"Fine, sir, fine. We shall get to the village tonight if we

move faster." There seemed a note of urgency in his voice.

"Yes," said Leon slowly. "It would be best to reach the village before you fall off your horse. Go gently then, lad, and try not to jolt that shoulder."

"I'll be all right, sir."

He moved off, shoulders bowed as if conserving all his strength in an effort to stay on the horse long enough to reach his home.

Leon dropped back to Judith's side. "He is in pain, no doubt of it, but he is determined to fall among friends."

"I hope we shall do the same," Judith said somberly.

"We will, if the boy can retain consciousness long enough for the people to believe that his injury was none of our doing. Keep close. I'll ride with the boy and hold him up if he flags." He called Angel's name in the darkness. "Guard," he ordered, pointing, and Angel fell in behind Judith's horse.

Long before they reached the village, the boy was reeling in the saddle. Judith saw Leon reach out, leaning sideways to put an arm about the slim shoulders. She heard the soft murmuring voice, encouraging the boy to one more effort, to keep his senses until they sighted the village. All would be well once they spied the first lamplight or candle flame.

The longed-for point of light came at last. The grass leveled into a well-trodden path running between small dwellings and goat pens. The goats themselves were invisible, but the bleat and scent pinpointed their positions. A torch flared ahead, and as the hooves of the horses drummed on the path, doors opened. Pitchforks and hammers caught the flare on their metals, men armed with staves rushed upon them. They were surrounded by surly faces and growling voices.

The torch bearer held the pitch flame aloft. A woman screamed.

" 'Tis our Gaston! They bring back his body," and she began to wail.

"Hush your noises, woman," bellowed a harsh voice. "Whoever heard of such a thing! They're left to scavengers and putrefaction." The man peered up, his eyes suspicious. "What is your business here? Is the lad dead? He looks mortal bad if he's not yet passed into the shades."

Leon raised his voice above the babble. "Gaston is still with the living and will remain so unless you talk all night and lose time in attending to his wounds. Fetch his kin and prepare a couch. Heat water and send a woman skilled in healing." He swung down from the saddle. "You!" his finger stabbed at a thick-set youth with a bovine stare. "Help me lift him from the saddle, and gently, mind, for he was sword thrust in the shoulder."

The villagers fell back, intimidated by Leon's tone. A middle-aged couple pushed their way forward, staring into the boy's white face. The woman clapped her hands over her mouth. " 'Tis truly our Gaston," she moaned.

"Then hurry yourself and prepare to receive him," Leon said briskly. "It is not yet time to mourn him. Go quickly."

His tone steadied the woman. "This way, sir. The cottage by the well. Fetch water, Pierre," she threw over her shoulder, and hurried ahead of Leon and the youth carrying the supine figure.

Gaston's eyes flickered open and rested on the torch bearer. "Friends, 'fore God. They saved me." His eyes closed wearily.

Judith slid from her saddle to follow on Leon's heels. She heard the boy's words and gave silent thanks. The crowd had looked on them with hostility. Who had they armed themselves against? Baron or duke?

The cottage door stood wide and the woman was hastily putting flame to rushlighting. Straw pallets lay in a far alcove, and Leon was directed there. He and the youth knelt, laying the boy down. Leon glanced over his shoulder and saw Judith. His expression relaxed and he beckoned her.

Judith smiled at the hovering woman. "Are you Gaston's mother?" At the woman's nod, Judith went on. "Since I know this wound, having dressed it before our journey, will you allow me to remove the bindings and lay it bare for your attention? You will, no doubt, be more skilled than I in the treatment of injury and chance hurts."

Leon and the youth stood back as Judith knelt by the pallet. The woman knelt beside her, her face full of foreboding. She stared appalled as Judith unfastened the blood-soaked tunic.

"He has lost blood, naturally, for that is a factor when swords are used, but the blood on his face is from a mere scalp wound and of little consequence. When we have washed it away, he will look the boy he was." Judith spoke evenly and smiled at the woman who seemed numbed by what she was observing. "He is a healthy boy and should recover quickly." She hoped she was saying the right thing and the sword blade had not severed any vital part. "A brave son, you have, Mistress, for though wounded, he guided two lost travelers to the safety of your village."

The woman roused herself as Judith laid bare the wound, and turned to the pan of water her man had set by the bedside. Other women entered, bearing cloths and jars. When the ministrations were finished, Gaston lay fresh and cleansed, slumbering like a babe and with a healthier color to his face.

Judith rose unsteadily, her eyes blinking as smoke from the rushlight caught her. She staggered, feeling unutterably tired, and was caught by strong arms and led to a table. Her stomach contracted as she smelled meat stew. How long was it since they had eaten? Her mind dizzied with hunger and fatigue. Was that Leon clamping her fingers round a warm metal mug?

"Drink," came the familiar voice, and she obeyed, coughing as the rough red wine sheared a fiery path down her throat. Blinking away the tears, she smiled at the blur of faces. The mug was replaced by a steaming bowl, a stew thick with vegetables. She stared at it, almost too tired to lift the wooden spoon, but the scent was irresistible. She ate slowly, only half-listening to the murmur of words.

Judith remembered little more that night, save being led to a pallet and having a blanket tucked over her. The pervasive odor of goat was in her nostrils as darkness overtook her senses.

The bleating of goats woke her. That and the numbness of a hand trapped under a heavy body. Leon? No, Leon did not make that snuffling, sighing noise. Her eyes opened to look straight into a pair of yellow ones. Angel gave a gusty sigh, his long tongue snaking out to rasp on her cheek.

She laughed. "Get off my hand, you brute. And where have you been all night?"

A figure turned from the table. "Beside you, where else?" Leon grinned. "You know the way he has of stalking right through any obstacle. Divine right, he believes, and none dare say him nay."

Judith sat up, stretching. "How is Gaston?"

"Doing well. Wolfing food and basking in his mother's attentions and those of a pretty young village wench. A hero's return, no less."

"Are they for the baron?"

Leon shook his head. "They're for themselves and want to be left alone. Do you feel strong enough to travel today? I sense that these people, though grateful, are uneasy with strangers here. They ask that we take all three horses when we leave, for they are too fine-bred to belong to villagers."

"Will Gaston be safe?"

"Safer with his goats than where we found him." He smiled. "I believe he will stay close after his adventure."

Judith joined Leon at table as Gaston's mother

brought in food. She beamed at them and set down a cloth-bound bundle.

"A little food for your journey, and my blessing on you for bringing back my son."

24

Judith and Leon left the village in the hills and struck north, heading toward France. The third horse had become an encumbrance, but could not be turned loose until they were many miles from Gaston's homestead.

With Angel ranging ahead, they rode for most of the day without encountering any habitation or sign of life. Leon's eyes moved constantly, although this hilly landscape was far from the city of Vallone.

"We are safe now, are we not?" queried Judith. "Surely the duke's men will be concentrating on the city."

Leon's eyes softened a little as he glanced at her briefly. "Truly, their aim is to raze the city to the ground and eliminate all opposition, but for that they need all the forces they can muster. It would not surprise me if mercenaries of all nationalities flocked to the duke's banner."

"In the hope of finding rich pickings in Vallone?"

He smiled and shrugged. "That is the nature of mercenaries. The scent of victory is a powerful inducement."

Judith glanced about her. The countryside lay still and deserted but they had not yet reached the plains they must cross. She looked again at Leon.

"If what you suspect is the case," she said slowly. "Then these mercenary armies may come from all directions, not simply over the river from France."

"You take my point," Leon said, turning in his saddle

to glance behind. "Vallone is land-locked with borders into Italy and Spain as well as France."

Judith felt her heart flutter and she, too, glanced back. "Is the duke so rich he can afford to hire all comers?"

"Rich enough, and he will be richer still when he takes the treasury and regains the ducal fortune. There will be no mercy for the baron or his followers."

Judith shivered in spite of the heat. "Thank God we are heading away from the city."

Leon made no reply but continued to scan the countryside. He slackened their pace as the hills softened into hillocks and ridges. The flat country lay ahead, the country they must cross before reaching the river. He did not confide his fears that over every hillock might ride a band of mercenaries. He knew enough of soldiering to accept the fact that gain was a greater spur to a foot-loose soldier than the sheer excitement of battle. Combine the two and all the riff-raff of Europe would be on the move to Vallone.

"Time to rest," he said, smiling calmly and keeping his tone even. "Now that we are leaving the hills behind, we must travel by night and hide by day. A rider can be viewed from a great distance over flat land." He did not add that the sight of a woman with a lone escort would contribute to the spice of a chase. "See that small copse?" Leon pointed. "Head for that. The horses must be rested for a few hours before we go on."

Judith nodded, she was tired, but what did that matter, as long as they reached the river. It might be less heavily guarded with all the duke's forces heading for the city. They would surely find somewhere to cross into the safety of France.

Angel joined them as they dismounted and loosened the girth straps. The horses bent to the thick grass and Angel flung himself down, tongue lolling sideways. Leon took the precaution of hobbling the horses before joining Judith under the shade of a tree.

She had opened the cloth-wrapped bundles from

Gaston's mother to reveal bread, goat-cheese, and thick slices of cooked meat.

Leon grinned at her expression. "Goat meat, naturally."

"Praise heaven they cooked it, for we are without means to cook."

"A generous parcel too. It should suffice for the few days we need to reach the river."

Leon agreed and tossed a slice of meat to Angel, avoiding a direct look at Judith. It sounded simple, a few days' ride to the river but Leon's instincts told him that life was never that simple. They had been lucky so far when only the duke's forces were in the field, but now with the influx of adventurers and opportunists, greater caution must be observed.

When they had eaten, Judith folded the parcel carefully and put it away in a saddlebag. Angel's yellow eyes followed her movements. She patted his head.

"You will eat when we do, my friend. I trust you, but not that much."

Angel seemed to eye her reproachfully, then he sighed and dropped his muzzle on his outstretched paws. He watched her fold the goatskin jacket into a pillow and lie down.

"Guard," Leon said softly to the dog and he, too, stretched out.

When they awoke it was dark, the air still and cool. Angel opened one eye as Leon rose and looked expectantly at the saddlebag, but Leon was removing the hobbles from the horses. There was no sound, save night noises, the flutter of a settling bird, the squeak of a tiny creature moving into shelter. It was safe to proceed and Leon woke Judith by stroking her hair gently.

"Come, my love, we must cover the distance by dark. At dawn, when we find a safe place, you may sleep the day away."

Judith rose and put on her jacket. "Do we still take the horse along?"

"For now, yes. We cannot risk it returning by chance to the village, nor can we leave it here to give a clue of our passing." He smiled down at Judith. "I will think of something."

Judith nodded, quite sure that he would. Her trust was complete, her future in his hands and once they were safe, she was determined never to leave him, whoever he was.

They rode through the remaining hours of darkness, keeping to the higher ground of ridge and hillock, in order to scan the way ahead. As grayness began to replace the darkness of night, Leon's eyes searched for a retreat. A barn, a derelict building, even another copse, but it had to shelter three horses as well. He must rid himself of one, perhaps two, but one had to be kept for quick movement. There was no safety on foot, although concealment would be easier.

As the ground flattened, small areas of cultivated land began to appear, attended by a huddle of stone or wooden dwellings. Halting the horses, Leon examined the buildings carefully, looking for signs of habitation. At this time in the early morning there was usually movement, a fire lit, a pan set to boil or a peasant setting out to his field. There was no sign of a cow or goat, not even a chicken scratching in the dust, yet Leon continued to watch. There was a slight ground mist, but not enough to hide any movement.

The peasants might have fled with their possessions and livestock to the dubious safety of the city; or perhaps the duke's forces had come and gone like locusts, leaving nothing behind. Whichever was the case, a discreet approach was indicated. Leon slid from the saddle, giving the reins to Judith.

"Stay here with the horses, if you please. The place looks deserted but we must not run the risk of coming upon another company of the duke's men, resting the night."

"Will you take Angel with you for protection?" Judith

asked, trying to see Leon's face in the half-light. Her voice was low and tense.

"No. It is best I go alone." He bent to the dog, whispering a command, then he was gone, soft-footed over the grass.

None of the buildings had been destroyed, Leon found, but signs of a hasty departure were obvious. Cupboards and drawers stood open, emptied of their contents, and the heavy ruts outside the door were evidence that a cart had stood to receive the goods. Leon's investigation of the other buildings proclaimed the same pattern of activity. The whole community had fled. He stood for a moment, deciding which building they should use, then returned to Judith.

He smiled up at her and saw the tension leave her face. "Quite deserted. We shall stay in the most obscure and poorest of the cottages." He took the reins of his horse. "Come, I will lead you round the back of the main house, for that is the one a traveller might naturally look to first, just as I did. If such happens, we shall receive notice and be on our guard."

His tone was so calm that Judith relaxed. The dwelling he had chosen had the advantage of a window that commanded the entire hamlet and was a little withdrawn from the rest. It was tiny but reasonably clean and Leon left her there while he went in search of any overlooked supplies. He returned triumphant. The villagers had fled in such a hurry that they had left cattle fodder in the barn and vegetables in the plot.

"No fire until tonight," he warned. "We must be content with the offerings of Gaston's mother until it is dark enought to hide the smoke of a cooking fire. The horses are secured in the barn. Now let us eat and rest."

It was dusk as they dug up and carried indoors the root vegetables from the plot. Judith had discovered a half-plucked chicken cast aside and forgotten in the panic. As she watched the bubbling pot of chicken and vegetables, she wondered what had spurred the

villagers into such a hasty action. Rumors of an invading
army sweeping the countryside? A command from the
baron, to bring in every able-bodied man to defend the
city? The men would respond, but they would be
reluctant to leave their families behind.

They ate well as the light faded and Judith added the
remains of the chicken to the bread and cheese of their
original gift. Leon had the horses saddled, and as the
light died completely from the sky, they moved on. One
day nearer to freedom, Judith was thinking, when Leon
touched her arm.

He pointed, wordlessly, and Judith scanned the way
ahead. Pin points of light dotted the countryside and
even from a distance she caught the scent of cooking.
The lights were so numerous that she blinked.

"The duke's men?" she queried.

"Anybody's men, at a price, I would guess." Leon's
voice came softly. "The duke's men are round the city.
These are those late-comers I spoke of before."

"Will they let us through if we should run upon them?"

Leon's hand reached out and caught hers in the
darkness. "My sweet Judith, you know little of the ways
of the common soldiery. The duke's regular army has a
certain discipline, but mercenaries are almost a law unto
themselves. They will greet you with delight, for you are
a woman and women have the value of scarcity during a
campaign. Do you wonder that men flee with their
womenfolk when such soldiers are on the march?" Leon
squeezed her fingers in a comforting gesture as a cold
chill ran through Judith.

"You are right, of course. I didn't think. So we must
avoid these men, too."

"Yes, and that will not be easy. See how they spread in
front, as far as the eye can see. If sentries are stationed
some distance from the fires, as is prudent with all
companies, the gaps in between will be insufficient to
allow three horses to pass unnoticed."

"What can we do?"

"Our only choice is to turn west and hope to find shelter before daybreak."

"But the river—?"

"The river lies beyond those camps and is, I suspect, more heavily engaged in transporting men and horses than it was when the duke's men crossed over. So west it must be."

For the remaining hours of darkness they moved west, the twinkling campfires stretching on and on, evidence of hundreds of men all intent on reaching the city.

"Could any of these mercenaries be for the baron?" Judith asked.

"Could a bird of prey be persuaded to leave its victim? Since they are not bound to the baron, they will profit by his fall, and fall he must with such a force against him."

Judith remained silent as they traveled on. She could only be filled with thankfulness that her arrival in the city had been delayed, thus delaying Leon's return, too. Their view of the burning city from the ridge above it had filled her with horror. How could men enjoy such slaughter as she had seen? she wondered. Yet Quentin, Leon and King Richard, too, were, or had been, professional soldiers. Wives and mothers were forced to accept these facts even if they did not understand the lure of soldiering held in their menfolk.

Quentin and Leon, her mind had said. Were they one and the same, or was her mind beginning to accept the possibility of two separate men? But how could he know so much of Tarrant if he was not Quentin? In their present predicament, it served only to tease the brain and was of little consequence. Neither she nor Leon might survive to reach France and the whole question would be academic. The only certainty now was the man riding beside her. This one she loved and would never desert.

Leon's hand touched her arm. "Make for that stand of trees, the one where the bushes grow thick."

Judith nodded and glanced to her right. "I see fewer campfires now. Have we passed the main concentration of mercenaries?"

"Perhaps, but not necessarily," Leon answered softly. "It may be that they have allowed their fires to go out, since dawn is no more than an hour away. We must be well in hiding by then."

They reached the trees and Leon nodded with satisfaction on observing the rough, thorny bushes.

"Good protection, there. Their horses will avoid them at all costs."

"What of our own? They will surely protest if we force them through."

"I was thinking of ourselves and Angel. The horses I will hobble in that thicket a hundred paces to the west. Two of them, anyway."

"Two? What of the third?"

He looked at her and in the slight lifting of the darkness, she caught his smile.

"This is where we rid ourselves of the third horse. Come, help me take off the saddlebags. They stay with you and Angel behind these thorn bushes. All our supplies will be safe. I shall be gone no longer than I can help."

"Leon." Judith's voice was intent. "For the love of God, tell me what you intend."

He took her face in his hands and kissed her lightly. "What better time than just before dawn to introduce an extra mount into the horselines? The lookouts will be tired and bored, having seen nothing all night. They may well have fallen into a doze since no alarm has kept them alert. Horselines are usually set up a short distance from camp. I have only to circle the nearest site and tie our horse to the end of the line."

"But there will be a guard on the horses."

"If I know horse guards, the fellow will be asleep amongst his charges, leaving them to waken him by becoming restive for some reason."

"You will take care?" It was a woman's plea but Judith had to make it. "I—I could not bear to lose you."

"I will take care," Leon promised, smiling. "Now give me your promise to remain hidden in these bushes, whatever you hear. On no account do I want you to reveal yourself. Keep Angel close and wait in silence. Promise me that."

"Very well, I promise."

Leon left Judith and the saddlebags in a small space encircled by bushes. With Angel beside her, Judith listened to the soft movement of the horses as Leon guided them to the thicket he had pointed out. After that there was silence.

Judith waited in growing tension as time passed. It seemed an eternity before she heard the soft padding of boots. She laid a hand on Angel's ruff. The fur lay flat and unruffled. He would know Leon's step, and his lack of tension communicated itself to her, so that she was able to remain calm as Leon came carefully between the thorny branches. There was a cheerful grin on his face and he swung a straw-covered bottle by its string loop. He squatted beside her.

"Would you believe it, that rascally horse guard was awake and in sore need of a gossip. A garrulous fellow but I managed to make my excuses and slip away."

Judith stared blankly into the dark, scarred face. "You—you talked to him? Did he not challenge you?"

"Why should he? Mercenaries wear no badge when they're about their own business. He assumed I was from a neighboring camp, doing a little bargaining on my own account. A fine horse, he says, and I agreed. An officer's horse, he asks, and I agree again but add that its owner won't be wanting it anymore and I had one of my own. Maybe, I say, there's some young sprig in the camp who might be wishful of buying a good horse. They're all mounted, he says, but his words come too quickly to be true."

Leon reached for Judith's cold hands. "Don't look so

worried, my sweet lady. It was obvious that he was as eager as I to come to terms before the camp stirred. A bottle of red wine and a gold piece he offered, so I took them kindly and we parted on the best of terms. He'll doubtless ask five gold pieces from some willing buyer and we're rid of the horse anyway."

Judith smiled her relief but asked anxiously, "Did he see you come this way?"

"Judith, dear heart, do you think me a babe in arms that I walked straight here?"

Judith leaned her head on his shoulder. "I should know you better than that. It was a foolish question."

Leon stroked her hair. "But a natural one. No, I headed out of sight then came back in a wide circle. I used all the cover available." He paused and his voice became sober. "What I saw on that journey gives no comfort."

Judith raised her head. "What is it? Bad news?"

Leon nodded. "The mercenary armies grow thicker on the ground. They stretch from the river halfway to the city. I doubt Angel himself could pass between their ranks unobserved."

Judith felt her heart contract. "You mean we cannot proceed on our western course without encountering them?"

"Exactly. Since west and north are now barred to us, we must go back the way we came."

"To the hills?"

"No. To the city."

25

Judith's eyes widened. For a moment she stared blankly at Leon. "You cannot mean it! Not into the city, surely?"

Leon smiled. "Since the countryside is thick with armed men, we shall be driven ahead, whether we like it or not, toward the city. No place in advance of his army will be overlooked when they seek shelter. We cannot pass through them, so what would you have us do? Surrender?"

Judith shivered. "No, never that! They would show us little mercy."

"Then it only remains for us to reach the city first and not be driven like goats in a panic, flying here and there in confusion. I think we must not waste this day in sleep but move out immediately before full dawn. It takes time for a camp to come alive. They will eat and prepare themselves in leisurely fashion. We shall have an hour or two start."

Judith nodded and climbed to her feet. What was tiredness compared with the treatment they might meet at the hands of the mercenaries?

Leon rose and picked up the two saddlebags. "Come, my dear, let me help you through the bushes." He looked anxiously into her face. "You are tired. I am sorry."

Judith forced a smile. "Tired, but not tired enough to fall off my horse." Her gaze moved to the straw-covered bottle and she said, almost gaily. "A draught of red wine would not come amiss, but since you have offered me none—'' She saw Leon's face relax into a smile.

"How very remiss of me to be so discourteous. Forgive me, my lady, and try the wine. I know nothing of its origins, so blame the horse guard if it proves unpalatable."

Judith raised the bottle and swallowed a mouthful. It was harsh and unmellowed but sent a stream of fire racing through her body. She gasped and held out the bottle to Leon.

"Fierce, indeed," she managed. "But it will serve to warm us."

Leon tilted the bottle and even he gasped. '' 'Fore God, it's as raw as a new recruit but we'll not abandon it.''

They moved quietly out of the thornbush shelter and toward the small thicket. Swiftly Leon saddled the horses while Judith kept her fingers over their soft muzzles, murmuring gently to quell any objection to being saddled so soon.

"Quietly now," Leon said as they mounted. "Follow at a walk until we are safely out of earshot."

In the gray dawn mist, they went slowly, drifting like phantoms until no sound was heard from any direction. The sky was lighter, the mist beginning to disperse as a hint of gold showed on the horizon. Leon spoke over his shoulder.

"We may risk a gallop now. We will head for that deserted village again. At least there was fodder enough for the horses and we may rest them awhile.''

They rode on in silence, mile after mile as the sun rose and moved high in its course. Judith glanced sideways at Leon's intent face. His eyes still scanned the countryside with a soldier's thoroughness, but she sensed that his mind was occupied far ahead with some plan of action for when they reached the city. Dear God, the city! The fire, the screams of men and horses, the savage clash of steel, were sounds and pictures she hoped never to see or hear again. Yet Leon was preparing to lead her into that inferno. What choice had she but to follow where he led?

The deserted village came into sight, and Leon slowed the horses. It looked exactly as they had left it, but he took the same precautions as before. Nothing had been disturbed. Judith slid a little shakily from the saddle, and Leon led her into the same cottage as before. After stabling the horses, he joined her. He knelt by the saddlebag, removing the cold food. Judith watched him tiredly.

"Eat first and then sleep," he said, arranging a bed of sacking.

"Is it safe?"

"Not very," he answered, smiling. "But I feel we are a few hours ahead of the mercenary adance."

The chicken and goatmeat were eaten, and Leon persuaded Judith to drink some more of the strong, red wine. She was too tired to notice that he took none himself. She lay back on the sacks and fell instantly asleep. Leon looked down on her for a moment, his expression gentle, then he repacked the saddlebags and took them to the barn. Angel lay in the cottage doorway, watching, as Leon hoisted himself, by way of a water butt, on top of the flat-roofed barn. It was a good position from which to view the surrounding country-side, and Leon allowed his body to relax but kept his eyes open. He thought of the girl asleep in the cottage. Was it right to take her back to the city where heaven knew what dangers lay? But there was no alternative. Gaston's people would not welcome a return, nor would any other hill village accept them.

He knew the city well enough, its alleys and canals, churches and squares, to believe that they might pass between the beleaguered forces and the encircling armies. She must be kept safe, and only he could do that, God willing. She had courage and spirit. She also had the heart out of his breast, but she was still Lady Tarrant or Madame la Baronne, and Leon de Foret was a nobody.

He kept to his post until the heat had gone out of the sun and dusk shrouded the landscape. He doubted if any mercenary army had traveled as swiftly as they had, for supply wagons slowed progress and, anyway, pickings would be easier in an already devastated city.

As Leon climbed from the barn roof, he took a last keen look round him. An odd pinpoint of light showed. Camps settling for the night, he guessed. That was good. They might risk their own fire now, and even if it was only vegetables in the pot, a meal and rest would revive them.

He was surprised to find Judith missing from the improvised bed. Before he had time to feel alarm, she came into the cottage, a basket of vegetables hanging from her arm.

"I thought to find you still sleeping," he said.

Judith smiled. "And I thought to have the pot well bubbling when you gave up your position on the barn roof." She set down the basket and eyed its contents ruefully. "Turnips and carrots only. It was a very small plot."

Leon grinned his relief at her light tone and began to build a fire. "Peasant food it may be, my lady, but a man in hunger does not complain of his fare."

"Indeed not," Judith returned, chopping the vegetables. "He will go hungry else."

Darkness had quite fallen when the fire was doused and the horses saddled. Judith strapped her belt about her tunic and touched the leather pouch lightly. She smiled up at Leon.

"I have jewels in plenty but dine on turnips. Who would believe I came by them honestly if I bartered but one piece for common fare?" She pushed back her dark hair, wrinkling her nose at the smell of their goatskin jackets. "Will I ever be rid of this aroma, I wonder?"

"Aroma?" Leon asked solemnly. "I detect none that differs from my own, yet mine might be the more powerful, I agree. Shall I ride to your rear, my lady?''

Judith laughed. ''That is not what I meant and you know it. We have no choice in the matter, so please ride at my side. I will not have you out of my sight for a moment, dear Leon.''

Riding hard through the night hours, they came at last to the place where Judith had dressed the boy Gaston's pierced shoulder before he led them up the mountain track. They drew rein and stared across toward the city. The sky still held the faint glow of smaller fires; the great conflagration they had seen before was just a memory.

Judith watched Leon's face as he studied the city carefully. He glanced at her.

''To be sure, all the wooden buildings and bridges will be gone, but the palace and churches are of stone. I imagine the baron's forces will hold them to the last. The duke may be content to wait until his siege towers are built. Since there will be little unburnt wood in the city, his men will need trees for towers and battering rams.'' He looked behind at the wooden slopes. ''And this is where they will come.''

Judith glanced about apprehensively but was comforted by all lack of sound. No campfires glowed on the hillside.

''Why here?'' she asked.

''The best hardwood is from this hillside. Beyond the city, the old trees have already been felled to make way for cultivation of the land. Since the duke's attack was launched from the north and east, I imagine he remembered the lie of his own land and took the need for wood into his consideration. And because of that, my dear, we shall be safer in the city than out of it, once morning comes.''

''By the west gate, of course.'' Judith drew in a deep breath. ''That's what you told the vicomte, is it not?''

Leon smiled. ''I'm afraid it is, but at that time it was meant to divert him.''

"He could be waiting for you still."

"Indeed he could, but he is a man of little patience and that was several nights ago."

Judith opened her mouth to speak, but Leon went on calmly. "I know you are about to tell me that he may have left troopers to guard the gate and will not be there in person, yes? I agree, but sentries get bored and careless with inactivity. We must hope that is the case."

"Can we not forget the city and take to the mountains? Must we walk right into the lion's den?"

"Our friends in the hills want nothing to do with us, remember? And the mountains are bleak and inhospitable. No, it must be the city, and before dawn at that. Will you trust yourself to me?"

Judith accepted that he was determined on this course and nodded. "Yes. I trust you. We live or die together. There is no middle way."

Leon looked into the steady blue eyes and faintly smiling face, illuminated by the pink glow of firelight. He felt a sudden fierce urge to turn into the hills and be damned to the villagers' hostility as long as this woman became his. But that would serve nothing in the long term. With that vast army of mercenaries, not only the city but the hills would be scoured for rebels, whichever side won the victory.

Leon quelled the urge savagely. True freedom lay beyond the borders of Vallone, and that freedom he must strive to give her. There was no middle way, as she had said.

"Come," he said, keeping his voice level. "We will continue to close with the city until we reach the west gate."

They walked their horses, keeping to the grass, with Angel prowling ahead. They reached the gate in the grayness preceding the rising of the sun. The city seemed quiet, and Judith expressed this view a little nervously.

Leon smiled. "It is best to fight an enemy one can see.

Each side will be consolidating its position for a new dawn attack when a man can distinguish friend from foe. Ambush is too easy in the dark, away from the comfort of the firelight. And men must sleep, too."

The west gate stood open and inviting. Beyond, they could see dimly the burned-out ruins of houses with only an occasional stone building left between areas of desolation. No light, no movement caught their eye, but that signified nothing to Leon. Sentries might be hidden anywhere amongst these ruins. No gate was ever left unguarded to allow the free entry of opposing forces. But which side held the gate?

"There will be guards," Leon said. "Stay here with the horses while I go down."

Judith stared at him. "Alone?"

"No, my dear. You will have Angel."

"I was thinking of you. Take Angel, please. Should you be surprised, he will play his part." As Leon hesitated, Judith pressed her point. "I am safe enough, mounted. You will be on foot. Take him."

Leon slid from the saddle and handed her his reins. "Very well. Await my signal."

Judith watched as man and dog merged into the grayness. She felt very much alone in this alien place. All she could do was wait and pray that both would return unharmed. She glanced about her constantly, aware that a body of men could be lurking on this very hillside, eyes watchful, and she would not even see them. The half-light was full of shadowy figures, stretching her nerves as she waited. What had seemed an empty hillside before could well be alive with armed men.

She fixed her gaze resolutely on the west gate. It was merely the absence of Leon and Angel, nothing more, that was fueling her imagination, she told herself.

The soft pad of Angel's paws came to her first, then the long black body appeared. Behind him walked Leon, and Judith clenched her teeth to hold back a gasp of sheer relief.

Leon held up his arms and Judith slid from her saddle into them, knowing that he must hear her heart pound against his chest. He kissed her gently on the brow and held her close for a moment.

"I saw no one," he said.

"You mean the gate is unguarded completely?" she asked, surprised.

"I said, I saw no one, which is not quite the same thing, but we must take our chances and find shelter within the gates."

They followed Angel down the incline, walking together with a horse on either side as a barrier against some surprise attack from the flanks. But none came, and they passed through into the city. It was lighter now, and Leon's hand rested on his sword hilt as he urged the horses onto softer ground, away from the shattered wood that would have crunched under their hooves.

It was obvious to Judith from what she saw that the duke's army had passed this way in a triumphal progress. Since the houses were poor, the alleys narrow, the soldiers would not have wasted their time looking for treasure but would have headed toward the old Ducal Palace and more prosperous areas of the city. This section had been devastated from habit, doors kicked in and furniture smashed.

A narrow canal, choked with rubbish, lay before them. Leon paused, eying the wooden bridge spanning it. Rough planking ran between the balustrades, and the bridge's width allowed no more than a single rider or two foot-travelers. Horses' hooves reverberating on the wooden planks would give signal to any sentry. But the canal must be crossed if they were to reach any of the stone-walled cottages.

He drew his sword, motioning Judith to remain where she was, then gripped the reins of his horse.

"Let me reach the far end," he murmured over his shoulder, "and I will hold the bridge for you. Retreat if I am attacked, and I will join you on the hillside."

God willing, he said to himself, and led his horse onto the planking. Despite the slowness of his movements, there was no disguising the thud of hooves, but he reached the other side without apparent attention from any direction. He beckoned to Judith and stood, sword ready, as she crossed, leading her horse.

Nothing stirred, no slinking cat or breath of wind disturbed the desolation. Not even a bird passed overhead. Like a city of the dead, thought Judith, with an involuntary shiver. But the city was not dead, she reminded herself, only perhaps this western part of it. As if to confirm her last thought, a trumpet shrilled distantly, a signal for men to rise, take up their weapons, and face a new day of conflict.

Leon glanced at Judith. "You heard that? The battle is not yet resolved. The baron will put up a stiff resistance, for he knows what awaits if the duke overruns him. There'll be no surrender."

They moved on, Leon's eyes searching every shadowed alleyway, avoiding those that hinted of being cul-de-sacs. He looked for a stone cottage, preferably one with a clear view in all directions and surrounded by wooden debris. No party could approach in silence with splintered wood crackling underfoot.

He glanced down a slightly wider alleyway and was tempted by the sight of such a cottage, standing apart from its collapsed neighbors. The far end of the alley was open and unbound by wall. He glanced at the sky. Soon the sun would rise, and they must find shelter before then. He made up his mind and turned into the alley. A glance behind showed him Judith's white, strained face. She needed sleep, just as he did, but first the horses must be under cover, somewhere nearby, and the doors of the cottage barricaded against intruders. Only then could he relax.

There was a tavern to one side of the alley, its shutters and door smashed, but the odor of wine still hung about it. It had been a half-timbered building, but the timbers lay split and scorched, and only the stone shell remained. What stocks of wine it had possessed were gone, from the evidence of the flagon-strewed floor.

They passed the silent tavern, drawing nearer to the cottage. Behind it Leon saw an outhouse, also of stone, and his spirits lightened. A good place to stable the horses, he was thinking when an instinctive sense of danger laid a cold finger on him.

Angel, ranging ahead and nosing into derelict buildings, paused, his body stiffening. A low rumble began in the dog's throat, cut short by the sound of a blow. At the same time a half-chocked cry from Judith behind brought Leon's tired mind alert. He swung round, then froze into stillness as he saw the blade of a dagger at Judith's throat.

At the same moment his arms were pinioned behind him and a twin dagger lay coldly against his own throat. He knew a moment of utter frustration. Where, by the Saints, had these men come from? The place had been deserted, he could swear to it. How could this ambush have happened?

The moment of disbelief passed and his mind cleared. How many? There was Angel's attacker, of course. Two men with daggers, two more holding the horses, and another, hands on hips, grinning at him from a bearded, dirt-grimed face.

"And who have we here, my friends?" the man said, looking Leon up and down. "Though you smell like goat-herders, you have not the look of them. Pray tell me, good sir, what brings you and Madame to our fine city?" His voice held mockery. "Or could it be that you are leaving our fine city?" He put his head on one side. "Tell me true, good sir, before I order your throats to be cut. Are you for the baron or the duke?"

26

Leon stared impassively into the bearded face, then let his cold glance move over the man's companions, seeking a clue to their own allegiance. Dear God, what a question the man had posed! If he gave the wrong answer, their throats would be slit, bodies left to rot. There was little to be learned from the men's appearance. All were ragged, dirty and bearded, faces taut and lined.

Judith's gaze passed Leon. She saw Angel and gasped. Her eyes flashed angrily. The dog lay in the doorway of a wrecked house, muzzle and forelegs roped. Clubbed, no doubt, for his yellow eyes were dazed and blood ran from a gash in his scalp.

"For the love of God, what harm has my poor hound done, that you truss him like a chicken?"

The man holding the blade to her throat blinked and took an involuntary step backward under her fury. She struck aside the arm holding the dagger and ran to fling herself to her knees beside Angel. The men watched her, uncertain what to do; then the leader looked at Leon.

"You've a spirited woman there. She cares more for that ugly brute of a dog than for these fine horses." He fingered the fine leather saddles. "Spanish leather, if I'm not mistaken, and corn-fed horses into the bargain."

One of his companions spat in the dust and eyed Leon malevolently. "They'll not find corn here, search as they might."

The undertone of bitterness in the man's voice was a slender clue, and Leon picked it up, his expression still impassive.

"Fine horses the duke had when he set out, but they'll be horsemeat before long." Leon's tone was casual, and the leader looked at him sharply.

"So you'll not be minding if we cut up your fine horses to feed ourselves?"

Leon shrugged, feeling his way carefully. "Supply wagons are crossing the river daily, but you'll know that, of course."

"And well-guarded, I'll be bound," burst out a young man.

"Hold your tongue," barked his leader and turned his glance on Leon. "Since you know so much, you must be a spy, so we'll make an end of you as you've no mind to answer my first question." His gaze moved to the man still holding the knife across Leon's throat.

"Hold back a second, friend," Leon said curly. "You've a mind too hasty and suspicious. Did you expect me to declare myself without knowing who was asking the question? If I'm a spy, I'm certainly not a fool into the bargain."

The leader hesitated. "You'll not deny these horses are come from France with the duke?"

"No," Leon said. "I don't deny that." He grinned suddenly. "But you've heard of theft, haven't you? Don't confuse horse with rider or you'll be short of many a comrade."

"You stole them from under the noses of the duke's men?" The leader was still suspicious, but now there was a hint of uncertainty in his voice.

"Along with a vicomte to give my lady and me safe passage."

"Safe passage out of the city?"

Leon sighed, sure of his ground now. "Were we leaving the city when you came upon us? Since you must have been watching the west gate, you could hardly fail to see us enter." He stared narrowly at the leader. "You lead these men. By what right, and what rank do you hold?"

"I am Otto Gerhardt, corporal in the city guards. And your name?"

"De Foret, Capitaine de Foret."

One of the men made a hissing sound through his teeth. "De Foret?" He peered closely at Leon. "By the saints, they said you were dead. Truly de Foret?"

"Truly. And you?"

The man shrugged. "Just Bruno, Capitaine. I possess no other name."

The knife had gone from Leon's throat and the men crowded round.

"You are maybe six," Leon said. "Where is the rest of your company?"

The leader, Otto, shrugged. "One in there to guard our backs." He jerked his head at the tavern. "The baron called all men to him to defend the palace. We, at the west gate, were too far distant to make the journey in time. Now there is no way through." He shrugged again philosophically. "So we guard the gate and harry where we can."

"I see. Seven men, and I make the eighth." Leon smiled. "A pitiful harrying force, Corporal, but we might pick off a few of the duke's men if we mount patrols toward the palace. Two patrols of four men. How does that strike you?"

The men looked eager. " 'Tis poor work here, Capitaine, until the enemy begins to flee. There'll be fine killings then, when the baron drives them out."

Leon nodded but kept his own counsel. The baron was bottled up in the palace, surrounded by the duke's men, and when that horde of mercenaries arrived, his straits would be even more dire. Well, he, Leon, was back in the city and, for better or worse, must lead these men against the ducal forces.

"Tell me, Corporal," Leon said, using the brisk tone of a soldier and an officer. "That cottage I was heading for.

Is it habitable?"

"Yes, sir, fair enough, but we use the tavern ourselves.
We've a couple of rooms in the stone end and place to
spare for you and the woman." His glance slid toward
Judith, who had removed Angel's bonds and was
cradling his head in her arms. "The wench could cook
for us and maybe make herself obliging in woman's
ways."

He brought his gaze back to Leon's face, and the
knowing smile faded as he met the icy stare from cold
gray eyes. Leon spoke slowly and distinctly, but under-
lying menace filled every word.

"As you implied yourself, Corporal, our goatskin attire
does not sit upon us naturally, but dismiss from your
mind the thought of my companion being obliging
wench or kitchen woman. She is a gently born lady, and
honor demands that I keep to the oath I swore as her
protector." His cold eyes traveled over the assembled
men. "Should anyone dispute my right, he has only to
say so."

Judith was at Leon's elbow. She had heard the conversation and now touched Leon's arm lightly.

"Do not glare so fierce, my love." She bestowed a
smile upon the company. "No man here will dispute the
right of husband to protect his lady wife when apprised
of the situation."

The corporal glanced uneasily from Leon to Judith.
"Your pardon, Madame, I was not aware—I thought—"

"Well, think no more on it, Corporal," Judith returned
crisply. "I will grant you pardon only if you provide me
with cloth and water to bathe the head of my faithful
friend. You can do that, surely?" Her brows arched in
question, and the man responded to the trace of
hauteur in her voice.

"Indeed, Madame, at once. I will send them to the
cottage."

By his tone, both Judith and Leon realized that here
was a man more used to taking orders than issuing

them. Leon strengthened their authority by saying over his shoulder as he made toward Angel, "Put the horses in the outhouse, Corporal, and water them. Bring the saddlebags to the cottage." He bent over the dog. "Come, my friend, up on your feet. I'm damned if I'll carry you, for you've the weight of a young horse."

Without looking back, they walked to the cottage, Leon's fingers deep in Angel's ruff as he guided the dog's stumbling steps.

"Heaven be praised," Leon said as he looked at the cottage. "This is the first reasonably whole door we've come across." He grinned at Judith as they entered. "And a solid dresser to bar it with when you're alone."

"Alone? Holy Mother, Leon, you were really serious about those patrols you spoke of to the corporal?"

"Of course. What else can I do but fight for the baron since they are aware of my identity?"

Judith sank onto a shaky-legged stool by the dresser and looked up at Leon. "We both know how the struggle will end, yet you propose to risk your life in what can only be a futile attack against the duke's men."

"Dearest—" began Leon, then stopped as he heard the feet crunch toward the cottage.

A young man came carryng a half-filled leather bucket of water, a cloth of uncertain age over his arm.

Judith rose and took them from him. "I thank you. Your name is—?"

"Sigmund, Madame de Foret." He smiled shyly from a round face covered by thick freckles and grime.

"I am obliged, Sigmund." Judith returned his smile. "Was it you who clubbed my dog?"

"Oh, no, Madame!" His tone was emphatic. "I don't hold with hurting animals. I'd have kept him quiet with these." He spread out a pair of large hands, palms uppermost. "I've held many a goat or sheep silent while they've been branded."

"You're a country boy, Sigmund?"

"Aye, Madame, and I wish—" He stopped, looking

fearfully at Leon. "But I'll be doing my duty, sir."

"I'm sure of it," Leon said pleasantly. "And the sooner we get this bit of bother over, the sooner you'll be able to go back home."

"Yes, sir, thank you, sir. I'll go and feed the horses now."

When he had gone, they bathed Angel's head. "Not too bad," commented Leon. "A day or so and he'll be back to normal." He straightened and took Judith's hand. "Let us now investigate our domain. There may be a bed of sorts for you."

The cottage boasted one lower and one upper room only. Downstairs, apart from the dresser, there were two stools and a table. Upstairs, a thin straw-filled palliasse lay on the floor and a few hooks adorned the walls. One small cupboard proved empty when Judith opened its door.

"I am doomed," she said with a wry smile, "to retain my goatwoman attire since my hope of finding some other garment has come to naught."

Leon smiled. "Come, let us finish our food, then I will consult the corporal while you rest upstairs."

"You will not go tonight, please, Leon, for you are worn to the bone yourself."

"Later perhaps, for a tired man is a careless one." He smiled. "I may well fall over my sword and give our position away, but I must know how this little band is armed and where the duke has positioned his forces."

Despite his injury, Angel's appetite had not lessened. They shared the remains of their food and Leon departed.

Judith stared about her. How drear and lonely she felt when Leon was absent, even for a short time. The thought of eight men attacking the soldiers of the duke appalled her, but they would see it as a duty. And if Leon, one night, did not return—the thought was too dreadful to contemplate. She shivered, hugging her shoulders with her arms. Without Leon to protect her, what was she but a wench to be taken by any man? Obliging in woman's ways, the corporal had said before she had proclaimed herself Leon's wife. Small protection if he was killed, but one thing she had determined on if fate went against them. She would not die a maid, but a woman who had lain with the man of her choice.

Water. Where had Sigmund obtained that bucket of water? Not from the choked canal, for the water had been clean. A well, then, somewhere, quite close. The boy had not been long after them.

In the shadow cast by the dresser, she glimpsed a small doorway. A back door to the cottage. That might prove of use if the duke's men came this way. She picked up the leather bucket and made for the door. Leon would not want her venturing down the main street, but there could easily be a well somewhere behind that had served the needs of the tavern and cottage and all those now-derelict ruins in between. The small door held a large iron key in its lock and turned with surprising ease considering its rusted and pitted appearance. And there, not ten yards distant, was the well, backed by a group of small bushes.

Judith went to the well, set the handle of the bucket onto the chain hook, and lowered away. The handle that drew up the filled bucket was smoothed by years of use. With an effort she steered the bucket onto the well's rim and carried it, slopping, back to the cottage. Angel's eyes followed her as she mounted the stairs. He was looking better, she decided, less dazed and cleaner for the grooming she had given his rough coat. For herself, she had the same aim in mind, and surely Leon would be grateful to strip and wash himself too. The vexing problem of clothes remained. Over cleaner bodies, they must necessarily put on the stained and goat-smelling garments.

Leon came two hours later and, finding no sign of

Judith below stairs, called her name in anxious tones
and pounded up the shaky steps. He stopped abruptly
as he saw her lying on the straw palliasse, her dark, wet
hair spread about, her body covered only by her old
gown.

"Thank God!" he said in a rush of words. "I thought
you'd wandered off or been spirited away by some
duke's man."

Judith smiled. "This is not a good place to wander in,
and should I have seen a duke's man, why, you would
have heard my scream a mile away."

He looked down on her. "There is something different
about you. What is it? I am at a loss to account for the
change."

Judith began to laugh. "Dearest Leon, you have seen
me so long begrimed, your mind is taxed by my
cleanliness. It is quite simple to comprehend." She eyed
him solemnly. "One takes a bucket of water and washes,
removing one's clothes, naturally."

He laughed, and Judith's heart turned over with her
love.

"But naturally," Leon said, "I remember that part." He
looked at the half bucket of water. "I've a mind to do the
same, then sleep the day through. The corporal has
promised to watch the place until he calls me at dark."
He picked up the bucket. "I will take this downstairs
and—"

"And come back up when you are clean?" cut in
Judith. "Or do you propose to find yourself a dusty
corner in which to sleep away the day?"

Leon looked a little startled by the caustic note in her
voice. "What would you have me do?"

Judith leaned up on one elbow and glowered at him.
"By all the Saints, Leon, you try my patience sorely. You
made no denial when I declared myself Madame de
Foret. Will your corporal not think it odd to find us
divided in sleep when he calls you? Especially as there is

no palliasse downstairs.''

Leon smiled. ''Truly, you have a valid point there, and that mattress is wide. I will not disturb you when I return.''

''Dear God above!'' Judith made an explosive sound. ''You disturb me constantly, and I begin to wonder why I love you.'' She stared at him moodily. ''Does honor still demand that you deliver me to the baron? If so, then I may tell you it will prove much harder than you anticipate, for I would as soon take Sigmund.''

Leon set down the bucket and began to strip off his clothes. ''You will not take Sigmund. I forbid it.''

''You forbid it? By what right?''

Leon smiled over his shoulder as he sluiced down his body. ''Have you not declared it yourself? I am your husband.''

''In pretense only.'' Judith lay down, staring at the wooden rafters. She heard the slop of water in the bucket and the sounds Leon made as he rubbed his skin with his discarded shirt. She heard the smile in Leon's voice as he spoke.

''I will hold you from the baron as I hold you from Sigmund or any other man save myself.''

Judith turned her head slowly. Leon stood naked by the bucket, rubbing his forearms on the shirt. She could not tear her eyes away from that lean, muscled body. Broad-shouldered and lean-hipped, the dark curling hair on breast and loins held her fascinated gaze.

''You're beautiful,'' she whispered. ''Like Adonis and Apollo—''

''And you, my heart, are Venus and Aphrodite.'' He came quickly to the mattress and lay down beside her, gathering her into his arms. ''The baron will soon be in the hell of his own making, but should he survive, I will not give you up. Will you take me as your very unlawful husband, Madame de Foret?''

Judith slid her arms about his neck and kissed his

mouth and cheeks. Her lips lingered on the scar on his temple. "I would have taken you weeks ago, my love, save for your ridiculous scruples."

Leon's fingers stroked her breasts and he laughed softly. "Scruples do not warm a man's heart like a loving woman." His hand smoothed the flat stomach, and Judith felt her breathing quicken as did her heart.

"And what decided you to abandon those scruples?" Judith asked, her limbs softening to his touch. "The corporal's suggestion that I become common property?"

"Not a bit of it, though I would have cut down the first one to lay a finger on you. My reasons are purely selfish and do me no credit."

"Tell me, then." Their faces were very close, eyes level. "Tell me why you have denied me until now that love which the simplest of peasant wenches can enjoy? Am I not a woman too?"

"Indeed you are, my love. I have been aware of it for many a week." His lips moved over hers and he was smiling into the blue eyes. "So many nights I have wasted in clinging to my fraying honor, but no more. I care nothing for the baron's cause, nor yet the duke's. I care only for you, my sweet Judith."

"This venture you plan with the corporal is quite mad."

"Quite mad, but there is no escaping it. I will come back, never fear."

And if you should not, Judith said silently to herself, I will at least have known the love of the man I love. At that point her thoughts scattered as her senses took command.

Her body seemed to melt into the palliasse and she no longer heard the rustle of straw as Leon caressed her thighs. His dark head bent over her, kissing and caressing, and she gave herself up to the magic heat of the flames that burned and burst in her like a torrent as their bodies fused in unbearable joy. She was blind and deaf to everything save the rhythm of Leon's body. The blood sang so loudly in her ears that her own soft moans went unheard.

27

Judith and Leon came awake together as the corporal's voice called hoarsely. Leon was off the mattress in seconds, his hand reaching for his sword. Then he relaxed at the man's words.

"It is dusk, Capitaine. I bring a pan of food for you and your lady. The patrol assembles at the tavern."

"Very well, Corporal. Give me ten minutes."

"Yes, sir." The sound of his steps faded, and Leon began to dress quickly.

Roused from sleep so abruptly, Judith felt a little dazed, then the real and frightening world flowed back into her mind. Leon was going into the city to seek out the duke's men and engage in bloody combat. Her love was so strong that just one night in his arms was not enough, it must last forever, and yet it might well be all she had to remember.

She rose too and began to pull on her clothes. Leon buckled on his sword belt and smiled.

"There is no need for you to distress yourself, my love."

"Would you expect me to sleep like some contented babe until you return? No, I shall join you for food, then lay out the vicomte's medicines and cloths and recharge the water bucket. There may be injuries," she finished flatly, avoiding his eyes.

"Yes, indeed," Leon said gently. "But I will take no risks, nor allow the rest of my patrol to do so."

They descended the stairs together and found the pan

of broth. As they ate, Leon looked at the dresser worriedly.

"I'd like that heavy piece to bar the door, but I doubt you have the strength to move it."

"We can do it together," Judith said. "You may not have noticed, but there is a back door and it has a key."

Leon's brows cleared. "Splendid. Promise me that you will lock yourself in after we are gone."

"Of course, after I have been to the well."

"There is a well?"

Judith smiled, almost gaily. "Did you suppose it a miracle bucket filling itself like the widow's cask of oil?"

Leon laughed and pushed the broth pan toward Angel, who cleaned it expertly with a long, pink tongue.

The dresser was hauled into place and Leon left by the back door. Judith heard his boots crunch over the wooden wreckage and he was gone. It was getting darker. She must fetch water first, then lock the back door. How long would the patrols last, and what on earth did four men hope to achieve except, perhaps, their own deaths? Later, securely locked in, the bucket refilled, she laid out the contents of the vicomte's saddlebag. A few pots and powders, a little cloth—a poor showing to treat a desperate wound. Young Gaston's wound had taken the greater part of the supplies.

For the sake of something to pass the time, Judith went through the dresser drawers and cupboards. The occupants of this cottage had not left in quite such haste as those in the country hamlet. There had been time enough, Judith thought bitterly, and unreasonably, she admitted, for them to pack everything of value. A small candle stub in the back of a drawer cheered her, but then she had nothing with which to light it. She shrugged. Perhaps it was as well. A light might attract attention.

A threadbare towel, a frayed headkerchief, and a chipped horn beaker were her only finds. Better than nothing, for a girl who possessed naught, save a pouchful of Tarrant jewelry, she acknowledged wryly.

It was full dark now, with only the gleam of moonlight making a pale square on the small high window. She sat down on one of the stools to wait. Angel yawned and spread himself out by the wall.

"Just you and me, friend," Judith murmured. "We might well be the last living creatures on this earth."

Angel yawned again and sighed gustily. Judith heard the thump of his tail on the wooden floor. It was comforting not to be quite alone, but her heart ached for Leon's return and she prayed silently that he would come back as whole as he had left. She laid her arms on the table and rested her head on them.

After what seemed hours, faint sounds reached her. Angel was on his feet, listening too. A soft tread of boots, then a tapping on the back door. Angel reached it first, and Judith dropped a hand to his ruff as she joined him. His muzzle was down, snuffling at the slight gap under the door. His tail thumped against her thigh as Leon's voice called softly.

Judith's hands trembled as she turned the large key. It was much brighter outside, and Leon stood outlined against the sky. He stepped forward and Judith almost fell into his arms.

"Thank God you are back! Are you hurt, did you find—"

"Let me in first," Leon said, grinning, "and I'll tell you all you want to know."

He locked the door behind him and took her one-handedly into his arms.

"You are hurt!" Judith said. "Your arm—"

"Not at all. Look closer. It's holding a bag. Let me put it on the table, then I'll have two free arms for you."

There was a clink as he set the bag down, then both his arms embraced her. He lifted his head. "Were you sitting in the dark?"

"Of course I was. What other choice did I have?" She

felt heady with relief and found herself smiling foolishly in the darkness. "Oh, I found an end of candle, but one needs some kind of flame to light it."

"And I left you too abruptly to think of it. I'm sorry. I brought food and a closed lantern from the tavern. Close those shutters while I light it."

Judith obeyed and heard the scratch of flint, then a soft flame glowed from the candle in the lantern. Leon set it in the middle of the table and produced a wrapped bundle from the bag.

"Sausage and bread, a few apples, and this." He showed her a dagger, still in its sheath and attached to a fine leather belt.

"Taken from one of the enemy," he explained. "I would have had his sword too, but his comrades were too quick for me." He laid the dagger down. "It's for you. You need something for your own protection when I am absent. Now let us eat and drink some of that terrible red wine." He paused. "I should have brought a mug from the tavern." He grinned cheerfully. "I'm afraid Madame must drink from the bottle again."

"I found a beaker," Judith declared triumphantly. "A little chipped, but it will suffice after I have rinsed it. I found a towel and headkerchief too, but never mind that. Tell me what happened. Was anyone hurt?"

"No, but a few of the duke's men were. A worthwhile patrol, I think. This kind of action makes them nervous."

Judith cradled Leon's dark head on her breast as he slept. Was it danger and the possibility of sudden death that made their love-making take on such urgency? In such moments, man and woman turned to each other for comfort and satisfaction of desire. Judith smoothed his tangled hair, smiling in the darkness before dawn. All those weeks when Leon had clung to his duty as escort for the baron's bride had not been wasted, for she had learned much of him.

Yet here he was, leading the baron's men into battle

for a leader in whom he had lost faith since his infamous killing of the old duke. Perhaps that fact and her own encouragement had broken down Leon's resistance to making her his own. After all, she thought cynically, the baron could not have expected a virgin widow, just a well-born woman. She was still well-born, and gave thanks that her introduction to bodily pleasure had been made by Leon, not by that self-styled baron.

Leon stirred in her arms and she knew he was awake. Her hands stroked the hard back, reaching down to the firm hips, and she let her fingers explore the muscled thighs, curling through the thickness of hair.

"Shameless hussy," he grunted sleepily, but she heard the laugh in his voice.

"Shameless, is it?" she asked softly. "Then tell me to stop this instant and I will obey, my lord."

"Too late, my sweet. You must suffer the consequences of your actions."

"Willingly, dear Leon, though suffer is not the appropriate word."

Leon's arms came about her, holding her close as his manhood asserted itself. For a moment they lay, breast and thigh together, then Leon's body covered hers and she took him into her, legs and arms clamped tightly about him.

Later, they lay, hand in hand, their faces turned to each other.

"I must get up," Leon said, "and attend to less serious business." He grinned and swung his legs over the mattress edge. He stood, stretching, then moved to where his clothes lay in a heap. Judith's gaze followed the lean, taut figure. They were so completely one, she had no thought of averting her eyes in modesty, any more than she thought of covering her own body from his gaze.

Angel's impatient snuffling at the door below caught their attention. "I'll let him out and see to the horses at the same time," Leon said. "No alarm, just his natural need to go outside for a moment."

He looked down on Judith, a faint frown between his eyes. "I can't help thinking of those mercenaries. They weren't far behind us. Most of them may follow the duke's tracks into the city, but some are bound to investigate this gate. I must talk to the men and plan an escape route."

"Isn't this cottage safe enough? It is stone-built."

"Our supplies of food don't run to a siege, my love, and a battering ram would have the place in ruins soon enough if they suspected it occupied. The same with the tavern. We must consider an avenue of retreat before the mercenaries arrive."

He clattered down the stairs, and Judith rose quickly to dress. Yes, she could see that an undamaged cottage might prove inviting, if only for shelter and without thought of it being occupied. Leon's words came back to her as they had looked at the mercenaries' campfires. They would welcome you with delight, for you are a woman, he had said. She shivered, pulling the goatskin jacket over her tunic. Downstairs, she saw the dagger, still in its sheath, lying on the table. Better that than be taken alive for the mercenaries' amusement. She pulled off her own belt and slid the loop of the sheath onto it, then buckled it on again. The original belt she put into the saddlebag with the vicomte's potions. There might be a use for it.

The back door was open and she moved outside. The outhouse door opened on this side of the cottage. That might prove useful if they needed the horses in a hurry. Angel was nosing about in the rough ground, and there was no sign of Leon. Judith moved to the well. Standing on its rim, she could see the west gate over the collapsed houses. She stared in other directions and imagined that she caught stirrings of sound from the city center. Distant plumes of smoke spiraled upward. Not the thick, choking smoke of burning buildings, but more like the campfires they had passed. Both armies must be preparing for another day of fighting, and the duke would have the advantage of his supply wagons. He could afford the time to starve the baron into surrender, but Leon had talked of siege towers, which implied the duke's wish to hang a healthy baron on the city gates, not an emaciated skeleton.

She looked toward the west gate again and tried to follow its progress. Several buildings appeared to have been constructed with or very close to the walls. The most distant one had a pitched roof and what might have been a bell tower built at one end. A church perhaps, or part of a convent. A footfall made her jump and cling to the bucket chain, but it was Leon.

"For the love of God, don't fall into the well," he exclaimed and crossed to her with long strides to grip her about the waist. "What do you think you are doing?"

"Looking at the lie of the land and keeping an eye on the west gate."

He swung her down, smiling. "The gate is under constant observation, and the hillside beyond."

There was a change in his tone, and Judith looked at him questioningly. "The tree-fellers?"

"Exactly. The duke is losing no time. He wants his revenge quickly." He looked over her head. "Tell me, did you see anything that resembled a church, on your survey of the land?"

"I thought I saw a bell tower, at least something square over a roof that might have been one, but it was too distant to tell if there was a bell inside."

Leon nodded. "The corporal mentioned an old priory built into the west wall. That could be the Santa Dominic. It was Spanish, but the monks died and Spain did not send out more. The corporal says it has been unused as long as he can remember."

"So, you are considering it a place to retire to, when the mercenaries come?"

"It's position is an advantage and, being deserted for so long, it should not interest any looter. Whatever it held of value must surely have gone back to Spain. The old duke would have held in respect any religious relics."

Leon stepped onto the stone blocks of the well rim and stared toward the old priory.

"A fair way from the gate, and it may well have several outer doors. Even a battle-crazed soldier will hesitate to destroy a house of religion." He glanced toward the cottage and the small open door. "I mistrust a place that has but one retreat to its credit." He smiled down on her. "And we cannot be forever moving that dresser." He stared again in the distance and nodded. "Yes, I think the old priory will serve us better." He stepped down. "I'll take a look at it and decide our best route."

"Can I come with you?"

"No, my darling. I want you safe here when I come back. There may be the odd straggler about, looking to find a little benefit for himself while the siege towers are being built."

They were moving back to the cottage when Sigmund appeared, carrying a bowl of food. He flushed with pleasure as Judith, glancing into the pot, smiled at him.

"It smells good, Sigmund. Did you cook it yourself?"

"Yes, Madame." He shrugged. " 'Tis only a bowl of oatmeal with a little honey added. Not fit for a lady, but we've little enough left." He glanced at Leon. "You spoke of supply wagons, sir. Would they be near enough to raid?"

Leon looked thoughtful. "We might try that, but not for a day or two. The first wagons will be too well guarded, I fear, for battle gives a man keen appetite." He studied the boy's face for a moment. "Tell me, Sigmund, what you know of the Santa Dominic."

"My grandfather talked of it, sir, for the monks still lived there in his time. Once a year he came to Mass, for our village is high on the hills. I always imagined those monks living inside the wall, when I was a boy. He talked of dark places underneath, but I have never dared go since it became empty."

"Will you come with me to look at it today? I fancy it will hold more protection than either cottage or tavern. That is," he went on carefully, "if the duke enlists the aid of foreign troops."

Sigmund's round face looked perplexed. "Foreigners, sir?"

"Soldier's of fortune, lad. There are many such about who could well be tempted by thought of profit to join this fight. For duke or baron, who can guess, but the city will suffer either way."

"Aye, sir," Sigmund said slowly. "And we'll not know friend from foe until it's too late."

"You take my meaning exactly," Leon said. "A man without true allegiance will take what he will, and who shall stop him? We are eight men. Can we hold the west gate against an army?"

"But if they're for the baron—"

"Well and good, Sigmund, but we have no badge between us. How will they know us for friends? Did you not take us for spies, yourself?"

"You're right, sir. Only the corporal had a badge, and that got torn away in a fight. We're none of us real soldiers but came to the baron's call." He looked from the cottage, down the alley to the shattered tavern as if with new eyes. He grinned boyishly. "Aye, sir, you're right at that. 'Tis not much of a place to hold for the baron. I'll come with you, sir, right gladly, for I've a fancy to see for myself this Santa Dominic."

It was late afternoon when they returned. Leon was satisfied with what they had found.

"A stout place with walls several feet thick but little left in the way of a gate. It's built into the wall but appears to have no entrance through it, which is a pity. However, the city wall has crumbled a few yards away, and we might chance the horses to graze outside. I doubt they'd be seen from the west gate."

"Is the place easily reached from here?" asked Judith.

"A few alleys and a turn over a canal bridge, but the tower is visible." He smiled. "No bell, I'm afraid. The Spanish must have taken it with them. There's a good view from the tower. I saw several camps."

Judith looked at him sharply. "The mercenaries?"

Leon nodded. "Must be. We'll move tomorrow."

"Tomorrow? Why not tonight?"

"Because we are short of supplies. I saw several wagons enter the city last night. Food is coming in, and tonight the duke's men will be well fed. We need some of that food if we're going to hold out in the Santa Dominic. Tonight, both patrols will be going out."

Judith stared at him, her heart growing cold. "You might all be killed."

Leon grinned and kissed her. "We shall be like shadows, my love. We are not intending to march together in a body. That would be foolishness indeed."

Judith sighed and clasped her hands together tightly. "You will do as you wish, I suppose," she said.

"I have to go, don't you see? Would you have me play the coward when these men know me for a baron's officer?"

Judith shook her head and tried to smile. "I understand, I really do, but the thought of losing you preys heavily on my mind."

Leon drew her to her feet. "It lacks an hour to dusk. Let us make better use of that time than by morbid thoughts of what may happen." He looked at her quizzically. "Is it not the traditional way of bidding farewell to a departing knight? Will you honor me with your love?"

Judith held him close. "You have it already, body and soul."

They ascended the stairs, arms about each other. The dying sun threw its beams over the straw mattress, and the golden light fell on their naked bodies as the act of love was performed. Leon was gentle at first, caressing the gold-edged body under his hands as if to imprint its lines on his memory. Then the depth of their love overcame them and they locked together in a fierce passion, blotting out time and place, past and future, in a maelstrom of the senses.

28

Leon de Foret, with Sigmund beside him, crouched against the low garden wall of a tumbledown cottage, watching the unloading of a supply wagon. Bruno and the fourth man in the patrol, Jean, were some yards distant behind the same wall. Long-poled pitch torches lighted the scene outside a stone barn where troopers were storing the sacks and barrels.

The night was sultry, without a breath of wind, and the soldiers sweated as they manhandled the goods off the wagon. Two pairs of hands were needed to carry grain sacks and roll the heavy barrels. The men wiped sweating brows between each bout of working. From the low mutterings and sour expressions, Leon deduced that they had been hard at work for several hours without a break. But these supplies, even if they could reach them, were too large to carry away in safety.

Leon glanced along the wall toward Bruno and Jean as another, smaller wagon rolled into view and stationed itself beyond the wagon they were observing. Bruno caught Leon's eye and nodded, jerking his head toward the newcomer. Leon touched Sigmund's arm and they moved, crouching, to join the two men. Leon peered over the wall. He could just see the rear of the second wagon. He patted Bruno's shoulder.

The man grinned. "I smell salami and fresh-baked bread. Maybe sent for those unloading the big wagon."

Leon nodded. "And maybe they'll not begrudge us sharing their supper." He looked at the heavy wagon.

"Almost empty. Wait until they're called away, and if you see a chance of getting to the small wagon, take what you can from it."

They waited as the last barrel rolled from the wagon. At that point, an older man appeared and the tired troopers fell into line and marched away. A new group headed for the smaller wagon. Most had discarded their tunics in the heat of the campfire but still retained sword belts.

"Let the first batch go," Leon ordered. "Then we'll stroll over and help ourselves. Don't load yourself with too much. It will rouse suspicion. Keep out of the light, if possible. I'll go first. Follow casually, don't hurry."

He slid over the wall and moved into the shadow cast by the empty wagon. As he rounded it, he saw two guards talking together at the head of the smaller wagon. He did not pause but slouched on, conscious of their idle glances. A sack with bread rolls caught his eye and he hefted it, pulling out a small bag with his other hand. It was soft, perhaps meat, then he turned and drifted past the large barn, out of the glare of the torch. Behind the barn, he doubled back to the low wall.

Sigmund was the second to return, a broad grin on his face. "I think I've got that salami, Capitaine, and a flagon of wine."

"Good lad. Do you think you could carry this lot back by yourself, straightaway? We can't chance its loss, if we have to make a run for it."

Sigmund nodded. "To the tavern, sir, or the cottage?"

"Better the outhouse where the horses are. Saddle them up and try to rope this load securely. Wait there for the rest of us."

Sigmund gathered the provisions together and melted into the darkness. Bruno came back with his hands full, but he was not grinning.

"Those two guards were eying me a bit sharp, sir. Best wait awhile until—" He stopped at the sound of raised voices.

There was challenge in the words, then the unmistakable voice of Jean, protesting, shouting back that his men were hungry, too. The noise increased as if other men had joined in.

Bruno half-rose, but Leon caught his shoulder. "Get this stuff back to Sigmund in the outhouse. I'll help Jean." Then he was over the wall, running, his sword free of its scabbard.

As he hurtled round the end of the wagon, he saw that both guards had drawn their swords. Behind them were other men, jeering at the guards, apparently amused by the spectacle of their harrying a lone man.

Leon raised his voice into a wild bellow. "Surround them, men! Come in on the flanks! Take them from the rear! Attack. Attack!"

His precipitate appearance, sword whirling round his head, sent the onlookers to flight, dragging out their swords as their eyes searched the darkness beyond the torch flares.

The two guards fell back. Jean's own sword hissed from its scabbard, and both he and Leon lunged for the stunned guards.

"Behind you, beyond!" roared Leon. "Take them, men!" His sword point sank into the shoulder of a guard. The man fell, his sword arm hanging limp, and blood welled from the wound.

Jean grunted with pain as a wild blow cut deep into his thigh. He staggered, and the guard leapt forward for the kill. Leon swung, and the man ran onto his sword, the point cleaving its way to the heart.

"Back to the wall," he gasped at Jean, then raised his voice again. "To victory, men! Cut them down like dogs!" Then he, too, drew back into the protection of the wagon and caught up with Jean.

The man was stumbling badly, his face white and sweating. Leon almost pushed him over the low wall, and they lay gasping for a moment in the darkness.

"On your feet, Jean," Leon snapped. "We must get

away while they're too confused to realize the extent of
the opposition.''

With an arm supporting the injured man, Leon forced
the pace through the alleys winding back to the street of
the tavern. Past the tavern to the cottage they
staggered, like two drunken men, until they reached the
door. Sigmund came out of the outhouse and helped
support Jean as Leon knocked and identified himself to
Judith.

She opened the door and stood back, her face pale as
she saw the blood soaking through Jean's breeches.

''See what you can do,'' Leon said wearily, and he and
Sigmund lowered Jean to the floor.

Judith drew her dagger and cut the thick cloth of the
breeches to expose the sword slash. She pressed her
lips tightly together to avoid exclaiming at the depth of
the cut. The man must have bled freely all the way back.
His skin had a bluish tinge already. How much blood he
had lost, she had no way of telling, but the flow must be
stopped. She took the threadbare towel and tied it
tightly above the wound, then washed away the blood
surrounding it. A pad, smeared with the vicomte's
unguent, was laid over the cut and she used the headkerchief to bind it into place.

''I can do nothing else,'' she said, looking helplessly at
Leon. ''We have no herbal pastes or mixtures of any
kind.''

Jean's eyes opened. ''I thank you, Madame. I come of
hardy stock. I will live if God wills it.'' His eyelids
drooped, and Judith felt her own eyes fill with tears.

''You are a brave man,'' she murmured, but doubted
that he heard.

Leon raised his head. ''Where's Bruno?'' he demanded
of Sigmund.

''Guarding the horses and supplies, Capitaine. He is
safe.'' The boy moved to the door. ''I will return to him
and—''

He broke off as Leon raised a hand. ''Wait. Listen.''

In silence, they all listened to the muted sounds in the alley. Booted feet, scuffling over stones, erratic movement without pattern.

Leon frowned. "Otto's patrol returning? Not without injury, I judge, from that unsteady gait."

The sounds came no nearer than from the tavern, and Leon moved toward the door. His hand was reaching for the handle when a scream of agony froze him. It was followed by a yell of triumph as steel clashed on steel.

"What in hell's name—" muttered Leon, and the sword hissed from its scabbard.

Sigmund's sword followed suit, but before they had the door open, all sound of battle died. A rush of heavy footsteps clattered away, the sound diminishing until only an eerie calm was left. No one spoke for a full minute, then Leon looked at Sigmund.

"Get Bruno. Go round the back of the tavern. I'll take the front. Watch your step, they might be lying in wait to discover our number."

Sigmund nodded. Leon glanced at Judith. "Lock the door behind us and keep Angel quiet."

Judith, too, nodded without speaking. She could not trust herself to utter a word, for it would only be a plea to have Leon stay here and not risk himself further. But his men were out there and he was their leader. How could he ignore that sound of swift battle? As the two men merged into the darkness, Judith turned the key in the lock and leaned against the door, feeling very alone and desolate. What if armed men were lying in wait, as Leon suggested? She shuddered and reached out her hands to grasp Angel's ruff. His tongue flicked over her wrist as if in comfort and his nearness steadied her.

Jean was lying very still, asleep or unconscious she could not tell. She squeezed out one of the vicomte's cloths in the water bucket and wiped his face. He was still alive, but his breathing was shallow. If Leon brought back—and dear God, he must come back—another injured man, she had no resources left to deal with any

serious wound. Perhaps the corporal's patrol had been
seen and chased to the tavern by the duke's men. The
briefness of that battle might have accounted for them
all, with Leon and Sigmund finding only corpses and
perhaps becoming corpses themselves.

She shook her head angrily, forcing her mind to stop
there. It was dark, she was alone, save for Angel and a
wounded man. Such imaginings were childish, the stuff
of nightmares. Of course Leon would come back. He
was not a fool but a trained soldier, a man who used his
mind, and not an unschooled country boy. She wiped
Jean's face again and examined the remains of the
vicomte's medications, as if there were more to
discover. The mattress, yes, that had a cover which she
could tear into strips for bindings. What else? No
curtains or hangings, and the only two things she had
come across were now binding Jean's thigh.

The soft tapping on the door, when it came, startled
her. She rose quickly from the stool. Angel gave a
throaty growl, and Judith paused, uncertain, her hand on
the key. Angel knew Leon's scent. Why did he growl?
For a moment she stood irresolute as Angel's muzzled
dropped and he snuffled at the gap below the door.
Feet shuffled outside, a murmur of voices, then Angel's
tail lashed Judith's leg. Relief flooded through her. Leon
must be there, but Angel had caught someone else's
scent first.

"Judith?" The whisper was certainly Leon's.

Judith turned the key and stood back as the dazed-
looking corporal was pushed into the room by Leon,
followed by Sigmund and Bruno. Leon guided Otto to
one of the stools and the man sat down heavily staring
blankly into space. Leon locked the door and took
Sigmund's arm. The youth was ashen-faced and shaking.

"Sit down, lad. Where's that red wine, Judith?"

She placed the bottle and the beaker silently on the
table and surveyed their taut faces. Even Leon was pale,
his eyes shadowed as if they had witnessed some

horror. But his hands were steady as he forced the beaker of wine into Otto's slack fingers.

"Drink," he said briefly to Sigmund and pushed the bottle toward the boy. "Don't go off into a swoon like some ravished maiden." His tone was harsh but it had the desired effect, and Sigmund raised the bottle, gripping it between both hands. Bruno, squatting on his haunches by the door, looked in better shape than any of them, physically, but his face, too, had a look of shock.

Judith could bear it no longer. "What happened? Where are the others?"

"There are no others," Leon said flatly. He turned a cold gaze onto the corporal. "When Otto has recovered his wits, he might care to tell us why the duke's men attacked the tavern."

Otto swallowed the contents of the beaker at one draught. He blinked and gasped, but a little color returned to his face as he heard the note of sarcasm in Leon's voice.

"We made a haul, Capitaine," he said slowly. "And were on our way back. We were clear of soldiers, and Luke says something about dining well on the duke's bounty." He paused.

"Go on," said Leon.

"Then he put his foot in a pothole and twisted his leg. He yelled and cursed out loud, his load going every way. We were ahead, but before we had time to do anything, there were duke's soldiers coming up to see what the noise was. We ducked into some bushes. They called him looter and knocked him about, said they'd cut his throat if he didn't speak true and tell where he was taking the stuff." He looked up at Leon. "We had to leave him, Capitaine. There were eight of them. We got out of the bushes and ran. We heard Luke screaming. He must have betrayed us, for the duke's men came straight to the tavern, dragging Luke with them. They cut his throat, then threw him in and rushed the place. Claude and Martin were butchered right off, and I got out through the roof." He looked pleadingly at Leon. "I couldn't take on eight of them."

Leon rested a hand on his shoulder, his voice kinder. "Of course not. You did the only sensible thing left to you."

Otto dropped his eyes to the table. "They said they'd be back at first light and find the rest of us. I think they were fearful of being ambushed in the dark."

"I think you are right, Corporal. That's why they made off so quickly after—after doing what they did to the bodies. Sheer barbarism."

Leon sat on the edge of the table swinging a leg. "So. They'll be back tomorrow to make a thorough search for rebels." He stiffened, and the leg stopped swinging. "And do you know what they'll find in daylight?" He nodded toward the unconscious Jean. "A trail of blood leading directly to this cottage!"

29

It was very quiet in the small room after Leon had spoken, but his words seemed to hang in the air like a menacing cloud. Judith, on her knees beside Jean, stared at the blood oozing sluggishly from the thigh wound. Of course there would be a trail, and by daylight, what better sign of a man's passing than by an easily followed track of blood? She turned her head slowly and looked into the faces of each man in turn. Haggard and dirty, the pattern of weariness was repeated on each face.

Five men, but one so hurt that he might not survive, were left to face the return of the duke's men, their ranks strengthened in the belief that a force of rebels lay at hand. Judith looked at Leon's thoughtful face. As if he sensed her attention, he glanced up, catching her eye. He smiled.

"I think we must reach the Santa Dominic without delay. I've no wish to be caught here like a rat in a trap with only that door between us and the duke's men. They might take it into their minds to return with torches, well before dawn." He stood up. "Sigmund, Bruno, on your feet. Bring out the horses and make sure those supplies are well secured." As the two men rose to the note of command in Leon's voice, he said more harshly. "Go out with your swords drawn and watch every shadow." They looked at him blankly for a moment. "'Fore God!" he snarled. "You may be country born, but move like soldiers, not village idiots! We're not done for yet."

Under the lash of his tongue, Bruno and Sigmund seemed to throw off the torpor of dejection and come alive. Sigmund even managed a grin.

"Very good, Capitaine."

He and Bruno unsheathed their swords and moved outside cautiously. Leon watched them from the open door, but they reached the outhouse safely. He turned back to Otto.

"Look alive, Corporal. You're supposed to set example to your men, not sit there like a brood hen."

Otto flushed and rose to his feet. "I'm all right, Capitaine. It was just seeing what they did—"

"Enough of that, Corporal," Leon interrupted briskly. "We'll mourn our dead in the proper place and that's the Santa Dominic." He glanced through the still-open door. "They're bringing the horses. Judith, you must ride behind Sigmund. He knows the way. Gather up what may be useful and stow it in the saddlebag."

As Judith rose, Otto looked down on Jean. "He looks in a poor way, Capitaine. With luck he'll be dead before the duke's men come." He shrugged and began to move, but Judith's angry voice stopped him.

"We're not leaving Jean here, Corporal."

Otto stared at her. "He'll not fight again. What use to take him?"

"Common decency, Corporal. From what you said, I gather that your comrades were subjected to mutilation, even before they died. Is that not so?"

"Well, yes, Madame—"

"And would you leave this injured man to suffer even more in his dying?"

"I—I was only thinking, Madame, he might not survive the journey."

"On the other hand, he might," snapped Judith, her eyes a hard, brilliant blue. "And whether or not, he will be on consecrated ground, not hacked to death in this cottage. Would you have that on your conscience,

Corporal, that you deliberately left a comrade in his hour of need?"

Leon was beside her, an arm about her shoulders. "Hush, my dear. Jean will not be left."

"But the corporal—"

"I am the one who decides since I am in command. I have no intention of leaving Jean, believe me. The second horse will carry him slung over the saddle. Pray heaven he stays unconscious during the journey, for it will not be a comfortable one. We must tie him to the saddle."

With difficulty, the four men carried Jean through the narrow doorway and laid him, face down, over the horse's saddle. Ropes bound round him and under the horse's belly were knotted. Judith pulled on her goatskin jacket and stuffed the few medicine supplies into a saddlebag. Sigmund swung himself into the saddle, and Leon helped Judith into place behind him, handing her the reins of the second horse.

He stood back. "Go gently and with caution, Sigmund. You have a precious cargo. We'll join you within the hour."

"Yes sir." Sigmund urged the horse forward, and Judith hooked the fingers of her free hand into his belt. She glanced back and saw the three men watching, then the shadows engulfed them and there was nothing but the clop of hooves and the breathing of the horses. Why weren't they following directly behind? There was nothing else to do at the cottage.

"How far to the Santa Dominic, Sigmund?"

"Half an hour at this walking pace, Madame."

Judith thought about it. "Then why did the capitaine say he would see us in an hour? A man may walk at the pace of these horses, surely?"

"Yes, madame, but I think the capitaine wishes to leave some surprise for the duke's men when they come."

"Surprise? What can he do?"

She felt Sigmund shrug in the darkness. "I don't know, Madame. He will think of something. Capitaine de Foret is clever."

"Well, I hope he's not too clever for his own good," muttered Judith.

"Pardon, Madame?"

"Nothing, Sigmund." She glanced back at the figure slumped over the saddle. He could be dead already, but she was glad that Leon had not taken the corporal's side. An injured man, still living, would be made game of by the more brutal of the duke's men. Angel padded behind the second horse, and, in spite of herself, Judith smiled. No more light-hearted forays in the vanguard for Angel. He had learned that lesson well and was too intelligent to want his head cracked again. Intelligent, but no coward, for he would attack if she screamed. She turned her gaze forward again. The bell tower might well be a landmark by day, but in the darkness, there was only Sigmund's sense of direction to rely upon. He had accompanied Leon, so they would reach the Santa Dominic in the half hour.

"We follow, Capitaine?" asked Otto, a little puzzled by Leon's silence.

"In due course," Leon said and glanced toward the horizon. There was no division yet between sky and earth. Two hours, perhaps, and the darkness would melt into gray. "Would it not be justice to arrange a surprise for the duke's men when they come at dawn?"

"Justice?" Otto frowned. "You say we should stay and fight?" He shrugged. "If you order it, Capitaine, but we shall be no match for them. There are three corpses already in the tavern."

"Then call it revenge for their deaths. Does your heart not cry vengeance?"

"Aye, Captaine." Otto's expression hardened. "One day, they shall pay."

"Not one day, Corporal, but this day. Listen to me, both of you." He looked at Bruno. "Bring all the hay and straw you can find from the stables behind the tavern. Strew it thickly on the tavern floor and here in the cottage. Rags and sticks, too, enough to make a blaze. Go now."

"Yes, sir," said Bruno and was off without question.

Leon turned to Otto. "Does the tavern cellar hold brandy or has all been looted?"

"Not all, Capitaine. They took what they saw and went on their way after putting a torch to the timbers. You want me to bring out all the brandy I can find?"

"Yes. Then follow Bruno as he spreads straw and soak it with brandy. They will expect a tavern to smell like one. Save some for the cottage floor."

Otto was beginning to grin, but a little doubtfully. "They will follow the blood trail to the cottage, Capitaine, but may not go inside if it is empty."

"It won't be empty, Otto. Do as I bid you now and don't waste time on talk. We have little of it to organize this charade."

Leon followed Otto's hurrying figure into the tavern and looked about him. He selected two half-empty flagons of wine, three metal beakers, and a wooden stool. Bruno eyed him curiously in the light of a candle, but said nothing.

"Spread it thickest round those broken benches," he ordered and turned out of the tavern.

In the cottage, Leon put the beakers and flagons on the table and set the three stools about it. He looked at the small, shuttered window and with his sword prised the shutters free, dropping them onto the floor. The closed lantern was on the table, too, giving off a soft illumination. Bruno came in, his arms full of straw bales. Soon, the small floor was ankle-deep and Leon nodded approval, both for Bruno's efforts and for the slight wind that was now coming in at the unshuttered window.

Otto arrived some moments later, a flagon in each hand. "Vallonese brandy, Capitaine. Strong enough to make a man burst into flames."

"Exactly what I had in mind," Leon said. "So save a little of it."

Otto poured the contents liberally over the floor. The two men straightened and looked at Leon. "What now, Capitaine?"

"The hardest part, I'm afraid. I hope you have the stomach for it." He indicated the three stools. "I want our dead comrades brought here. Luke, Martin, and Claude. Their bodies must die again for the cause."

"Burn them here?" asked Bruno, his eyes wide.

"Yes." Leon's voice was hard. "Their souls have already fled. Their remains are empty husks of decay. Should we leave them to the mercies of scavenging dogs or give them the right to exact vengeance from those who took their lives?" he looked from one to the other. "Choose now, for there is a lightening in the sky. Do we run like rabbits and leave our dead unavenged?"

"No, we do not!" It was Bruno who spoke, his eyes fierce. "What use their lifeless bodies?" He crossed himself. "Their souls will commend us and God will understand." He turned and blundered out of the cottage.

Otto nodded. "So be it, Capitaine."

The three corpses were brought to the cottage, their bodies already stiffened by death. Blood had dried in dark patches, and their faces were unrecognizable under the dagger cuts. It seemed as if every man of the pursuing force had shared in the hacking and slashing of bodies from which the life had already gone.

The bodies were arranged on the stools, their arms laid over the table. Three heads leaned together, sightless eyes open, the flagons and beakers forming a centerpiece. Without knowledge, one might have supposed them three men deep in conversation. Leon took the flagon from Otto and emptied the remains over the dead men.

"What now, Capitaine?" asked Bruno in a hushed voice as they backed to the door.

Leon picked up the lantern and closed it up to guard the candle from the night breeze. He bent and picked up a handful of the soaked straw and thrust it into the neck of his shirt. It lay cold and soggy against his skin.

"I mean to climb onto the roof and lob the lantern through the window when the carrion arrives."

Otto said. "It's a pitched roof, Capitaine."

Leon smiled for the first time that night. "You're right, and damned uncomfortable I shall be. Let us hope the enemy comes before full light and mistakes me for a chimney stack or gable end."

"A good plan, Capitaine. And the door?"

"We lock it from the outside. They won't be able to resist the lure of a locked door. They'll be bound to believe something's afoot and break it down. When they rush upon our departed comrades, I'll smash in the lantern. If things go to plan, I'll make my escape in the confusion."

Otto nodded. They left the cottage, and Leon locked the door, tossing the key into the bushes.

"I'll fire the tavern, sir. I've a bunch of candles tied together and with wicks at both ends. Should make a nice blaze between us, God willing." They exchanged grins, and Otto went on. " 'Tis only a two-man job, sir. Sigmund and your lady may have greater need of a pair of strong hands to help with Jean."

"True, Bruno. It's time you retired from the scene. You know the Santa Dominic? Go now and join the others. Do what you can to help Jean."

"Very good, sir." Bruno half-turned then paused, listening.

Leon touched his shoulder. "Be off at full speed, Bruno, and keep my lady safe between you. I think our guests are about to arrive."

As Bruno merged into the grayness of the coming day, Leon turned to Otto and held out his hand. "To your action station, my friend, and may the goddess of fortune smile on us today. We'll meet up at the Santa Dominic."

Otto grasped the hand and nodded. "God be with us too, Capitaine." Then he was gone, moving swiftly to the rear of the tavern.

Leon hauled himself onto the roof of the cottage with the aid of a water butt. The tiling was cold and damp from the night air, but with a leg on each side of the pitch, the lantern clutched firmly, he squirmed forward on his stomach until his head was hanging over the small window. He took a firm grip of the lantern and peered down.

The sky was much lighter. He could distinguish the sides of wrecked houses, the tavern down the street, and the track along which, hopefully, the duke's men would come. They might approach round the back of the tavern, but Leon doubted it. Too many cramped alleys and broken walls where ambush might lurk. As he waited he thought of Judith and remembered the beauty and joy of their loving. It was a memory he would take to the grave if this desperate plan failed. It must not, he vowed, for there was no safety here for any woman, well-born or not. They would wait, of course, but as the hours faded, one into another, so her hopes would fade. He began to worry. Why the devil had he not told Sigmund what to do if neither he nor Otto made it to the Santa Dominic? Bruno, even; he should have sent some message by him. It was too late now. He must trust Sigmund to get her out of the city and to his own hill village. The boy would surely do that if he found himself and Bruno the lone survivors. Both country-born, they would accept the inevitable, the uselessness of further resistance.

His eyes saw the pitch torches approach, and he

shook himself angrily, forcing his mind to work. He was not dead yet, he must keep his mind on the job in hand. Settling himself securly on the roof pitch, he pulled the damp straw from his shirt, cradling the lantern in the crook of his other arm as firmly and as gently as he would a newborn babe. Resting his chin on the point of the roof, he lay quite still, watching.

The duke's men, perhaps twenty of them, flanked by torch bearers, were proceeding cautiously along the earth track. Their steps were muted, and each man held an unsheathed sword. Steel glinted in the torchlight. Another sound emerged, coming from the rear of the advancing men. The clop of hooves, the jingle of bridle made Leon peer beyond the men. A mounted officer?

They came nearer, and Leon discerned the single horseman. He blinked as something sparked in the gleam of a torch. A jewel, perhaps? Gold and braided epaulettes? Unlikely for a fighting officer who usually dressed as plainly as his men. He blinked again as a face swam into his vision. Holy Mother, it was the vicomte, the man he had promised to meet by the west gate! He bit back a grin. Well, here they were at the west gate, but it had been a promise he had no intention of keeping, at the time he gave it.

The gallant vicomte, the officer who led his troops from the rear and used his sword only on dying men. He had been dissuaded by his sergeant from hanging Leon as a horse thief. There would be no dissuasion this time if Leon fell into his hands alive. The nearest beam would see him choking out his life, the vicomte watching, honor restored.

The troops halted, fanning out in front of the tavern. The vicomte's querulous voice floated on the faint breeze from a safe distance, rippling the uneasy quiet of the dawn.

"For the duke, men! Charge the place. Death to all rebels!" He still sat his horse, waving the sword with its glittering, jeweled hilt. Fine horse, thought Leon absently, and one which will carry the vicomte away, the moment battle is joined. Battle? There was only Otto in the tavern waiting, as he was, for the rush of soldiers.

The vicomte raised his voice angrily. "Charge, I say!"

The body of men surged forward. Booted feet thumped into the tavern, the sound muted by the layers of thick straw. Leon heard furniture crash, the sounds of shattering glass, the yells for the duke deafening in the low-ceilinged room.

"Now, Otto, now!" he muttered, and, as if it was a personal signal, a whoosh of flame answered him. The yells turned to cries of alarm as the brandy-soaked straw erupted. Blue flames illuminated the interior, catching at splintered wood. Smoke rose then, and cries turned to screams as men fought to get out of the narrow doorway. Others, with better sense, flung themselves through casement windows, rolling scorched or burning onto the track.

Leon tore his gaze from the scene and looked to the rear of the tavern. Was that fleeting shadow Otto? He prayed it was as the grayness took it from view. Run for your life, Otto, he willed. The search will be on when the shock wears off. He looked to the front of the tavern again. At least half a dozen men were lying groaning, their clothes almost burnt off their bodies. He hoped that the murderers of last night were amongst them. The vicomte was even farther away than before, but his voice came strongly.

"Search the area, immediately. The ruffians cannot have got far."

The men milled about, belatedly running to the rear of the tavern.

"This way, my lord vicomte, this way," muttered Leon, but the men seemed intent on closing with the tavern.

A torch dipped toward the track, and its holder shouted. Faces turned toward him as he pointed with the long-poled torch. "Look, look! A trail. They went that way."

Leon stared down at the blood trail. The morning mist had bedewed it, leaving it as shiny as if it had been freshly made. A shout of triumph went up, and men rushed to examine it. They seemed not to find it incongruous, leading as it did from the front of the tavern where they had recently assembled. No man raised a suspicious face. Perhaps they assumed the fire-raisers to have mingled with their own desperate rush to escape.

Leon lay very still. Had a man looked up, Leon would surely be spotted, for the dawn grayness was draining fast from the sky, but every eye was fixed on the ground. The soldiers passed from view, moving slowly to the two doors. The dresser still barred the front door, but Leon hoped they would focus their attention on the smaller, less solid, back door. Yes, they were collecting about the back door. Good. There was a thump as if a heavy shoulder had thrust at it. More thumps and a crack of wood. The door was giving. He tensed, opening the window of the lantern away from the street.

Thump, creak, a splintering of wood. They were almost in. Wait, he told himself, for the cry of triumph as they saw the men round the table. The door gave suddenly, crashing back on its hinges to thump against the wall. A wave of sound flung itself out of the window under his body. The hand clenching the brandy-soaked straw unclenched and he thrust the bundle into the lantern. The candle flame reached greedily and the lantern became a ball of fire. Leon leaned forward as far as he could, gritting his teeth as the flames licked his fingers. Holding the lantern at arm's length, he swung and lobbed it neatly through the high window.

Off balance for a second, he tried to recover but knew he was falling.

30

To lob the lantern cleanly through the high window had taken his right arm at full stretch, the left hand gripping the ridge of the roof. As his booted feet strove to find hold on the damp tiles, all he felt at first was the grim satisfaction of an archer hitting the bull at first shot. Had the lantern bounced off the sill into the street, the three butchered men inside the cottage would have been denied just vengeance.

His boots left the tiles, his body swung like a pendulum, one hand still gripping the roof while his right hand sought the rough stone sill. Then he let go of the roof hold and grabbed for the sill, two-handed. Should have made a cleaner job of removing those shutters, he thought, as wood splinters tore at his fingers on their way to the stone sill. He drew himself up, hooking an elbow over the sill until he was hanging on the stonework. Then he looked into the room.

By some strange freak, the lantern had cartwheeled, coming to rest on the table between the shoulders of two of the dead men. The horn slats of its windows exploded into fragments showering the corpses. Blue flames shot across their backs, catching beards and hair until they became human torches. The soldiers, crowded into the small room, were frozen into attitudes of stunned disbelief that men could sit calmly while flames devoured them. Horror held them motionless as hair, flesh, and clothing melted into nonhuman shapes and the stench of burning bodies was appalling.

Then, one after another, the skeletal corpses seemed to rise and fall back, crashing to the floor. The soaked straw caught and flames sheeted across the room. A man screamed. Stunned disbelief was gone, replaced by the basic survival instinct of every living creature, man or beast. The small doorway was jammed by men, fighting like animals to escape the inferno that now had the cottage in its grip.

Men fell, screaming, hair and uniforms alight, skin scorching in the heat. The old dresser, feet deep in straw, groaned, cracked, and shot out spurts of flame that ran angrily up to the roof beams. A scene from hell, thought Leon, and as the roof tiles began to crack in the uprush of hot air, he came to himself and realized that he must now look to his escape. He dropped to the ground and ran, crouching round the side of the cottage. Men were still tumbling out of the door, faces wild with panic. Some threw themselves down, rolling to extinguish smoldering tunics. A man stumbled across Leon's path, beating at his clothes. Leon cannoned into him. The man glared from a smoke-blackened face, his eyes suspicious.

"The well," Leon shouted, pointing. "Get water. There's a bucket. Come on."

The man reached out. "Wait. I don't know you—"

But Leon was past him, running toward the well. "Don't waste time, you fool. Men are dying and you would have my name and rank?"

The man was quick on his feet and right behind Leon as they reached the well. He was no dullard either, for as Leon put himself at the far side of the well, the man said, "Not so fast, whoever you are. That was your face at the window, I'll take my oath on it."

"Take the bucket instead," Leon snapped, thanking God that the half-filled bucket was suspended on its chain.

He swung the heavy bucket across the well-head. The man raised an arm to deflect it, but the swing had enough weight behind it to take him off balance. He staggered, and Leon leapt for the bushes, crashed through, and began to run.

There were no shadows now, the day was alive, all grayness gone. This was not the direction he had taken with Sigmund, but it would serve until he was sure no pursuit was mounted. One could not make straight for the Santa Dominic if the duke's hounds were at his heels. He ran on, jumping obstacles, skirting buildings, and always listening. With luck, the duke's men might be too demoralized to instigate immediate search parties. Two incidents of unnatural fire-raising would make them approach with great caution, and the vicomte was not a man to spur his troops into high valor.

Leon paused at a street corner, gasping for breath. It was very quiet. He doubted there would be any pursuit for a lone man who might lead them into another ambush, but he could not relax his vigilance yet. He looked about him. There was a collapsed house with its chimney pointed skyward like an accusing finger. That was what he needed, a high point from which to survey the area. With all the twisting and turning he had done, he was unsure just how far he had come from the cottage. The blackened stonework looked sound. It did not tremble as he began to climb, using broken projections as footholds.

He reached the chimney pot and, keeping it level with his face, scanned the surroundings. It was a completely alien landscape. Where the devil was he? He grinned to himself. Even a tired fool should be able to tell east from west when the sun was scarcely risen. And he called himself a capitaine, a leader of men? He craned his neck round the chimney pot, feeling the rough stone of the chimney stack score his already sore hands. He could not see the west gate, but what he could see brought a surge of relief. Not a hundred yards away, the bell tower of the Santa Dominic showed white against a background of green, wooded hills.

He turned his gaze away from the bell tower and scanned the way he had come, probing every building and bush through narrowed eyes. Nothing moved, no sound of life, nor glint of sun on steel. At last he was satisfied and climbed down from the chimney. Even then, he approached the Santa Dominic with wariness. It stood silent and gray, watching his coming with the solemn blank eyes of age. Were other eyes watching? He glanced up at the bell tower. Was that a movement he had caught out of the corner of his eye? He drew his sword. If the duke's men were here, he would not be taken alive, he vowed, and bounded forward between the old gates, swinging his sword in a wide arc. But there was no one in the courtyard, no armed men behind these walls.

A heavy door creaked, and he swung, half-crouching to face it. Judith stood framed in the doorway holding onto Angel, her eyes brilliant, her mouth curved into a smile of welcome. He ran for the door, sheathing his sword, his own face splitting into a wide grin that reflected the one looking over Judith's shoulder. It was Otto's face, grimy and singed. Beyond him stood Bruno showing strong white teeth.

Leon bounded up the steps and swept Judith into his arms. He kicked the door shut with his heel and said, half-laughing, but still with the grin on his face, "We're like a convention of village idiots grinning at nothing, but all the same, I'm glad to see you got away, Otto. You too, Bruno." He looked down at Judith, whose eyes had never left his face. "And you, my lady? You made the journey without mishap? Where is Sigmund?"

"Watching over Jean." Judith spoke huskily, only half-believing that she was in Leon's arms again. "You were so long after Otto, I thought—"

"Imagined, my love, that is all. I had to wait until the searchers reached the cottage."

"The cottage? Why?"

Leon looked quickly at Otto and Bruno. Each gave a

slight shake of the head. Good, they had not told her of the macabre setting out of the corpses.

"The trail left by Jean, remember? It ended at the cottage, but I wanted to know in which direction they might continue the search."

Otto scratched his bearded chin. "Did things go to plan, sir?"

Leon nodded. "Perfectly, and it's my belief they'll draw off until they've a larger force to sweep the area." He looked at Judith. "The officer in charge was our old friend, the vicomte. Not a man to risk himself with a small force."

She glanced up, startled. "The vicomte? Holy Mother, if he catches you, Leon, he'll not rest until you're hanged. Did he see you?"

"No, and I'd as soon not become reacquainted with His Lordship." He looked at Otto. "You don't by chance have any of that brandy with you? I've a powerful thirst on me, and why are we standing here, gossiping like old women? Is there no food to be had? I've an appetite on me, too."

Otto grinned. "Come this way, sir. We've better than Vallonese. Sigmund lifted a flagon of French brandy when he went foraging. There's bread, a whole cheese, and a cooked haunch of beef. Your lady served us as we arrived but kept her eye on the brandy." He grinned cheerfully.

"And quite right, too," Leon said. "I'll have no drunkards under my command."

They moved into the body of the hall where Jean lay on a bed of old cassocks. Sigmund rose.

"Welcome, Capitaine." He smiled briefly, then looked down at Jean. "I think he fails, sir. Madame has done what she could, but the sword cut went nigh to the bone."

Leon knelt by Jean. The man's face seemed shrunken and the skin devoid of blood. A tinge of blueness was on his lips. Leon saw the thick padding that Judith had obviously contrived from the remains of Jean's shirt, but the blood still seeped, discoloring the cloth.

Judith knelt beside Leon. There was a helpless note in her voice. "He has not opened his eyes since we brought him here. Without proper attention, I fear he will drift into death."

"There is nothing you can do, my dear," Leon said, drawing her to her feet. "He will go without pain if God sees fit to take his soul."

They walked to a side bench, and Judith poured brandy into the chipped horn beaker she had put in the saddlebag. She laid out the food, then sat beside Leon.

As he ate, he questioned the men. They had searched every inch of the old monastery and found two doors, one leading into a kitchen garden, the other into a stableyard where the monks had kept mules, according to Sigmund's grandfather. The two horses were there, he said.

"And the bell tower? I thought I glimpsed someone up there."

"Very like, Capitaine." Sigmund grinned. "Madame has been up those stairs a dozen times since Otto arrived."

Leon smiled at Judith. "A good view from there, is it not?"

"Very good," Judith said, without smiling. "I saw trees being felled by the score. The duke will soon have his battering rams and siege towers for the palace."

Leon looked round at the assembled men. "And when that task is accomplished, there will be troops enough to scour the outskirts for rebels."

It was the quiet Bruno who spoke. "We are but four men, Capitaine. Even if we could hold this place, what would it achieve, if the baron is taken?"

"Less than nothing, my friend, and would be useless sacrifice. We must accept that the duke will triumph, for there are mercenary camps outside the city. My lady and I passed them on our way in."

"You said naught of mercenaries before, Capitaine." Otto protested.

Leon smiled. "The knowledge would not have lifted your spirits. As it was, we made a fight of it in fine fashion and disposed of a few of the baron's enemies. We will not break out now, we must accept that."

Sigmund's eyes held a hopeful light. "Do we leave the city then, sir?"

"There's no other course. As Bruno says, we are but four men. There are no stout gates, and even this old place would be no match for a siege tower, should they suspect it of harboring rebels."

Otto's shoulders slumped in dejection. "So, it is the end."

"For the present, Corporal. Who knows? The country may rise against the duke if he rules as his father did." Leon rose and stretched, clapping Otto on the shoulder. "There may be work yet for you, old war-horse, but for now a strategic withdrawal is indicated." He turned to Sigmund. "It would be wiser to tether those horses on the hillside, below some hillock, where they'll not be seen. Their presence here would give us away."

Sigmund nodded. "Yes, sir. I recollect that gap in the wall. I'll move them now."

"We'll take watch about in the bell tower," Leon went on. "I'll go up now. Get some sleep, the rest of you."

Judith walked with Leon to the foot of the steps leading to the tower. He stopped and laid a hand on her cheek.

"You too, my love. Your eyes are eating up your face."

Judith smiled. "Talking of faces, your own is hard to discern under that coating of grime. And your hands are cut and burned, just like Otto's. I have nothing left to dress your wounds."

"They'll heal soon enough. What do you think of Jean's chances?"

Judith shook her head, her eyes troubled. "The

journey here brought on fresh bleeding. He is far too weak to be moved again, and where would we take him?"

"Maybe God will take him first, my love. Try to sleep now. We are safe enough for a day or two."

He forced his legs to carry him up to the bell tower. The morning sun made him blink and the scene swam dizzily for a moment. God, he was tired, but so were they all. A day's rest and food, a little breathing space, then they must seek the safety of the hills. He scanned the countryside, seeing the trees fall with terrifying rapidity. Teams of axe-men must be hard at work. The duke was taking no chances on the baron escaping. Through the ever-widening gap left by the felled trees, he saw workmen splitting logs, measuring and hewing them into sections. For the uprights of the siege towers, he supposed, then his eye caught something else.

He frowned, trying to recall where he had seen something like that before. Had they been used in Poitou? Yes, that was it. King Richard of England had caused them to be built as he was laying siege to the castle of Chaluz. Two solid uprights, strengthened at their bases by diagonal supports, a contraption of ropes and pulleys, a trebucket—yes, that was the name—a giant catapult! More effective than either battering ram or siege tower, for its load of rock could be hurled high into the air, to fall with devastating results inside any besieged place.

He leaned his elbows on the parapet. Chaluz? Had he been at that battle? Some knowledge of it lurked behind his conscious mind but refused to be summoned into the open. It was a long time since he had taxed his mind with the question of identity. And was it worth pursuing now? Tomorrow, or very soon, he might be just another corpse, like those pathetic three in the cottage. Had anyone known their names or where they had come from? No decency of Christian burial was observed on a battlefield. He looked again at the construction of the trebucket. It would take longer to erect than a siege tower. Balance and weight, the right lengths of rope and the creation of buckets to hold the missiles, and the counter weight must all be judged to a nicety.

He stirred as footsteps echoed up the stone stairway. Sigmund's head came into view. He grinned cheerfully.

"My watch now, Capitaine."

"The horses? Are they safely out of sight?" Leon asked, rubbing his tired eyes.

"Yes, Capitaine." Sigmund's head swiveled, and he positioned himself behind Leon. "See that copse, sir, outside the wall? You'll only be glimpsing the treetops from here, but the horses are tethered there. A bit of a stream and grass in plenty. I hid the saddles under a bramble by the water's edge."

Leon nodded. "Well done. The less we leave lying about, the easier it will be to remove all traces if we observe the enemy's approach."

"You think they'll quarter this area soon, Capitaine?"

"Sure to." Leon turned back to the hillside. "See what they're doing with the felled trees? They're swarming like ants to build those towers and rams."

Sigmund peered. "Yes, I see them, Capitaine," he said soberly. "So many men the duke has brought with him." He narrowed his eyes into the sun. "What's that thing beyond, on the flat ground?"

"Did you ever toss stones as a boy, with sling or catapult?"

Sigmund looked startled. "Why, yes, sir. Do you mean that thing is—?" His voice faded and he peered again.

"The biggest catapult you ever saw, lad. Keep a special eye on that and report to me if you see them moving it."

"That I will, sir," Sigmund muttered, his gaze fixed on the contraption. "That's a right deadly weapon, so it is."

Leon moved down the spiraling staircase and into the hall of the monastery. Bruno and Otto lay on wooden settles, their tunics pillowed under their heads. Both slept soundly. Leon looked for Judith. She was sitting beside Jean, eyes closed and slumped uncomfortably in the angle of a wall. He moved, soft-footed, toward her. Angel raised yellow eyes and his tail began to move. Judith's own eyes opened, dazed and unfocused for a second, then she smiled.

Leon knelt down. "You've chosen an uncomfortable position, my love. Why aren't you stretched on a settle like the others?"

"How can I leave Jean? I have water here in case he wakes."

Leon looked into Jean's face. It had aged beyond recognition, his pallor that of one already dead, but he still breathed.

"You can do nothing more for him," Leon told Judith gently. "Go to a settle and sleep." He rose and lifted her. "You need your own strength. Remember, it is a long way to France and safety. I don't want you falling from the saddle when we move."

He led her to a settle and watched as she lay down. "I will stay by Jean."

"France?" Judith murmured. "Are we ever likely to reach it?"

"Keep that thought alive in your mind. We shall reach it, God willing, for there's nothing to keep us here when we've rested. Our fight is fought."

There was no response, and Leon smiled. Asleep already. That was good. She would need all the strength and courage at her command when they left, for it might prove a hazardous journey. He lay down beside Jean, listening to the faint breathing of the dying man. He dropped swiftly into sleep.

At dusk they were all awake, still filthy but refreshed. They ate the cold food and finished the French brandy.

"Is there a well in the yard?" asked Leon. "Our smell, if nothing else, will give us away."

"No, sir," Sigmund said. "The monks must have

brought their water from the stream I mentioned. I
fetched a bucketful when Madame and I arrived. Shall I
go again? It's not far."

"I think not," said Leon. "Those tree-fellers are
covering the hillside. They might find the horses, but I'll
not risk you falling into their hands. We have what
remains in the bucket for drinking and will be gone by
dawn." He looked round at the men. "Does anyone
disagree with that decision?"

Heads were shaken. "'Tis best, I suppose," Otto said,
then a faint grin lit his face. "We put an end to a few of
them and scared a lot more witless."

The atmosphere lightened, and the three Vallonese
began to talk of their villages until a choked cry from
Judith stopped the flow. They all turned and watched
her rise from Jean's side.

"He's dead. Jean is dead! He just—just slipped away."
She covered her eyes for a moment, feeling a constric-
tion in her throat at the sheer futility of Jean's death.
"And what did he die for? Tell me that!" Her voice was
muffled, but the words came distinctly. "For the baron,
that monstrous man who will care naught for Jean's
sacrifice."

Leon came to his feet swiftly and drew Judith into his
arms, holding her face against his breast.

"Hush, my love, say no more. It will do no good. Jean
fought for his beliefs and died for them. Let him rest in
peace, I implore you."

Judith felt her wits reassert themselves as the shock of
discovery lessened. Leon's words had held warning. Her
mind cleared. Of course he was right. These men
thought she and Leon were for the baron.

She drew back from Leon and regarded the three
men. Sigmund and Bruno looked perplexed, but it was
Otto who stared, eyes narrowed and suddenly full of
suspicion.

"Monstrous man, Madame? To speak of our lord
baron in such terms is traitor's talk." He moved his stare

to Leon, his eyes hard and probing. "You were uncommon shocked, I recall, when we took you in the alley by the tavern. For all your quick tongue and fine ways, it's maybe two traitors we're harboring!"

31

"Traitors?" Leon's voice was hard and derisive as Otto's fingers crept to his sword hilt. "Do you forget the duke's men we accounted for?"

"And lost four of our own, including Jean," Otto returned sourly.

"Have a care, Corporal." Leon's tone became low and measured. "Did I lead them to the tavern or hang back from the job we did? Was my lady not caring for Jean's hurt?"

"Aye, but—" There was a hint of uncertainty now in Otto's voice and Leon pressed on, an edge of curtness to his voice.

"I suggest you release your hold on your sword, Corporal, before my own sees the light. It has served me well for many a year and will do so again should you hold to your doubts."

Angel, sensing the tension, had padded to Judith's side. His eyes, yellow and unblinking, were fixed on Otto. The man's hand dropped from his sword hilt and he shrugged.

"Maybe I spoke a mite hasty, but Madame's words were harsh."

Judith had herself under control now. She spoke coolly. "You are a soldier, Corporal, and made oath to the baron. I am a woman and did no such thing. Jean is dead. Will his wife or mother mourn him the less for dying in the baron's service? Will the widows of the duke's men not rail against the leader who called their men to battle? Dead is dead, Corporal. How it comes is of no importance. You must allow a woman her feelings."

Otto relaxed. "You're right, Madame. You cannot help being female."

Leon's mouth twisted into a faint smile. "For myself, I prefer it that way, Corporal."

Otto glanced at him, then he too smiled and gave Judith a sheepish look before turning away.

As dawn crept grayly over the land, Judith stirred, feeling cold and stiff. Her spirits were low as she stared at Jean's body. Poor man. If only she had been able to save him. She remembered his brave words. Even a man of hardy stock bled like any other, and the wound had been grievous. Rousing herself, she moved to the food supply. There was little of that left. Six mouths, including Angel's, had taken their toll.

There were stirrings from the pews and settles as men roused themselves. Leon came down from the bell tower where he had stood the last guard of the night. Looking round at them all, Judith thought she had never seen such a disreputable body of men, all filthy and ragged. Nor could she excuse herself, for she too must look like some wandering tinker woman. She shrugged and laid out the food. She met Leon's anxious gaze and smiled, forcing gaiety into her words.

"Good morning, my lord. A slice of venison or the poached salmon? Perhaps you would care for quail's eggs or trout with almonds? There's fresh-baked bread and a splendid country cheese."

Leon grinned. "Why, ma'am, I confess to a small appetite this day. A little cheese and bread, if you please."

"Then please help yourself, for my wrist aches with the effort of hacking through that very stale bread. The cheese is in reasonable condition although it has grown a protective coat."

The men gathered round, sawing at the bread loaves and hard cheese. Leon looked about thoughtfully. The hall was dim and shadowed.

"There must be a crypt," he said. "Since I have yet to see a headstone anywhere." He looked at Sigmund and smiled. "It would be too much to suppose your grandfather knew of its entrance?"

Sigmund shook his head. "He was a simple peasant, Capitaine. Only the monks would know."

"Then we must search for it." Leon glanced at Judith. "Jean will lie in holy company this day."

Sigmund stuffed the crust of his breakfast into his pocket. "My watch, Capitaine. That thing you showed me is growing apace. I have never seen its like."

He was off up the bell tower steps, and the rest of them spread out into the hall to search out the crypt entrance. The monastery had many archways and narrow corridors, bordered on each side by small, cell-like rooms. Judith shivered in the dark, airless rooms and wondered how the monks had survived such bleak conditions. Their bones must have ached in the damp atmosphere, hands and feet blue and swollen in the winter's chill.

All corridors seemed to lead nowhere but to the outer walls of the building. She wandered through a refectory, a primitive kitchen, and back to the hall. She was puzzled by her lack of success and came upon the men who also admitted defeat.

"We seemed to have searched every inch," Leon said. "Why would the monks be so careful as to hide the crypt entrance? I don't understand it. Spain took back its treasures, there can only be coffins down there."

"Perhaps the monks regard them as treasures, but not in the earthly sense," Judith suggested. "They would revere their dead brothers' souls as treasures for heaven."

Leon looked at her keenly. "Sealed up the entrance, perhaps?"

"Or disguised it against such intrusion as we plan."

Leon nodded slowly. "Maybe that is the answer. Spain could well have sent an envoy and escort to be certain of retrieving everything of value. So we must look again in all the unlikely places."

"What's the point of wasting time, Capitaine?" Otto grumbled. "If those old monks were so clever, we'll never find it."

"Would you have us leave Jean to the rats?" Judith asked hotly. "We must find it! If the monks were here for hundreds of years, they'll have worn a path over the flagstones. There must have been scores of burials, even hundreds."

"The stones are all worn, Madame," Otto said in a belligerent tone. "Where would we begin?"

Judith bit her lip and stared down. Weeds and grass grew about each stone, and stronger growths beneath lifted and tilted flatstones. She lifted her shoulders in a hopeless gesture. The only indented stones she could see led to a tall, boxlike structure by the altar wall. What might once have been curtains hung limply over the opening. It was impossible to guess what color they had been, but their very fragility suggested that a touch would have them fall into dust.

Otto followed her glance. "A confessional box, Madame, must have a track to its door since all folk are sinners. The monks would hold confessionals for the townspeople, I suppose."

Judith frowned. "One box, one father confessor. That must have taken time. Why not many such boxes? Would the townspeople wait hours to confess their sins?"

She turned to look down the aisle. "There is scarce room for two abreast here. Coming and going would be difficult. Far easier to have the confessionals near the door where the hall widens."

Otto shrugged. "You can see the grill between the partition. It's a confessional box, all right."

"I don't doubt it for a moment." Judith moved closer to the box and peered between the curtains, the cloth only held together by years of dust and neglect. "But I wonder why, since it is so close to the wall, the fathers did not utilize the wall and build only two sides, with the curtain forming the fourth side."

The men moved closer. Leon peered over Judith's shoulder. "That back panel is carved mighty fine. There is a depth of wood to it."

"For the benefit of the townsfolk who could scarcely see it when the curtains were drawn?" asked Judith, looking into Leon's face. "Could the monks have kept this confessional for themselves alone?"

"By the Saints!" Leon said, staring. "That rich panel down the center puts the rest of the box to shame." He withdrew his head and moved to the side of the box.

"Take the other side, and draw your sword, Bruno, and I will do likewise from this side. Run the blade behind the side panel. Watch the panel, Otto. If our swords show, I believe my lady has discovered the door to the crypt."

Judith and Otto watched the elaborate back panel, Otto skeptical but Judith hopeful.

"Now, Bruno."

Two sword points glinted as the blades swept down. The old curtains shivered, throwing out dust motes, and the side panels of the box creaked. The curtains sighed and collapsed, sending up plumes of dust.

"It's a door," called Leon in triumph. "Help us move the box, Otto."

Judith joined in, and the tall box was pulled away from the wall. They all crowded into the space behind and stared. It was certainly a door with iron-strapped hinges and a heavy drop latch on the other side. Only the wooden paneling had been visible from the curtained side. A cursory glance might have noticed nothing more, had the curtains been in good condition.

The three men were grinning at her. "Well done, my

love," said Leon. "Now Jean may rest in the holiest of places."

They pushed the box farther away, and Leon lifted the latch. Dank, musty air swept up a flight of stone steps. There was an involuntary shiver from them all. Angel, who had been watching this strange activity with interest, sneezed and peered down the steps into total blackness. He sneezed again, much louder, and the sound seemed to echo and rumble into the distance below. Judith clutched Leon's arm.

"It sounds to be a very large crypt," she whispered.

"A lot will have died over the centuries," Leon whispered back, then looked at her, his lips twitching. "Why are we whispering? There's no one to hear."

Judith smiled nervously. "I don't know. It seems respectful to whisper with all those holy men down there."

Leon nodded. "We need candles. It's as dark as pitch."

"Altar candles," Bruno said. "I came across some in a cupboard."

"Good man," Leon said. "There must be candle holders, too. Have you both got tinder boxes?"

The men nodded, and after a few moments, Bruno returned with a bundle of old, dried-out candles. He pulled out his dagger and began to trim the wicks. "With luck, Capitaine, a few should have tallow enough in them to burn."

Candle holders of rough iron were fitted with candles and lit in turn.

They all stared into the gloomy depths as if unwilling to take the first step into the long-undisturbed sleep of the monks.

"We must do it for Jean," muttered Leon and began to descend slowly, holding the candlestick aloft.

They followed his cautious progress, the flames flickering over damp, lichen-covered walls. It was very cold, the air musty and unused. The steps ended and a passage stretched before them. Their boots disturbed grit and dust deposited by many years of neglect from wall and roof. The passage angled away in a slow curve, and Leon thought they must be under the main structure, the cells and refectory. It was a wide passage, much wider than the aisle above ground and wide enough, Leon supposed, for the carrying of corpses. The passage opened into a hall, high-roofed and wooden-beamed. Numerous alcoves led off the hall, but this appeared to be journey's end. No passages extended in any direction.

The alcoves lay in deep shadow. Leon held up his candle and peered into one. It was more of a short passage than an alcove, he realized, perhaps twenty feet long. Each side was shelved from floor to roof, each shelf a depth of two feet or so. Lying head to toe along the entire length of the shelving lay shrouded forms.

Leon backed out of the alcove. He did not believe himself to be unduly superstitious, but some of those shapes were so lifelike they might have sat up and asked his business in these hallowed precincts. The other alcoves told the same story. All brothers of the Order, together in death as they had been in life.

He stared about the hall. Between each alcove stood a stone sarcophagus, embellished by carvings. Judith was examining the wording of one. She glanced up as Leon approached.

"The priors or fathers of this Order must be contained within. This inscription is in Latin, but so worn it is hard to read his name or year of death."

Leon nodded. "Perhaps he will not mind if Jean joins him. All the shelves in the alcoves are full, and we cannot leave Jean to lie on the floor."

Judith's startled look faded and she nodded. "Yes, there is evidence of rodents. It would be too horrible to leave Jean at their mercy. Were the—the bodies of the monks undisturbed?"

"They appear to be, but the monks were clever at

embalming their dead.''

Judith laid a hand on the sarcophagus. "This holy man will surely not deny welcome to another soul.''

Leon looked at Otto and Bruno. "Do you agree?''

They nodded, faces somber in the candlelight.

"Set candles about, Judith," Leon said. "And we will slide open this lid.''

With their daggers, the three men dug the dust of ages from the rim of the stone lid. After that, it swung with surprising ease. The body below was a mere handful of bone and cloth. They stared silently.

"He has long gone to his reward," Judith said in a hushed voice. "But I will stay with him until you return with Jean. Angel shall hold vigil with me.''

As the men's footsteps receded and the stillness descended, Judith looked about the hall. She felt no fear in this place of the dead. Why should she? They had all been holy men, striving for perfection in life and accepting peace in death. What would they have thought of the present conflict? She imagined them tending the sick and praying for the souls of dying men, while despairing of man's inability to live in peace.

Angel rose to his feet, and Judith lifted her head to listen, then hurried to the foot of the stairs, a candlestick raised. They were bringing Jean down. Bruno came first, holding Jean's legs. He had been a large-boned countryman, and the combined strengths of Leon and Otto were needed to negotiate the uneven steps as they supported his shoulders and torso. Judith moved down the passage ahead of them until they reached the hall.

Even in the chill of the crypt, she could see the sheen of perspiration on each face. Judith bent into the sarcophagus and gently moved the old bones aside as Jean was laid down. Otto blew gustily and wiped his brow.

"A fair weight was our Jean, God rest his soul.''

Judith looked for the last time into the peaceful face of the man she had scarcely known and said a silent prayer. The lid was swung into place. The burial chamber was exactly as before, except for the presence of one man, not of the Holy Order of monks.

"Time to go," Leon said. "Collect the candlesticks. We're later than I had—" He stopped as he heard running footsteps echoing along the aisle. Sigmund's voice, high with panic, called.

"Capitaine, where are you—a patrol—they're coming."

Leon leapt for the corridor and bounded up the steps. "Here, Sigmund. The door by the altar, behind the confessional box."

Footsteps raced down the aisle. Leon caught him as he almost fell down the steps. The boy was white and shaking.

"They're all around. I was watching the gates, but they came from behind—through the gap in the wall, I think. I ran down straight away from the tower."

"Be calm, Sigmund. Are they in the courtyard?"

"Yes, sir. They'll be inside any minute. What shall we do?"

Bruno and Otto were on the steps behind Leon. "Back into the crypt," Leon said. "Sigmund, help me pull the confessional box to shield the entrance. With luck they won't look behind, for we can't latch the door. Quickly now, move as if the devil himself was on your heels."

They hauled frantically at the box, trying to position it as it had been before, but they needed to leave enough space to allow themselves entry through the crypt door.

"All right, Sigmund. Down the steps now. It's not good, but it's the best we can do."

The courtyard was ringing to the sound of booted feet. Any second now the soldiers of the duke would fling open the main door and leap inside, swords at the ready.

Leon pulled the crypt door as close as he dared, for there seemed no inside latch to match the heavy one outside. Why should there have been? Those who went down were unlikely to rise and demand freedom, and

the crypt door must have stayed wide open while the
last rites were being observed.

He followed Sigmund down the steps. They
assembled in the hall by the sarcophagus wherein Jean
lay.

"Draw your swords, men, and take up stations, each
to an alcove. Leave the first on each side empty. That
may be enough to reassure any searcher. Judith, take
Angel and go to the farthest one. Keep him from
growling if you value your life."

"You think they'll come down here, sir?"

Leon gave Bruno a grin. "Maybe not, but we must be
ready if they do! Find your places now and I'll snuff the
candles. Attack when I give the word, and God be with
us."

Judith caught his look of tenderness toward her, then
the last candle went out. She crouched with Angel on
the dusty floor, holding his head to her breast, ready to
quell the slightest sound he made. It was darker than the
darkest night, and she wondered how far the crypt
extended underground. To the monastery wall or the
city wall? Did the monks tunnel on, building new alcoves
as the number of dead increased? Did it matter anyway,
since that number might increase by five persons and a
dog before the sun was high?

She concentrated on the sounds above. A great
stamping and running of many feet, shouted orders, and
the crash of overturned pews. Did they think to find
rebels squeezed beneath? She tried to think of anything
that might give them away. The food had been finished,
but what of the empty brandy bottle and the horn
beaker? Would they be noticed? The old cassocks on
which Jean had laid. The blood might have dried. She
controlled a start of fear as a voice bellowed louder than
the rest. It seemed to roll down the steps and
reverberate through the crypt. It was followed by a
thunderous crash of splintering wood. The confessional
box. Dear God, had they discovered the door behind it?

She pressed Angel's head closer and stared toward the hall. It was less dark, surely? A grayness seemed to hang over it. They must have pulled open the crypt door to allow this slight illumination.

A man's voice shouted and sounds were hushed. They were there, listening, at the top of the steps. Perhaps they would go away, not daring to invade the ancient burial place. Then she heard cautious steps and knew they would dare. The light grew brighter. They were coming with torches and drawn swords. Soon they must reach the curving passage leading to this hall. Once here with their bright torches, there could be no hiding place. Four swordsmen against a company of duke's men, what chance had they? Jean would not be alone anymore.

The hall became flooded with light and the footsteps ceased. She imagined the soldiers looking about, peering cautiously into the first alcoves, empty of the living but full of the dead. A voice, slightly more distant, came to her. A nervous, querulous voice, as if its owner had ventured no farther than the foot of the stairs. That voice was well-remembered from their previous encounters. The vicomte, himself, still hunting rebels in the rear of his men.

"Have you found anybody, Sergeant?"

"Hundreds, sir, but they're all dead," came the laconic reply.

"Of course they are, you fool. It's a crypt, isn't it? You know I meant rebels."

Judith heard the sergeant sigh. "Will we open every coffin, sir? There's room enough for a handful of villains in each."

The vicomte must have detected the note of patient resignation in the sergeant's voice, for his words came angrily and closer to hand, as if he had braved the passage.

"Do your duty, Sergeant, and be quick about it. It's devilish cold down here."

"Yes, sir. All right, men. Half of you go round the walls. The rest of you start on those coffin lids."

Judith shrank back into the shadows, holding Angel firmly. It was hard to control her breathing, for she recognized the voice of the sergeant, too. The same man Leon had disarmed before taking the vicomte hostage for the soldier's good conduct. The sergeant was a professional soldier. He would not forgive Leon's deception. Any second now, there must come a shout of discovery from one of the searchers.

The harsh grating sound of a coffin lid being disturbed was suddenly muted by a thunderous voice that boomed and swept about the crypt.

"Go! Let our dead brothers sleep in peace!"

Although Judith knew the voice to be Leon's, the deep, sepulchral tones sent a shiver of fear down her back. Disembodied, accusing, the words hung in the air. Their effect on the duke's men must have been equally chilling. Startled cries, the clatter of boots, had them making a panicky rush for safety until the sergeant's loud command halted them.

"A trick, you fools! Can the dead speak? Look you at the footprints in the dust and the fresh grease from these candles."

"Attack!" roared Leon, and four men burst from the sheltering alcoves, hurling themselves violently onto the momentarily bemused soldiers of the duke. The advantage of surprise was a small one, but Leon had judged it well. The four men slashed and stabbed with their swords, advancing abreast and driving the soldiers back into the passage where free play with their sword arms was hampered.

"Back, back, you dogs!" Leon's voice boomed, his lips drawn back in a wolfish grin.

Those beyond the four flashing swords broke, and a mad scramble for the steps was not impeded by the vicomte. He had scuttled already to the head of the stairs and stood white-faced and shaking like a man with the ague.

The sergeant tried to rally the men with curses and threats, but the retreat was in full flight. He stood his ground at the foot of the steps, parrying and slashing, but his support dwindled. A sword thrust took him through the upper arm, and his own weapon spun from his hand. He stood, panting, glaring defiance. Otto raised his sword, two-handed, to deliver the deathblow, but Leon's words halted him.

"Put up your swords, men." His eyes met those of the sergeant, whose own eyes widened in recognition. "You're a gallant fighter, Sergeant, a better man than he who calls himself Commander. I'll not cut down an injured man as he would. Go, Sergeant, and tell that foppish gentleman I'll not deal so leniently with him should we meet again."

"Nor he with you, you may depend on it." The sergeant's face was twisted with pain, but he managed a smile. "I thank you, sir, as one soldier to another." He turned and began to pull himself up the steps, the four men close behind.

The vicomte stared down at the advancing party, then his eyes probed beyond as if expecting to see a following army in the shadows. His gaze fell on Leon and his eyes bulged.

"Holy Mother of God! You! Tarrant!"

He pivoted on his heel and whirled away. A thud, the sound of a heavy latch dropping into place, then the darkness became absolute.

32

The five men stood quite still in the darkness. Leon broke the silence, and his voice held sardonic amusement.

"A little hasty in his ways, your Commander, Sergeant. He mistook our good intentions and has lost for himself a brave man. Another minute and you would have been above ground."

"He cares only for his own skin," came the sergeant's resigned voice. "What is the loss of one sergeant to him? He'll convince himself he scored a brave victory and bottled up a hundred rebels, losing just one of his own men."

"Not just any man, Sergeant, but you. He'll rue the day he deserted you."

Leon spoke over his shoulder. "Move down the steps with care, Bruno, and ask my lady to light the candles, then bring one here and I'll help the sergeant."

"Your lady, sir?" The sergeant sounded surprised. "You have your lady down there?"

"Naturally. Where would I leave her in safety? The city is in conflict and the countryside alive with the camps of the mercenaries."

"I take your point, sir. I thank God my own wife is safe in Limoges."

A candle flame illuminated the darkness, and they heard steps in the passage below. Bruno looked up from the foot of the steps, and Leon held the sergeant's arm on the slow descent. With Bruno leading, they gained the hall.

Judith looked at them, and the sergeant smiled ruefully.

"We meet again, my lady, and I am your prisoner this time."

"And a wounded one, Sergeant. How bad is your arm?"

"A flesh wound only."

"Take off your tunic, please. I have no salves, but I will bind it if you will sacrifice your shirt."

Leon removed the sergeant's dagger belt and scabbard, helping the man ease out of his tunic. The shirt was reasonably clean, and Judith tore it into strips, padding and binding the wound. It was not bleeding as copiously as Jean's had been. With luck, the cut would heal.

"That's the best I can do until we—" She paused, then continued. "Until we get out of here."

No one spoke in contradiction. They were trapped in the crypt. The only way out was through the door the vicomte had slammed. He was unlikely to open it again. Perhaps he had already gone, secure in the knowledge that his victims were as good as dead. She looked around at the men, all sitting in attitudes of weary dejection, their backs against the stone coffin.

Otto was staring at the vicomte's sergeant, his expression unfriendly.

"Why did you have me hold my hand against him, Capitaine?" he muttered. "I could have killed him on the steps, for sure."

"I know you could, but I was hoping they'd leave the door open long enough to drag the sergeant through. We could have rushed them and made a fight of it at the entrance."

"That fine-dressed fellow recognized you, Capitaine."

"Unfortunately, yes. We have met before."

"As long as he shut you in, he didn't care about the sergeant, here."

"That's true." Leon smiled at the sergeant. "My apologies, friend."

"So." Otto was pursuing his own line of thought. "What's to stop me finishing him off now?"

"My sword arm, Corporal," Leon said. "Only barbarians kill injured prisoners."

Otto scowled. "He's still the enemy."

"Not so, Corporal. This crypt is the enemy now, and we are as much like prisoners as the sergeant. What good would it serve to despatch a man here?"

"He'd be company for Jean," Otto growled.

Leon sighed. "Save your blood lust for later, Corporal. Put your mind to the thought that the air here is less fresh than when we brought Jean down. That sarcophagus is old and cracked. Would you double the scent of death?"

It was true, Judith realized, there was a sweet, sickly smell in the air. She had been unable to account for it until Leon's words brought understanding. Poor Jean was already in a state of decay. She shivered. It must happen to them all if the crypt remained sealed, and there was no earthly reason why the vicomte should return or anyone else show interest in a long-abandoned monastery.

"How goes the battle up there, Sergeant?" asked Leon, pointing upward with his chin.

The sergeant's mouth twisted. "Well enough for the duke, I hear, but our Commander, as you know, has a partiality for staying in the background." He looked at Otto defiantly. "The baron's cause is lost, but he'll fight to the last man in his peasant army. He knows what lies ahead, so he won't surrender."

"We kept watch from the bell tower," Leon went on. "The woods were being stripped for siege towers and trebuckets. I assume the duke will build more than one of the latter.''

''He plans several, I'm told. He brought skilled men to operate them, men with an eye to balance and range-finding.'' The sergeant smiled thinly at Otto. ''The usurper will come under a hailstorm of missiles when they get the range on the palace. 'Tis pity such a fine palace must suffer, but the duke will rebuild the home of his ancestors.''

The two men eyed each other with open dislike. To prevent the flaring of tempers, Leon stood up and took a candle from the sarcophagus. ''While we still have light to spare, I suggest we make a thorough search of the crypt. There might be a door we've missed in passage or alcove.''

''Why should there be?'' grumbled Otto as he climbed to his feet.

''I don't know, Corporal,'' Leon said patiently. ''Which is why I suggest we look. Times change over the centuries. Spanish priests may not always have been accepted by the duke's predecessors. It is worth an investigation, at least. Or do you propose to sit here until starvation turns us into fit companions for the dead already at rest here?'' He clicked his fingers at Angel. ''Come. Your nose is keener to scent a breath of fresh air.''

Their search revealed nothing. Each alcove held only the shrouded bodies. The stone walls of the passage were solid, plain and uncarved, no protuberance that might hint at a secret opening. Leon went up the steps to examine again the inside of the crypt door. The iron-work was smooth, and the wood, so elaborately carved on the other side, was plain and fitted so closely that not a vestige of light or air penetrated. It would take a battering ram to break through that, he mused, but how could men swing a ram if all were on steps of different heights? And battering rams were not usually part of a crypt's furnishings. He rejoined the men in the hall.

"We'll leave one candle burning to conserve our supplies. Find a corner to sleep in, but keep your swords to hand. If anyone comes, we shall hear the door." He looked at the sergeant. "How's the arm?"

"Well enough, sir. Your lady has gentle hands."

Leon nodded somberly and moved to Judith's side. He drew her into a shadowed corner and they lay down, trying to find comfort on the cold, stone floor. They lay in a close embrace, and Leon remembered their other embraces and sighed.

"To die in a crypt while still in full health is not the future I had planned although the company is the same."

"If we must die, at least we are together," Judith murmured. "But tell me of the plans you had. It will serve to pass the time."

"I hoped to find my true self by retracing my steps as far back as I could remember. This diversion into the city has given my mind no time for deep thought."

"And when you had found yourself, what then?"

"To hold you to me before a priest and bind you fast by my side."

Judith laughed softly. "I am bound fast to your side, with or without a priest. Unless you put me away, I shall never be far from you until death."

"Dear God, if there was only some way—" Leon began, then stopped abruptly.

"What is it?" Judith asked, and even as she said the words, she heard it, too.

The men were sitting up, their expressions inquiring. Distant thuds and a slow rumble as of falling masonry reached them. Faintly at first but growing steadily louder, the rumbling continued.

"A thunderstorm?" Judith hazarded.

"No," Leon said with conviction. "Sergeant," he called. "It sounds as if your duke has got the trebuckets at work. What do you make of it? Could it be so?"

"It could, sir, but—" The sergeant's voice held doubt

"—but would we hear it so far from the palace?"

Sigmund was on his feet, staring at Leon. "That trebucket we saw, Capitaine, on the hillside. It hadn't moved while I was on watch, save to take on more shape."

Leon frowned. "The range would be too long to hit the palace."

The sergeant listened to the heavy bombardment for a moment, then he spoke dryly. "But not too long for this place, Capitaine."

"This place? Why would—" Leon paused, looking hard at the sergeant, whose face held wry amusement.

"By the Saints, Sergeant, you cannot mean the vicomte would bombard this holy monastery!"

"Why not, sir? If he orders the bombardment of this place, who will dare disobey? The monastery must be reduced to rubble to wipe out the nest of rebels concealed within, he'll say." The sergeant's voice became bitter. "One or a hundred, it's all the same to him. I know him too well, sir. He's a man to bury his mistakes if he can't pass them onto others. Since I'm not at hand to take any blame, he'll tell a brave story and be rid of one who was witness to his cowardice."

They all listened intently. A pause between each thud was obviously the time taken to reload the bucket. A shattering crash above their heads brought a cloud of dust out of the stonework. There was the sound of falling masonry.

"The bell tower, Capitaine," Sigmund said, wiping streaming eyes. "I think we are directly beneath it."

"I think you are right, Sigmund. It is—or was— a good target for an experienced man. A pity they can't aim at the crypt door."

They all stood by the old sarcophagus, awaiting the next blow. It came with a thunderous crash, showering them with dust. The stone walls seemed to shiver and creak ominously.

"What the devil are they loading with?" muttered

Leon. "These walls are at least six feet in thickness."

No one answered. They waited for the next assault. It came with a booming crash that filled their ears like the ringing of bells, an intolerable, echoing sound that reverberated through the entire crypt. As the noise died away, another took its place, the rattle and thud of splintering stonework, slab grinding on slab with weary acceptance.

The bombardment went on, blasting and weakening the old structure. A metallic crash had Leon leaping for the passageway. For the briefest of moments he saw the crypt door twist and buckle, then the steps were gone in a vast upheaval of stone. In a choking fury of dust the passageway erupted. Leon staggered back, blinded by flying particles. When he could, at last, clear his vision, he found himself staring at a solid barrier of rock from floor to roof. He cursed the vicomte long and fluently as he coughed and wiped streaming eyes. For a second the way had been clear, then this avalanche of rock had descended. He turned back into the hall.

"The passage is blocked," he said briefly. "Half the monastery lies between us and the crypt door. There's no way out."

He leaned against the sarcophagus of the Father Prior. Judith moved to his side, sliding her arm about his waist. There was no need for words. They all accepted the verdict. No way out, no escape. The last flicker of hope had died. Even so, the vicomte had not finished with them. The bombardment went on, and they crouched by the sarcophagus as one of the alcoves of dead monks collapsed into an obscene heap of rubble and bone.

Judith laid her face against Leon's chest as skulls rolled over the floor.

"Dear God," muttered the sergeant. "Has he not done enough? Is it a wasteland he wants, without a stone left standing?"

"I imagine he has that in mind," Leon said. "He'll take no chance of allowing anyone to claw their way out of here.''

Another alcove caved in, and the sergeant's voice came through the fog of dust. ''There'll be precious few missiles left for the palace if we are privileged to receive the greater part of the stockpile. The duke will not be pleased with him.''

''That, I would like to see,'' Leon said dryly, then pulled Judith closer as a slab of rock fell, splitting apart a sarcophagus a few feet away. She choked back a cry as a bony skull slid into view.

Hypnotized by the sight of the rolling skull, the five men and Judith instinctively strained back against the old prior's coffin. There was a grating sound as the sarcophagus moved. Bruno scrambled to his feet, shaking and dust-streaked.

''It's collapsing,'' he cried. ''Just like the other. I don't want to fall on Jean.''

''Nor I.'' Otto declared, coming to his knees. ''If the floor caves in—''

''Wait,'' said Leon. ''The floor is sound enough, the coffin is in no worse shape.''

''But it moved, Capitaine.'' Sigmund was on his knees, too, staring.

''Yes, it moved. I accept that. But why?'' Leon frowned and laid his hands on the lid. He pushed. A faint grating sound followed. He looked round. ''All of you. Lay on your hands and push.''

''What for?'' asked Otto. ''It will only prove we can move a coffin.''

''A coffin this size and carved from solid stone? It must have been built down here, for no dozen monks of frugal habits would have the strength to carry it down. Do you doubt your own strength, Corporal? Stand back if you do and wait for the vicomte to turn you into one with the monks already here.''

Otto scowled at the sarcasm and laid his broad hands on the coffin.

"Gently, now," Leon said. "There may be a drop beneath."

At each cautious heave, the sarcophagus moved, turning slightly sideways.

"Stop," Leon said quickly. "There's some sort of opening beneath. Move to the ends and watch your footholds."

They obeyed and jumped back swiftly as the sarcophagus swung into a half-circle and ground to a shuddering halt. A stench of rotting undergrowth rose through the dust-laden air. They stared into the depths.

"A candle, someone." Leon's voice was hushed, and Judith held out the lighted candlestick.

"By all that's holy, it's a stairway!"

The men peered down, and Leon gave a croak of laughter. "They were not so simple-minded, after all, these holy fathers. It looks like an escape tunnel. The secret of it could well have been handed down from one prior to the next."

He grinned round at them. "Even priests have their enemies when countries fall into conflict. Monasteries have been sacked before now by barbarian overlords." He looked down the steps. "This Order had the foresight to make provision for that. Please God, they kept the route in good condition."

Another alcove disintegrated in a shower of stone, and Judith took a candlestick, holding it toward Leon, who put his own candle flame to its wick.

"We can be no worse off down there than up here," she said shakily. "You have two faithful adventurers in your train, my lord. Come, Angel." She glanced at Sigmund, whose expression was half-fear, half-hope. "Your village will not be reached if you remain here. Nor yours, Bruno. It is our only chance. Will you throw it away?"

"No, Madame. That we will not. Lead on, Capitaine."

"You follow me, Otto, and we will both hold to our

sword hilts in case this way is known. My lady and the sergeant to follow, then Sigmund and Bruno."

Leon began the descent carefully, watching each step. The steps surprisingly dry, considering the dankness, and they numbered twenty. A tunnel led into darkness. Leon waited until all of them were down the steps, then entered the tunnel. It ran curving downward for a considerable distance, then began to rise. The undergrowth smell became stronger, and lichen grew thickly on the walls. The noise of the bombardment grew fainter, and Leon grinned at Otto.

"So far, so good. Let us hope the vicomte stays on target."

Otto grinned back, all his hostility gone. "I'll swear I can smell God's fresh air, even from here. We must be beyond the city wall."

"Amen to that, Corporal, and well beyond, I hope."

As they moved up the slope, it became steeper and the vegetable smell sweeter. Soon, green living bushes dotted the tunnel and the blackness was lifting. Gray light began to filter toward them, and Leon called over his shoulder for the candles to be snuffed out. He and Otto doused their own and handed the candlesticks to those behind. The two of them drew their swords. A short way on the grayness turned into heavily shadowed daylight. Leon halted the party.

"Wait here. The corporal and I will scout ahead. If all is clear, I will whistle for you to come."

He looked round at the dimly seen faces. Judith's was pale and strained, the sergeant's tight-lipped and running with perspiration, pain evident from his shoulder wound. Sigmund's young face looked dazed, but Bruno nodded to Leon.

"If you need another sword, Capitaine, I will come."

"If I do, I shall call, Bruno. Meanwhile, guard well our little party."

The track they followed was broken by rock, the

bushes thickening into an almost impenetrable barrier ahead.

"Beware we do not come upon the duke's men at work, Otto."

Otto nodded, and they moved on warily. There was no sound of axes. They could still hear the vicomte's bombardment, but the sound was muted, as if it came from another part of the hillside. Leon tried to work out the direction, but both passage and track had curved. He looked up. There was the sky above, that clear blue sky he had thought never to see again. A sense of excitement gripped him.

"Those old monks, Corporal, would not be foolhardy enough to end their escape route within sight of the city. I would guess they pointed it toward the Spanish border, since they were men of that country."

"And well up the hillside, Capitaine, to give them view of any pursuit."

"Exactly, Corporal. It's my belief we shall find ourselves looking down on the vicomte's trebucket."

They grinned at each other, and Otto chuckled.

"That would be a rare sight, Capitaine. To watch the vicomte pounding the Santa Dominic to rubble while those he thought to bury looked on."

Leon smiled. "Let us push on and see if we are right."

They came to a thicket of bushes and crawled through on hands and knees. The hillside lay empty, the mountains of Vallone stretching eastward. Lifting their heads above a ridge, they stared down. The city was distant, but the flat ground on which the trebucket stood swarmed with small figures staggering under loads of rock, two men to each boulder, as they filled and refilled the bucket. On a small rise to one side stood a gesticulating figure. The mouth opened and closed, but the two watchers heard no sound. They were too far away to hear more than the dull thudding of missiles on stone.

The Santa Dominic had barely a stone left standing. The whole once-proud edifice was a heap of desolation.

"Will he not give up, the madman?" growled Otto. "Does he think a living soul could crawl out of that?"

"Let him be, Corporal. I think the duke will be on his way to discover what target needs so much destruction. The vicomte will answer to the duke for the waste of missiles. Let us call up the others before the confrontation. We'd best strike toward Spain, then turn into the hills well above the city."

They retraced their steps to a point where Leon's whistle might be heard. Bruno appeared first, his sword unsheathed. He grinned with relief as he saw the two men.

"Praise God, you are safe, Capitaine. You were gone so long I was hard put to restrain Madame from coming in search of you."

"You did well, Bruno." Leon smiled at Judith and ran his eye over the others. "There is quite a climb now, so that short rest will have done you good. Lead on, Otto. I will help the sergeant."

Otto set off and Leon slid an arm round the sergeant's waist. "Lean on me, friend. You're hardly in good condition for a stiff climb."

"I'll admit that to you, Capitaine," the sergeant gasped, "but not to your bloodthirsty corporal. He'd put me down like a dog." He glanced sideways at Leon. "Why do you trouble yourself with me? Am I not your enemy, too?"

"To be honest with you, Sergeant, I support neither side in this conflict. Oh yes, it is true I held rank in the baron's army and held fast while I thought him a man of integrity whose only desire was to free the peasants from the old duke's harsh rule. I believed he had dealt honorably with the duke and his household. I learned the truth from a goatherder when I returned from a mission in France. I am not a Vallonese, so I forswear allegiance to a tyrant. You gave my lady and me shelter one night when I sought to carry her to safety, so for that I am in your debt. How could I allow you to be despatched by the corporal?" He looked into the sergeant's face. "And what of you, my friend? Will you return to the service of a man who left you to die?"

The sergeant gave a faint grin. "And be hung as a deserter? That's the way His Lordship will tell it, I'll take my oath. Since I am presumed dead, I've a mind to head back to Limoges. I'll not fight any more with this shoulder."

"A wise decision, Sergeant."

They said no more until they had reached the high point of the hillside, overlooking the city. The vicomte seemed, at last, to have been persuaded to end the bombardment, and in the stillness they could hear birdsong.

"We'll rest until dusk, then make for a hill village," Leon said. "We need food and water, and the sergeant's shoulder must be attended to." He glanced at Sigmund and smiled. "Any ideas, Sigmund?"

The boy nodded. "I know of a village not too far away."

Leon read the doubt on his face and said quickly, "We'll not be welcome, I know, but we'll not ask for lodgings, just a little help."

"Yes, sir." Sigmund nodded his relief. "I've a cousin thereabouts. He'll be sure to help."

They lay down in the shadows of the bushes, seeking what comfort they could. Leon took his place beside Judith. "Are you all right, my love?"

Judith licked dry lips and tried to smile. "Yes, but my mind is plagued by thoughts of fresh water, or even that terrible red wine you had from the horse-line guard."

Leon put an arm about her shoulders. "Sleep now, my love, and at dusk I promise to head for the nearest stream."

Despite their discomfort, sleep overcame them with the relaxing of tension. Judith opened her eyes some hours later to the lengthening shadows and the twittering of birds settling for the night. One by one they came awake to blink gritty eyes and shake the dust from their clothes.

Judith pushed back her hair. It felt rough and matted. Her skin had the texture of old canvas, she reflected wryly, and glanced about her. The sergeant's face was gray with fatigue and pain. The others looked little better than filthy brigands. Leon, Otto, Bruno, and—she glanced round quickly. There was one missing. Sigmund. Where was Sigmund? Surely he had not deserted them while they slept? Sigmund was to lead them to the village where his cousin lived. The hill stretched out above them, empty now of all human form. And Sigmund was gone, swallowed up in the gathering twilight.

33

"We should go, Capitaine," Otto declared.

Leon shook his head. "It is not dark enough yet. We cannot risk being seen if the duke has lookouts on the city walls."

"And what if the lad brings back a troop of soldiers to bargain his life for ours?"

"He wouldn't do that," Judith said vehemently.

"Then what is it that keeps him away?" Otto returned, scowling. "Why should he slip away in the first place if not to betray us?"

"What has he to gain? We are free of the city."

"A price on every rebel's head and you ask that, Madame?" Otto stared at Leon. "I'm in no mood to wait until the rope is about my neck, Capitaine. I'll take my chance alone."

"Very well, Corporal. I have no power to detain you."

Otto nodded briefly and was gone.

"How about you, Bruno?" Leon asked. "You are free to go if you wish."

Bruno shook his head. "I don't know this part of the country, sir. I will wait for Sigmund. He'll not betray us, whatever the corporal says."

"It might be wiser to move our position and stand guard until full dark. We must move then whether or not he's back."

They moved along the bush line, Judith helping the sergeant, whose wound had stiffened. Angel, padding beside Leon, stopped suddenly and lifted his head.

381

Leon caught the movement, dropped his hand to the dog's ruff, and they all stopped, listening. Leon's fingers tightened on his sword.

"Horses," he whispered. "Keep very still."

The clink of a bridle came to them and the soft but definite approach of hoofbeats. There was a pause, and someone gave a low whistle. The notes were the same as Leon had used to summon the party up the hillside. He repeated the whistle, but his hand stayed firmly on his sword hilt.

"Capitaine? Where are you? It's Sigmund."

Motioning the others to stay where they were, Leon went forward cautiously. On a lower slope of the hillside, he saw Sigmund's upturned face, each hand gripping the bridle of a horse.

Leon stared. "Sigmund?"

"Yes, Capitaine." The boy's teeth showed in a grin as he saw Leon's amazement.

"By all that's holy. I'd forgotten the horses, lad. So that's where you've been."

"I did not forget them, Capitaine. I could not leave any dumb beast to fend for itself."

"But you were away so long. Did you have trouble finding them?"

"No, sir, but there were some soldiers climbing over the ruins of the Santa Dominic. I had to hide until full dark." He grinned. "My trouble then was finding the saddles. All bushes look alike at night." He turned and fumbled in a saddlebag. "I found an empty flagon by the stream's edge. Here, sir."

Leon began to laugh softly. "You're a marvel, Sigmund. Our throats are as dry as old rushes." He moved down to relieve Sigmund of the flagon and one of the bridled horses.

The warmth of his welcome from the rest of the party had the boy grinning in scarlet embarrassment. No one told him of Otto's suspicions, only that the corporal had decided to strike out alone. The arrival of Sigmund with water and horses had put fresh heart into them all. Judith and the sergeant were helped into the saddles, and the three men escorted them, with Sigmund in the lead.

Two hours later they came within sight of a small village. Sigmund led them to a run-down barn.

"If you wait here, Capitaine, I will rouse my cousin." He merged into the shadows.

Within half an hour he was back with a large man and a very old woman.

"My cousin, Rudy, and Tante Maria," he explained. "She is skilled with wounds and will tend the sergeant." He spoke to Rudy in some patois Leon could not understand, but the man nodded and went away, returning with a leather bucket of water and a basket of bread and cheese.

"There is little to spare, Capitaine," Sigmund said apologetically. "And Rudy hopes you will not bring trouble to the village."

Leon smiled at the large man. "Please thank your cousin for his generosity, Sigmund, and tell him that we stay no longer than is necessary for Tante Maria to clean and bind the sergeant's wound."

The large man nodded, satisfied, and Leon looked down on the sergeant. A candle had been lit in the shelter of the barn wall, and in its light Leon watched the old woman bathe and bind the sergeant's shoulder with a quick dexterity that belied her years. She muttered as she worked, and Sigmund smiled.

"She says the wound is little, though it hurts you sore, but that will pass and the flesh is good."

"I am greatly obliged to the lady," the sergeant said, easing back into his tunic.

When they had eaten and drunk, the sergeant and Judith remounted the horses.

Leon looked at Sigmund and Bruno. "This is where we part, my friends. You are back amongst your own people. May all go well with you."

The two men nodded. "God speed you, Capitaine," Sigmund said. "Bruno and I will find our way from here."

Leon swung up behind Judith, who lifted a hand in farewell.

"Limoges, you said, Sergeant?" asked Leon as the dawn came up slowly.

They had ridden all night, occasionally resting the horses, but had seen no campfires. The city was far behind and no doubt full of mercenaries by now. They crossed the river without hindrance.

"Aye, sir, and I begin to see the landmarks before me. I'll be there before nightfall." He looked at Leon. "Where are you and your lady headed, sir?"

"Poitou, Sergeant. I have business there."

"Then we, too, part company before noon. I'll be home tomorrow, anyway, even on foot."

Leon smiled. "Keep the horse, Sergeant. It is one of the duke's, after all. I'll buy another at the nearest town."

"That's kind of you, sir, and I won't say no."

They parted at a fork in the track, and Leon set his and Judith's horse toward Poitou. Judith glanced over her shoulder into Leon's face and smiled.

"I hope you will halt at the first stream we see. No one will sell you a horse, looking as you do. Our clothing cannot be helped, but a little less dirt on our faces would be advantageous."

Leon laughed. "You are right, my love. They would set the dogs on me, for sure. Where's Angel, by the way?"

"He appears to have found the stream we seek."

Judith lay on her back beside the stream, refreshed and relaxed. Beside her lay the belt holding the dagger and the jewel pouch. The goatskin jacket, shaked and pummelled, still smelled of goat as, she was convinced, she did herself. But that was a small worry. They were free of Vallone and in France. She opened her eyes and smiled at Leon.

"Come, my love," he said, drawing her to her feet. "Just a little farther. There must be a town ahead where we may lodge for the night and buy clothing."

Both were found in a small French market town. Leon's glib and indignant description of being set upon and robbed by Vallonese bandits, combined with his most arrogant and imperious manner, convinced the suspicious landlord that he dealt with quality. The best bedchamber was put at their disposal and cans of hot water brought up. Judith bathed and washed her hair clean of accumulated smells while Leon went to market.

He returned with garments of plain but good quality. Judith slipped into the new shift and tunic gratefully. She tossed back her damp hair as she strapped on her belt and jewel pouch. She smiled up at Leon.

"You have good taste, Leon. Perhaps you have purchased female attire before?"

He laughed, his teeth white in the dark face. "Not to my knowledge, and I would rather not repeat the experience, for the good wives of this town eyed me in a curious fashion."

"A wealthy goatherd may be new to them," murmured Judith. "An object of curiosity, wouldn't you say, for there was no disguising your occupation."

Leon's brows rose. "I never thought of that." His eyes lit with amusement. "How soon one becomes accustomed to the smell. Now, go downstairs, woman, and leave me to rid myself of the taint."

When he joined Judith in the tiny dining room, he came to her relaxed and smiling, unlike the hard-eyed Capitaine de Foret of the last few days. He looked younger, the lines smoothed from his face as if part of a burden had been lifted.

Angel lay under the trestle table, resisting all attempts by the landlord to remove him to the barn. He knew his place, and that was by her feet. He was not to be dislodged. The landlord served him food where he lay.

As they ate, new travelers arrived, entering the dining

room, amidst a babble of conversation.

"The city, you say?" the landlord remarked, setting down wine. "And in full view, too. Well, I'll not confess to sorrow, for many have passed this way with naught but the clothes on their backs, and tales of treatment to make you cringe."

Leon caught the landlord's eye. "What news is this? What city?" he asked.

The landlord came close. " 'Tis well you and your lady are safe in France, Monsieur, for these travelers bring news of Vallone. The baron is hanged from the city gates in full view of all, and the people celebrate the return of the young duke."

He looked at Judith, who had paled. "Forgive me, Madame. This talk of hanging has distressed you, but his punishment is fitting for he did the same to many others." He bowed and moved away.

Leon pushed Judith's goblet toward her. "Drink a little wine, my dear, and put all thoughts of Vallone from your mind. Come, I will take you upstairs. It has been a tiring journey. A good fire and a soft bed will do much to ease your mind."

They entered the bedchamber, and Leon set down the candlestick given to him by the landlord. He glanced at the bed and smiled.

"A softer resting place than we have had for many a night, my love. A goose-feather mattress if I'm not mistaken."

Judith slid her arms about his neck. "Then take me to it, my lord. I care not whether it be straw or goose-feathers as long as you share it with me." A laugh rose in her throat. "See how brazen I have become, like a kitchenmaid luring a stableman into her embrace."

Leon laughed too, holding her close. "And he so lovesick no lure is required." He moved his hands and began to unbuckle Judith's belt. The jewel pouch fell to the floor with a thud, and Judith's new tunic and shift followed it. Then she was lifted and laid gently on the bed. Leon's clothes dropped beside hers, and he joined her. He leaned on one elbow, appraising the slim body frankly, running gentle fingers over her breasts and stomach.

"Does your kitchenmaid please you, my lord?" Judith asked demurely.

"Like no other ever did or ever will," he answered solemnly and smoothed back the cloud of dark hair on the pillow. "I will fight the world to hold you."

Judith lifted a hand to his face. "You hold me now. Let the world wait until tomorrow, for I cannot."

Leon's lips were on hers as he pulled her close, so close that not even a goose-feather from the mattress could have come between them. There was no need of the fire in the bedchamber grate, for the heat of their joined bodies spread into a consuming fire. Judith felt her limbs melt in glad acceptance of Leon's strong manhood, her body arching to his as the passion of their loving swept past and future into oblivion. There was only now and the urgency of this moment.

The sun woke them as it streamed through the small, latticed window of the bedchamber. Judith turned her head on the pillow and found Leon watching her. He smiled and reached for her hand, his eyes warm but thoughtful. She knew what lay on his mind.

"How can you find your true self, my love?" Judith asked. "What way is there?"

"I must go back to the monastery in Poitou where Leon de Foret began his known life. I will take you first to Marquise and leave you in the care of Sister Ulrica."

"Please let me go to Poitou with you. I could not rest easy without you."

"I will return to the convent."

Judith held him close. "If the secret lies with the monks, I would like to be there." She tried to smile into his face. "Should you discover you have a wife elsewhere, you may think it best not to return."

Leon looked startled. "By the Rood. I had not thought of that! Perhaps I should hope to be Tarrant, after all."

Two days later, they reined in their horses before the gates of a long, low building, stone-walled and moss-encrusted. Leon raised his eyes to the bell tower, remembering the peal of its bells, then the soft chant of voices. He urged his horse to a walk, and they moved between the gates into a courtyard to dismount by the main door.

A young monk answered his knock and guided them into a hall. As they waited for his message to be conveyed, Leon stared from the side window, seeing the patch of grass beneath the chestnut tree, the place where he had sat so many times in blank, unseeing solitude, fighting the pain in his body.

He turned at a step behind and looked into the face of Father Ignatius. The old man, still gaunt with tight-drawn skin over his cheekbones, came forward smiling at them both.

"Good day, my son. You asked to see me. How may I serve you and Madame?"

Leon took a deep breath and stepped closer to the monk. "Father Ignatius, do you remember me? I was one of the wounded brought here from the battlefield."

The monk spread his hands. "So many battles, my son, it is hard to remember."

Leon felt despair touch him. "The spring of 1199, Father, when King Richard of England died outside the castle of Chaluz."

"I remember hearing of his death, but those wounded did not come here. There was fighting enough to the south of Chaluz to fill our beds." He frowned and came closer to Leon. "Come, walk in the garden with me. My eyes are not good and there is more light there."

Judith followed the two men, and Leon paused on the patch of grass and looked up into the chestnut tree.

"I sat here often, Father. There were others, soldiers of Vallone. I left with them."

The old man peered into his face, hearing the quiet desperation in Leon's voice. "What is it you want to know, my son?"

"Who am I, Father? My mind is tortured by memory as if I had two lives. I must know my past to find my future."

He moved his head restlessly, and a shaft of sunlight through the leaves of the tree touched the white streaks in his hair and the cruel scar that ran from his temple.

The old man nodded. "I remember you now. We fought hard to save your life and, with God's help, succeeded. We healed your body, but your mind was distressed." He smiled gently. "You told us you were Leon, not once but many times as if to test my memory."

"Leon? One name only?"

They had moved away from the tree toward a stone seat set under a hedge. Leon sat down and placed a hand over his eyes. The old priest eyed the drooping shoulders silently, then sat down beside the man. They both seemed to have forgotten Judith, who stayed in the shadow of the chestnut tree.

"And yet, a curious thing, my son, which comes back to me." Leon raised his head and stared fixedly at Father Ignatius as he went on. "The name you gave us so often came sometimes like a question. Why should that be?"

Leon said slowly, "It is a name well enough." He shook his head. He had hoped for so much on their journey here, but he was still Leon. "Perhaps I sought to test my own memory, not yours," he finished, then looked at the priest with a frown. "De Foret? Did I call myself that, too?"

"No, my son. It was the place where you were found. Men lay thick amongst the trees of the forest. You gave us no name save Leon, so I gave you the name of de

Foret, a good, sturdy name. Forgive me if I was wrong to do it but you knew no other to take into your rebirth. Only a poor peasant has one name, but a gentleman boasts two." He nodded at Leon's inquiring gaze. "Oh yes, my son, your birth was gentle. It showed itself in many ways. Our patients were men of many nationalities. Men from the Low Country and men from England. Do you recall your birthplace?"

Leon shook his head. "I assumed I was French, yet I found the English tongue coming to my lips, but what does that signify? A soldier may acquire many tongues."

"But not use them as fluently as you did with the Englishman."

Leon stared at him. "What Englishman?"

The priest shrugged. "I knew not his name, but he wore the emblem of Coeur de Lion. He spoke much in his delirium, poor fellow, but the fever's grip was too powerful to be denied."

"And I spoke to him?"

"Listened would be more apt, for your mind was feverish, yet he seemed to gain comfort from your presence and the words you spoke."

Leon rose and began to pace restlessly as if he could not rest easy in one place. "But Vallone, Father? You said Vallone would see me again."

"You had their badge on the sleeve of the tunic round your shoulders when the brothers found you."

"Ah yes, of course. My own was ruined and it was cold. I remember taking it from a corpse. So that is why I found myself in company with those returning to Vallone. But I am no nearer to solving this riddle than I was." He took a few paces away. "Dear God, if only I had not discarded my own tunic—"

Father Ignatius rose, his eyes bright with thought. "Would your recognize it, my son?"

Leon turned quickly. "What do you mean?"

"When a patient is tended, his clothes are stripped

from him and kept in the storeroom. When a man recovers, he reclaims his clothes."

"And if he does not recover?"

"We retain them for those who come seeking their lost ones. Those who know not if their kin is in life or death. The brothers gather all such things from the battlefield."

Judith, watching from the shelter of the chestnut tree, saw the leap of hope in Leon's eyes. She stepped forward. Leon turned and held out a hand. His fingers tightened on hers.

"Father, this is Lady Tarrant. Her husband was with Richard of England, but not at Chaluz."

"I knew him so little," Judith said huskily. "I thought—we thought—"

Father Ignatius looked at the clasped hands. He smiled. "I understand. Come."

They followed him into a small room laid out to shelving. In one corner a few swords lay rusting, and the air was musty and cold. Jerkins and breeches lay folded on the shelves, an assortment of footgear nearby.

"Those things we give to the poor who pass our way, but the tunics and surcoats we keep in this chest." He raised the lid. 'We clean them as best we might to lessen the distress of those who search through them. Some we could not match with our dead and wounded, for men in panic cast off their badges and allegiance when pursued by the enemy."

Judith looked at the pitiful relics of battle, pierced and slashed cloth that had once contained the strong, healthy bodies of fighting men. Her eyes misted. "And what of the men who die nameless and unclaimed?"

"We give them Christian burial and in our own consecrated ground. A stone cross without inscription is the most we can do."

Judith's hand moved slowly in the chest, disclosing a tunic that barely hung together, so many cuts had it sustained. Her gaze was caught by the badge of the

Plantagenets, but below it was another. Her heart jerked as she looked on the flash of Tarrant color.

"Dear God," she breathed, reaching for the tunic. "How came it that Lord Tarrant's messengers missed this place?"

"We were but a small Order, my lady, and perhaps the messenger knew only the name which we did not. Had they come, they would have seen as you see now." He looked at Leon questioningly. "Does this garment say anything to you, my son?"

Leon frowned at it. "There are many cuts in the fabric. Too many, I think, for the wounds I sustained." His tone was hollow with despair. "Holy Mother of God, I must be someone! If I am not Tarrant, then who am I?" He pushed the tunic aside angrily. "Those colors I thought mine are not. There is still a flaw in the arrangements."

The old priest looked at him with sympathy. "The mind is strange, my son. Since your own mind was emptied of memory at the time, the words of the Englishman entered therein like rain on parched grassland, creating false thoughts that were not your own. Open up your mind again and let us see if true memory returns. The secret must lie in this chest, since your body does not lie in our graveyard."

He lifted out the tunics, one by one, commenting on each. "Vallonese, Flemish, French, Austrian, and this from Brittany. The lord himself came from—"

"Nantes!"

The word came suddenly to Leon's lips and fell into the silence between them. Leon looked startled as they stared at each other.

"Nantes," he repeated and took the tunic from the priest's hand, staring hard at it, as if it would give up its secret. A small badge on the shoulder was stitched with two interwoven letters. There was no flash of color.

"These letters, Father. Did the lord from Brittany give you his name?"

"Hugo de Vane, my son, an Englishman who followed

Count Geoffrey from Anjou to Brittany. He mourned his only son. Put on the tunic, my son, and see if you have discovered your true self."

Leon rose hesitantly, discarding the tunic he had bought in the south. He slipped into the tunic with its sword-slashed sleeves and stared down into Judith's eyes. They were glowing brightly.

"It fits you, Leon, as perfectly as if it had been made just for you."

Leon looked dazed. "De Vane," he muttered, then turned to Father Ignatius. "A tunic, but no grave to show the lord. Did he not find that odd?"

The priest frowned in thought. "Strangely, he was cheered by it, if I remember aright. He declared that I had lifted his hopes and the arrogant young cub would return in his own good time."

Leon grinned. "That sounds like him, the old lion. He said the same when I went off to the Holy Land." He stopped and looked at the priest. "Can it really be? My mind is filling with memories at last, now that I have cast out all remembrance of Tarrant's words. I told you I was Leon, again and again you say, but I could go no further. Now it comes back I am Leon de Vane of Nantes." He gripped the priest's hands. "You have given me back myself."

His smile died as he gazed on Judith, holding Quentin's tunic to her breast.

"Where is he buried, Father? Will you take us to him?"

The priest nodded, and Leon lifted Judith to her feet. "Let us pay our respects to a brave man."

They followed the priest into a shaded area set about with bushes. A row of crosses paid tribute to the fallen soldiers. Father Ignatius pointed to one of them.

"Where it is known, we have their names carved. It can be arranged, my lady."

Judith nodded. "He must not lie in an unmarked grave." She knelt, feeling only sorrow that a vital life had been cut short. He had chosen his path as Richard had done. God rest them both.

She slipped the Saracen Stone over her head. In his delirium he had spoken of Farida, the girl who had been more to him than his wife. It was a small gesture, but she could make it. She hung the Stone by its golden chain over Quentin's cross, then looked up into the startled eyes of the priest. "It was his, brought from the Holy Land. It is fitting that I leave it here in the place where he came to God. Use its worth as you wish, in gratitude for the care you took of him and those like him." She stood for a moment at the grave side. "I will send a message to Lord Tarrant."

Father Ignatius walked with them to the horses by the main door. Angel rose from his sprawling position in a path of sunlight, and his unblinking eyes rested on the priest. He moved, soft-footed, and thrust his muzzle under the hand of Father Ignatius, his tail thrashing the air.

Judith stared in surprise. "He is usually most suspicious of strangers, but he greets you as a friend."

The priest smiled and ran his fingers over the dog's head. "I am no threat to him and he knows it, for his mind works simply by instinct." He smiled at Leon. "It is not so simple for the human who claims a higher intelligence. Our instincts are less direct, hedged about by custom and self-interest, the rules of our civilization. Would that men had the simplicity of beasts."

As they clasped hands at leave-taking, Father Ignatius gazed on Leon quizzically. "You came to us clean-shaven, my son, save for a night's growth of beard."

Leon smoothed a hand over his chin. "Did I, indeed?" He laughed. "This beard belongs then to Leon de Foret. Leon de Vance shall be clean-shaven when he returns to Nantes. God bless you, Father."

"Go with God, my son and daughter." Father Ignatius stepped back and raised a hand in farewell as Leon de Vane and Judith Tarrant walked their horses between the rusted gates of the monastery.

For a long time they cantered in silence, each absorbed in thought. How strange, thought Judith, truly twice widowed, yet never a wife. Two husbands whose trade was war, knight and peasant but equal at the final reckoning. Lord Tarrant had lost both his sons. His line must die with his own death.

Leon drew his horse closer to Judith. He reached out, taking the reins and bringing the horses to a halt. He took her hand in his and regarded her from somber gray eyes.

"I am eight and twenty years old, unwed and unbetrothed. Would you do a bemused and newly discovered Leon de Vane the honor and kindness of taking him in marriage, for he loves you most desperately?"

Judith's hand turned in his, and she swayed in the saddle toward him until their lips met. "I will, my lord, for I love him beyond all hope of recovery." She drew back a little, a smile lifting the corners of her mouth. "Do you, perchance, have goats in Nantes?"

The gray eyes filled with amusement. "Indeed we do, but they dwell, dear love, in the far pastures and are strictly forbidden the precincts of the castle." He lifted her fingers to his lips and put the reins back into her hands. "We can reach Nantes by sundown and marry tomorrow, if you've a mind to it."

Judith urged her horse forward. "I have a mind to it." She threw the words over her shoulder, laughing, and met Leon's answering grin.

A wild elation surged through Judith and she threw her horse into a headlong gallop. The same elation was reflected in Leon's face as he caught her up. Even Angel sensed the atmosphere, for he barked and pranced like a pup, but kept the pace with ease.

Shoulder to shoulder the two horses thundered along the road to Nantes, both riders filled with a fierce desire that a wedding should take place on the morrow in the castle of the de Vanes.

Make the Most of Your Leisure Time
with
LEISURE BOOKS

Please send me the following titles:

Quantity	Book Number	Price
_____	_____	_____
_____	_____	_____
_____	_____	_____
_____	_____	_____
_____	_____	_____

If out of stock on any of the above titles, please send me the alternate title(s) listed below:

_____	_____	_____
_____	_____	_____
_____	_____	_____
_____	_____	_____

Postage & Handling _____

Total Enclosed $_____

☐ Please send me a free catalog.

NAME_____
(please print)

ADDRESS_____

CITY _____ STATE _____ ZIP_____

Please include $1.00 shipping and handling for the first book ordered and 25¢ for each book thereafter in the same order. All orders are shipped within approximately 4 weeks via postal service book rate. **PAYMENT MUST ACCOMPANY ALL ORDERS.***

*Canadian orders must be paid in US dollars payable through a New York banking facility.

Mail coupon to: **Dorchester Publishing Co., Inc.
6 East 39 Street, Suite 900
New York, NY 10016
Att: ORDER DEPT.**